Sign up for our newsletter to hear
about new and upcoming releases.

www.ylva-publishing.com

THE
FIFTH
SURGEON

Faith Prize

Acknowledgements

There is a saying that writing is a solitary activity, and for me, truer words have not been spoken. I wrote *The Fifth Surgeon* without telling anyone because I was afraid nothing would come out of it. I thought that I would quit halfway through, or write it and hate it, or worse, write it and be the only one who loves it.

When I finally gathered the courage to let someone read my work, I put my trust in the right person—Astrid. It's still surreal to me that she wanted to publish the writings of one so inexperienced in the craft as myself and I will be forever grateful she took a chance on me. Her invaluable input, advice, and support shaped the story into the book I am so proud and excited to share with you.

My editors made the narrative flow much more seamlessly than it was. Hayley showed tremendous patience in teaching me how to transform the thoughts in my head into words on the page. She asked my cool and reserved surgeons, "And how does that make you feel?" so many times that I'm pretty sure she'd earned an honorary degree in psychology by now. Julie smoothed the very sharp edges of my story, making me sound a lot more eloquent than I actually am. Michelle not only fixed the grammar but pointed out a few small but crucial details that would have forever haunted me had they gone to print.

None of this would have been possible without the incredible Ylva team that was responsible for me falling head over heels with lesbian fiction, and then inspired me to do my best when writing a book of my own.

Dedication

In memory of my grandmother,
who passed on to me her love of romance novels,
and whom I miss terribly.

Chapter 1

The Five Ps

NADIA HEADED TO THE EMERGENCY department to see a new consult, but her thoughts stayed in the cardiac intensive care unit on the patient in bed eleven—a forty-five-year-old man with end-stage heart failure. He was Singh's patient, but everyone in the cardiothoracic surgery department knew him. After a heart transplant five years ago, his body was rejecting the donated organ, and he was now back on the waitlist.

But it wasn't his medical history that was on Nadia's mind this morning. It was the look of despair on his wife's face that seemed to have taken permanent root there. She knew as well as any physician that there was no guarantee another suitable donor heart would be available in time to save her husband's life. With every passing day, his chances of a happy outcome exponentially declined.

"Nadezhda!"

Nadia froze in her tracks at the familiar cheerful voice calling to her from the conference room. Setting her jaw tight, she turned to face Ashley Rylan, one of the attending surgeons. Well, not just an attending surgeon but the chief of the cardiothoracic surgery department where Nadia was doing her fellowship training.

Rylan was nothing one might expect from a surgeon. She was bright and sweet and tried to be everyone's friend, often at the expense of quality training.

Nadia bit back a sigh. Despite her lack of authority, Rylan was still her boss, so she stepped into the room.

Two dozen elementary school children silently stared at her, electrifying her nerves.

"What are you doing right now?" Rylan asked, her blue eyes big and desperate.

"I'm on my way to the emergency department for a consult," Nadia replied, hoping that would end the discussion. She would have walked away at that point too, but she reminded herself again that Rylan was her chief. She waited out of respect for the title, not the person.

Rylan looked out into the hallway again. "Jack, come in here."

Was Rylan planning to bring the entire healthcare team in the room?

"Nadezhda, you remember Jack, the med student who is rotating with us this month?"

She didn't, so she remained motionless, holding her lips in a thin line.

"Why don't you let Jack see your consult and then brief you on it?"

Nadia nodded tightly. Having the student do the consult would create more work for her.

"Great." Rylan beamed, apparently ignoring Nadia's utter lack of enthusiasm. "I have an emergency, but I'll be back in ten minutes, tops. These students are here to learn about being a surgeon. It's a career awareness trip." She paused, then added more quietly, "Be nice," before she hurried away.

Nadia turned to the medical student, anger simmering under her cool exterior. Jack was just another child Rylan had foisted upon her. "The patient is in the ED, room fifteen."

Jack pulled out a notepad and waited with his pen poised in the air. Nadia crossed her arms, tapping her fingers against her skin. If remembering the room number was already too much for him, she dreaded finding out what sort of report he would give her.

Finally, Jack spoke. "How old is the patient, and what is the chief complaint?"

Nadia's first instinct was to tell him, but teaching wasn't about giving students the answers. "That's for you to find out and tell me."

The children giggled and Jack's face grew pink.

"You have fifteen minutes," Nadia said. "Do a focused H&P, and I want to know if you think he's an operative candidate. Go."

Jack had the good sense to leave immediately.

Nadia turned to face the remaining children, her jaw setting harder. What could she possibly tell them? She couldn't tolerate most adults, and kids required even more patience. Her own school experience had been unnerving. She had never fit in as a student. People mistook her direct manner for rudeness, and she rarely corrected them.

"Are you a nurse?" one boy asked her, his chest puffed out like a bird.

She narrowed her eyes at him. "Why do you think so?"

"Because Dr. Rylan called you by your first name."

"Observant, but wrong."

The other children giggled and the boy looked down.

"To you, I'm Dr. Keating. And it appears I'm going to be the one talking today about careers in surgery. Now, how many of you—"

"If you're a doctor, why did Dr. Rylan tell you what to do?" another student tentatively asked, her big brown eyes peeking out from underneath her bangs.

"Because she's my boss."

"Aren't you both doctors?" She scrunched up her nose.

"Yes, but she's an attending and I'm a fellow." Nadia looked around at the children's blank expressions. They were here to learn about surgeons, and it would be Nadia's fault if they left this place as ignorant as when they had arrived. She walked to the whiteboard and picked up a marker. "There's a hierarchy in—"

She stopped. They might not understand complex words. "The surgical department in a hospital is like a pyramid. At the top is the head of surgery, the chair." She wrote the word at the top of the board. "He or she is a fully-trained surgeon who oversees all surgical subspecialties." She drew a few lines branching downward. "Below the chair are chiefs in charge of different divisions. Can anyone give me an example of a surgical specialty?"

The children continued to stare at her blankly. They didn't seem to be following at all. Finally, the same boy who had asked if she was a nurse said, "Neurology."

Nadia smiled, pleasantly surprised. "Is your mother or father in medicine?"

"My aunt is."

Nadia nodded. "Good guess," she encouraged him, wanting to spare the boy another round of giggling from his classmates. While there certainly was such a thing as stupid questions and answers, putting oneself out there shouldn't be discouraged. "But neurology is what's called a medical subspecialty. Its surgical counterpart is neurosurgery. Physicians treat patients with medications, physical therapy, and some nonsurgical procedures, but only surgeons can operate on them."

She wrote *chief* and *neurosurgery* on the whiteboard, then added a few more examples.

"Dr. Rylan is one of these chiefs. Did she tell you what kind of surgeon she is?"

The children furrowed their brows as if they were solving a complex mathematical equation.

"She's the chief of cardiothoracic surgery. That's a surgeon who operates on the heart and lungs."

Nadia drew a few more branching lines. "Under each chief are what we call attending physicians. They've completed their training and are responsible for treating their patients as well as supervising all treatments given by any doctors-in-training on their service. The chair and the chiefs are also attending doctors who take care of patients. They just have administrative duties in addition to their attending role."

The children were watching her intently. Some had their mouths open, and others looked as if they had forgotten how to blink. Most of them probably weren't following well, but everyone seemed engaged on some level. Nadia smiled. The task Rylan had foisted upon her wasn't as terrible as she'd thought it would be.

"And below the attendings are the fellows like me. We're doing advanced training in a subspecialty. Below fellows are the surgical residents, who are usually still practicing general surgery." She wrote *fellow* and *resident* on the board.

"You're a fellow?"

"Correct. I operate on patients, but there is always an attending in the room with me." She added *intern* to the board. "And you may have heard of interns. They're fresh out of medical school. They're at the bottom of the pyramid, and everyone above them can tell them what to do."

"Including us?" one girl asked.

Nadia chuckled. Even at this age, power was attractive. "No. Sorry." She added *students* at the very bottom of her diagram. "When you're a student, you need to listen to what you're being told."

At this remark, some of the children stuck out their lower lips. Nadia could relate. She had little tolerance for the hospital hierarchy. She was smarter than the chair, the chiefs, and all the attendings combined. She had a level of expertise from years of research that surpassed her training level, yet, she had to listen to everyone above her in the pyramid.

At that moment, Jack reappeared, studying his notes. He had to present a concise narrative of the patient's complaint. Nadia had to judge his presentation, examine the patient herself, and verify the facts presented, simultaneously treating the patient and enhancing Jack's medical knowledge.

It was a lot of responsibility, but it had its benefits. Nadia looked at the class and said, "He's just a medical student. You can be in charge of him."

The class cheered loudly. Jack looked up from his notes, startled.

Before Nadia could ask him to summarize the case in front of her audience, Rylan returned, flushed and out of breath. She looked at the laughing children with arched eyebrows and parted lips.

"Um, thanks." Rylan recovered her composure and smiled.

Nadia's inner child itched to reply, *See? I could be nice if I wanted to.* Instead, she kept her poker face. "I'm going to see my patient now." She glanced at Jack. "Follow me."

The class giggled again.

As she walked away, Nadia heard a girl proudly declare that she wanted to be in charge of surgery when she grew up. She smiled. Despite Ashley Rylan's inconsiderate disruption of her work, if Nadia had inspired at least one child in that room, her time had not been entirely wasted.

Ashley's head pounded, her feet felt like lead, and every muscle in her back ached when she finally made it home at the end of another long day at the hospital. It was after ten o'clock.

There was a time when physical exhaustion didn't hurt her spirit, but lately, she was in a rut. The days, weeks, and months blended together in the same repetitive cycle: work, sleep, work, and sleep again. Ashley looked around her empty apartment. The silence was deafening.

She dropped her keys in the small wooden bowl on the cabinet by the entrance, her gaze lingering on the gift from her ex-girlfriend. Maya had thought Ashley would be less likely to lose her keys if she had a designated place for them. She had been right. Ashley couldn't remember the last time she'd had to search for them in the morning.

Her chest ached with the memory. After two years together, Maya had decided that Ashley's work schedule didn't leave room for romance.

She swallowed the lump that formed in her throat. Maya had asked her to choose between her career and their relationship. Ashley regretted the question but not her choice.

Her phone chirped, interrupting her thoughts. She realized she had been staring at the damned bowl for several minutes. Maya had left eight months ago. There was no point in dwelling on the past, and it only added to Ashley's exhaustion.

The text message was from the hospital. Ashley scoffed and typed her reply, confirming the patient's medication orders. She tossed her phone on the coffee table next to the sofa and dragged herself to the bathroom to get ready for bed. Her chest tightened with every step. For the last few months, all she had done was wake up, go to work, get home too late and too tired to do anything, and go straight to bed. It was the same suffocating routine. Her heart ached for change. Even though the gratitude of a patient still gave her a thrill for a job well done, depending on cardiothoracic surgery to breathe meaning into her one-dimensional life was turning into a fragile lifeline.

She crawled under the covers and opened her laptop. As tired as she was, she didn't want to end her day in the usual fashion. She had an overwhelming need for a change.

Her friend Pari had told her it was high time Ashley found a new girlfriend. Recently, Pari had even taken it a step further and set her up on a dating website. While Ashley had no interest in disappointing another woman with how little of her time she had to offer, perhaps she could find someone to talk to who wasn't a colleague, someone who could help her break out of her routine.

She opened the website's page and typed in her login, but her finger hovered over the *enter* key. Her pulse quickened at the thought of putting herself out there. Still the alternative—closing her laptop and going to bed—made her stomach twist.

Ashley closed her eyes and breathed deeply. Finally, she snapped them open and with a decisive tap hit the *enter* key and navigated to her profile page.

Her burst of courage fizzled. She had forgotten how little information had been posted on her *About* page. Not even a picture. Not surprisingly, there were zero new messages.

It was disappointing, but Ashley reminded herself that sharing information would only draw attention when she wasn't really ready to reciprocate.

She scrolled through several new profiles. There was one like hers with no photo. Ashley's gaze lingered on it. If this person had no interest in completing the profile, perhaps she had similar reservations about committing to a relationship. She clicked on the link, her heart beating more loudly.

The page had less information on it than her own, *if* that was even possible. The description was of a thirty-two-year-old female who was fit and who had dark brown hair and eyes.

And she was online.

Curious. Why would anyone go through the trouble of creating a profile on a dating site and provide so little information?

Before she could change her mind, she typed,

Hi.

The woman replied immediately.

Do you have sex with men, women, or both?

Ashley pushed her laptop aside and jumped out of bed. She had misread the woman's motives entirely. Clearly, she wasn't looking for friendship.

Ashley stared at the blinking cursor on the bright screen, her mind racing. She had wanted something different, but maybe this was *too* different. The safe choice was to log out and go to sleep.

She remained frozen in her place. Part of her wanted to know where this conversation might go. It was a controlled environment. What harm could it do to exchange a few more lines?

She took a deep breath and climbed back into bed, retrieving her laptop. She typed her reply and waited, a little amused. Lately her only adventures had been in the operating room, but that was about to change, even if it was only in an anonymous online conversation. She hit *Enter*.

acr_34: Women.

MargaretBulkley: In the past 2 months, how many partners have you had sex with?

Ashley snorted. That question was even more direct than her previous one. And why was the time period so specific? Two months seemed rather arbitrary. Whether she was driven purely by curiosity about this woman or by the prospect of speaking to someone outside of work for the first time in months, Ashley didn't know. She typed another one-word reply.

acr_34: None.

MargaretBulkley: In the past 12 months, how many partners have you had sex with?

This time, Ashley scoffed. The conversation was beginning to feel like an interrogation. She tapped her fingers on the mattress as she considered whether or not to reply.

acr_34: One. How about you?

MargaretBulkley: What do you do to protect yourself from sexually transmitted infections or HIV?

What the hell? Ashley got out of bed again. Being direct was one thing, but this felt more like an annual physical exam than talking to a potential partner.

She went to the kitchen and poured herself a glass of cold water. She was getting flustered, and not in a good way.

Why did everything have to be so complicated? Her career interfered with her relationships, but she loved her job too much to let it go. Her lack of personal life bothered her but maybe not enough to even chat anonymously with a woman she might never meet—a woman who stubbornly refused to conform to any predictable pattern of someone on a dating website.

Ashley returned to the bedroom to consider her options. One, she could put an end to this bizarre chat and go to bed. She had to get up by five in the morning for an eight-hour OR case. Going to bed would be the adult thing to do.

Or, option two, she could keep answering the woman's questions, despite how one-sided and plain weird the conversation already was.

She went over the questions again in her mind. They were weird, yes—but perhaps they weren't all that random.

Margaret had asked about her partners and protection from STDs. Ashley sat on the edge of the bed and picked up her laptop again. She opened a new browser page and typed in *questions about taking a sexual history*. As a cardiothoracic surgeon, she rarely needed to ask her patients about these sorts of things, but she had learned in medical school that there was a guide to important questions to cover. She clicked a link on a healthcare provider's website called *The Five Ps of Sexual Health*. It offered a way for physicians to organize relevant questions. The categories were partners, prevention of pregnancy, protection from STDs, practices, and past history of STDs.

Ashley read the questions in each of the categories. They were identical to what the woman had asked. *How curious.*

But that didn't mean *MargaretBulkley* was a doctor. Anybody could look up questions to assess STD risk. It was just that nonmedical people rarely did.

Ashley stroked her chin. Giving direct answers hadn't gotten her anywhere, so it was time to change tactics.

acr_34: Isn't it a bit early to have this talk?

MargaretBulkley: Given the intent of this conversation, no.

Ashley smiled. She had finally gotten Margaret to break out of the questionnaire.

acr_34: So you are capable of writing lines that didn't come out of a medical textbook.

MargaretBulkley: Would you answer my question?

acr_34: Why should I?

This time, Margaret didn't answer immediately. Several minutes passed without a response and Ashley's smile faded. Maybe she had gone too far. Then: *ping*!

MargaretBulkley: What's your email?

Ashley huffed. She wasn't about to give her actual email address to a stranger. Fortunately, Pari had created an alternate email when she set up the account.

acr_34: acr_34@gmail.com

MargaretBulkley: Not trusting me with your real email?

Ashley's smile returned. Margaret sure was direct. And perceptive.

acr_34: I thought you'd approve. You're all about safety, aren't you?

MargaretBulkley: Check your email.

Ashley opened the attachment—and froze.
What did she expect?
A picture of the woman, perhaps?

Certainly not the results of an eleven-panel STD test. Ashley frowned. She was used to interpreting all sorts of patient data in her professional life, but she didn't expect to review a medical test in her personal one.

The report indicated that the samples had been collected a week earlier, and the results were all negative. The personal information was redacted. *So probably not Margaret Bulkley, huh?*

As she studied the document, one thing became clear—Margaret, or whoever this person was, didn't want to answer personal questions, even though she kept asking them. Ashley smiled, amused. Her fingers flew across the keyboard as she pointed out the flaw in Margaret's plan.

acr_34: You can't seriously expect me to manufacture an STD report just because you have one.

MargaretBulkley: And that's why I am asking you questions, to assess whether you should get one before we have sex.

Ashley laughed out loud. She leaned back against the headboard.

acr_34: Sex? Isn't that a bit presumptuous?

MargaretBulkley: Isn't that why you messaged me?

Ashley laughed even more loudly. This woman, who had yet to say anything resembling a normal conversation, didn't lack any confidence in thinking where this was all heading.

But Ashley didn't work that way. She didn't know anything about Margaret except that she apparently had a clean bill of sexual health. What an odd first thing to know about someone who wasn't her patient.

acr_34: I don't have sex with women I don't know.

MargaretBulkley: Is emotional attachment important for you?

acr_34: Isn't it for you?

MargaretBulkley: No.

The instant response deflated Ashley's mood. She tapped her fingers against her laptop while she considered what to say next.

Was there any point in continuing the conversation? They seemed to have very different goals.

Yet, how many people interested in a one-night stand wrote in full sentences and looked up safe-sex questions?

Ashley had never slept with a woman she didn't know well before, but where had that gotten her? She had been alone for over eight months, and her personal life was nonexistent. Perhaps it was time to try something new. At least a noncommittal relationship meant a woman wouldn't be disappointed with how unavailable she was because of her job.

With a surrendering sigh, Ashley decided to give Margaret what she was asking for.

acr_34: I've never had an STD. My last relationship lasted two years and ended eight months ago. I've only ever been in long-term monogamous relationships. That's all I'm willing to share for now. You'll at least have to buy me a drink before I tell you any of my "practices."

Ashley held her breath as she waited for a reply. She kept rereading the message she'd just sent, wishing she had skipped the last part. It had been intended playfully, but in retrospect, it sounded as if she was asking her out for a drink.

MargaretBulkley: There doesn't seem to be any point in continuing this conversation. I'm not interested in being your girlfriend.

Ashley rolled her eyes. This woman had a talent for making good things sound bad. *I must be insane to still be interested.*

acr_34: Who said anything about a girlfriend?

MargaretBulkley: So you think you can handle having sex with someone you don't know and will never meet again?

Despite not even knowing what this woman looked like, Ashley pictured clearly the mocking smile on her face. But she wasn't some goody-two-shoes. She could do casual. And it was thrilling to think of proving Margaret wrong.

acr_34: Of course I can. So what's next? Do we exchange photos?

MargaretBulkley: Anyone can take a good photo. It doesn't mean they look good in person.

Ashley chuckled. Margaret seemed to have an opinion about everything.

MargaretBulkley: Let's meet in person. This Friday at 8:00 p.m. at a public place. A bar, perhaps. This won't be a date. There will be no food. One drink and we talk. I'm not interested in your real name or what you do for a living. If there's a mutual physical attraction after the drink, we have sex.

Ashley rolled her eyes again. Margaret needed to loosen up. A lot.

acr_34: Deal.

They exchanged cellphone numbers and details about where to meet. Then Margaret went offline.

Ashley's fingers froze in mid-sentence. She scoffed for the millionth time tonight. She snapped her laptop shut and set it on the bedside table.

Why had she agreed to meet this insane woman? It was totally out of character for her. The entire exchange felt so impersonal.

Was she really about to meet up with a stranger just to have sex? Just because the stranger had challenged her to do it?

She rubbed her temples. Second-guessing herself made the stifling loneliness she'd been feeling for months creep back in her heart.

But maybe somehow, meeting up with a woman who demanded a no-name one-night sexual transaction was a step in the right direction. Or any direction. At least it would break her routine and remind her to try harder in her romantic life. Heck, if she put in one-tenth of the effort into her personal life that she put into her work, maybe she wouldn't feel so lonely every night.

As she fell into sleep, she made a mental note to ensure that her Friday night was work-free.

Chapter 2

Eligibility Criteria

NADIA MADE HER WAY TO Pari Singh's office, her stomach flipping with every step. The closer she got to Friday evening, the more uneasy she became. But she was determined to go through with it, and to hell with her fears and nerves. She raised her hand to knock on the door, then paused.

"I can't be on call this weekend. It's the only time I get to see my kids."

She recognized the hostile voice as belonging to Peter Williams, one of the senior attendings. His loud protests signaled that she should wait.

"This is the schedule we all agreed on, Peter. Each attending is on call one full week of the month. All seven days. You don't get to decide at the last minute you won't do weekends and use your family as an excuse. We all have lives outside this hospital. Why should you be special?"

A smile flickered on Nadia's lips as Singh held her own against Williams. Her voice was calm but firm, carrying considerably more authority than the one of her noisy colleague. She was the director of the cardiothoracic fellowship program, and as such, Nadia's direct supervisor.

"I never agreed to be away from my family so often. Every time I'm on call, there's one emergency after another. It's outrageous. If you truly cared about your own children, you'd understand where I'm coming from."

Nadia rolled her eyes. She sometimes wondered if Williams had had children for the sole purpose of using them as an excuse in moments like these.

It wasn't unusual for senior attendings like Williams to feel entitled. Surgeons rarely bothered to be nice, especially with each other. They were forward, abrupt, and sometimes downright immature. Nadia understood why—after working for twenty hours without any rest, people tended to forego pleasantries and jump straight to the point.

"Don't go there." Singh's voice was like ice. "Don't bring my kids into this."

"The chief has no children," Williams continued as if he hadn't heard. "Why don't you make her do it? It's not like she would object. She's a pushover."

"Peter! I expect you to show more respect for your colleagues. Just because Ashley got the position you wanted doesn't mean you can be a sore loser. Besides, we both know you use your family as an excuse. What is it you'd rather be doing this time? Playing golf with Bratton? Or another night out drinking with him? Or did you convince another nurse to sleep with you?"

"It's none of your business what I do in my personal time," Williams growled.

Nadia pictured the flushed expression on his face after being called out, pushing down her sudden feelings of twisting guilt. Her situation was nothing like his. She straightened up, focusing instead on how few had the guts to be so blunt with him about his indiscretions. Nadia admired Singh's directness. It was one of the characteristics she shared with her mentor.

"But as you so astutely point out, Bob and I are old friends, so there's nothing you can do." Williams had regained his confidence. Robert Bratton, the chair of surgery, was in his back pocket after all. "I'm not working this weekend, and that's final. You can either let the patients die or take the calls yourself if you want to protect your little protégé of a chief. I don't care. I'm turning my phone off."

Williams burst out of Singh's office and smirked at Nadia as he passed. She stared after him until he disappeared.

Despite his behavior, Williams's threats were just that—threats. After he was rested, he would probably stay on call next weekend. He was a jerk, but he pulled his weight.

"Keating, what's up?" Singh's expression relaxed when she saw Nadia. Her long raven-black hair had been let down from its usual tight ponytail and covered the shoulders of her beige blazer. "I hope you're not here to tell me you won't be working this weekend either."

"Of course not, Dr. Singh," Nadia said. She kept her tone deliberately businesslike. "I emailed you that research paper you asked for, and I just rounded on our post-op patients. I took care of their med orders and spoke with the nurses. Do you need anything else before I head out for the night?"

"What? No late-night research? That's new."

Nadia's nerves surfaced again. She hoped Singh wouldn't notice the heat she felt on her cheeks. Regaining her composure with a tight smirk, she recited Singh's own words. "We all have lives outside this hospital."

"You weren't supposed to hear that. Residents and fellows should dedicate one hundred percent of their time to their work." Singh chuckled. "But I suppose I don't need to tell you that. You put in more hours than your other three colleagues combined."

Nadia shrugged. "I try to do my part." She wasn't sure if being called a workaholic counted as a compliment or not.

"Since when are you so humble?"

"Just because I'm the best fellow doesn't mean I can't be humble." Singh rolled her eyes as Nadia's smile challenged her to disagree.

Nadia was the best cardiothoracic fellow in this hospital, and she didn't see a point in hiding that she knew it. She was probably going to be the best surgeon on the West Coast or even in the entire US very soon. But only a crazy person would say so to their program director. Nadia knew the game too well to go that far. Blind respect for your superior was a critical factor for a successful career.

Nadia hesitated, then added, "I have to admit I'm glad I won't be working with Dr. Williams this weekend." Respect was one thing, but bonding with a beloved mentor over a shared dislike was permissible. There were so few people that Nadia could tolerate at work, she allowed herself the occasional familiarity with Singh. Within reason, of course.

"Hm. What makes you think I won't ask the chief to be on call? I know how much you'd like that."

The sarcasm was not lost on Nadia. It was a toss-up whether working with Williams was worse than working with Rylan. One was an incurable chauvinist, and the other was simply weak. Nadia couldn't stand either trait.

"Actually, I think you should make Dr. Rylan do it. She needs to take some responsibility around here. But for selfish reasons, I would rather you worked yourself."

"Flattery will get you everywhere." Singh smiled. "You're in luck this time. Ashley is going to a private matter tonight that I don't want to interfere with. But I may still ask her to help out over the weekend, so play nice. I don't want to hear any complaints from the nurses."

"I have never not *played nice*, Dr. Singh. It's just that she's so…positive and energetic all the time. It's exhausting."

"You are aware she's my friend."

Nadia kept a straight face. "This was the nicest possible way to say it."

"You are so full of it." Singh laughed. "You'd better get out of here before you say something we both regret."

"Call me if you need me."

Nadia pivoted and exited the office with an eerie feeling of anticipation rising in her chest. This would be the first time that she had left the hospital before seven p.m. since she had started working there seven months earlier. Her heart's wild beats echoed in her ears. Her hands trembled, and her breath caught in her throat at the thought that she was about to do something she had never done in her life. She was going to have sex with a woman.

Nadia walked into the bar and was bombarded by loud music. *Good.* She wasn't looking for conversation tonight.

She scanned the crowded room, resisting the urge to turn and run out. Her stomach had been in knots all day. Leaving now would untwist those knots, but it also meant that nothing would change.

Nadia stepped into the noisy room. She wanted to do this. Her heart hammering against her sternum tried to prove her wrong, but she simply tightened her fists and resolve and took another step.

She normally didn't scare easily. The last time she had felt this nervous was seven years ago when she had delivered her first national talk to a room full of surgeons. Since then, a lot had changed, and Nadia was no longer that frightened girl with no title to her name. Now she was the confident surgeon who inspired fear in her junior colleagues. It was better that way. Keeping people at a distance meant she wouldn't be disappointed.

She closed her eyes, breathing slowly in and out. Her innate respiratory rhythm could be overridden by a voluntary pace. By controlling her breathing, she told herself that she was in control of her body, not the other way around. If she believed it, her heart rate should return to normal rhythm.

She had practiced this breathing technique many times in the past before correcting the mistake of a doctor, a medical student, or a research assistant. It had also helped her gain emotional neutrality before delivering bad news to a patient.

She thought she had outgrown the need to use a calming technique during social situations, but given her current emotional state, clearly, she was wrong. She frowned. Admitting she was wrong, even to herself, was nearly as bad as her heart stubbornly refusing to slow down.

Tightening her fists harder, Nadia found a table in the shadows of the far corner of the bar, where the music was at a tolerable level, and sat. She ordered two drinks, took out her cellphone, and typed,

I'm here.

Before she could change her mind, she hit *Send*.

Ashley froze when she caught herself twirling a lock of hair in the reflection of the taxi's window. She was tangling it, making it worse. She dropped her hands onto her lap and chewed on her lip instead. She fidgeted in her seat. Meeting a strange woman whom she knew nothing about—other than her STD panel—for a one-night stand was the craziest thing she had ever done.

Her phone chirped, bringing her back to reality. She looked at the screen and cursed herself for being late for her blind date. *If one could even call it a date.*

Despite pushing herself all day to finish on time and Pari helping her out, Ashley had still spent the last two and a half hours at a last-minute emergency meeting to discuss the politics of patient satisfaction surveys. She scoffed. Administrators had no idea what qualified as an emergency. Now, finally, she was on her way to the bar.

She had convinced herself that she wanted this blind date, but that didn't stop her from freaking out. What if they didn't like each other? Or worse—what if they *did* like each other? Would they go to Ashley's place or Margaret's place? Or to a hotel? And what would happen after? Should Ashley just…leave?

To still her racing thoughts, she resorted to what usually helped her through stressful situations: she forced herself to envision the best possible outcome. She would like this woman. They would have a great time together. Ashley would get out of her rut and her life would become more interesting. And perhaps she would find something more meaningful in the future.

Her phone chirped again. The message read,

I'm here.

Ashley's stomach clenched in a fresh wave of anxiety. She felt paralyzed with fear. *What if she leaves before we even meet?*

The thought scared her even more, and she finally forced herself to act. She checked the street signs, then typed,

Running late. I'm so sorry! I'll be there in 10.

———— •••• ————

The time that elapsed after Nadia sent the text were the longest two minutes of her life. Her heart pounding, she read the return message and scowled. The only thing worse than someone being late was someone who groveled about being late.

She set her phone down on the table. There was no point in replying to the text since she had nothing nice to say. Forcing herself to take a few deep breaths again, she decided to simply wait…patiently.

No one had said she had to like this woman.

Nadia tapped her finger on the table next to the untouched drinks. Normally she wouldn't waste her time with sexual frivolities, but she wanted to experience this once so she could put it to rest.

It was how things worked. Curiosity compelled people to seek new experiences. The unknown activity created an adrenaline rush. Once the fantasy was fulfilled, the novelty was gone, along with the desire to repeat the experience.

The online conversation last night had piqued her interest. The woman had used full, coherent sentences; she was just a couple years older than Nadia, making her age appropriate; and she had an unremarkable sexual history. The deciding eligibility criterion was a mutual attraction. If there was a physical spark, tonight's encounter would be the final chapter of this story. Nadia was ready to get it over with.

At 8:14 p.m., precisely ten minutes after receiving the text, Nadia looked up, searching the entrance for a blonde wearing a long black coat. Instead, a familiar face entered the bar.

It was Ashley Rylan. *What is she doing here tonight?* Of all the places she could be, why would she come to the same bar as Nadia?

Nadia balled her hands into fists again. Rylan's appearance left no doubt in her mind that she had to leave. If Rylan saw her, she would undoubtedly smile cheerily and strike up a friendly conversation.

Then Nadia had an even worse thought. What if the woman she was meeting showed up before she could get rid of Rylan, who was her boss after all? The thought of anyone from work learning about her plans doused her curiosity like a cold shower. She had kept her professional and personal lives separate for years, and that wasn't about to change now. She deliberately compartmentalized her life for structure, security, and comfort.

Tonight was a mistake.

Nadia picked up her phone and quickly typed,

Something came up. I have to go.

She hit *Send* and waved at the server to settle the bill.

As soon as Ashley entered the bar, her phone chirped. She read the message and sighed. Given how anxious she was, it should have been a relief to cancel her plans but it wasn't. Her heart sank at the thought of going back to her empty apartment alone.

Was her date having second thoughts? Or was there another reason?

Ashley scanned the room and was surprised to find one of the CT surgery fellows at a table in the shadows. Nadezhda Keating was trying to get the attention of a server who was busy at a nearby table.

Ashley stared in disbelief. She had pictured Nadia's life outside the hospital as a dark void. She should probably walk away and leave Nadia in peace, but she couldn't take her eyes off her. It was like witnessing proof that the Loch Ness monster existed.

She took a step in her direction, then paused. Nadia was an extremely talented doctor with a promising future, but she was also the epitome of arrogance. Ashley couldn't remember ever seeing her exhibit a single positive emotion. So while saying hello would be polite, Nadia would almost certainly be unreceptive.

When it came to her junior fellow, Ashley was convinced of two things: Nadezhda Keating was destined to do great things, and being agreeable was never going to be one of them.

Still, Ashley wondered, *Why is Nadezhda here tonight?*

Coincidences were possible, but scientists rarely attributed results to chance. She considered the evidence as her heart began to race.

Nadia matched the description of the woman she was supposed to meet tonight. She had straight brown hair, and she was wearing a black V-neck sweater. She also had two drinks in front of her and no one sitting next to her. And she was about to leave, something her date had told her she would do.

Ashley gasped. She could be way off, but something inside her urged her to test her theory. Her feet started moving before she could reconsider. She pulled out her phone and typed a text message, but rather than hit *Send*, she pocketed it, her thumb poised over the button.

Nadia braced herself as she watched Rylan approach. She had just paid the bill, but it was too late to escape the encounter. Nadia had no desire to talk with Rylan at work, much less outside of it. With skill that comes from years of practice, she adjusted her features into its usual expressionless mask.

"Nadezhda, what a surprise," Rylan said, smiling woodenly.

Nadia nodded. "Dr. Rylan."

Her phone, still on the table, vibrated. The screen lit up:

You'd better find a way to make it up to me.

She looked up to find Rylan staring at her phone intently. *What for?* Refusing to entertain the question, Nadia stood up and pocketed her phone. "I was just leaving."

As she started to walk past Rylan, the woman grabbed her arm and pulled her into earshot. "So how do you plan to make it up to me?"

Nadia's heart processed the information faster than her brain. It began to pound so loudly, she was convinced everyone in the bar could hear it. She stared at Rylan like a deer in the headlights, but there was no impending collision that would end this catastrophic moment.

Finally, her mind caught up. Ashley Rylan, the chief of her cardiothoracic surgery department, was the woman she had picked to have sex with.

Chapter 3

Testing a Hypothesis

"We should talk," Ashley said after a long pause.

Nadia stood motionless, her expression unchanging. She reminded Ashley of a patient in a catatonic state.

"Sit down." Ashley's tone was surprisingly authoritative, but the realization that her date was a surgical fellow she was responsible for had caused her jaw to set and her vocal cords to tighten. The sooner she shut down this HR disaster of epic proportions, the better.

She tugged on Nadia's arm, and Nadia sat back down. Wordlessly, she circled the table and sat across from her.

This wasn't how things were supposed to go. Tonight was supposed to be a fun, carefree night. Instead, Ashley was facing her subordinate whose expression suggested she might have sustained an acute stroke.

She picked up one of the drinks—scotch with no ice—from the middle of the table, drained half the glass, and put it down. She gazed at Nadia who wasn't blinking.

Clasping her hands was no good; she couldn't keep her fingers from fidgeting. And for the love of God, why did Nadia still show no signs of life? Her face was blank, her eyes unresponsive.

As the silence lengthened, it became more strained and unbearable. What had possessed Ashley to agree to this meeting in the first place? She cursed herself for letting loneliness overtake her reason. There was no excuse for being in this situation, and with Nadia, of all people.

"Look, I didn't know it was you. Of course I didn't. I only figured it out when I saw you here."

Nadia blinked once, slowly, but said nothing.

"For God's sake, Nadezhda, say something!" It was unprofessional to yell at a subordinate. It showed poor self-control, and typically, Ashley never did that. But Nadia's comatose state alarmed her. Were her thoughts so horrible that they could cripple a woman trained to perform optimally under stress?

Finally, Nadia's gaze sharpened and she met Ashley's eyes with cool intensity. "Dr. Rylan, I do not know what the appropriate thing to say in this type of situation is." Her voice was monotone, even more expressionless than usual.

"It's Ashley." Nadia's look made her want to squirm in her seat. "Please call me Ashley."

Nadia stared at her, unblinking.

The painful silence between them drew out again. Ashley finished her drink, hoping the alcohol would numb her embarrassment and calm her nerves. But to her complete horror, Nadia's new frozen state included glaring at her. She clutched the empty glass.

Ashley had never been good at confrontation. And trying to talk to Nadia right now was worse than taking her oral board exam. At least then the intimidating surgeons had attempted to be pleasant.

Maybe she should just leave, put some distance between them so that they might both process the situation.

Still holding her gaze, Nadia pushed the second drink toward Ashley. "I'm on call."

Ashley picked up the drink and drained the glass. It was the first act of kindness Nadia had ever shown her. Perhaps Ashley was facing a human after all. "Why did you order drinks, then?" She asked the first question that popped into her head.

"Are you asking if I'm an irresponsible physician?"

So much for being nice. Nadia's murderous expression made Ashley regret she had thought, let alone asked, the question. But it wasn't her nature to fight fire with fire. "No! Of course not."

Ashley looked down at her empty glass. Perhaps leaving would be the better option. But something made Ashley want to stay, even though she could think of nothing to say that would relieve the tension.

"I didn't know you liked women," Ashley blurted out before she had the good sense to stop herself.

The wall that was Nadia's face didn't crack. "I keep my private life private."

"Right."

Her minimalistic answers weren't helping the situation. "I don't exactly broadcast my sexual orientation, but I don't hide it either." Why was she even explaining herself to her junior fellow?

"I wasn't aware you liked women." Nadia looked away with an unmistakable discomfort.

Ashley blinked. Nadia had volunteered saying something instead of giving clipped replies to Ashley's statements. And her reaction—another unexpected show of emotion, however slight. *So…closeted.*

Nadia cleared her throat. "Not that it matters. It's none of my business."

She met her eyes again, looking at Ashley with the usual arrogance. Ashley shifted in her seat. She doubted she would ever look at Nadia the same way again. If the circumstances were different—*very* different—she probably would have slept with Nadia tonight. *She's a very attractive woman.* Ashley immediately pushed down the thought, scolding herself for having it in the first place.

"It's certainly not my place to discuss this with anyone," Nadia added, her tone shutting down further discussion on the topic.

"Right," Ashley said. "Good to know."

"I hope I can rely on the same discretion from you?"

How could Nadia maintain such a stone-faced expression? And how did she make it look so sexy?

Ashley frowned, equally mad at her inappropriate thoughts and at Nadia's question. "I'm surprised you'd even ask me that. Why would I want to tell anyone about any of this?"

"I don't know what you may or may not do, Dr. Rylan."

Nadia's use of her formal title, a painful reminder of how wrong the situation was, made Ashley wince.

"For example, why did you think it was appropriate to even approach me tonight?" Nadia continued.

She kept her eyes locked on Ashley. *Christ.* Her confidence made chills run down Ashley's spine. "I didn't know it was you."

"You did when you saw me. You could have walked away."

"I suspected. I wasn't sure."

"So testing a hypothesis was a sufficient reason to embarrass me?" Nadia delivered every word with clinical precision.

"What?" The accusation set Ashley back on her heels. She never intended to embarrass anyone.

"You could have simply walked away. I would have never known, and you could have pretended you didn't either. Life would go on as usual."

"I, uh…" *The statement made sense.* "I should have. I didn't think it through. I just acted. I'm sorry."

Nadia cringed.

"But you aren't a victim here," Ashley added.

"I'm the one in the compromising position."

"We're both in a compromising position! And it's far worse for me."

"I told you I won't tell anyone."

"And I'm not going to tell anyone either," Ashley said, jabbing the air to punctuate her words.

Why was she having so little faith in her discretion? She had never gossiped or given any reason for Nadia to think so little of her.

"But *you* know." Nadia's hard exterior showed a slight crack. She looked—unsettled. "You know something about me I would have never told anyone at work. It's…humiliating." She spat out the word as if it left a bad taste in her mouth.

This is the emotion she chooses to portray? Ashley rolled her eyes. Nadia certainly had a flair for the dramatic.

"Big deal. So the great Keating gets horny like the rest of us. Get over yourself."

"Stop," Nadia hissed.

They stared at each other, neither willing to look away, although it took every muscle in Ashley's body to hold her ground.

"*We* are not doing this." Nadia glared at Ashley.

"Oh, we're definitely not doing anything," Ashley snapped. "I'm going home. We won't speak of this again."

"Agreed."

Ashley dug into her purse for her wallet.

"It's taken care of," Nadia said.

Ashley's hand froze. "I had the drinks. Let me pay for them." It didn't seem right to let Nadia pay; as a junior fellow, she earned considerably less than Ashley.

"Really?" Nadia raised her eyebrows. "You think it's appropriate to give me money?" Her voice was charged with anger. "Haven't you embarrassed me enough for one night?"

Again with *her* embarrassment. Ashley scoffed. "Fine." Every one of her attempts to make this situation tolerable had been met with hostility. There was no point in trying to be nice. "Goodnight, Nadezhda."

Ashley marched away, wishing she never had to see Nadia again. *What a total disaster.*

Nadia tossed in her empty bed, punching her pillow in frustration. She squeezed her eyes shut as if she could order herself to sleep. As a surgeon, she had learned to fall asleep anytime, anywhere. But tonight seemed to be an exception.

The evening at the bar had been a disaster. What were the odds that the woman online would turn out to be the chief? *Damn Rylan!*

Nadia rolled over restlessly, blindly grabbed the second pillow, and threw it across the room. Deciding to deal with one problem at a time, she shifted her focus back to the moment Rylan had appeared at the bar. The audacity! How dare she approach her looking so stunning tonight? That dark green blouse perfectly framed her body and matched her expressive blue eyes that shone even in the dim light. Nadia scoffed. *Who cared how Rylan dresses or what color her eyes were?*

In fact, Rylan's fashionable outfits drove Nadia insane. She wore scrubs only in the OR. Maybe if she didn't put so much effort into her wardrobe, she would be a better surgeon.

Professionally, Rylan was too sweet, too weak, and too timid to be a leader. Nadia had seen a different version of her at the bar, a version she had liked—well, *tolerated*—a little more, but she was still the same insecure people pleaser who consistently failed to impress her. Professionally speaking. The rest was irrelevant.

It was best to pretend the catastrophe at that bar had never happened and focus on her job as she had always done. It was two days before Nadia had to work with Rylan again. Something stirred in her at the thought, but she quickly pushed it down. There would be no more thinking about any people outside this bedroom tonight.

Nadia drew the covers over her head and squeezed her eyes harder. She would count sheep all night long if that meant keeping away unwelcome thoughts.

Ashley shut the door and leaned back against it. Other than making a fool of herself, she had accomplished nothing tonight. Now she was not only alone but also frustrated and embarrassed.

She scoffed. Nadia had acted as if she were the only one who was embarrassed, and as if that were the worst thing in the world. In the seven months they had worked together, Ashley had never seen her so upset. In fact, Nadia rarely showed any emotion at all. Seeing a new side of her made Ashley's stomach flip. Worse still, Ashley was more bothered thinking she had made Nadia uncomfortable than she was about her own feelings.

As she put on a T-shirt and pajama pants, she tried to shake her disappointment. If anything, she had learned tonight that she shouldn't try to change her life. She should just focus on what she was good at—surgery.

She picked up her laptop and sat on the sofa. She could do nothing to change what had happened, but she could avoid future misunderstandings. Blind dates, or hookups, or whatever this was called, were clearly not for her.

She clicked on the website, intending to delete the damned dating account that had gotten her into this trouble. Instead, she clicked on Margaret Bulkley's profile. She visualized Nadia's image in the empty silhouette.

Nadia had looked so different tonight out of her blue scrubs and into a V-neck top that tempted Ashley's eyes to wander. Not that the alternative, Nadia's steely face, was easier to endure. The mere thought of those striking high cheekbones that had seemed sharper than ever and those imperial brown eyes enhanced by her black eyeliner made Ashley shudder even now.

Ashley had never seen Nadia wear makeup before. It must be the reason she had been so inappropriately distracted tonight.

Not that she needs makeup. Ashley groaned. Why did she keep thinking of a woman she didn't want and could never have?

Shaking off her intrusive thoughts, Ashley deleted her account. It was for the best. Her routine was safe, if boring. It meant nobody got hurt or embarrassed or whatever. She would forget what happened tonight and go back to thinking of Nadia as nothing more than her junior colleague. Her life was not meant to change and that was that.

Her future resolved, Ashley dragged into her bedroom to face another night alone.

Chapter 4

Saying Something Entirely Inappropriate

Ashley ran a hand through her hair. She would rather be anywhere than at work right now. Actively avoiding a surgical fellow while running a surgical department was stressful. Her commitment to professionalism was tested daily, but especially so at this moment.

Friday morning began with the usual daily rounds, where doctors checked on their patients. The doctors-in-training presented the cases, and Nadia seemed to be presenting every single one of them for no other reason than to test her resolve.

Ashley struggled to keep Nadia out of her thoughts. She had known Nadia for months, but after last week's fiasco, she realized that there was more to her than her work performance.

True, Nadia was typically direct and often skipped *please* and *thank you* when she talked to coworkers, but her actions showed her to be kinder than her words. She would always help the OR staff move the patient back to bed, or she'd put a patient's socks back on after an exam. Instead of ordering a nurse to bring a pillow to a coughing patient to lessen the pain from a chest incision, she would fetch it herself.

And it wasn't only her newly discovered bedside manner that Ashley found intriguing. It was also the way Nadia attempted to puff up her flattened hair with her fingers after wearing a surgical cap for hours that was endearing. Or how she always had her scrub top neatly tucked into her pants. Or the fact that she clipped her ID badge to the base of her V-collar, drawing Ashley's gaze to a place she had no business noticing.

Ashley would rather not pay attention to any of those things. They reminded her of how her heart skipped a beat whenever she was around Nadia.

"Patient is a forty-three-year-old male, pre-op, here for a VSD repair." Nadia began presenting the next case.

A ventral septal defect meant the man had a hole between the chambers of his heart and would need surgery to fix it. Ashley nodded at the presentation of the patient's condition. She studied the patient, the monitoring equipment—looking anywhere except at the speaker.

If Ashley thought she had been so taken by Nadia at the bar because of her tipsy state or Nadia's dressy appearance, she was very much mistaken. Her sober mind found the junior surgeon even more attractive in her blue scrubs. But saying this out loud would be entirely inappropriate.

"Four months ago, patient presented with shortness of breath—"

Why did Ashley have such a hard time looking at Nadia? She was struggling to act professional even though Nadia seemed to handle being around Ashley just fine. It was as if Nadia were trying to prove they could still work together despite what had happened.

"Physical exam revealed a grade four harsh diastolic murmur…"

Nadia looked at Ashley intently every time they talked. And every time Ashley looked back, she felt as if she were doing something wrong.

"In the setting of worsening cyanosis, pulmonary hypertension, and…"

It was as if Nadia hoped Ashley would say the wrong thing so she could shoot that murderous expression at her again.

"He is scheduled for closing the opening tomorrow morning…"

Ashley's jaw tightened. She had no right to be annoyed at Nadia. After all, she was the one who had first said *hi* in that chat, who had insisted they keep talking, and who had agreed to meet with her. And Nadia had made it abundantly clear that Ashley was at fault for approaching her.

"Dr. Rylan?"

The question interrupted Ashley's musings. All four fellows were waiting expectantly.

"Uh, Nadezhda?" Ashley asked, her cheeks heating. She had no clue what Nadia had just said.

"Do you agree with the pre-op treatment plan?" Nadia asked, a smug half smile dusting her lips.

"Uh…yes." Ashley cursed herself for not listening. She straightened up. "Are we done here?"

"We are, Dr. Rylan."

The group scattered to their next tasks. Ashley followed her senior fellow.

"Hey, Dan." She lowered her voice. "What medications did Nadezhda mention for the last patient?"

"Just the usual, plus sildenafil and antibiotics for IE prophylaxis. You seem distracted. Can I get you a coffee or something?"

Ashley smiled easily at the thoughtful fellow, declined the offer, and circled back to the intensive care unit. She had avoided talking to Nadia privately so far, but she needed to let her know to add one more therapy for that last patient.

She found Nadia talking to one of Peter Williams's patients. Peter was the senior surgeon that Nadia was assisting today. Ashley approached her at the patient's bedside.

"Nurse, when is the doctor coming?" the patient asked Nadia. "I want to ask him a few questions."

Ashley rolled her eyes. Fewer people these days assumed that the women in a hospital must always be the nurses, and when it happened, it was hard to know whether to laugh or get offended. She had started wearing business attire under her white coat instead of scrubs to avoid patient misconceptions.

"I'm the doctor. I'll be assisting Dr. Williams with your surgery today. What are your questions?" Nadia's voice was even, the words rehearsed.

"You're the doctor?" The man stared at Nadia's ID badge. "Nadez—" He gave up on pronouncing her name. "Did you get your degree from the Soviet Union?"

Ashley sighed. Sexism wasn't the patient's only virtue. *Charming.*

"My name is Dr. Keating. I earned all of my degrees in the United States," Nadia replied with the same measured voice. Her ability to control her emotions in these circumstances was impressive. "Do you have any questions related to your surgery?"

The patient's gaze shifted back to her badge. He seemed even more confused.

"You don't have an *MD* after your name. What kind of doctor are you?"

"The *surgical* kind," Nadia snapped.

Insulting Nadia's gender or nationality hadn't bothered her, but it seemed questioning her credentials did. Ashley stifled a smile.

It was time to speak up. "Hello, I'm Dr. Rylan." She stepped in. "I'm the chief of the cardiothoracic surgery department. May I steal your doctor for a moment?"

"My doctor is Peter Williams," the patient said. "I haven't seen him yet. He keeps sending me his lackeys." He waved in Nadia's direction. "But now that I'm talking to a *real* doctor, would you mind answering my questions, sweetheart?"

Sweetheart? Really? Ashley smiled stiffly. "Mr...?"

"Zimmerman," Nadia supplied.

"Mr. Zimmerman, I don't know your case as well as Dr. Keating does. This is a teaching hospital, and the fellows, like Dr. Keating here, manage the patients preoperatively, not the attendings. I can promise you all of our fellows are extremely qualified doctors. You are in excellent hands."

"Then can I get another—what did you call it—fellow?"

Ashley's smile slipped a bit. "Do you have a problem with Dr. Keating?"

"She's not even an MD," he said. "I don't know what this DO means, but it doesn't sound like a real doctor."

"It stands for doctor of osteopathic medicine," Ashley explained. "Both DOs and MDs are licensed to practice the full scope of medicine and surgery in all fifty states."

"Isn't that like a chiropractor? I'm having heart surgery; I don't need my neck cracked."

Ashley bit back a retort. The man had no redeemable qualities. No wonder Nadia had snapped at him. "I doubt Dr. Keating can help you with any neck pain. She specializes in cardiothoracic surgery. And she's very good at it. You should ask her your questions."

The patient narrowed his eyes. "If it's all the same, why didn't she just get an MD?"

Ashley glanced uncertainly at Nadia. She needn't have worried—Nadia was smirking, waiting for Ashley to respond.

"Osteopathy is based on a different philosophy. DO schools focus more on preventive medicine, patient-centered approach to care, and promoting the body's natural self-healing through musculoskeletal manipulation techniques. But that is too complex to get into right now. The bottom line is osteopathy is something extra, not something else." Ashley smiled, hoping she had explained it sufficiently.

The patient grimaced. "Patient-centered care?"

"It means we care more," Nadia deadpanned.

Ashley choked back a laugh, trying to make it sound like a cough. If DOs cared more, it was certainly hard to tell from Nadia's attitude.

"Mr. Zimmerman, there is no one better qualified than Dr. Keating for your surgery. The head of surgery himself recruited her personally for this fellowship. Let her do her job, and you'll see for yourself."

"Well," the patient said slowly, "if the head of surgery thought she was good—"

"Excellent!" Ashley stepped toward the exit. "Now may I steal her for one second?" She gestured for Nadia to follow her out of the room, not waiting for a reply.

"God, I can see why Peter is avoiding this guy. Didn't the Soviet Union dissolve in '91?"

"I didn't realize you knew so much about osteopathic medicine." Nadia's lips quirked slightly.

"I don't, but I researched the topic for your fellowship interview." Ashley returned the teasing smile. "But you seemed to be allergic to anything DO, so I dropped the subject."

"You prepared for interviewing an applicant? Shouldn't it be the other way around?"

Ashley chuckled at her challenging tone. She liked this sarcastic side of Nadia much better than the angry one. "I didn't exactly want to ask the great Nadezhda Keating unintelligible questions. Your reputation preceded you even then."

Nadia actually smiled at that. Ashley had never seen Nadia genuinely smile before and couldn't stop from staring back. It was equal parts addictive and frustrating.

"What?" Ashley asked.

"You always say my full first name. Why is that?"

"I don't know. I saw your full name on your application. I guess it stuck." *And I like saying it.* "Would you prefer I call you Nadia?"

"No," Nadia said. "I like it when you say it."

Ashley's pulse quickened at this admission. And Nadia's intense gaze made her head spin. The connection was unsettling, yet she couldn't look away.

Then Nadia's eyes shifted and she cleared her throat. "Dr. Rylan, what did you want to talk to me about?" Her face was once again indecipherable, her tone businesslike.

"Yes. Uh, would you start inhaled nitric oxide in bed nine?"

"The VSD patient?"

"Yes." Ashley tried to sound confident, as if she weren't guilty of inattention earlier. She was the attending physician; there was nothing wrong with adding a therapy.

"Even though you agreed with the preoperative medication plan less than fifteen minutes ago *without* the iNO?"

"I changed my mind." Ashley felt heat rising to her cheeks.

"You always add iNO for hypoxia and pulmonary hypertension. Changing your mind would be to skip it."

Of course, Nadia wouldn't just let it go. "I changed my mind back." Why was Ashley even arguing? She was the one in charge. "Just do it, Nadezhda."

"It's already done." Nadia smirked. "I added it when I placed the pre-op orders. It was clear you weren't listening to a word I was saying. I skipped it to test you. You failed."

"Very funny." Ashley looked away, mortified. She should have been paying attention. She had hated it when she'd been the trainee and her teachers had only half-listened to her. She had vowed never to be *that* attending.

"You've been avoiding me." Nadia stepped closer, lowering her voice. "And you can't even stay focused when we're working together. I was afraid this might happen."

"Nothing is happening. Don't flatter yourself."

"It's hard not to when you were practically drooling all over me this morning."

"There was no drooling!" Ashley bit her lip, regretting her high-pitched denial. She looked around, confirming that their conversation was still private before adding, "And even if there was, it certainly wasn't over you."

"Why weren't you paying attention, then?" Nadia's mocking tone didn't match the playful glint in her eyes.

Ashley smoothed her white coat. Denial wasn't working. Nadia didn't ask easy questions, and Ashley couldn't very well admit to thinking of her. "Look, I'm sorry I didn't pay attention. I trust you to do a thorough job, but this isn't a good excuse. I shouldn't lose track like that. I won't do it again." Hopefully, sincerity would suffice instead of an answer.

Nadia leaned even closer. Ashley breathed in her scent: a mix of a floral shampoo and something that was uniquely her. She couldn't care less who got the last word anymore.

"You still haven't answered the question. This is telling."

"You're impossible!" Ashley scoffed, taking a step back. "I'm going to do my job now. You should do the same."

She pivoted on her heel and walked away, a grin on her face. She should be annoyed, but she was happy that Nadia had moved on from her embarrassment at the bar.

Nadia sighed and rubbed her temples. She was too distracted to edit her manuscript. With every little noise, she lost focus. The wall clock seemed to tick more loudly than usual, and it made her want to throw the damn thing out the window. Every time she heard footsteps outside her lab, she glanced at the door.

Why was she so distracted today?

It was almost eight p.m. Her clinical work for the day complete, she thought she might finish up one of her research papers.

Except her mind kept drifting back to this morning, summoning Rylan's tempting image. Her killer stiletto boots and tight black skirt that barely covered her knees occupied Nadia's thoughts and fueled her imagination.

It was criminal. *Why did she have to dress so damn sexy all the time?* And why did Nadia keep caring what Rylan wore?

Nadia considered their conversation that morning. Rylan had bothered to learn about osteopathic schools to accommodate Nadia's diversity. It was…unexpected. And it gave her a warm feeling she was reluctant to acknowledge.

Even more alarming was the way Nadia had let her guard down. She had smiled and teased instead of scowling behind her usual wall of indifference. But she couldn't help it. Last week, Nadia had been fueled by shock and anger. But, true to her word, Rylan hadn't told anyone anything and had kept her distance. So Nadia's fears had faded, giving way to a strange desire to spend more time with her. She tested Rylan at every opportunity simply because she was amused—and endeared—by Rylan's fretful expressions.

Nadia shook off her reverie. She had written half a sentence since she'd gotten to the lab and had done nothing but think about the chief she couldn't stand only a few days ago.

She looked out the window. The daylight had already faded, and all she saw was her own reflection. She should either get to work on the paper or go home, but neither option appealed to her.

She looked around the empty lab. Why couldn't she get that morning's conversation out of her head? Rylan had been so tolerant with the bigoted patient, even defending Nadia's choice of medicine, a choice that she herself preferred to ignore.

It didn't mean the bright, cheery chief really understood her.

Anyway, Rylan's personality was irrelevant. Nadia was not looking for an emotional relationship. Her heart had been fooled into taking an interest in the experimental subject. It was probably a psychological response to finding out her attractive chief was not only a lesbian but also available. No doubt that night would have ended differently if they didn't work together.

But they did work together. Nadia slapped her hands on the desk. And now Rylan was plaguing her thoughts.

Nadia tapped her fingers softly on the desk. Her goal had been to fulfill a sexual fantasy. Maybe Rylan was the best woman for the job after all. Maybe their professional relationship wasn't really a barrier. It might even help simplify things: Rylan would never date a subordinate, but perhaps she might agree to a night with no strings attached so they could get it out of their systems and focus on their work. And that type of arrangement was exactly what Nadia had offered to her on the chat thread.

Yes, Nadia could see the benefits of a night like that. It would eliminate this fascination she seemed to have developed for the chief—new experiences losing their luster when done and all. It was logical.

There was only one problem: Rylan would never go for it. She was the chief. She would stay away, and rightly so.

And she had.

She would never start anything anyway, said the small voice at the back of Nadia's mind.

What if Nadia initiated it? Would Rylan follow her lead?

Nadia closed her laptop. Second-guessing wasn't in her nature. She was Nadia Keating. She chose her training programs. She led groundbreaking research projects. She received millions of dollars in grant money to fund her ideas. She wasn't about to wait around to be asked out.

Taking a deep breath, she headed to Rylan's office. *This ends tonight.*

Ashley stared at the bane of her existence—the attendings' call schedule for the coming month. Trying to work it so everyone would be happy was the hardest part of her job. Most of the attendings were such divas, and fighting with them over shifts was more draining than completing a twelve-hour surgery after a full day of clinic.

Peter randomly chose when to honor the schedule, and Michael refused to cover for anyone outside his week of commitment. Pari tried to jump in and help, but she was a transplant surgeon, and she had to drop everything else anytime an organ became available. That meant Ashley covered multiple shifts and worked extra hours virtually every weekend. It was enough to make her blood pressure spike and her head pound.

Ashley looked at the clock. She was supposed to wrap up an hour ago, but matters unrelated to work were making it hard to concentrate.

It was Nadia who was distracting her. On the one hand, she could relax a little, knowing Nadia wasn't angry with her. On the other, obsessing about Nadia's feelings had drawn more of Ashley's attention to her. And she liked what she saw.

Ashley shook her head. Such thoughts were inappropriate. As the chief, she needed to lead by example. Fraternizing with subordinates would be taking advantage of them, and it was utterly wrong.

But what was there to take advantage of?

The surgical fellows were mature adults. They were highly trained, and they knew what they were doing. Fellows didn't expect preferential treatment, regardless of the situation.

Besides, Nadia wasn't a typical fellow. She was knowledgeable, experienced, and independent, more so even than some of the more seasoned attendings. She did what was needed with minimal guidance.

If taking advantage of a subordinate wasn't an issue, then why was it a bad idea to get to know Nadia outside work?

"We should have sex."

Ashley whipped her head around, her thoughts skidding to an abrupt halt. Nadia was standing tall in front of her, arms crossed. Ashley blinked. "Excuse me?"

Chapter 5

The Aortic Catastrophe

THE SCANDALOUS WORDS ECHOED IN Ashley's ears. Overwhelmed, she could do little else but ask Nadia to repeat what she had said.

"I thought I made myself clear." Nadia held her stance.

Before Ashley could even begin to collect her thoughts, her phone rang. She grabbed it, welcoming the interruption. "Rylan speaking."

"Hi, Ashley. It's Mary."

Ashley went into full alert. The nurse manager *never* called unless she needed Ashley to respond in person.

"We have a patient already in the OR with an acute type A aortic dissection. According to Hayes, an aortic catastrophe is imminent if we don't operate now. I've got anesthesia and nursing ready, but I need a surgeon."

Ashley glanced at Nadia, who had leaned over and was watching her intently.

"I'm not on call tonight." Ashley tried to focus on Mary rather than her audience. "Peter is. He switched weekends with Pari, remember?"

"Peter is about to do an urgent CABG that arrived earlier today. Their patient is still not in the OR, and it will take him at least five hours without delays before he can do another case. This patient doesn't have five hours."

Ashley sighed. Mary sounded as irritated as Ashley felt. "Who took the consult?" Ashley looked up hopefully. Nope, Nadia hadn't moved. She forced her attention back to the call. "Why is the patient already in the OR?"

"Pari saw the patient and she was going to do the surgery, but a last-minute heart donor offer came in from Portland for her ICU patient. The transplant is scheduled in two hours. Before you ask, Michael is opening for her, so he can't do the case either."

Ashley pursed her lips. Just because it was Mary's working shift didn't mean the rest of the world should also be working.

"Okay, tell anesthesia to hold off on sedating him. I want to look at his chart first. I'll be there in five minutes," Ashley replied evenly. At least she could avoid the awkward conversation with Nadia.

"What's going on?" Nadia asked as soon as Ashley hung up.

"Acute type A dissection. Hayes referred him for immediate surgery. Peter is doing CABG, Pari is getting a heart for her ICU patient, and Michael is opening for her." Ashley brought Nadia up to speed, still avoiding eye contact. She needed time to sort through her feelings about Nadia's suggestion—well, order—before she responded to it. It was so... direct. Talking about an imminent surgery was safer. Actually, the surgery wasn't safe, but it *was* safe to keep to a professional discussion.

"The patient in bed eleven is getting a heart?"

The question effectively pulled Ashley out of her internal ramblings. She nodded.

"Good for him. I don't think he has much time left otherwise." Nadia paused and visibly swallowed. "Do you need help with the surgery?"

Tension tugged Nadia's nerves and she fought down the impulse to run. The fact was, with the attending surgeons already engaged, the other three fellows would be assisting them. So Nadia was the only one left to help, despite not being on call.

She wasn't entirely sure what to feel about assisting Rylan. On the one hand, she had never enjoyed working with the chief, but on the other, this could be an opportunity to prove to Rylan that they could work together effectively. That they could keep their professional and personal lives separate.

"How old is the patient?" Nadia asked before Rylan could respond.

Aortic dissection was a serious life-threatening condition. It was a tear in the wall between the layers of the largest blood vessel branching off the heart. If the weakened wall gave, the patient would bleed out in seconds. Rylan would want to give the patient the best chance for survival. Of course, that could only mean she would want Nadia to assist.

"Uh…" Rylan pulled up the patient's chart on her computer. "Forty-two, with a heavy smoking history but no CTDs or other comorbidities."

She was making eye contact with Nadia again. Switching topics seemed to have eased her apprehension.

"Hm, he is young. No Marfan?" Nadia asked.

"No ectopia lentis, no family history of the disease." Rylan looked up at her with a pinched expression. "So, no, no diagnosis of Marfan."

Nadia picked up on Rylan's annoyance. She had said no CTDs, meaning the patient had no connective tissue disorders, which included Marfan syndrome. Asking if there was Marfan was a question more suited to an intern, not an attending.

But if Rylan's feelings were hurt, that was Rylan's problem. Nadia had learned the hard way that assuming anyone who wasn't her did their job properly set her up for failure. Whether they were subordinates or superiors, she double-checked everyone's work.

"But you don't have to do this," Rylan said, her tone polite but strained. She had finished scrolling through the CT images and looked up at Nadia. "It's your night off. I can ask one of the general surgery residents on call to assist me."

So maybe Rylan wasn't bending over backward for Nadia to assist her. *Huh.*

Nadia straightened up, biting back her instinct to tell Rylan to suit herself and leave. Despite her wounded ego, she was determined to prove to Rylan that she could be a team player.

"Well, as it turns out, my plans for the evening just fell through." Nadia looked at Rylan pointedly. "Also, you need a competent assistant surgeon to give the patient the best chance of survival."

Rylan rolled her eyes, and amusement threatened to break Nadia's serious façade. She had intended to humble herself by saying that the patient would need a competent *assistant surgeon* instead of outright saying he would need at least one competent *surgeon,* period. Judging by Rylan's reaction, it was clear her humbling efforts had been in vain.

Before Rylan could answer, Nadia's phone rang.

She pulled it out and waited. "It's probably Mary calling to ask if I'm available to assist you. What would you like me to tell her?" She kept her gaze on Rylan, the only sound her still-ringing phone.

She didn't really need to ask for permission. Nadia was here to get experience in different surgeries. Whether or not Rylan was comfortable with Nadia being in her OR should be irrelevant.

Finally, Rylan spoke. "Yes. Tell her you can do it. And thank you." She smiled stiffly.

"Don't mention it." Nadia accepted the call. "Keating speaking... Yes, I can do it. I'll be there shortly."

"Hey, listen..." Rylan said after Nadia hung up. "What you said earlier about—"

"Dr. Rylan, there's a human life in your hands right now." Nadia shut her down. She was set on proving they could work together. It wasn't the time to return to the earlier conversation. On a deeper level, Nadia wasn't prepared to deal with however Rylan chose to finish that sentence, not when she had to focus on working with her right now. "Diverting your attention to anything else is irresponsible. We'll continue our conversation later. Let's go." She waited impatiently for Rylan to get up.

Rylan cleared her throat but made no move.

Fighting the urge to snap at her, Nadia asked, "What is it?"

"I can't exactly walk into the OR in stiletto boots."

Of course not. What an absurd statement. The OR nursing staff certainly wouldn't appreciate Rylan's sexy black skirt either.

Oh.

Nadia blushed when she realized that Rylan was simply waiting for Nadia to leave so she could change into her scrubs.

"I'll go get things started in the OR. Don't take forever."

She hurried out, hoping the harsh admonition would hide the fact that she suddenly couldn't stop wondering what Rylan wore underneath that elegant outfit.

By the time Ashley entered the operating room, the patient was on the table and the anesthesiologist and his resident stood ready to put him under. Jose and Melissa, the nurses for the case; Charlie, the perfusionist;

and Jack, the medical student were also waiting. Nadia, wearing a skullcap that hid her glossy dark hair, was studying something on the computer in the corner.

Ashley stared at her, thinking of what she had said earlier. Nadia had got what she wanted—they would be spending the night together. It wasn't what Nadia had meant, of course, but, still, the irony was not lost on Ashley.

Nadia looked up and zeroed in on her.

Ashley shook off her gaze, grateful her mask covered her warming cheeks. This was not the time to analyze her conflicting emotions. Nadia had offered to help simply because that was what good fellows did. The more cases they were exposed to, the better surgeons they would be. The fact that Nadia had never offered to work with Ashley before didn't mean anything.

She approached the patient. "Hello, Mr. Freidhof. I'm Dr. Rylan. I'll be doing your surgery tonight. I trust that my colleague, Dr. Singh, has explained to you what we're about to do?"

"I don't want to die." The patient's words were a little slurred from the preoperative sedative, but the plea was clear. Despite the calming drug, fear darkened his drooping eyes.

"I'll take good care of you, Mr. Freidhof. I'll do everything I can to get you through this." Ashley touched his hand. "I'll talk to you again after you wake up."

She looked up and nodded at the team to proceed with the anesthesia induction.

Ashley held the patient's hand as he faded into unconsciousness, never looking away from his face. A familiar sense of pressure weighed down on her, yet her gaze and touch never faltered. This man's life was in her hands. Every decision she made during the surgery would affect him.

"Nadezhda," Ashley said as soon as the patient was sedated, "would you mind exposing the right axillary artery for the bypass while I do the midline sternotomy?" She kept her voice professional. Whatever their personal relationship was, there were clear boundaries in the OR. Despite her pulse quickening, Ashley was determined to treat Nadia as she would any other surgeon-in-training.

"Certainly, Dr. Rylan."

Without another word, the two went to scrub in.

It was this ritual that cleansed Ashley of any doubt she might have and washed away thoughts that didn't belong in the operating room. Despite being acutely aware of Nadia's presence next to her, her heart rate slowed down and she focused her mind. Tonight was about Aaron Freidhof.

Everything else will have to wait.

———————— ••• ————————

As she mapped with her fingers the incision point in the soft tissue below the patient's right clavicle, Nadia took in the surgical team. Rylan was on the left next to the patient's head, gowned and gloved, a headlight and loupes on her head. Nadia stood opposite in similar attire. Next to her was Jack, the third-year medical student, then Jose, the scrub nurse. The anesthesiologist and his resident worked behind the sterile drape at the patient's head, and Charlie, the perfusionist, primed the bypass machine behind her. Melissa, the circulating nurse, was at the computer station, updating the patient's chart.

Nadia's gaze lingered on Melissa a moment, grateful she wasn't the one so far away from the operating table. She would have to write her own case notes later, but right now she was scrubbed in and part of the action. A familiar thrill coursed through her system.

"Why is the axillary artery preferentially used in acute type A dissection, Nadezhda?" Rylan asked as she skillfully drew her scalpel down the midline of the patient's chest.

Nadia scowled. The warm feeling of the moment before turned to frost. While it was appropriate to test a trainee's medical knowledge during surgery, she didn't appreciate being used as a teaching moment for the medical student. Or at least she hoped that was the reason Rylan had asked such a basic question.

And since when did she think anything Rylan did was *skillful?*

"It's a safe method to provide antegrade blood flow during perfusion and cooling." Nadia spoke with detached confidence. A lesser fellow would have stopped at that, but she continued with additional information, even quoting *Sabiston and Spencer's Surgery of the Chest* for no other reason than to show off.

"Very good." Rylan glanced up at Nadia, her eyes crinkling with the smile under her face mask.

Resolutely, Nadia fought the sense of reward the damn smile triggered. Instead, she zeroed in on Jack's rather overzealous suctioning with the Yankauer tip.

"Stop."

She grabbed the Yankauer, cleared blood from her field of view, and adjusted its position at the edge of the incision.

"Nadezhda…" She heard Rylan's warning, barely above a whisper.

Nadia gritted her teeth, reminding herself she was going to play nice tonight. She took a calming breath. "Keep the field clean. Don't suction unless you can't see what I'm cutting. Right now, you're clashing with my Bovie."

The kind tone sounded like Rylan's, but it was Nadia who had explained. *Great.* Now Rylan was turning her into a nice person.

She was distracted from that thought when Jack obstructed her field again.

"Like this?" he asked eagerly.

Glancing at Rylan, Nadia silently communicated her displeasure. Why was the student assisting her and not helping with the midline sternotomy? She watched the artful rhythm between Rylan and Jose: as the surgeon dissected, Jose kept the sucker poised and ready to suction away accumulated fluid. As soon as a bleed appeared, he stealthily cleared it so Rylan could see what to cauterize.

Nadia took the Yankauer out of Jack's hand again to clear her field. "Watch how Jose is doing it."

Jack's shoulders slumped, and Nadia scowled. The OR was no place to feel sorry for yourself.

"Thank you, Dr. Keating. I didn't expect such high praise from you. You've made my night," Jose teased.

Everyone in the room, including Rylan, chuckled. Nadia's scowl deepened.

Rylan's attention returned to the patient. "Chest saw."

Nadia took the sucker away from Jack again and positioned it at the top of Rylan's incision to siphon off the newly pooled blood. Then she requested the Dacron graft from Jose while assisting Rylan with stopping any sternal bleeds. Once she had her graft in hand, she focused back on her own small incision below the right clavicle.

Confused about whether to assist Rylan or Nadia, Jack kept moving his sucker from one incision to the other.

"Make sure to suture the perfusion graft to the true lumen, Nadezhda," Rylan instructed, keeping her focus on the midline incision. "Jose, can I get a DeBakey for Jack, please?" Then, to Jack, she said, "Grab the forceps and retract the pericardium opposite to me so that we can expose the heart and aorta."

Jack dropped the Yankauer in the sterile pouch in front of him and grabbed the forceps that Jose handed him.

"No, don't let go of your sucker," Rylan said softly. "Keep it in your left hand and the DeBakey in your right."

Nadia rolled her eyes. Rylan's patience with Jack was maddening, as were her unnecessary instructions to Nadia. "There's only one lumen at this level, Dr. Rylan," she said through gritted teeth.

If Rylan had bothered to spend more time with her in the OR, she would have known that having Nadia as an assistant was equivalent to having another skilled surgeon in the room. Rylan should save the basic OR training for the medical student.

Not that she had ever bothered teaching any of them how to properly assist. Nadia's eyes widened with horror as she saw how Jack held the forceps. Apparently, it was more important for her to be liked.

"Place the DeBakey between your thumb and index finger with the shanks resting near your metacarpal-phalangeal joint," Nadia ordered Jack. It was all she could do not to add that if he didn't know the primary instrument grips, he shouldn't be in the OR.

Jack stared blankly at the forceps. *Silly boy.* The answer wasn't written there.

"Hold them like a pencil. Like this." Jose grabbed a set of forceps and demonstrated the proper grip.

Nadia completed her task and helped Ashley establish circulatory support. Ashley smiled under her mask. Maybe she had been wrong earlier to hesitate accepting Nadia's offer to help. She was the consummate professional. She stuck to her task, keeping dialogue to a minimum. It enabled Ashley to focus on her work.

They switched places. Ashley moved to the right, where the lead surgeon typically stood. Jack followed Nadia to the left side.

The surgery was going without a hitch. Nadia anticipated what Ashley needed and expertly provided the necessary retraction and suction. A mentor had once told Ashley that the first step to becoming a great surgeon was to be a good assistant. If one could anticipate the surgeon's moves, then one could do them. If the statement were true, Nadia would be a brilliant surgeon one day.

Someone entered the OR. From her peripheral vision, Ashley saw the newcomer move to the head of the table and take a peek from behind the anesthesia drape.

"Imagine my delight when I found out I'm not the only one losing sleep tonight." The honeyed voice with the slight Indian accent gave away the newcomer's identity.

"What happened with your transplant, Pari?" Ashley asked, still working on mobilizing the aorta.

Nadia raised her head.

"Eyes back here, Nadezhda. I need your help."

"The heart was crap. I turned it down." Pari's voice seeped with disappointment. "That's why I'm here, actually. I need to talk to Keating."

"What's going on, Dr. Singh?" Nadia asked without looking up this time.

Pari peered over the sterile drape. "My ICU patient is on maximal life support and on the verge of multiorgan failure." Her voice cracked. "Can we get him signed up for your ex vivo trial? Maybe we can find him a marginal heart sooner."

Nadia examined the bypass connections for leaks that Ashley knew weren't there. From what she had heard, the patient was simply too sick, and Pari was asking for a Hail Mary transplant. Ashley tightened her grip around the DeBakey forceps in her hand. There was nothing she could do to change the outcome. Chances were this man was going to die. Soon.

Ashley stole a quick glance at Nadia. Why was she still quiet? Ashley knew that Nadia held Pari in high regard. Why wouldn't she? Pari was a remarkable doctor and an extraordinary transplant surgeon. Ashley had learned a lot from her too.

So why did her stomach twist to think that Nadia had more respect for Pari as a surgeon than she did for Ashley?

"Patient doesn't meet the screening criteria," Nadia finally said matter-of-factly. "This is his second transplant, and we don't enroll re-dos. Chance of survival is greatly reduced, and comparing them to first-time transplants would result in a negative bias." Her words were robotic, devoid of emotion. She lifted her head. "I'm sorry, Dr. Singh. It won't work."

"Can't you request an exception for humanitarian reasons?" Pari asked softly.

"He won't qualify," Nadia replied in the same indifferent manner.

Ashley frowned at the clipped response. Was Nadia really that heartless?

"But in case I'm wrong, I'll submit a formal request first thing in the morning. The odds of getting it approved are slim."

Well, what do you know? Ashley smiled. *She's human after all.*

Then again, Nadia had a soft spot for Pari. Ashley doubted she would have agreed if anybody else had asked, including her. Especially her. She knew this, but it had never seemed that important before. She forced herself to focus on her surgery.

"Excellent," Pari said, relief in her voice. "It's three in the morning now. Let's meet at seven to go over his chart. Breakfast is on me."

Ashley straightened up. Her patient was on the bypass machine. They had dissected the aorta away from the structures surrounding it in record time, and the team was waiting to complete the systemic cooling. Ashley stole a look at her friend, still on the nonsterile side of the drape.

Pari was typing on her phone. She looked up and met Ashley's gaze, warmth reflected in her dark eyes. The fact that Nadia had helped Pari feel better made Ashley want to reach out and squeeze the hand that Nadia had resting on the patient just inches from her own. Her muscles twitched, but she resisted the urge.

Pari huffed, interrupting Ashley's thoughts. "Li couldn't understand why the donor heart looked so bad. The echo images showed great function." She chuckled joylessly. "I told him it was like dating: anyone can take a good picture, but that doesn't mean they look good in person."

Remembering their bizarre online conversation, Ashley glanced at Nadia, who quickly looked away.

"Ready to cross-clamp?" Nadia asked the perfusionist. She was back to all business.

Right. Ashley followed Nadia's gaze behind her, not trusting that her surgical mask was sufficient to hide her amusement.

"Give me two more minutes. We're at 34 degrees Celsius," Charlie replied without looking up from his notes. He was completely unimpressed by Nadia's impatience.

"Jose, let me see the aortic clamp again," Nadia said.

Ashley stifled the urge to laugh. She had already checked that the clamp was the perfect size and shape for the job. Nadia was obviously trying to busy herself.

"Speaking of dating," Pari continued, "how did your date go last week?"

Nadia froze with the clamp in hand. Ashley's laughter died in her throat. Pari had a knack for choosing the most inappropriate moments for a girl chat. She probably would never have asked in front of Nadia if she had known who Ashley's date was. Or maybe she would have. Trying to guess Pari Singh's social responses was like tossing a coin and predicting heads or tails.

"Dr. Singh, there's a human life in my hands right now." Flustered, Ashley blurted out verbatim the words Nadia had used earlier. She grabbed the clamp from Nadia. Maybe it wasn't such a bad idea to double-check that it was the right instrument.

The barely audible scoff that escaped Nadia's mouth made Ashley smile despite her fidgeting hands.

Pari looked closer to see if they were doing anything important. She snorted. "You certainly have a flair for the dramatic. Does that mean you hated your date?"

"No, it doesn't," Ashley muttered. She could feel heat rising in her cheeks.

"It went well, then?" Pari pressed on, oblivious.

The OR was silent except for the rhythmic beep of the pulse oximeter alarm. Everyone waited to hear the response, including Nadia. Ashley pictured the mocking smile behind her mask.

"Pari, I'm busy." Ashley gestured at the patient field with her free hand. "Don't you have a husband to go home to?"

"He's sound asleep. He won't care where I am until it's time for dinner again." Pari's husband did the cooking and took care of their children most of the time. Asking his wife the bare minimum—attend dinner—wasn't the outrageous statement Pari was making it to be. "I'll take a nap in your office. Your sofa is much more comfortable than mine. When you're done here, you can tell me all about your date."

"You can cross-clamp now," Charlie said as Pari stepped back behind the drape.

Ashley rolled her eyes. Why couldn't he have said that thirty seconds earlier? She gripped the clamp that was still in her hand. "I won't be telling anything," she muttered loud enough for Nadia to hear.

———————— •··• ————————

Nadia mentally ran through the remaining surgical steps. It was easier to focus on dissecting the pathology instead of regretting the way she had answered Singh's question. She had heard the desperation in her mentor's voice when she asked for help with her patient. But science didn't care about emotional investment. She wished Singh understood that.

"Nadezhda, can you explain what technique we use to suture this anastomosis?"

Nadia gritted her teeth. Whoever had said, "there are no stupid questions" was a fool. Nadia's mind wandered back to a couple weeks earlier, when she had asked those elementary school children simple questions and encouraged them despite the wrong answers they had given. But that was different. Rylan had no excuse to treat her like a child. It was patronizing. Nadia didn't need to prove she belonged in the OR. Part of her even wondered if Rylan was asking her questions to figure out what to do next rather than teach Jack or test Nadia's knowledge.

"This is called the Griepp trick." Nadia kept the annoyance from her voice as she addressed Jack. "See how we rotate the beveled end of the graft so that this end opposes the greater curve of the arch? Right here, near the…?" She pointed to a vessel and looked at Jack, waiting for him to identify it.

Jack's blank stare made Nadia's face twitch. He probably had no idea if they were operating on the patient's brain or heart right now. He had been with them for over a week, and it seemed as if he had learned nothing. His lack of knowledge reflected poorly on his teacher, Rylan.

Nadia swallowed the harsh words she was thinking and waited for Jack to say something.

"Near the brachiocephalic artery." Rylan jumped to his rescue.

Nadia pressed her lips together. The reason Jack never learned anything was because Rylan kept doing him a bear favor, like in the fable about the bear that tries to help his master chase a fly away from his face by throwing a boulder at him, killing him in the process.

After taking a deep breath, she carried on with the explanation. "Once completed, the graft tucks tightly into the natural curve of the arch and prevents the lesser curve from being too long. What do you think happens if the graft is too long, *Jack?*"

"Uh…it would…uh…" Jack stammered, eyes darting around the room aimlessly.

"If it's too long, the graft will kink, impeding the blood flow," Rylan answered with a cheery voice.

With a poorly stifled sigh Nadia gently pulled on the two suture ends to bring the aorta and the graft together. Jack wasn't going to learn anything tonight.

"What's next, Nadezhda?"

Is that a teaching question, or does she seriously have no idea what to do next? "The graft is clamped," Nadia said, handing the clamp to Rylan.

"Now what?" Rylan asked.

Does she expect me to spell out the entire procedure for her?

Nadia pushed down her resentment and recited the remaining steps. Rylan's glimpse of authority might have been sexy at the bar last week, but now it was getting on her nerves.

Maybe Rylan was testing her, trying to prove that having sex with her would be a mistake. The thought made her grip her instruments more tightly.

"The aortic annulus is markedly dilated," Rylan said after assessing the pathology. "We'll do a composite valve graft root replacement." She asked Melissa for additional materials.

For real? Nadia frowned. She couldn't let this one go. She had wanted to prove to Rylan that they could work together, but not at the expense of a patient's quality of life. "Dr. Rylan, we should do a valve-sparing aortic root replacement. The David reimplantation method would work better." Nadia made her objection respectful but firm.

"Jack, what Nadezhda is proposing is a technically challenging procedure that requires extended bypass time and increases the postoperative risks for the patient," Rylan replied in an equally polite but firm manner.

Surely, Rylan knew the David method was a better option—unless it was too technically challenging *for her*.

"Putting in a mechanical valve requires lifelong anticoagulation medication, increasing the risks for the patient, *Jack*. His quality of life will be affected." Nadia stared directly at Rylan. "Please reconsider, Dr. Rylan."

No one in the room made a sound. It was unheard of for a doctor-in-training to argue with an attending in the middle of surgery. Nadia's heart pounded as she realized the gravity of what she was doing. But the patient's needs mattered more to her than obeying rules.

"Jack, Nadezhda's proposed surgery has aortic regurgitation fifteen percent of the time and may lead to heart failure." Rylan stared back at Nadia as Jack quietly looked at his hands. "Heart failure will affect the patient's quality of life. Wouldn't you agree, *Jack*?"

"I...I guess," Jack stammered, his voice barely a whisper.

"The. Heart. Will. Be. Fine." Nadia glared at Rylan.

"No, it won't." Rylan spoke with the voice of absolute authority.

Nadia maintained her stance despite the chills running down her spine. She was certain that her procedure was the best one for the patient. Anger rose in her like fire, and she pulled back her shoulders. "He'll tolerate mild regurgitation. And I can assure you there will be none—since I'm operating."

The team gasped as one voice. The anesthesiologists were peering at them over the sterile drape, and Melissa had stopped in her tracks.

"Nadezhda, you can either assist me with *my* surgery, or you can leave my OR." Rylan spoke softly but every word was delivered with stark finality.

And with that, Nadia lost the battle. Rylan had made it clear that she wouldn't reconsider. Nadia's body shook with barely restrained anger.

She placed her instruments in the sterile pouch in front of her, backed away from the table, and tore down her bloody surgical gown. "Good luck with the operation, Doctor. I hope for the patient's sake that your ego doesn't cost him his life."

She turned and headed for the exit.

The last thing she heard was Rylan asking Jack to adjust the OR lamp so she could see better.

"Like this?" Jack asked.

And the entire room erupted with "Don't touch anything!"

Nadia looked back to see Jack's bloody handprint on the nonsterile part of the lamp. He had raised his hands in surrender.

She huffed. *Fucking circus.*

Chapter 6

Surgery is Complicated. Dating is Simple.

Alone in the hallway, Nadia focused on her breathing. Her head was pounding with rage and exhaustion, and her next shift started in less than four hours. Despite that, she couldn't abandon Rylan with an inexperienced assistant.

Nadia could have handled the situation better. It wasn't like her to act impulsively. But she had let Rylan get into her head.

She closed her eyes. The right thing to do had nothing to do with Rylan. It was to ensure the patient's safe and successful surgery. But she couldn't go back. She doubted she could calm herself enough to focus, even if she managed to tolerate the procedure Rylan was doing. That left only one course of action.

Resolved, Nadia pushed into the operating room next to the one she had just left.

"Dan, scrub out and go assist Dr. Rylan in OR five. She's halfway through a composite valve graft replacement. I'll assist Dr. Williams." She used a tone that left no room for questions.

Her senior colleague looked up and studied her before turning back to the attending. "Dr. Williams, would that be all right with you?" he asked.

Peeking over the drape from the anesthesia side, Nadia estimated the bypass surgery would be finished in less than two hours. Maybe she could still get a nap before her official workday began.

"Oh, I'm sure we can manage without you, Dan," Williams said, his voice sickeningly silky. "Having the lovely Dr. Keating in my operating room is always a pleasure."

Williams was nothing if not predictable. His shameless flirting was how she got away with interrupting his surgery. Still, the fact that Williams's advances persisted despite her total lack of interest made her skin crawl.

Dan stepped back and removed his gown. Nadia followed him to the substerile room to rescrub.

"Dan? Don't tell Rylan I sent you." Nadia regretted the way she had handled the situation, that she hadn't changed anything, and, most of all, that she had abandoned the patient. But she wasn't sorry for walking out on Rylan, and she didn't want Dan's appearance to be seen as an apology.

"What would you suggest I tell her?" Dan asked, raising an eyebrow. "Not all of us can walk into a room and start ordering their superiors around." A faint smirk hinted on his handsome face.

He had a point. "Tell her you're done with Williams's case and would love to learn her method of repairing an aortic dissection. She'll be too flattered to question you."

Dan nodded. He understood her better than most people at the hospital did.

She had known it would be easy to get him to switch places. It was no secret that Dan liked operating with Rylan. He praised her work ethic and teaching methods, stopping just short of declaring his undying love for her.

That last thought made Nadia's chest tighten, and her attention locked onto Dan. He looked at her with those tranquil brown eyes and smiled.

Nadia looked away. The physiological response was illogical. Why would she care that Dan had a hopeless crush on their boss?

Rather than spend more time analyzing her reaction, she washed her hands at the sink and returned to the OR.

"Keating, I knew you couldn't stay away for long."

Instead of replying, she quickly gowned and gloved herself and took the vacant spot opposite Williams. Wordlessly, she grabbed the sucker, cleared the oozing blood, and inspected the sutured grafts. Williams flirted shamelessly every time they worked together. She had learned to ignore it most days.

"Isn't tonight your night off?" Williams glanced at her. "I can't imagine a pretty girl like you would choose to be here because she couldn't find a date."

Really? A girl? She could be home sleeping right now instead of deflecting the advances of her married colleague. Nadia took a deep breath, let it out slowly, and focused on her work.

The things she did for Rylan.

It was almost dawn by the time Ashley got back to her office. Her entire body ached.

The procedure had taken a long time, but the patient was stable. She was grateful Dan had miraculously appeared at just the right time. His training would be complete in a few months, but he was already an excellent surgeon.

"What time is it?"

Ashley turned toward her sofa. "You're still here?"

Pari sat up, squinting in the suddenly well-lit office.

"It's six thirty. I have an hour before rounds. Mind if I take my sofa back?"

Pari yawned and stretched. Her high cheekbones stood out against her face, puffy from sleep. "How did it go?"

"It went well..." Ashley leaned against the door frame, looked at the paperwork on her desk, and then back to Pari. "If you don't count Nadezhda making a scene and storming out in the middle of the surgery."

"She did what now?" Pari was suddenly very attentive.

Ashley dropped next to Pari on the sofa. "We had a...disagreement over whether to do a valve graft repair or a valve-sparing procedure." She bit her lip to stop herself from saying more. She didn't have the energy to relive that moment.

"Let me guess: you wanted to replace the valve, and she wanted to save it with the more technically challenging procedure."

Ashley frowned. "Are you saying I can't do a complex surgery?" She kept her voice low and steady despite the sudden anger at Pari's implication. It was bad enough having Nadia challenge her; she didn't need it coming from her friend.

"Not at all. You know as well as I do that staying in the OR longer than necessary is asking for trouble. 'Technically challenging' is not a good term in my book."

Ashley searched Pari's face before sighing heavily. She had let Nadia get into her head. That was the only explanation for why she suddenly felt insecure.

"Sorry for getting defensive, Pari. I'm still upset I let her talk to me like that."

"Freaking osteopaths." Pari chuckled. "They always think the least artificial approach is the best one. I'm surprised they haven't already invented a massage for a ruptured aortic dissection."

"Osteopathy is not massage," Ashley said. "You know she'd kill you if she heard you say that, right?"

Discussion of Nadia's osteopathic medicine degree was considered off-limits in the hospital.

During her fellowship interview, Ashley had experienced firsthand how Nadia reacted to even the slightest suggestion that her training was different from everyone else's. When Ashley had asked her what qualities she would bring to the team as a DO physician, Nadia had barraged her with examples of her research accomplishments, her MD-accredited residency, and a chilling glare that had dared her to disagree. It had been a very hostile interview. If not for the chair's nonnegotiable insistence, Ashley would never have accepted Nadia to the program.

"What did you do?" Pari's question brought Ashley back to the moment.

"About Nadezhda's behavior? I told her to get out of my OR."

"Ballsy." Pari stood up and went to help herself from Ashley's tea stash.

Ashley frowned at the blasé response. "You don't want to ask me why I chose to replace the valve? Nadezhda's procedure is the standard of care after all."

"Nope. I'm sure you had your reasons. Keating should have listened to you." She rummaged in the drawer for a paper cup.

Ashley dropped her head against the back of the sofa. She wished she could be as sure as Pari that she had made the right decision. Not about the surgery but about kicking Nadia out of the OR. Maybe she could have explained why she had chosen the procedure instead of arguing with her.

No. Ashley's mind rebelled at the thought. Nadia's attitude had made her blood boil and her tolerance for teaching evaporate. Nadia had been wrong to question her. It was the job of the primary surgeon to call the shots, and the assistant's job was to assist. Nadia knew that. She was arrogant, but she had never crossed the line before.

So why had she?

It could be that it was a coincidence. Or it could be that Nadia no longer considered Ashley to be her superior. If that were true, it would only complicate matters more. It was why Ashley needed to keep her distance.

She closed her eyes and rubbed her temples. "I don't know why your star pupil has to be so difficult."

"I thought we weren't supposed to have favorites."

Ashley scoffed. "Like that would stop you."

"Fine. I admit a technically flawless, transplant-orientated, type A personality is my idea of a good student. She's far from perfect, though. For one thing, she has major delusions of grandeur. Enabled even further by doctors telling her she'll likely be the next surgeon who wins a Nobel Prize. Her ego is bigger than the size of this hospital."

Ashley opened her eyes and looked at Pari. "She had never opposed *you*." It was true that Nadia liked Pari better. Even though it was in a strictly professional capacity, it still made Ashley's chest ache just as much as her head did. Not that she cared to admit it.

"That's because she knows I wouldn't tolerate this sort of nonsense. You were right not to let her have her way. You don't answer to her, and you shouldn't have to justify your decisions to her. There is a hierarchy for a reason." She stirred some sugar into her tea. "Anyway, you micromanage. I bet that's why she hates you so much."

"I don't micromanage her." Ashley crossed her arms. "She's a junior fellow in her first year of cardiothoracic training. Everyone assumes she already knows everything because of her research accomplishments. I just want to help her so she doesn't make any big mistakes and ruin her career before it begins."

"Here is where you're wrong." Pari joined Ashley back on the sofa, blowing on her steaming tea. "She might be a first-year fellow, but she sure knows her way around a scalpel. I bet she sees your attempts to teach her the basics as beneath her intellect. She's really quite extraordinary. And you know that means a lot coming from me."

Nadia was indeed extraordinary. *In more ways than one.* The more attention Ashley had paid to her this past week, the more she realized that there was more to Nadia than her professional achievements.

"Enough about Keating. When I asked you how it went, I was referring to your date last week. Margaret Bulkley, was it? Was that her real name? Was she really British?"

Ashley groaned. They had talked about Nadia enough already.

Williams's case had wrapped up, and Nadia waited for the patient to be transferred to the intensive care unit. Williams was an excellent technician when it came to the operative aspect of surgery, but his lack of interest in postoperative management was what gave surgeons a bad name.

As soon as the chest bone had been closed he scrubbed out and left. Nadia had taken her time to make sure the incision edges opposed each other perfectly to minimize scarring. After the patient was transferred, she stayed by his side until the postoperative chest X-ray was done. She took pride in taking the extra steps to ensure the patient was stable before she handed his care to the nurse. It gave her a sense of fulfillment.

Having confirmed that the X-ray and lab results were satisfactory, she headed to the doctors' lounge for a thirty-minute nap before she met with Singh about her heart transplant patient.

Dan caught up with her on the way. "Thank you for giving away your dissection case. I can't believe you let it go for a routine CABG. And with Williams, no less." Nadia tried to ignore him, but he continued, oblivious. "Dr. Rylan's technique in repairing that dissection was exquisite."

Nadia dug out a clean napkin from her pocket and handed it to him. "What's that for?"

"To wipe the drool off your face," Nadia said mockingly.

Dan pushed her hand away and straightened up in his walk. She had probably offended him. Nadia wanted to laugh. It was so easy to get under his skin.

Still, it wouldn't do for people to think he had a crush on Rylan. They might assume he was just another entitled white man who thought he could hit on female colleagues. But Dan was nothing like Williams. He was diligent in his work and took extra time to make sure his patients were comfortable. Nadia had great respect for him. She decided to soften her approach. "Did she say anything about me?"

In hindsight, Nadia had done exactly what she'd set to prove she wouldn't do. She had been unprofessional, reckless, and emotional. Her face cringed with staggering displeasure. She had accomplished nothing.

"You mean other than about you yelling at her that she was doing the wrong surgery and then leaving in the middle of the case?"

"I didn't yell," Nadia snapped.

"Whatever. She didn't even say that. I got the scoop from Jose."

Nadia frowned. That was odd. Rylan was usually chatty. The fact that she hadn't said anything was an ominous sign. Nadia picked up her pace to get to the lounge.

Dan matched her steps to catch up. "I think you misjudged the situation." His closed expression gave her no clue as to his thoughts. "I suggest you read her op note. You may regret your actions."

Nadia nodded though she doubted she would regret anything. She would rather have nothing to do with Rylan at this point, but her curiosity would win in the end. Once she was rested, she would take a look.

Inside the quiet, dimly lit lounge, Nadia set an alarm and stretched out on one of the sofas.

"Why are you so interested in my dating life all of a sudden?" Ashley darted her gaze around her office. Usually, she'd welcomed her friend's curiosity and shared personal details about her life. But while she wanted—no, needed—Pari's perspective on this, she had promised Nadia she would be discreet. Even talking about her without mentioning her name felt like a betrayal. Nadia was so private, so closed off. She would hate it if Pari somehow found out the identity of Ashley's blind date.

"Because I'm your friend and I care. And because ever since you broke up with that awful woman a year ago, you've hardly gone out at all."

"It was eight months ago, and Maya wasn't awful. There's no such thing as an awful kindergarten teacher." Ashley said half-heartedly. Maya was a bit...theatrical, but she truly believed that working with children was the most important job in the world.

She had liked Maya at first, but the relationship had quickly turned into one of convenience: Ashley had clung to Maya because she didn't want to be on her own again.

"Your ex was a nut job. She made it sound like pulling a Lego out of a toddler's nose was the most heroic act on earth." Pari shook her head. "And she made that claim in a room full of surgeons, for God's sake. I can't believe you were with her for as long as you were. You're too nice."

"That…" Ashley hesitated. No matter how the relationship had ended, she still instinctively wanted to defend the woman she had spent two years with. But this time, she was at a loss for words. Truth be told, they had only lasted as long as they did because Ashley was busy most of the time, and Maya was fun—in small doses.

Jesus. Maybe she *was* too nice.

"In any case, I only worked last weekend so you could have your date. I think I deserve details." Pari nudged Ashley. "So spill."

"It's complicated." Ashley hoped the cliché would work.

Has it ever?

"Complicated is doing a composite valve graft replacement," Pari argued. "There are certain specific steps. Resect the native valve. Choose the right prosthetic size. And even when you do everything right, you still end up with an unaccounted Ray-tec and—"

"Wait. You left a sponge in a patient?"

"Of course I didn't," Pari growled. "The fellow had thrown it in the trash, so the nurse didn't count it. It cost me an extra hour to get a portable X-ray and go through the trash twice. Idiot."

"Please tell me that idiot was Nadezhda."

"Sorry." Pari grinned. "It was Dan. Keating has always been technically flawless. She once spotted a needle I almost forgot in a patient."

Of course she did. Ashley rolled her eyes. Why did Nadia have to be so perfect all the time?

"My point is that surgery is complicated. Dating is simple."

"You haven't been on a date in twenty years," Ashley said, unconvinced. "Things have changed."

"Nonsense." Pari waved her hand. "Dating is based on two simple principles: one, did you like her? And two, did she like you?"

"It's not that simple, Pari," Ashley protested. "Liking or not liking isn't that straightforward." Truer words were never spoken when it came to Nadia.

"O-kay, let's try a simpler question. Did you find her attractive?"

That was simple. "Yes."

"Good. Obviously, she found you attractive, unless she's either blind or a nut job like your ex."

Ashley snorted. "My friend, you're great for my self-esteem."

"Did you sleep with her?"

"Pari!" The heat rose in Ashley's cheeks. "How is that relevant?" She had been so good at avoiding thinking about Nadia's earlier proposition all night.

"Chemistry is important."

Oh, there is plenty of chemistry, in a polar-opposites-attract, yin-and-yang sort of way. Ashley looked away. Thinking of how Nadia had looked that night at the bar made her heart stutter. But no matter what contact her body might crave, her mind demanded restraint.

She looked at Pari. Maybe she could offer one small detail without violating Nadia's privacy. "Actually we, uh, we got interrupted. I was with her yesterday when I got called."

Pari beamed. "I'm all ears."

Time to crush her enthusiasm. "But she was very clear from the start that she wasn't looking for a relationship. And she wasn't too happy when I left." That was kind of the truth. *Minus the part where she followed me to the operating room and told me I'm an incompetent surgeon and I kicked her out.*

"Oh, sweetie, you must have really liked her to agree to this. You were never wired for one-night stands. It's a sure way to get your heart broken." Pari took Ashley's hand.

Ashley pulled it away, frowning. Why did people assume she was a naïve romantic? "My heart is fine. Sinus rhythm, great ejection fraction, all in all, in fantastic shape. I appreciate that you care about me, but I know what I'm doing." It was time to end this conversation. She looked at the clock. "Speaking of broken hearts, don't you have a meeting with Nadezhda so she can fix your patient's?"

"Good point. I better head there now. Keating is so punctual. You know how wound up she gets when people are late." She gulped the remainder of her tea and stood up. "But we aren't through talking about the new woman in your life. I'm sure she'll call you for another date. You got interrupted so you could save a human life. Who wouldn't want to go out with a hot-shot surgeon?"

A hotter-shot surgeon, perhaps?

Pari threw away her cup and hurried out.

Ashley thought about what Pari had said. She doubted that Nadia would want to contact her in the future.

Well, unless it was to send Ashley a detailed article on why her aortic dissection procedure was the wrong one. She snorted, then covered her face with her hands. Why couldn't she have chatted with any other woman online? No matter what Pari said, dating was a lot harder than surgery.

Chapter 7

The Possibility of Being Wrong

NADIA KEATING WAS NOT OFTEN wrong. In fact, she couldn't remember the last time she had made a mistake. That being said, she sincerely hoped she was wrong when she had told Singh there was nothing they could do for her patient.

Singh was rarely emotional. She projected a cool and powerful exterior that earned universal trust from patients and colleagues alike. Nadia, too, appreciated and admired those qualities in her.

Today, however, she hated her mentor's ability to keep her feelings in check. Because it made watching Singh let her emotions bleed that much harder to bear.

She had asked Nadia to get her patient onto a study he didn't qualify for. Experimental drugs and devices were tightly regulated by the Food and Drug Administration. If certain criteria were not met, the patient would not be approved for the medication, no matter how lifesaving it claimed to be.

The rules were there for a reason. What if the drug was harmful instead of helpful? There were many examples of drugs and procedures damaging or killing people throughout history.

The FDA process made sense to Nadia. Still, when the person who had taught her more in seven short months than she had learned in her five years as a resident asked, Nadia had to try.

So she was using the humanitarian device exemption loophole.

Nadia and Singh met early and went over the patient's chart, constructing a well-thought-out argument for why the institutional review board should approve their request. They wouldn't. It was the grim reality Nadia had made peace with, but Singh refused to acknowledge how hopeless the request was. So Nadia ignored the sinking feeling in her chest and focused on the paperwork.

"Done. I'll call the analyst first thing on Monday to ask for an expedited review."

Singh dipped her head slightly in acknowledgment. The gesture made Nadia forget how tired she was after pulling an all-nighter and assisting on two separate surgeries.

"Ashley told me what happened during the aortic dissection case." Singh scowled. "You were wrong to challenge her."

Nadia held back an exasperated sigh. Of course, Rylan had told her. They were best friends. "I recommended what was best for the patient. He was too unconscious to advocate for himself." She held her head high. She was right after all.

"I don't want to hear excuses. He wasn't your patient, and it wasn't your place."

"You would have done the same."

"Argue with a superior?" Singh tilted her head. "Perhaps. But argue with Ashley, who is a brilliant surgeon? Never."

Nadia held her tongue. There was no point in continuing this conversation. The patient's valve had been replaced. It was done, and talking about it wasn't going to change anything.

Then Nadia remembered that Singh had asked Rylan about her mystery date. If Rylan had told her about their OR fight, could she have told her about that as well? She leaned forward. "What exactly did she tell you?" She winced at the way she'd phrased that. If her nerves weren't so frayed from working all night, she might have thought of a more subtle way to ask.

"Why? Do you think she exaggerated or misrepresented the situation?"

"No. I meant…was that all you two talked about?" Nadia's pulse quickened. She might be alerting Singh to things she didn't suspect.

"What are you getting at?"

Despite Singh's frown that was a mixture of irritation and confusion, Nadia breathed easier. Rylan seemed to be honoring her promise to be discreet. *Good.*

"Nothing." Nadia looked away. Singh wasn't a mind reader, but she could be very astute. Better to quit while she was ahead. "I have to go deal with some research stuff." Nadia winced again—she sounded like an idiot. "I'll keep you posted about the patient in bed eleven." She got up to leave before she could embarrass herself any further.

"His name is Michael Sanders," Singh called after her.

———————————

It was late Sunday afternoon when Nadia finally got to her lab and dropped into her chair with relief. Her head throbbed and her muscles were stiff in protest of having worked all weekend.

She logged in to check her emails. It seemed that her OR stunt had attracted the attention of Jason and Li, two of the other fellows in the department. They had declared her insane through a series of texts with childish emojis.

They had a point. Shuddering at her stupidity, she knew she had gone too far. She had lost control around Rylan. But even now, thinking about her maddening and deeply flawed surgical decision made Nadia's blood boil.

On the bright side, judging from Jason and Li's comments, Rylan hadn't said much to either defend or condemn the incident. Nadia relaxed, and she smiled smugly. Rylan must have figured out she was wrong and—more importantly—that Nadia was right.

Remembering Dan's words from earlier, Nadia opened the electronic medical record of the aortic dissection patient and looked it over. He was stable, awake, and in good spirits. According to the chart notes, he thanked the entire hospital for saving his life. Nadia rolled her eyes. *Somebody should teach the medical students what information goes in a progress note.* Besides, she doubted he would be grateful once he realized he would need lifelong anticoagulation therapy, thanks to Rylan's choice of procedure.

Nadia next opened the operative report and scanned the document. She froze.

She read the diagnosis, then read it again. The patient had Marfan syndrome.

She slammed her hands against the desk. *Damn it.*

This one small detail changed everything. It was why Nadia had specifically asked Rylan if the patient had this condition before the case. And Rylan had denied it. Nadia's nostrils flared. If this were true her proposed repair would have been the right choice. But in patients with Marfan syndrome things were more nuanced.

Nadia's gut twisted as she recalled Rylan carefully examining the echocardiography images and the heart's structures repeatedly. She had been weighing in on what the right surgery for this patient would be. And given the poor quality of the native valve that would only worsen over time, Rylan had made the right choice.

Still glaring at the computer screen, Nadia didn't wonder how Rylan had found out about the diagnosis. This was irrelevant now. Nadia should have asked why she wanted to do this surgery before assuming it was the wrong one. Even though Rylan hadn't offered an explanation, Nadia should have asked. Because while both of them had refused to back away from their narrow views, only one of them was at fault—the one who hadn't trusted her attending. Nadia slammed the desk harder, her palms stinging.

She *was* the one who was wrong.

"Dan." Ashley greeted the fellow standing in front of her office. "I didn't realize you were waiting. Please come in." She had promised earlier to meet with him to discuss his professional aspirations.

Dan fidgeted in the middle of her office, glancing at the open door.

"Close the door," Ashley said, moving to sit behind her desk. "We have important business to discuss, and I don't want any interruptions."

Dan nodded tightly, and after closing the door sat in the chair across from her. "I'm grateful for you taking the time to meet with me, Dr. Rylan. I know you're probably tired from working all weekend."

"I'm busy and tired all the time, Dan. But your future is important." She smiled effortlessly. It was easy to be nice around nice people. "Besides, I would have been a great deal busier if you hadn't helped me with that dissection case. Your timing was impeccable. But then again, you always go above and beyond what is expected of you. You have the qualities of a great attending."

"Uh…thank you." Dan looked down. "But it was Nadia who asked me to help you. I wasn't completely honest when I said the CABG case was over." He looked up at her. "She took my place so I could assist you."

"I see." Ashley kept her face neutral as surprise stunned her. That was so unlike Nadia. The last time she had done something nice was…well, Ashley couldn't remember Nadia ever doing something nice for her. She masked the smile the realization invoked by clearing her throat. "Thank you for telling me."

"I'm glad she asked me." He smiled, revealing a perfect set of teeth. "And I'm impressed with your interpretation of the clinical history of that patient. Figuring out that he had Marfan when none of the other doctors knew was remarkable. Even Nadia didn't pick up on it."

Ashley frowned. "Nadezhda doesn't know everything. She isn't an all-powerful deity." *Even if she thinks she is.* "Although there was nothing impressive about my assessment, I assure you. He didn't seem to meet the criteria for the diagnosis. But his primary doctor called me just as I was heading to the OR to tell me that he had the FBN1 mutation."

"Aortic root dissection and FBN1 mutation are sufficient to establish a diagnosis of Marfan syndrome." Dan nodded. "The patient is lucky his doctor called you."

"Indeed."

Of course, Dan would see it that way. He was such an easygoing guy. Ashley was sure if Nadia were here, she would criticize someone for not presenting this information sooner. She smirked. Oddly, she preferred Nadia's brash personality to Dan's affable nature. "So you understand why I decided to do the more aggressive procedure?"

"Of course. I suspect Nadia will not be happy when she finds out she was wrong to doubt you. You're amazing." Dan looked at her intently.

Ashley looked down, busying herself with papers on her desk. While she took pride in her work, compliments—even professional compliments—made her feel awkward.

Dan cleared his throat. "Dr. Rylan—Ashley—would you like to go out for drinks sometime?"

Ashley's head snapped back up. Had she heard him right? She blinked.

"You're asking me out?" Ashley's voice rose in high-pitched disbelief. "On a date?"

"Yes, I am."

Wringing her hands, Ashley scrambled for words. "I'm the chief and you're a fellow. It would be inappropriate."

"That will change soon." He looked at her with puppy-dog eyes.

Her heart broke. Why was he springing this on her now?

He leaned forward. "My remaining time here is a formality. I've already passed all my exams. If the professional status is what bothers you, I'll wait and ask you again after I graduate. And if—"

His voice droned on, but Ashley was no longer listening. She should be straight with him. Well, not straight. And certainly not with him. *Ugh.* Ashley raked her fingers through her hair. If only he would shut up so she could think of what to say.

"I really like you, Ashley. I've liked you since—"

"Dan, I'm gay."

His mouth snapped shut. Ashley swallowed, grateful she had the silence she needed to think.

Why was she having so much trouble lately maintaining a professional conversation?

Dan had done both his residency and fellowship training in this hospital. He had been working here for almost eight years. They had attended Christmas parties and social events together. Maybe if Ashley had brought a plus-one to any of those events, she wouldn't be looking at the pained expression on his face right now.

"Are you saying this to let me down easy?" A frown distorted his saddened features.

"I wouldn't lie to you about this." She pulled back her shoulders and held his gaze firmly. This conversation couldn't go any further. "I hope we can continue to maintain a good *professional* relationship."

Dan sat back in his chair, resigned. "I'm sorry for putting you in an awkward position, Dr. Rylan. I'd like to forget this conversation ever happened." He was polite but distant.

Ashley's chest tightened. She ignored it. He had dropped it, and that was what mattered. After all, surgeons were masters of detachment.

"Of course." She nodded. "Now, I believe you were here to talk about your career goals?"

"Correct." He cleared his throat. "I'd appreciate your opinion about some of the places that have offered me a job. Would you take a look?" He handed her a piece of paper.

She forced a smile. She still had an urge to get away, but she had promised to help him.

This was going to be a long meeting.

———— •••• ————

As soon as Nadia read the committee's response to the request for the patient in bed eleven, she called Singh. Her disappointment would pale in comparison to Singh's. Sanders had been her patient for over four years.

"I just saw it." Singh didn't bother saying hello. Her voice had lost its usual lilt. "You must have pulled some major strings to get it reviewed so quickly."

"I'm sorry it didn't change anything." Nadia kept her voice even despite the sense of failure that gnawed at her.

"Can you believe what they said?" Singh scoffed. "They don't feel it will make a difference, and he's going to expire regardless of their decision."

They had written, *We feel we would only be prolonging the patient's suffering.* Nadia was torn between condemning and admiring their honesty. The wording of the rejection letter was cruel. But were they wrong? A second transplant didn't guarantee success.

"Assholes," Singh muttered bitterly. It appeared she was too upset to see it that way. "What right do they have to deny Michael this chance? They're wrong."

"Not all patients make it," Nadia said bluntly.

It wasn't the comforting words her mentor needed to hear, but it was the truth. Nadia swallowed back the despair threatening to choke her. *This was the nature of transplantation*, she reminded herself. A donor organ was the candidate's best hope for survival. Some made it to transplant. Some didn't. If they grieved for every single patient who didn't make it, they'd drive themselves insane within a year.

Singh cleared her throat. "I was wrong to hope this one would beat the odds."

Nadia tightened her grip on her cellphone. "This isn't over. He's still alive."

She hung up before frustration overwhelmed her. She had failed both Singh and her patient. There was nothing more she could do for them. Her heart was breaking, and her mind turned to the person who had been in her thoughts all weekend: Rylan. Maybe there was at least something she could fix today.

"Why didn't you tell me the patient had Marfan?" Nadia barked. She stood with her arms crossed in front of Ashley's desk. Again.

Ashley sighed. "I don't have to justify my decisions to a first-year fellow." If Nadia had expected a kinder welcome, she shouldn't have barged in so late in the evening, demanding an explanation. After her meeting with Dan that morning, she was in no mood for another battle with Nadia's sense of entitlement. Despite acting as if she owned the hospital, Nadia was the one at fault here.

Nadia closed the door, then turned back to face Ashley. "No, you don't. It was wrong of me to question you. I'm sorry." The words were mechanical and unconvincing, like a poorly rehearsed line. There wasn't even an ounce of remorse in them.

Ashley huffed. "Tell me something, Nadezhda. Why did it take you three days to apologize? Was it because I was right or because you were wrong?" Ashley rarely spoke in such a cold and measured tone. But she was angry and not ready to let it go.

Nadia said nothing, fueling Ashley's anger even more. Nadia clearly had no respect for her, and it made her blood boil. "God, you're unbelievable. In what universe do you think it's acceptable to be so insolent? What if the patient had become unstable and I needed your help?"

Nadia snorted. "Oh, I'm sure Jack—"

"Stop it! I don't want to hear another word about the medical student."

Nadia held Ashley's gaze defiantly but said nothing.

"Nadezhda Keating does what Nadezhda Keating wants. Is that it? Is that why you thought you could challenge me in *my* OR?" Ashley jumped out of her chair and circled her desk to face Nadia. "You aren't the one in charge here. I am. Is that clear?"

Nadia's face flushed, but she remained silent.

Ashley balled her hands into fists, digging her feet in the ground. *Damn Nadezhda's arrogance!* She had no right to be angry after coming in with a pathetic excuse. "Dr. Keating, answer the question."

"It is clear," Nadia replied at last, through gritted teeth.

Ashley stood face to face with her, close enough to feel her warm breath on her face. She shivered. Before she could step back, Nadia abruptly stepped forward and kissed her.

The act caught Ashley completely by surprise. She was scolding the arrogant fellow, not flirting with her. And Nadia looked furious.

Or did she? Had Ashley misinterpreted the physical signs of arousal for anger?

For a moment, she surrendered, fully appreciating Nadia's lips. Unlike her demeanor, they were soft and warm. *Burning.*

Nadia held Ashley's head firmly, drawing her deeper into the kiss. Moaning softly against the pressure of Nadia's tongue, her lips parted. Her body lit with fire, screaming to lose herself, to experience firsthand the skills of the infamous surgeon.

Then her mind caught up, and she pulled back. She looked at Nadia, breathing heavily. This was wrong. Ashley was Nadia's superior, and Nadia had shown her absolutely no respect from the beginning. And they were fighting. A new surge of anger crushed Ashley's arousal. "You haven't learned a thing, have you? You just do what you want."

Nadia looked down. "I thought this was what you wanted."

Ashley snorted. "What I want is for you to stop acting like you're in charge of everything!"

"Okay." Nadia locked the door and closed the window blinds, isolating them from the already empty building. She looked at Ashley, who was frozen in her spot, with those dark brown eyes that conquered worlds. "You be in charge, then."

Ashley blinked. Nadia was still dictating the rules. Despite knowing that, Ashley took a step forward. And another. It was as if she was being pulled by an invisible rope. The fresh memory of Nadia's lips on hers dissolved reason. Despite her mind roaring in protest, her body was on autopilot, craving the Nadia experience.

She pushed Nadia against the nearest wall. The woman's eyes bored into her, continuing to challenge her.

Ashley was still angry, yes, but anger wasn't the only reason her heart pounded wildly. The thought of having Nadia made her dizzy with desire. Besides, Nadia was offering.

Before she could reconsider, Ashley kissed her. This time, she didn't hold back but poured all her craving and frustration into it. Their mouths fit so perfectly. Ashley pressed against her, feeling pleasure she hadn't felt for a long time.

And it was pleasure that was different than any she had felt before. Ashley pushed her tongue deeper, desperate to hear Nadia moan. At the same time, she throbbed with the need to take her own pleasure. She wanted to give and deny Nadia everything. A simple kiss had never had such an effect on her before.

Nothing is simple about Nadezhda.

With great effort, Ashley pulled away. Despite her burning hunger, she had to make sure Nadia still wanted this. She looked into her dark eyes and saw only desire in them. And it fanned her own fire.

Emboldened, she slipped her hand into Nadia's pants, moving past the layers of clothing until warm wetness welcomed her. Ashley hummed an approving sound. *So responsive.*

Nadia gasped as Ashley slid her finger inside her. She closed her eyes, then opened them abruptly as Ashley withdrew her hand. She raised her wet finger to her mouth and took a deliberate lick. Still watching Nadia, she hummed again. "Delicious."

Chapter 8

The Taste of Power

Nadia closed her eyes again, softly gasping at the word Rylan had breathed. It was hard to keep her cool as arousal dulled her control. But Rylan's bold moves drew her like a moth to a flame, and she could not have resisted even if she'd wanted to.

When Rylan headed to the sofa, Nadia moved to follow.

"Stay."

Nadia froze. Rylan smiled cruelly, making her shiver with need. Her heart pounded, but she had agreed that Rylan was in charge, so she employed great discipline as she struggled with the simple task of remaining still. Rylan sat on the sofa like it was her throne, regarding her thoughtfully.

"Clothes off."

Nadia swallowed hard. Her hands twitched.

"Don't make me repeat myself." Rylan's closed-off expression revealed nothing and demanded everything.

Nadia swallowed again though her mouth felt dry. Why did she feel so shy all of a sudden? When she had kissed Rylan, she fully intended to take her clothes off.

The continued pounding of her heart drowned out any thought. With rigid moves, she pulled the scrub top over her head while the fully dressed Rylan watched. Nadia removed her scrub pants, then her bra and underwear.

"Look at me," Rylan commanded.

Nadia looked up. Under the spotlight, her naked skin burned as Rylan made a show of examining her body thoroughly. She got up and circled Nadia as a vulture would its prey.

Interesting choice of foreplay, Nadia thought, but her attempt at sarcasm failed. Her clitoris throbbed. Her knees shook. What a cruel punishment it was to just stand still and do nothing. And how much it tested her resolve to surrender her beloved control.

As Rylan continued her inspection, Nadia itched to reach out and touch her. Her muscles tensed with the effort to remain frozen on the outside. Inside, her blood felt like molten lava.

"I didn't believe you when you said you'll let me be in charge," Rylan said. "I'm happy you meant it." She took Nadia's hand. "Because the thought of bringing Nadezhda Keating to her knees"—she leaned in with a taunting smile—"has me soaking wet."

Nadia gasped. Her legs trembling, she allowed herself to be led to the sofa.

"Well?" Rylan looked at her expectantly.

Looking into Rylan's icy eyes, Nadia remained frozen.

"On your knees."

Her legs already weak, Nadia was almost relieved to comply with the command. *Almost.* It was still an act of submission. But her reservations were quickly overridden by the thought that she would be allowed to touch Rylan soon. She got on her knees.

Rylan looked down at her before she sat back on the sofa. She reached out and stroked Nadia's breasts with her hand, roaming possessively. Nadia held her breath.

"You had no interest in apologizing tonight, did you? It was just a means to an end."

Nadia tightened her jaw. Objecting would only kill the mood.

"What did you picture us doing instead?"

Nadia said nothing. Her attention was focused on the invisible lines that Rylan was drawing down her lower abdomen.

"Did you imagine me touching you here?" Her right hand cupped Nadia's sex.

The exquisite touch elicited an instant moan.

Just as quickly as she'd introduced her hand, Rylan retracted it. She sat back regally, holding Nadia's gaze. Her face was perfectly smooth and indecipherable. "Am I to interpret your lack of communication to mean that you have no desire to be pleasured?"

Rylan's mocking voice was intimidating and every bit as thrilling as the touch of her hand had been. Nadia had never heard her talk this way before. She had never known herself to be so shy either. Apparently, kneeling in front of Rylan had that effect on her.

"It's probably for the best," Rylan continued, "because I'm in the mood to be pleasured rather than to please."

Nadia gasped softly as the words sent a jolt to her core. *Since when is she so good at controlling a situation?*

"Would you like to crawl between my legs and show me how obedient you can be?"

Her lips barely parted, forcing out the faintest of sounds. "Yes." Despite her nerves, she was fully capable of *vocally* communicating if that was what Rylan's imaginary rules demanded.

Rylan's triumphant smile was intoxicating. "Now, that wasn't so hard, was it?" Her taunting suggested she knew exactly how hard it was. She parted her legs slightly. "Remove my panties."

Nadia moved forward, relieved to shift positions, and slipped her hands up Rylan's tight skirt. Her heart rate quickened as the touch captured her senses. Rylan's skin was soft and smooth, and touching it was *like touching silk.*

Nadia found the hem of Rylan's bikini bottoms and slipped them off. Then, breathing heavily, she ran her tongue against her lips in tortured anticipation, waiting for the next command.

Rylan pulled up her skirt and moved her legs apart a little more. "Proceed."

Indeed, the woman is talented.

Nadia had slowly and thoroughly explored Ashley's anatomy. Her initial teasing had progressed quickly to delivering intense, *and very effective,* stimuli. Ashley quivered with the rising heat in her core. She raised her hips and pushed herself forward, craving more. The mere thought of Nadia between her legs nearly brought her over the edge.

"Stop," Ashley gasped.

Nadia stopped immediately. Her newfound submission only fueled Ashley's fire. She gently pushed Nadia away and stood up. "Lie down on the sofa."

Nadia promptly complied, sending fresh currents of desire throughout Ashley's body. She had been following Ashley's commands without objection. The feeling of power was heady.

If only she could be this compliant during business hours.

She gazed at Nadia lying on the sofa. Her brown eyes, usually intimidating, were now dark with desire.

Ashley's breath hitched as her gaze ravaged Nadia's body. The woman was stunning. The blue scrubs didn't do her justice. Underneath them, she hid a body worthy of a yoga commercial. Her legs and arms were long and toned. Her flat abdomen was firm, hinting at the perfect balance between femininity and strength. Her breasts were full and round, and her areolas made Ashley's mouth water.

Nadia's face was flushed. Ashley couldn't tell if it was because of embarrassment or due to her dedicated efforts thus far.

Towering over Nadia, still fully dressed, albeit sans panties, Ashley held her gaze as she slowly lifted her skirt. Her heart was pounding, and blood was rushing to her slick folds.

Nadia looked unblinking into her eyes, making her head spin. For a moment, Ashley felt a connection deeper than lust, as if Nadia were a piece she didn't know was missing.

Breaking eye contact, Ashley pushed the thought away and returned to the moment. She straddled Nadia, moving upward until she was directly over her face. She reached out and grabbed a handful of Nadia's hair.

Had she ever been that rough before?

Nadia's ragged breath landed hot on Ashley's sensitive flesh, extinguishing the flicker of doubt in her mind. She was laying absolutely still, waiting for instructions. Drunk on the power Nadia was giving her, Ashley let her instincts rule her. "Continue," she breathed.

She moved her hips back and forth, her primal urges taking over. Nadia gave a guttural moan against her clitoris, the vibrations making Ashley cry out in sheer pleasure. Nadia felt so good underneath her, she wanted it to last forever. Relaxing her grip on Nadia's hair, Ashley slowed down to savor the moment.

Immediately, the pressure intensified as Nadia wrapped her arms around Ashley's legs and drew her closer. That was all it took to push Ashley over the edge. An explosion of pure bliss enveloped her senses, and her muscles tensed and spasmed with an unbelievable release. She bit her lip to muffle her cries as she rode out her orgasm.

Releasing her grip completely Ashley stretched out and lay down next to her. They panted together in the silence.

Wow, that was…*wow*. Ashley's mind had checked out a while back, and her excitement grew stronger as she felt Nadia's smooth skin pressed against her.

After regaining some composure, she pushed herself up to a sitting position and turned slightly to face her, not ready for this to end. "Go sit on the desk," she said, her voice husky. Nadia was inspiring her to act assertively. She even added, "Now!"

Nadia rolled off the edge of the sofa and walked over to the desk, looking down.

Ashley approached her slowly, taking in the beautiful picture in front of her. She clicked her tongue. "What am I supposed to do with you?" She placed her finger under Nadia's chin and pushed it up to meet her eyes. "You've been so naughty."

She loved Nadia's newfound shyness. It was so unlike her that it felt more intimate than anything else they had done tonight. Ashley's entire body tingled in agreement.

With her free hand, she stroked Nadia's inner thigh, moving higher until her fingertips lightly brushed against the folds of Nadia's smooth sex. The wetness there made her lick her lips.

For me?

Keeping her touch feather-light, she traced the soft—*and so very wet*—skin and withdrew. Driven by Nadia's growing failure to suppress her gasps and moans, Ashley kept repeating the teasing action.

"We should work on your communication skills, *Dr. Keating*. You used to be a lot more articulate."

At that Nadia gasped and blushed, and thrusted forward, seeking more of Ashley's touch and fueling her sense of power. She looked so desperate, so ready for the pleasure Ashley wanted to give her.

Not yet. Ashley abruptly withdrew her hand.

Nadia reached for it, but Ashley waved her retreating hand out of range. "I did not give you permission to touch me, did I?"

Indignation showed on her face, but she said nothing.

"Hands behind your back."

Nadia's jaw tightened, but she complied. Ashley smiled. It showed she understood this was going to be a lesson on trust. Nadia didn't trust her to do the right surgery; would she trust her with this?

Not that I can make Nadezhda do anything she doesn't want to. "Good. Let's begin."

Ashley plunged two fingers into Nadia's wet center and placed her thumb on the sensitive tissue above it. Nadia shut her eyes tight and groaned, exciting Ashley beyond words. *All for me.* With every thrust of her fingers inside Nadia, Ashley was rewarded with more heat, more wetness, more ragged breathing. She knew it wouldn't take long for Nadia to reach her completion. The needy sounds rang in her ears, and made her redouble her efforts, desperately wanting to hear Nadia come for her.

Drunk with power over Nadia's reactions, she breathed, "You are not in control here. I am. I make the rules and you will comply." The words had double meaning: the sexual one and the one where Nadia didn't oppose her attending.

Nadia growled in her ear, thrusting her hips harder against Ashley's fingers.

The sense of authority charged Ashley's desire, driving her mad with excitement. "I decide if and when you'll have your pleasure." She stopped moving her hand and locked eyes with Nadia. "Ask me to continue."

For a moment, Nadia's heavy breathing was the only sound filling the room.

"Rylan, please…" The strained whisper broke the silence.

Wait, what?

In an instant, Ashley's ardor cooled. Why did Nadia still stubbornly refuse to call Ashley by her first name?

Ashley couldn't have sex with a woman who hadn't even once said her name.

Well, she most certainly couldn't possibly *continue* having sex with a woman who hadn't even once said her name.

Fortunately, the power to immediately change such impertinence was in her hands. Literally. Ashley smiled. "If you want me to continue, say my first—"

Her phone's ringtone startled her out of her thoughts. She almost growled in frustration. "Don't move an inch."

Her phone was on her desk, within reach. She grabbed it with her free hand. "Rylan speaking."

"Hi, Ashley, it's Mary."

Ashley held her breath.

She withdrew her fingers, hearing a restrained gasp escape Nadia's mouth. Her chest tightened at the impossibility to do anything about it. Nadia remained sitting on her desk obediently, making Ashley's body roar at the inviting sight. She tightened the phone in her grip, spun away from temptation, and forced herself to listen to Mary's words.

———— •••• ————

Ashley sighed as Mary kept talking. It was a patient with a large blood clot to the lungs, and no other attending surgeon was available to do a possible emergency embolectomy. Had it been anything else, Ashley might have finished what she started. But patients with emboli could die in the blink of an eye, and that trumped her office activities.

"Page the MCS team and tell them to set up for a bedside VA-ECMO. And let Dan know he'll be assisting me. I'm on my way."

She hung up, but despite her promise, her feet stayed rooted to the floor. The last thing she wanted was to leave.

At least she'd had her completion first.

She turned to face Nadia, solemnly remembering that she had not yet had any. Nadia had already pulled on her bottom scrubs and bra and was retrieving her top from the floor.

At least I won't have to tell a naked woman I have to leave, Ashley thought bitterly.

"So you have a PE consult?" Nadia was back to her usual self, her tone cool and matter-of-fact. She passed Ashley the box of tissues on the desk.

"I do." Ashley averted her eyes as she wiped the moisture from her hand. Up until now, she had let her body dictate her actions. But that was over, and she had to face a reality she very much wished to avoid dealing with. "The patient is stable, but she isn't responding to anticoagulation." She looked around for her panties. "I have to go." She couldn't possibly walk around the hospital without panties. *Where are they?*

"I know." Nadia handed her what she was looking for.

"Thanks." Ashley pulled them on, still avoiding meeting Nadia's eyes. "Uh…" She finally looked up. How did one gracefully address what had just happened between them? "Thank you."

Nadia tilted her head.

Oh, God. Ashley blushed furiously. "Thank you for apologizing for the OR incident," she clarified hurriedly. "I'm not going to hold it against you this time." The clear professional message should encourage Nadia to behave in the future.

"That's it?"

Or not. "What else is there to say?"

Ashley grabbed a pair of scrubs from her desk drawer, removed her boots and skirt, and put the pants on.

Nadia watched her dress, staring intently, then looked away. "Look, I shouldn't tell you how to do your job."

Ashley chuckled. "But you will anyway?"

"Only if you would consider it a friendly piece of advice rather than crossing a line."

Still wearing only her bra, she faced Nadia. "This should be good. I'm all ears." She picked up her scrub top.

"If you want to be taken seriously, you shouldn't let fellows run your OR." Nadia's voice retained its characteristic even tone, but the words were rushed. She was still avoiding looking at Ashley.

"What exactly are you suggesting I do?"

Ashley pulled on her scrubs, left her office, and headed to the restroom, Nadia following briskly behind her.

"If I were you, I wouldn't let my trainee get away with a private apology after pulling a public stunt." She said the words casually, as if they were discussing the actions of a third party who had nothing to do with Nadia.

What was she getting at? Surely, it couldn't be a selfless attempt to help Ashley recover her reputation. Ashley gave an amused scoff. *Is Nadia even capable of altruism?* She considered Nadia's words as she washed her hands in a way befitting a surgeon.

"Are you saying I should make you apologize in front of everyone?"

"Dream bigger."

"I should...uh"—Ashley felt the heat rising to her cheeks again—"discipline you?"

Nadia exhaled noisily. "For God's sake, you shouldn't be trying to guess the answer."

That wasn't what had made Ashley hesitate, but the nuance appeared to elude Nadia. Ashley cleared her throat to mask her flustered enjoyment at Nadia's single-mindedness and then dried her hands. "Fine. Consider your OR privileges suspended for the next three weeks. Happy?"

"Of course not! I don't want to be out of the operating room for three weeks. It will hurt. But that is the point."

"What point, exactly?" Ashley walked over to the elevator and impatiently pushed the button.

"This needs to happen for you to get some respect around here."

"You're doing this for me?" Wide-eyed, she searched Nadia's serious face.

"Don't ever repeat this to anyone."

Ashley grinned. When Nadia had entered her office earlier, it had put her on edge. But she was hardly mad at her anymore. Because of multiple factors, one of which might have to do with elevated endorphin levels because of a certain afterglow phenomenon.

"Seriously, don't say a word. I have a reputation to maintain." Nadia continued to look perfectly serious, but her eyes sparkled.

"Okay, we'll try it your way. I'll play the hard boss. You seem to enjoy it."

Nadia scoffed. "I must be losing my mind."

"What just happened"—Ashley bit her lip—"was...interesting." *So much for grace.*

"I normally don't let other people be in charge."

"Oh, really? I hadn't noticed."

"Cute." The dry tone didn't support the statement. Still, Nadia appeared dangerously close to a smile.

"We should probably talk about it."

"What's there to talk about?" Nadia crossed her arms.

Ashley smiled despite the sharp look Nadia shot at her. "How about, I'm sorry we got interrupted before I could…reciprocate?"

The elevator finally arrived, and Ashley stepped in, fighting the urge to stay and continue the conversation. She had a sick patient waiting for her.

"And I'm sorry for the way I behaved in your OR. Let's call it even."

"I'm happy to make it up to you next time," Ashley suggested playfully.

Nadia's face hardened, making Ashley's stomach drop. As the doors began to close, she added, "This was a one-time thing. It will never happen again."

***

Ashley walked to the emergency department, Nadia's words repeating on a relentless loop in her mind. *It will never happen again.*

Why not? Having sex with Nadia had been different and unexpected, but it had also made her body vibrate with an almost-forgotten desire.

Ashley's jaw tightened as anger rose in her. How could Nadia be so compliant one minute and so damn stubborn the next?

Then a new thought twisted her insides with dread. Ashley had been so lost in the moment, she hadn't considered that it might have been…too much. What if it had been a blatant abuse of power on her part?

Maybe it was Ashley's fault that Nadia didn't want them to do this again. Maybe she had done the wrong thing by responding to her kiss and everything that had happened after it.

"Dr. Rylan." Hayes approached her the moment she entered the emergency department. His face was pale, but his eyes were wide and alert. "Patient went into cardiac arrest. We're working on resuscitating her, but there may not be a point if you think she's not eligible for surgery. What do you want us to do?"

Ashley sifted through the possibilities, or rather through the lack of options available to the patient. They were running out of time. A cardiac arrest upon presentation predicted a poor outcome. The patient's survival was one in four at best. And that was optimistic.

Maybe it was the endorphins still in her system, or maybe she felt the need to do something right, but she said, "Let's get her pulse back and go to the OR stat."

She clenched her jaw and followed Hayes. She was going to get this right.

Chapter 9

Everything is About Sex Except Sex

"Did you know Rylan was a lesbian?"

"Excuse me?" Nadia's voice was a notch higher than she wanted it to be despite her effort to sound indifferent. She lifted her head.

Dan had joined her at the table in the cafeteria, interrupting her solitude. *Pity.* She thought she was doing a great job pretending to read a journal article she had printed out. In reality, she was thinking about the same woman Dan was referring to. Since their indiscretion last week, she had been losing an unacceptable amount of sleep because of her.

"She told me she was gay. Is this a known fact?" His tone was sharp and strained.

Nadia narrowed her eyes on him. It didn't look as if he had slept much. His hair was disheveled, his eyes were bloodshot, and he hadn't shaved in a couple of days. It all supported Nadia's hypothesis that he had spent the weekend drowning his sorrows in alcohol. Naturally, he was suffering the consequences of a hangover.

He looks like a wet puppy.

Nadia fought the urge to smile. Knowing someone else was affected by Rylan was strangely satisfying. And wrong. Her heart was also heavy with empathy for her comrade—after all, they had both succumbed victims to the charms of the same pretty blonde.

Clearing her throat, Nadia chased the conflicting thought away. She shouldn't tolerate this *the-chief-is-gay* conversation. "I don't think Dr. Rylan would appreciate you asking people if she's a lesbian." Nadia didn't want to lie to Dan, but gossip was in poor taste and unkind, and she would have none of it.

"I'm not asking just anybody," Dan said. "I'm asking you because I know you're discreet and because you seem to know everything about everyone."

Of course, Dan's statement was inaccurate. She had only recently found out Rylan was a lesbian. Nadia paid attention to which doctors had spouses and children, but that was only so she could decide if she wanted to do research with them. Family people were often torn between being in the hospital and attending some second-grade recital about the *Prince Frog* or something equally appalling.

"No, I didn't know." She delivered the lie with conviction. *It wasn't entirely a lie.* Besides, it was none of Dan's business.

"Good," Dan said. "I'm glad I wasn't the only one fooled."

"Fooled?" Bile rose in Nadia's throat. "There isn't some diabolical plot to make people believe she's a heterosexual woman humbled to be considered by any man who would give her a drop of attention. Stop obsessing over her, and let her fuck whomever she wants."

Nadia fought to control her breathing. She told herself she was annoyed that she was defending Rylan rather than at Dan's thoughtless remark. Because that would mean she wasn't emotionally invested in Rylan.

Dan studied her. "Sorry. I take it back." He raised his hands in surrender. "You know I didn't mean it that way."

Nadia sat back in her chair, her anger dissolving. Who could stay mad at a wet puppy?

"I just can't believe how oblivious I was. You know, at times I thought she might even be interested in me. In the last couple of weeks, she's asked me to assist her with every case. And she's always so happy and relaxed when we work together. We have great chemistry in the OR. I anticipate her moves and assist her without her having to ask. I can't believe it was all in my head."

To be fair, it wasn't *all* in his head. Lately Rylan had worked closely with Dan. But her proximity to him was because she was running away from Nadia rather than running toward him. Nadia shifted in her seat, telling herself it was what she wanted Rylan to do. But the more time that passed without them talking, the more the unwelcome ache in her gut grew.

Besides, if one ignored the constant irritation, the power struggle, and the overwhelming disagreements, Nadia had better working chemistry with Rylan than Dan could ever hope to have.

Nadia rolled her eyes. Who was she fooling? She hated working with Rylan.

"Uh, sorry again," Dan said. "Didn't mean to bring up surgeries. It must be hard getting benched out of the OR for three weeks."

She hadn't been thinking about it, but since he brought it up, she did miss being away from the action. Operating helped her put things into perspective and calmed her stormy mind. It was another piece in her life that was now missing.

She bit back an irritated sigh at all the unsettling thoughts that kept resurfacing with this conversation. *Thanks a lot, Dan.*

"Doesn't bother me," Nadia said evenly. "For the past week, I've been working on something big; something I've wanted to do ever since I was in med school. So it's been time well spent. Besides, two more weeks, and I'll have served my sentence."

Dan smiled at her. It was probably meant to be reassuring, but it only sparked more irritation. She didn't need his pity.

"I still can't believe Dr. Rylan suspended your OR privileges, even though you were wrong and she was right."

Nadia narrowed her eyes. "Even a broken clock is right twice a day."

Dan chuckled. "Even with that attitude of yours, I still can't believe it. I thought Dr. Rylan was too nice and patient to do it."

She didn't do anything. Well, not without some help, anyway. Leave it to Nadia to come up with the brilliant idea to harden up the chief's image at her own expense. She sighed. She only hoped her sacrifice would not be in vain and Rylan would win some respect.

Nadia frowned at her own flawed thoughts. It was hard to believe she, Nadia Keating, had put Rylan's needs first. Why did she even care?

"It isn't like you to just roll over either." Dan studied her.

Uh-oh. Nadia tried to swallow against a sudden dryness. "It doesn't matter if Dr. Rylan was right or not. I was wrong to argue with her in the OR. She only did what anyone in her position would do. There's a reason surgery isn't a democracy. I had to be reminded of that." *And the Oscar for best remorseful performance goes to...*

Dan nodded, taking the bogus statement at face value. "She's kind and nice and yet strong and decisive when she has to be."

Nadia snorted at the lovesick proclamation. "You can't still be hoping to be with her."

He looked at her with those sad puppy eyes and denied nothing.

"Oh, stop." Nadia shook her head. "Don't tell me you think she's a lesbian only because she hasn't met the right guy yet. And you're the one who is going to sweep her off her feet and take her to heterosexual heaven." Nadia laughed. "That never works. If she told you she's gay, she meant it." *And I confirmed it.*

Dan sank down in his chair and guilt tugged at Nadia's conscience. Maybe she shouldn't have been so blunt with him. He was a good man, and Nadia was only too aware that she was projecting her own resentment onto him. He was just a guy with a hopeless crush on an unattainable woman.

Nadia bit her lip. She was just as guilty. She had avoided Rylan for an entire week.

She had her reasons, of course, and they could all be summarized by the *it's complicated* cliché. Being with Rylan wasn't what she wanted, needed, or could have right now.

Maybe ever.

Nadia took a deep breath to combat the tightness in her chest. She refused to speculate. The whole thing was supposed to have been a silly experiment to take care of her need for novelty.

But it hadn't worked. In fact, her entire body ached with need to be touched by Rylan again.

She looked at Dan, who openly reflected the feelings she worked so hard at concealing. There was nothing she could do to silence her own heart, but perhaps she could help to heal his. She tried to think of something comforting to say.

She drew a blank.

While they sat in companionable silence, Jason and Li, the other two fellows, joined them. Nadia greeted them with a scowl. Why did everyone assume they could just invite themselves to her table?

"What are you two talking about?" Jason asked.

Nadia glanced at Dan, hoping he had enough sense to keep his mouth shut.

"Uh, as a soon-to-be attending, I intend to join the antirejection multicenter drug study Nadia is participating in. I was asking her about the start-up requirements." It was a semiplausible story.

"Exciting," Jason said sarcastically. "I prefer to focus on actual surgery once I complete my fellowship. Research is for lab rats."

Nadia studied him with pursed lips. Shredding him to pieces would be a welcomed distraction. "It's a clinical trial. If you're unfamiliar with the term, it means actual human participants are involved. In our study, the participants are very sick—often dying." Nadia shuffled her papers, aligning them in a neat pile. "Would it be better if PhD doctors treated these patients?" She paused for him to respond, but he said nothing. Under her cool mask a gloating thrill quivered inside her. "But why stop at excluding patient research from your resumé? If you can outsource patient management entirely, you can stick only to the technical part of surgery. Maybe you'll win an award for advancing the field one day." Her words cut through the tense silence. "Or would that count as devolving surgery back to its barbaric roots?"

Jason opened his mouth to speak, then closed it again. Neither Li nor Dan jumped to his defense.

"If you love cutting so much, you should have become a butcher. I heard the training is considerably shorter."

The bouts of laughter that came from Dan and Li strengthened the impact of her words. There was nothing else she wanted to say to either of them. She pushed her chair back and walked away. Fraternizing with her colleagues was a fool's errand.

Her departure was intercepted by one of the CT surgery attendings. "Keating, I'm glad I found you." Michael Miller stepped in front of her. "The patient in bed seven had an aortic valve repair surgery yesterday, but her chest tubes' output is still high. She must be bleeding from somewhere. We need to go back to the OR for exploratory surgery. Are you free to assist?"

"Dr. Miller, as you are well aware, I'm not supposed to be in the OR this week." Nadia was pleased her voice betrayed none of her sadness.

"Oh, come on, Nadia. I'm sure Ashley will understand," Miller said tightly. "My patient is in critical condition."

Nadia held her lips in a thin line. Miller's sense of entitlement meant he thought he could disregard Rylan's authority as chief. *Not this time.* At least not if Nadia could help it. "If you clear it with Dr. Rylan, I'll be more than happy to assist you. But if your patient is in such critical condition, I suggest you ask one of the other fellows," she said, gesturing at the table she had just left.

He glanced at the fellows there, taking in Dan's hangdog expression, Jason's overzealous smile, and Li's confused demeanor. None of them at that moment inspired confidence.

Turning on her heels, Nadia added, "I'm sure one of West Coast's finest will do while I'm out of service."

She walked away before Miller could say anything else, her fists clenched in her white coat's pockets. Two more weeks of suspension. Two more weeks without seeing Rylan. Two more weeks to get her irrational feelings in order. And she would get them in order. If she focused on her research hard enough, maybe she would forget what touching Rylan felt like. Or what her scent was…or how she tasted. Nadia pushed the thought down, clenching her fists more tightly. Two more weeks to forget what she couldn't have.

―――――― •·• ――――――

Ashley went to Pari's office for their usual Monday lunch, carrying two salads, a cup of coffee, and a cup of tea. They had begun the tradition seven years earlier when Ashley was still in training, and it continued whenever their schedules allowed.

Today her feet were dragging, but not from fatigue. Last week's after-hours office encounter laid heavy on her heart and made everything she once enjoyed difficult to endure.

"Come in. I'm almost done with this email."

Ashley set the food and drinks on Pari's desk and numbly waited for her friend to finish typing.

Her email finished, Pari picked up the salad closest to her. "Thanks. I'm starving."

Looking at her salad, Ashley pushed around a piece of broccoli with her fork. She had no appetite.

"Thank God for these lunches or I'd never see you. Ever since you decided to play the hard boss, we've been a fellow short in the OR," Pari said between bites.

"Sorry I had to ground your star pupil. Perhaps if you had taught her some manners, I wouldn't have had to." She spoke with more anger than she intended. Nadia's unwillingness to even talk to Ashley made playing the mean chief who suspended discordant fellows much easier.

"Don't worry about it. I prefer to work with Keating, but Dan has been an adequate replacement, though lately he looks like a kicked puppy. Must be girl trouble, if you ask me."

Ashley cringed. Dan's dejection was also her fault.

Pari continued, seemingly oblivious to Ashley's reaction. "Jason has been less than impressive so far, but I'll whip him into shape by the time he graduates. I think you made the right call suspending Keating, although I was surprised you had it in you."

I didn't. It was Nadezhda's idea. A stabbing pain gripped her heart.

"It's been good for her to have a time out," Pari said. "Although she's been so engulfed with her latest research project, I suspect she's learned nothing."

"What project?" Maybe Nadia had a legitimate reason for dodging her all week.

"Something about reinventing the way we do transplantation. Whatever the hell that means. She's been very vague about it."

Great. Ashley gave up trying to eat and sipped her coffee. *A fake project for a fake excuse.*

"But enough about work. Tell me, how is your dating life going? Did you hear back from your one-night stand?"

Ashley crossed her arms. "I don't want to talk about it."

"She never reached out?" Pari gave her an empathetic look. "That explains why you've been so down lately."

"No, it's not that. She did contact me." *She came to my office and apologized.* "But she made it clear she wasn't interested in a relationship." *We had sex, she left, and we haven't spoken ever since.*

"She must be insane if she doesn't want to date you."

"Thanks." Ashley forced a smile. Pari's comments were always a great confidence booster.

"Why are you so miserable about a one-night stand, anyway? Was she *that* good?"

Ashley blushed. Sex with Nadia Keating was addictive. Even though Ashley had been exposed to the drug only once, and even though she knew it was bad for her, she craved more of it. Memories of that night flashed through her mind every time she saw Nadia. And even though they never spoke, every time, Ashley tensed with anticipation and her heart rate quickened. She knew that particular drug's withdrawal effects would continue for a long time.

"I've never seen you at a loss for words before. That good, huh?" Pari teased. She finished her salad and reached for her Darjeeling tea.

At that moment, Ashley realized that she didn't owe Nadia anything. She would be discreet about the details, of course, but there was no reason not to talk with Pari about the encounter. Unlike Nadia, she wasn't made of stone. "She was…memorable, yes, but that's not what's bothering me. Have you heard the expression, 'Everything in the world is about sex except sex. Sex is about power'?"

"Sure. Kevin Spacey said it in *House of Cards*."

"Actually, I've heard it attributed to Oscar Wilde, although that's unlikely too."

Pari shrugged. Like her favorite pupil, she rarely thought she was wrong about anything. Ashley shook her head with amusement.

"Anyway, it never made sense to me before. I figured it must be some heterosexual battle of the sexes or whatever. But when I was with, uh, that woman, I got it. Sex with her was great, but it had nothing to do with love. It was raw lust and desire, purely physical. And it was about power. I wanted to possess her, to control her. I've never felt anything like it before. And because she was someone who was normally in charge, it was even hotter when she took orders from me."

Pari tilted her head at Ashley.

Ashley looked down. Had she overshared? They had talked about sex before. And Pari always wanted details.

"I can't picture it." Pari's lips twitched despite visibly trying to keep a straight face.

"What?"

"You dressed in leather with a riding crop."

Ashley rolled her eyes. "It wasn't like that. There were no…accessories."

Pari burst out laughing. "Yes, ma'am. Whatever you say."

Was the thought of Ashley being in charge *that* funny? "Stop!" Ashley smiled in spite of herself. "You're missing the point."

"Sorry, sorry. What was your point?"

"Well, given that it was…edgy, I think I might have crossed a line. We didn't discuss…limits." Hot blood flooded Ashley's cheeks. The more she tried to explain it, the more BDSM it sounded. "And now she won't speak to me."

Pari nodded, her face turning serious. "Now I see why you're so bothered by it. You're worried you might have abused your power during your role-play." She paused and then clicked her tongue. "Ashley, I wish I had something more comforting to tell you, but unless you want to spend the next hour dissecting your sexual encounter, I think you should just let it go. She wasn't interested in a relationship in the first place. Don't beat yourself up over something that's passed. You're a good person. Let it go." Pari gave her a gentle smile.

If only it were that simple. A lump of unspoken words stuck in Ashley's throat. Pari would never understand unless she knew the full story, and Ashley could never tell it. She was bound by discretion not to share all the details.

Ashley slumped deep in her chair, dejected. Even if they didn't work together, Nadia wasn't easy to forget—if Ashley even wanted to. But what she did want more than anything was to make things right between them.

Her jaw tightened with determination. She would have to talk with Nadia or she would never escape the mental vines that clutched at her.

Chapter 10

The Unattainable Woman

It was just sex. Nadia stared at the source of her turmoil, her heart rate quickening just at the sight of Rylan sitting a row in front of her.

It was easy to hide from her when she wasn't allowed in the OR. Nadia stayed in her lab. She worked on her research. That was it.

But Monday afternoon, she had to attend the weekly meeting of surgeons and interventional cardiologists who were forced to pretend they didn't hate each other.

Nadia focused on the video on the large projector screen that showed a heart's vasculature that disappeared and reappeared as contrast dye streamed through the arteries. Despite being one of the worst coronary angiograms Nadia had ever seen, her face didn't flinch. She had long ago learned to approach such cases with acceptance. There was only so much medicine could do.

"I'm telling you if we stent the LM, the OM1, and the RCA, the patient will be as good as new." The senior interventional cardiologist, Stefan Kowalski, stabbed his finger in the air.

Hardly. Nadia bit back a scoff. The heart was tragically trying to do its job, and it was failing. Miserably.

"You can't be serious, Stefan. Even if you revamp all his coronaries with your metal monsters, this man will still die. He should have been on my transplant list yesterday." Singh scowled through her glasses.

Nadia glanced at the wall clock. Only ten minutes had passed. It felt like ten hours. Interventional cardiologists and cardiac surgeons were always fighting over patients. Why the administration had decided they should be friends was beyond her.

Nadia looked at the video again. She agreed with Singh. That heart was good for nothing. A transplant was the patient's only hope for prolonging his life.

"It won't work, Pari," Kowalski argued. "Why offer him something he may not survive waiting for when we can put in stents today?"

"Bypass surgery is superior to stenting in multivessel disease," Williams said immediately.

And so it went, the same dance routine every single time. The surgeons would cry out that a triple-vessel disease warranted a bypass surgery. The cardiologists would wave some random paper as if it were the Holy Grail and argue it supported their claim for stenting. The surgeons would rebut the validity of the paper, and the cardiologists would act offended that their integrity had been questioned.

Eventually, it would escalate into an outright war where everyone pointed a finger and questioned the ethics of their colleagues, declaring that they alone cared about the good of the patient.

Nadia sat back in her chair. This discussion would take a while.

"Why don't we try an LVAD?" The soft voice was drowned in the shouting match between Williams and Kowalski. These meetings always ended with a pissing contest between those two. The noise was getting on Nadia's nerves.

"Shut up!"

As soon as Nadia yelled, she realized three things. One, she needed to learn to tolerate her attendings better. Two, Singh had shouted out the same words at the same time. And three, everyone was staring at Nadia.

She cleared her throat. "I believe Dr. Rylan had another suggestion."

Nadia cringed at her own kindness. Why did she care enough to interfere? She should have let Singh defend Rylan.

"Right." Rylan spoke a little more loudly. "Thank you, Nadezhda," she said without making eye contact. "I suggest an LVAD while we do his transplant workup if CABG or PCI are both too little, too late."

The discussion continued for another twenty minutes. Nadia ignored the twist in her stomach, stubbornly deciding that Rylan not looking at her for the rest of the meeting was for the best. She leaned back in her chair again and crossed her arms, reminding herself to stay quiet. The doctors forgot she was even there—except Singh, who threw the occasional baffled look at her as if she were from another planet.

Just great. Her mentor must think she was mentally unstable.

"Nadezhda, wait. We need to talk."

Nadia kept walking. Rylan was making it impossible to keep her distance. Her outburst during yesterday's meeting had poked holes in Nadia's resolve to pretend that nothing had happened between them. But playing nice hurt them both. They couldn't be together. As much as she mourned for Rylan's touch, a relationship would never work. They were simply two women who'd had sex. Once.

Did it even count as once if they had been interrupted?

Nadia pushed down the thought. It was best to stay as far away as possible.

But Rylan hadn't gotten the memo. She caught up with Nadia as she waited for the elevator. "I'm sorry," she said.

The words grated. Rylan apologized too much.

Nadia said nothing. She wanted Rylan to leave before her body gave her away. The fine hairs on her arm already stood at full alert, every nerve recruited to take in Rylan's presence.

She focused on her breathing, telling her body to stand down. There would be no encore performance. She had set clear parameters: *one* encounter. Anything more was dangerous.

"I'm sorry for whatever I did wrong." Rylan persisted with her apology.

Nadia turned to face her. "Dr. Rylan, I have no idea what you're apologizing for."

"Call me Ashley. And I obviously did something wrong. You're avoiding me."

Nadia balled her hands into fists. Standing so close to Rylan made her heart race. She wanted to touch her arm and assure her she had done nothing wrong. In fact, if Nadia objectively evaluated that evening, Rylan had done things very right.

The elevator doors opened. Singh, Dan, Jason, and Li stepped back to make room, and Nadia rushed in it. To her angst, Rylan followed.

"Nadia, hi." Dan smiled at her.

She nodded, her stoic expression unchanging.

The men exchanged pleasantries with the chief. After that, no one spoke. Nadia moved as far away from Rylan as possible in the limited space, settling next to Jason, half-hidden behind his broad shoulders.

Finally, Li said, "We're going to see the new Da Vinci in action!"

Great. She was missing a robotic surgery case as a direct result of doing something *nice.* Nadia forced her face to remain expressionless as misery gripped her heart.

Rylan caught her eye. "The robot will still be here in two weeks."

Nadia frowned. Rylan was only making things worse. She didn't need or want her sympathy.

"So despite Keating coming to your rescue yesterday, she's still in the doghouse?" Singh spoke to Rylan as if Nadia weren't there.

Nadia's jaw tightened as she refused to look away or be bothered by this conversation.

Rylan glared at Singh but didn't say anything.

"Aren't you going to the PR meeting?" Singh asked Rylan.

"It's in ten minutes. But, uh, first Nadezhda asked me to approve a purchase for her research project."

Nadia stood still, wishing she was invisible. Why did Rylan have to involve her in such a transparent lie to Singh, the only doctor in the hospital whose opinion of her mattered?

"You should go to your meeting, Dr. Rylan. I may not need that approval after all." *And you need to focus on your work and quit chasing me.* "As you know, my research grant outweighs the departmental budget by twofold." Nadia raised her chin. She had good reason to be smug. It was a true statement. Rylan could have come up with a less idiotic excuse if she wanted people to buy it.

"But you do need my approval to get clinical clearance for the use of the equipment."

Nadia flinched with distaste. It was true. Her new device needed to be medical grade. And it was clear Rylan wasn't going away. Might as well get the conversation over with. She held Rylan's gaze, her lips pressed into a thin line. "Certainly, Dr. Rylan."

The elevator reached the OR level, and Singh left for the Da Vinci surgery. The three fellows followed her like a flock of ducklings.

Without the audience, Nadia turned away, ready to ignore whatever Rylan wanted to say.

She said nothing.

Nadia snuck a glance back at her—Rylan was fidgeting with the button on one of the sleeves of her tailored navy-blue shirt. Despite Nadia's best efforts, her gaze traveled upward. The color of Rylan's shirt was a stark contrast to her pale skin, and she had left open the top two buttons, revealing just a hint of the swell of her breast.

What was under that shirt? How could it be that Nadia was intimately familiar with the sounds Rylan made when she orgasmed but had no idea how to answer that question?

Nadia faced forward again. It was useless. No matter how hard she fought to keep her mind off of Rylan, it rebelliously kept straying to their shared evening. Nadia had replayed it over many sleepless nights. Everything had happened too fast and with too many clothes on Rylan's part. It had lacked some critical components, such as being able to map out Rylan's anatomical landmarks. Instead, their time together had only created an intense longing for more, a longing she struggled to ignore constantly.

Nadia glanced over at Rylan again. She was still fidgeting with that damn button. "For God's sake, let me do it."

She rushed across to Rylan to help her for the sole purpose of removing her own temptation.

"You'd think a cardiothoracic surgeon would have better dexterity," she muttered, hoping the harsh comment would somehow lessen her realization that she would much rather be helping Rylan unbutton that shirt.

Rylan sighed. "Would it kill you to do something nice without adding an insult to it?" She withdrew her arm but not before Nadia had secured the button.

The elevator finally stopped on the ninth floor, where Nadia's lab was. She charged ahead without looking back, but Rylan followed closely on her heels. When they reached the lab, Nadia handed Rylan a document from her desk.

"What's this?"

"You wanted to sign for a medical-grade device."

Rylan sat down and scanned the paper, then looked up at Nadia. "And if I don't sign?"

Nadia shrugged. "You can do what you want. I intended to ask the chair anyway. I thought you might want to do something productive since you've come all this way."

Rylan looked at the paper again. "So you want to get an organ bioreactor?"

"I *am* getting an organ bioreactor." Nadia punched the words with conviction. "I need it approved for clinical use."

"You intend to grow tissue for human use?" Rylan's brows kneaded as she tried to piece together the scant information Nadia was giving her. "Do you have research approval for that?"

"No. It's not a clinical trial." Nadia tried to be nonchalant. "Yet. But if it becomes one, I can use this same device."

"You're saving the department money?"

"You're welcome."

Rylan huffed. She reached to the breast pocket of her shirt, as if she had her white coat on, but her fingers grazed the smooth fabric of her shirt instead. "Got a—?"

Before she could finish the sentence, Nadia handed her a pen.

Their fingers brushed, and Nadia's disloyal heart instantly fluttered. Ignoring it, she forced herself to focus on the paper Rylan was signing.

After it was done, Rylan faced her with a half-smile. "So there is an actual project you've been working on? It wasn't an excuse to avoid me?"

The direct question prompted an internal smile that never made it to Nadia's lips. She considered pointing out that she excelled at multitasking and could do both. Instead, she schooled her features into well-rehearsed neutrality. "Dr. Rylan, I don't know what you did during your surgical training, but I haven't gotten this far by pretending to do work."

The look of hurt in Rylan's eyes made Nadia almost regret her words, but she pushed past it. In situations of emotional distress, only a true master could maintain self-control.

"Tell me, is this passive-aggressive attitude a hardwired part of you, or is it something I can turn off?"

Nadia continued to hold her gaze, unmoved.

"And for the love of God, it's Ashley!" She glared at her. "I didn't come here to discuss your work performance. Why is it so hard for you to call me by my first name?"

"Because we're not friends, *Dr. Rylan*." Nadia's mask was firmly in place. She held Rylan's eyes with equal intensity. It was time to set clear boundaries. "You're my boss, and I'm your student. Anything else would be an inappropriate overfamiliarity."

"Really? That's where you draw the line of propriety?" Rylan threw the paper on the table. "Having sex with me is allowed, but calling me by my first name is heresy?"

Why couldn't she understand? This conversation was only hurting them both.

Nadia's mask cracked, and her chest rose with frustration. "You told me you could handle a one-night stand. Why aren't you *handling it*?"

Rylan's mouth snapped shut. She blinked, her stubborn expression morphing into one of mere hurt that clenched Nadia's heart. Rylan looked down at the floor. "Because, Nadezhda," she said, her voice low and steady, "most people have emotions that cannot be turned off on demand. We can't all be robots like you."

Nadia's nostrils flared. She wished she were a robot. It would be easier to not have emotions than to work so hard to hide them. "A surgeon should have a better hold on her emotions."

Rylan looked up to meet Nadia's gaze. She said nothing for several long seconds. "Forget it. I'm sorry I even bothered to talk to you. I'll stay out of your way and you stay out of mine for the next two years, and everything will be just perfect!"

Nadia met the outburst with stubborn determination and a steely indifference. "Agreed."

Rylan's face lost its momentary scowl. "Why do you have to be so"—her voice almost faded into silence— "you?"

Nadia stared at her. She lacked the will to fire back a hurtful comment or pretend like nothing bothered her. Pushing down the urge to say something soothing or reach out, she simply stood there.

Rylan sighed softly and left the lab without saying another word.

Still frozen in her place, it occurred to Nadia that every time she spoke with Rylan lately, one of them stormed out hurt.

She shook her head as if to chase the thought away, walked over to her desk, and sat down. She stared into the black computer screen. *This is a good thing*, she told herself over and over, hoping she would believe it. She was finally left alone to focus on her work. It should bring her comfort.

She continued to sit rigidly in deafening silence. A nagging feeling chipped away at her consciousness. Maybe she had hurt Rylan the same way Rylan had hurt Dan. She balled her hands into fists until her short nails bit into flesh. *Except I'm not the unattainable woman in this story.*

Chapter 11

High Velocity, Low Amplitude

WHAT THE HELL AM I doing? Despite her awareness of her own self-sabotage, Nadia continued to stride toward the chief's office, a medium latte in her hand.

The fact that she had spent yet another sleepless night bothered by her latest encounter with Rylan made her grip the paper cup until its shape threatened to give away. She immediately relaxed her hand a little. Whatever this woman was doing to her, it couldn't be good for her mental health.

Her chest tightened, combatting her wayward heart's flutters. She shouldn't care that she had upset Rylan, and yet here she was, ready to apologize. Again. This time, she wasn't even sure she had done anything wrong.

The door was open. Nadia knocked on the door jamb more loudly than she'd intended.

Rylan visibly stiffened when she saw who it was and Nadia reflexively scowled. *A great start.* Nadia walked in without waiting for an invitation that was unlikely to come and placed the coffee on Rylan's desk.

Craning her neck to see past Nadia, Rylan asked, "What is this?"

"Relax, your admin assistant is on a break. And I promise not to kiss you again."

"Oh." Rylan stared at the cup.

"It's a truce offering," Nadia added somewhat more softly. "I figured you could use some caffeine. You look tired."

"Your romance could use some work."

Nadia flinched, as if the word were a scorching fire. "It's a *friendly* gesture. That's all."

"Oh?"

"I told you I'm not interested in a relationship with you. I've been very clear about this. It would never work." Nadia spoke to convince Rylan as well as herself. "But we must work together, and right now we're not doing that. It's my fault. I should have talked to you instead of shutting you out."

"That's…big of you."

Rylan's morose look made Nadia's jaw tighten. What else did she expect her to say?

At least after she sipped the coffee, Rylan grinned, her mood visibly improving. "It's a triple-shot latte. My favorite."

Nadia tried to look as if she wasn't pleased Rylan had noticed. "Don't get too excited. I know all the attendings' coffee drinks."

"Ah."

"Singh drinks Darjeeling tea unless she's slept less than two hours, then she switches to espresso shots. Williams takes his coffee black without sugar, and Miller pretends he doesn't need caffeine but drinks two or three cans of Coke a day when he thinks nobody is looking."

Rylan raised a perfectly shaped eyebrow. "So I'm not special; is that it?"

"Well…" Nadia stepped closer, as if about to reveal a great secret. While her defensive instincts screamed at her to confirm the statement that Rylan wasn't special, her open face with that amused look made Nadia, for some unfathomable reason, want to be honest with her. "I've never gotten coffee for any of them. Learning the doctors' drinks is just a habit I picked up as a medical student. You'd be amazed how easy it is to get on a physician's good side by bringing them a cup of coffee."

"That's what this is? Trying to get on my good side?"

Nadia chuckled. "I'd be a fool to let the chief of my department stay mad at me."

"I'd never let my personal feelings interfere with my professional judgment." Rylan's gentle eyes were fixed on her. "I won't compromise your career."

"I know," Nadia added softly. Of course, she knew that, but hearing Rylan actually say it brought a curious warmth inside her. Distracted by the feeling, her next words slipped past her defenses. "And yet, it felt wrong that you were upset with me." She cleared her throat and looked away. "You didn't do anything wrong, by the way. I was the one who initiated and terminated our…private relationship. I see how keeping you from having a say in it might have been frustrating."

"You refused to talk to me for a week. *Frustrating* is putting it mildly."

"I didn't want to lead you on. I thought shutting you out would be easier for both of us." Nadia fought the urge to wrap her arms around herself, as if she could protect her exposed heart. "I could have handled it better."

Rylan stared at her drink. "So I didn't do anything wrong during… uh…?"

"No," Nadia said firmly. "You didn't."

"I don't know what got over me. I didn't overstep, did I?" Her timid eyes searched Nadia's. She looked so vulnerable, so worried, and nothing like the woman who had commanded Nadia to take her clothes off and pleasure her.

Nadia held the fragile gaze as she said in a cool, low-pitched voice, "Like you can make me do anything I don't want to."

Rylan's posture finally lost its rigidity.

It was curious that she was so bothered by the fact she might have done something wrong during sex. The thought that Nadia had let her feel that way tested her resolve to stay indifferent.

"But I want to make one thing clear," Nadia added. "My only agenda that night was to apologize to you."

Rylan smiled. "I know that. Otherwise you wouldn't have suggested I suspend your OR privileges. Sorry I had to leave before you could…uh…" She blushed.

Nadia raised a questioning eyebrow, adding to her fluster. *She's so damn cute trying to talk about sex.* "You apologize too much."

"Sorry." Rylan's lips curled up.

Nadia laughed out loud. This was dangerous. She cleared her throat, recalling the reason Rylan had left that night. "I'm sorry that embolectomy patient you operated on didn't make it."

Rylan's face instantly darkened. "I suppose you want to tell me I shouldn't have bothered with the surgery."

"It's quite clear now the effort was futile, given the outcome."

The hurt in Rylan's eyes made Nadia want to take the words back. She shouldn't have brought up the subject. A surgeon never got used to patient death, although most got better at hiding their feelings. But Rylan wasn't a typical surgeon. She cared deeply and openly for every single patient. Nadia had never liked seeing vulnerability, but that didn't stop the urge to comfort her.

"Even if the patient had lived," Nadia said, "you'd be criticized that the surgery was unnecessary because she might have survived with medical therapy alone. Since she is brain dead, you are chastised that it was a desperate attempt. Embolectomy is a controversial surgery. It's declared a failure before an incision is even made."

"And what do you think I should have done?"

Nadia gave her best know-it-all smile. "Oh no, Dr. Rylan, I'm not going to comment on what you do in *your* OR. I learned that lesson."

Rylan returned the smile. "You absolutely shouldn't when we're in the middle of a surgery. But I do welcome respectful feedback outside the OR. What kind of a chief would I be if I shut down people's opinions all the time?"

"The no-nonsense kind?" Nadia said before she could stop herself.

"You think letting people express an opinion is a waste of time?" Rylan frowned. "Do you plan to run your OR as a complete dictatorship?"

The thought of running her own OR, once she became an attending surgeon, crossed Nadia's mind frequently. "People tend to doubt one's leadership if one is indecisive. Besides, most people have nothing to contribute to a discussion; they only talk for the sake of talking."

Rylan shook her head. "How can you be a doctor and have such a low opinion of humankind?"

"I'm a surgeon. A superiority complex is in the job description."

"And I suppose I should feel the same to meet your criteria of a good surgeon?" Rylan challenged.

Nadia opened her mouth, but before she replied, she reconsidered and shut it tight. It was a trick question. She shouldn't go anywhere near it. "I think you did the right thing by doing the embolectomy," she said instead. "You rushed her to the OR immediately. The fact that she coded on the way was unavoidable. You couldn't have predicted she wouldn't wake up."

Rylan nodded with glassy eyes. "I knew her heart would stop again. I could have opened her up at bedside instead of having her transported to the OR."

"Now, that would have been insane." If Rylan was about to second-guess herself, which she absolutely shouldn't, she could at least offer a more plausible alternative. "Performing open-heart surgery outside the OR is a fool's errand. Unless you think a postmortem autopsy is a surgeon's job?"

"You're probably right." Rylan rubbed her forehead.

"What's wrong?"

"Oh, it's nothing. Just a nagging headache."

"Ah." An outrageous thought crossed Nadia's mind. "You know, a lot of surgeons suffer from tension headaches." Despite the staccato beat in her chest, her voice was calm. "All that headlight gear makes your neck muscles tight. I can take a look, if you'd like."

Rylan snapped her head up. "You want to treat my headache?"

Nadia nodded.

"With, uh, osteopathic techniques?"

"I can prescribe Percocet, if you prefer the allopathic approach," Nadia said dryly.

Two deep furrows nestled between Rylan's delicate eyebrows, making a twinge of nerves flicker in Nadia's gut. Maybe she shouldn't have offered to help.

"I don't want you to crack my neck."

Rylan's quiet voice made Nadia bite back a huff. Seeing her reluctance and desire to agree for the sake of agreeing was typical for Rylan. What was atypical was Nadia's sudden determination to help Rylan despite her protests. She told herself it was only because she felt guilty for the way she had acted this past week and nothing else.

"If a patient comes in with chest pain, do you immediately book an OR?" Nadia asked.

"Of course not."

"Then why not let me examine you first? You may not even benefit from a cervical HVLA."

"HV—what?"

Nadia chuckled. "It stands for high velocity, low amplitude. It's what we prefer to call 'cracking necks.' And I understand if you don't want me to take a look. I won't be offended."

"It's not that I don't trust you. It's just you never talk about any DO stuff. I don't know how good you are. And it's my neck on the line here."

Rylan's squirming made Nadia purse her lips to hide a smile. *Perhaps she's only capable of dominance during sex.* "It sounds like you don't trust me," she taunted. "How about I palpate your back and neck muscles to assess the problem first? Then we can talk about treatment options. I promise I won't do anything you're not comfortable with."

"Uh, okay."

"Lie down on the sofa." Nadia kept a straight face, despite recalling the same words used when the roles were reversed.

Rylan blushed but complied. Nadia knelt behind her and reached for her neck. She focused on her work despite the conflicting urges to withdraw and bury her fingers into the soft skin playing a tug-of-war game in her mind.

Still, she couldn't resist one final dig. She leaned closer to Rylan's ear and whispered, "Do you need a safe word?"

"Why didn't you choose to practice osteopathic medicine? I'm sure you know how good you are at it." Ashley tried to distract herself from the fact that strands of Nadia's hair that had escaped her ponytail were brushing against her face.

Nadia guided Ashley's head and arm into a contracted position and instructed her to relax. Apparently, the so-called strain counterstrain technique helped release spasmed muscles. It might have worked better if Ashley hadn't been so aware of Nadia's hands on her upper torso.

"I'm good at a lot of things." Nadia was so close that her breath warmed Ashley's ear, sending shivers down her spine. "It doesn't mean I intend to make a career out of every single one of them."

"But you love showing off what you're good at," Ashley teased. The tension in her neck and shoulders had dissipated along with her headache. "Why do you never talk about osteopathy?"

"Relax." Nadia gently squeezed her arm. "I never intended to be anything but a surgeon. Osteopathy is all about noninvasive healing."

"Surgery and osteopathic medicine aren't that different."

"Mm, do tell."

Perhaps arguing with somebody who had a degree in one of the fields and was brilliant in the other was not a good idea. Ashley decided not to reinvent the wheel. A wiser person had said it far better than she ever could. "Surgeons have no influence on the healing mechanisms. The most accurate sutures would not suffice definitely if the organism were not capable of making its own repairs."

Nadia slowly returned Ashley's head to a neutral position and sat up. Ashley turned a little to find her leaning back on her heels. She held herself rigid, despite her face remaining neutral.

"It's from Alexis Carrel, the surgeon who pioneered vessel suturing," Nadia said.

"I'm surprised you know the quote." Then again, Nadia knew everything when it came to surgery.

"And I suppose what you're saying is that surgery and osteopathy preach the same philosophy?"

"Exactly. It's all the same idea. We're all healers, trying to explain the world from our different perspectives, but at the end of the day, it's the same world we're trying to explain. Ideas are bound to overlap."

"I'm curious," Nadia asked with an almost amused voice. "How is it that you read Carrel's book? It's not exactly part of the med school curriculum."

Ashley racked her brain, trying to remember. "I think somebody recommended it to me at a conference some years ago."

Nadia kept her poker face. "Do you remember who it was?"

If this was a quiz, Ashley was failing. Clearly, Nadia knew the answer. "Maybe somebody said it during one of the morning presentations. You know how they try to make them inspirational."

Nadia snorted. The unexpected burst of emotion made Ashley raise her eyebrows in surprise mingled with confusion.

Nadia cleared her throat. "Yes, I suppose these talks tend to sound more like legendary epic tales rather than historical facts." She tilted her head. "You don't remember the speaker?"

Ashley shrugged. "Not really. It was a long time ago."

Nadia got up from where she knelt, slowly walked to Ashley's desk, and hoisted herself up on it, crossing her arms in front of her.

Heat crept up Ashley's cheeks as she recalled the last time she had seen Nadia in that position.

"I must say my ego is quite bruised," Nadia said teasingly. "I'd have thought I was more memorable than a man who died seventy years ago."

Ashley's mouth dropped open. "You were the speaker?"

"Why are you so surprised?"

"You never mentioned that we've met before."

Ashley tried to remember meeting Nadia at the conference. She had probably met thirty different people that day and had since attended many other conferences. Still, her chest tightened with disappointment. How could she have forgotten such a memorable person?

Nadia shrugged. "We spoke briefly before my presentation. You didn't seem to recognize me when we met again at my interview. Why would I want to point out how forgettable I must be?"

Ashley looked away. *Forgettable* was the last word she would use to describe Nadia. "I'm sorry I didn't remember you." She looked back at her, smiling weakly. "I guess that explains why our interview was so hostile."

Nadia pursed her lips. "I admit my feelings might have been a tiny bit hurt."

Ashley knew Nadia well enough by now to see that, past her cool façade, it must bother her a great deal. She would have to make it up to her.

Nadia jumped off the desk and made her way to the door. "I should get back to work. You should too." She glanced at the empty coffee cup. "Are we okay?"

Ashley smiled. "We are."

———— •••• ————

Ashley looked at her reflection in the mirror again, anxiety toying with her nerves. A light blue shirt and tailored black slacks accentuated her figure. The high heels gave her confidence.

She needed it. Nadia was coming to her office again. She had offered to do some more of her osteopathic treatment after Ashley had *casually* mentioned her headache had returned. The truth was her head and neck muscles felt great, and she had been headache-free since the last time Nadia treated her. But admitting that would deprive her of Nadia's addictive touch.

"I hope I'm not interrupting." Nadia appeared like clockwork.

"Not at all." Ashley smiled, the butterflies in her stomach accelerating their flight. "I've been looking forward to it. The last treatment was amazing."

"Not amazing enough to last two days though." Nadia walked in and resumed the familiar position on top of Ashley's desk.

Ashley dropped her gaze. *Was Nadia doing this on purpose or was she unaware of her actions?* She licked her lips. It had to be intentional since nobody ignored furniture intended for sitting by accident. Right?

Ashley leaned against the nearest wall, too nervous to sit down. "How come you went to a DO school if you are so anti-osteopathy?"

"It's not that I'm against it; it's just not what I saw myself doing." Nadia's flat tone betrayed no emotion.

"So what happened?"

Nadia studied the floor. "I did get into some good allopathic schools, but…"

Ashley waited patiently, letting Nadia gather her thoughts, and hoping to see her let her guard down in return.

"I didn't want anything or anyone to get in the way of me and my medical training. I made that very clear to the man I was with at the time. But when I got accepted to a medical school in a different state, he said he'd follow me to the end of the world."

Nadia liked men too? Or maybe it had taken her some time to figure out her preferences? Ashley pushed down the question in her mind and waited for Nadia to continue. Given her long and uncharacteristic pauses, she could tell it was difficult for her to talk about.

"He was supportive, caring, and so charming. I was swept up in the fantasy of having this incredible person by my side. He was willing to support me unconditionally through med school, and I promised in return to be too busy to pay attention to him."

Another pause followed. He sounded like the dream partner, and Nadia clearly had cared for him. Her voice was still guarded, but her face was soft and her eyes were warm and affectionate as she described the man's virtues. An inexplicable knot twisted in Ashley's gut.

Nadia cleared her throat. "Then his mother was diagnosed with stage four breast cancer. It only seemed fair for me to make some sacrifices. I applied and was accepted to the only local medical school. It happened to be a DO school. We stayed in the city. He moved in with his mother. She passed away thirteen months later."

Ashley stared, speechless. Nadezhda Keating had changed her plans to support another human being through a difficult period. She hadn't seen this coming. Pregnancy, tuition issues, even alien kidnapping was more plausible than Nadia's explanation.

Her cold factual delivery lacked the usual romance of such a grand gesture, but the fact was that she had potentially sacrificed her chances for a career in her chosen field because of a man. Surgical residencies were highly competitive and tended to prefer MD applicants. Sure, a DO could do anything an MD could in theory, but in reality, the majority of DOs ended up practicing family medicines.

"Don't look so surprised," Nadia said lightly. "I do perform acts of humanity every now and then."

"You stayed because of a relationship?" Ashley could only muster this question as her mind was blown away.

"It was the right thing to do. And to be honest, I liked the school more than I thought I would."

"What happened to him after his mother died?" Ashley asked before she could stop herself. Did she want to know?

Nadia brushed invisible lint off her scrubs. Then her head snapped up, her expression as indecipherable as ever. "That's not how this works. I told you something personal. Now it's your turn."

Ashley smiled. It was a fair statement. "What would you like to know?"

"When did you...know?" Nadia's eyes were on the floor again.

Ashley filtered her inner smile into an expression that resembled ignorance. "Know what?"

Nadia met her gaze. "You enjoy making me say things that make me uncomfortable, don't you?" She smiled, breaking her stoic look.

"I don't know what you're talking about." Ashley's facial muscles failed her too.

"When did you first know you were attracted to women?" Nadia clarified, a quiver in her voice betraying her cool demeanor.

"I've always known." Ashley bit her bottom lip. Keeping her answers short would force Nadia to ask more *uncomfortable* questions.

"You mean you've never...?"

"Never what?" Ashley savored the discomfort written all over Nadia's face. Seeing her carefully constructed mask fall made Ashley's head spin in delight. "I said I would answer your questions, but you have to ask them first." She was very much enjoying this new sense of power.

"You've never been with a man?"

"No, I haven't."

"But then how can you be sure you aren't attracted to them as well?"

Ashley blinked. She didn't expect such a naïve question from someone like Nadia. *She doesn't know everything after all.* "Have you ever done an orthopedic surgery?"

"No. How is that relevant?"

It was refreshing that, for once, Nadia was the clueless one.

"If you've never done ortho or neuro or plastics, how do you know you wouldn't like them better than thoracic surgery?"

"I always knew I would be a CT surgeon. I didn't see the point in considering other specialties."

Ashley smiled. "I didn't see the point either."

A look of understanding crossed Nadia's face. She leaned back on her hands. "Do I have to continue with the twenty questions? I believe I told you a story."

Nadia's directness made Ashley laugh. She had a point, of course.

"I had my first relationship when I was sixteen. I thought we were in love, but being gay wasn't easy in my school." Ashley shrugged, trying to dismiss the sudden sense of tightness in her chest. It was in the past. "In the end, she chose the quarterback. They became prom queen and king, and I was left pining over a straight girl."

"I'm sorry."

Such an automatic reply was exactly what Ashley expected from Nadia. It was the line every medical student learned to say when delivering bad news. In a typical Keating style, it was devoid of empathy. Nadia had probably always been the one to break up with someone and never the other way around.

Shaking the feeling of insecurity that threatened to overwhelm her, Ashley waved her hand. "It's the biggest cliché in the book. It was a long time ago, and I'm over it. What about you? What was your first experience with a woman like?"

Nadia sat up straight, her expression hardened, and Ashley squinted slightly in a futile effort to read her thoughts. Just as she opened her mouth to speak, Ashley's cellphone rang.

Swallowing a groan, she shot a murderous glare at the wall clock. It was almost seven at night. Why did everyone assume she was available all the time?

She hurried over to her desk and reached across Nadia to pick up the phone. In doing so, her arm brushed against Nadia's thigh, and her heart instantly leaped at the recurring moment between them. "Rylan speaking," Ashley squeaked, her voice giving away her discomposure.

"I need a favor." Pari rarely bothered with the customary hello. "There are two transplants happening tonight, and I'm a surgeon short for the organ recovery. I can't send Li on his own. The lungs are marginal, so I need someone who knows what they're doing."

"You want me to recover for you?" Ashley tried to interpret Pari's words.

Pari burst out laughing. "When was the last time you did a recovery? Four, five years ago? Thanks, but no thanks."

Ashley rolled her eyes. A simple no would have sufficed.

"I need you to let Keating go. I know she's benched, but this is important. You can discipline her some other time."

"Hold on a second." Ashley muted the phone. Nadia was watching her intently, her piercing dark eyes making her lose her train of thought. "Uh." She blinked the spell away. "It's Pari. She needs you to procure a set of lungs for her."

The faintest scowl crossed Nadia's face. "And?"

"And she's asking me to release you from suspension." Despite her better judgment, she wanted Nadia to be involved in the decision.

"You can't be seriously asking me what you should do," Nadia scolded.

Ashley rolled her eyes again. Nadia had mistaken inclusion for indecision. "Hey, this was your ingenious idea. And now the department is short-staffed because people think I'm too sensitive to stomach a little discourse in my OR."

Nadia scoffed. "Believe me, I'm already regretting trying to improve your image."

The harsh words made Ashley's irritation yield to guilt. Ashley loved being in the operating room. Any surgeon did. And Nadia had given it up for her.

She must have looked pretty pathetic because Nadia sighed. "Let her know I can do it, but make it appear like you had the last word."

After considering the advice for a moment, Ashley unmuted the call. "Fine. Nadezhda can go." She watched Nadia's face. "But do not let her assist for the implantation. She goes. She brings the lungs back. She doesn't step foot in the recipient's OR."

Nadia smiled approvingly, matching Pari's enthusiastic "Yes, ma'am" reply. Ashley hung up, interrupting Pari's thanks.

"Not bad," Nadia said. Her softened eyes raked Ashley's face, settling on her lips.

Neither one of them spoke, and for a moment it seemed like Nadia was about to lean in and—

Instead, she shifted away. "I better go get some sleep before the case." She made no move to leave.

Finally, Ashley became very aware of the deafening silence that surrounded them. "Thank you."

"For what?"

"For sharing your story with me."

Nadia opened her mouth but no sound escaped, and she pressed her lips back together.

Ashley watched her, hoping to glimpse the woman behind the mask again.

The silence built again but it was broken when a phone rang, tearing at Ashley's eardrums and shattering the fleeting moment. This time it was Nadia's.

"Keating speaking… Did you clear it with Dr. Rylan?" She looked at Ashley mischievously. "In that case, yes, I can do it. What time do you need me? …Got it. I'll be there." Nadia terminated the call and jumped off the desk. "I have to go." She pulled out a small plastic bottle from her pocket and handed it to Ashley. "These are for you."

Ashley examined the bottle. Ibuprofen. She looked at Nadia quizzically.

Nadia gave her a Mona Lisa smile. "For your headache."

"Right!"

"You should be more consistent with your symptoms if you want to be believable," Nadia said. "Or just come up with a simpler pretext to see me next time."

With a burning face, Ashley struggled to say something clever. Or say anything at all.

Fortunately, Nadia didn't wait for a reply but pivoted on her heel and left.

Ashley stared out after her, then chuckled. Of course, Nadia had called her out. *She loves having the last word.*

Ashley stretched out on the sofa and sighed.

What was she doing?

In just a few short days, she had learned more about Nadia than in the previous seven months. It was an apt metaphor for Nadia's osteopathic technique. What was it called again? High speed in a short distance? Something like that.

But the rush of giddy excitement was mixed with a shiver of fear.

Ashley rubbed her eyes. Stars and colors flashed and swirled before her. Her mind was at war with itself: she both wanted and didn't want to grow closer to Nadia. But while her mind was muddled by mixed desires, one thing was clear—the void in Ashley's heart disappeared whenever she was with Nadia.

Chapter 12

The Extraction

NADIA'S PHONE PINGED, AND SHE grabbed it eagerly. Her excitement quickly fizzled out. It wasn't Rylan. Disappointment turned to guilt and gripped her like a cold hand. She had to quit misleading Rylan—everyone.

Yet, her heart jolted every time she and Rylan were close, or even if she just thought of her. *Pathetic.* It wasn't like her to be so self-conscious as she was around Rylan. She shoved the phone back in her pocket. The message wasn't work-related. It could wait.

When the car stopped moving, Nadia glanced out the window. They had arrived at the small private airport. She had barely registered the trip. Her thoughts had been too preoccupied with the mess she had gotten herself into.

"Hello, you must be Drs. Keating and Wei." A man read the names from an itinerary sheet. "I'm John. I'll be your pilot tonight. We're going for the, uh…extraction?"

Nadia smiled. "I've never heard anyone refer to an organ procurement that way, but yes, we are. I'm Dr. Keating." The three parties shook hands, and the doctors followed him to the small private-jet parking lot.

Despite the appearance of luxury, there was nothing glamorous about their form of travel. As expected, the aircrafts kept getting smaller and smaller.

"Are we going by plane or boat?" Nadia deadpanned.

John chuckled. "It's only a fifty-minute flight. The SF50 will suffice."

Li and the pilot loaded the equipment, giving Nadia a moment of silence. Once they had boarded, Li kept up a steady stream of conversation. Nadia gritted her teeth. He was a good man, but he had the tendency to ask too many questions. Instead of entertaining him, she wanted to focus on the unresolved issue of why she was allowing herself to be so close to Rylan. Nadia pulled up an article about lung recovery protocol on her phone and pretended to read it as they took off. Even after that, Li tried to chat with her, but it was impossible to maintain conversation above the roar of the engine, and he finally lapsed into silence. Nadia stared at the article, but all she saw was Rylan's easy smile. She shook her head to erase the image.

She was developing feelings for the subject of her one-time experiment. Taking a deep breath she hoped to break the suffocating grip around her chest. Spending time with Rylan was like a disastrous vortex she couldn't escape. She shook her head. This irrational yearning had to stop.

Deliberately changing the rhythm of her breathing to deep, slow breaths, Nadia reminded herself that she was in control. She forced herself to relax.

Despite her inner turmoil, she knew there was more to Rylan than she had originally thought. She was almost ready to admit that she might have judged her prematurely. Professionally speaking, of course.

The thought that she might have been wrong again made Nadia frown.

Rylan was indecisive and lacked essential skills when it came to surgery—that hadn't changed. But Nadia might have overlooked some of her redeeming qualities. For one thing, Rylan was open to considering feedback or advice from anyone. Nadia herself found it impossible to take advice from most people, let alone subordinates. That Rylan could do so was admirable. Plus, she was trying to be more assertive. That thought alone made Nadia smile.

Friendship. Her thoughts kept circling back to that word. That must be what she was experiencing.

Very well. They could be friends. Having a resolution—even one that wouldn't withstand the test of time—set her mind at ease. She could simply enjoy Rylan's company instead of dissecting her feelings. And now that she had decided that friendship was permissible, Nadia would help Rylan become a better surgeon. Because that meant spending time with her would be purely altruistic.

The plane landed and taxied to the hangar. John cut the engine. "Welcome to Arcata, California."

The flight, along with Nadia's frivolous musings, was over. Now it was time to get to work.

"We probably won't be back for two or three hours, John. Someone from the organ network will contact you to tell you what time we need to take off."

Nadia, Li, and John gathered the equipment and headed to the waiting vehicle. The luxurious SUV was warm and smelled of leather and air freshener. Nadia gazed through the window at the white airplane they had just left and smiled wryly. Despite being cramped into a small plane, there was a certain benefit to not passing through checkpoints, waiting in line, and dragging luggage.

Unlike the plane ride, the drive—sadly—was not a quiet one. The driver enthusiastically told Li about the joys of living in Arcata. Something about a vintage charm, beautiful redwood forests, and easy-access beaches. *God, she sounds like a tourist brochure.*

Nadia crossed her arms and refused to participate in the conversation. And she did judge Li for talking about sightseeing. It was almost one a.m., and they were about to harvest the organs of a poor college student who had gotten drunk on his twenty-first birthday and fallen down the stairs.

It was a familiar story that tugged at her heartstrings every time, testing the extent of her trained apathy. Somebody died before their time, and even though other people would benefit it was still a devastating tragedy.

That reminder of the limitations of transplantation was why Nadia hadn't wanted to become a transplant surgeon. By operating on people, she wanted to cure them. Donors were past saving. There was nothing she could do to help them.

But seven years ago, a cardiothoracic resident had changed her mind. When she had shared with Rylan all those years ago her well-thought-out argument that immunosuppression was a barbaric solution to the rejection problem, Rylan had shook her head, calling Nadia's views naïve. Nadia had taken it as a challenge that lit a fire inside her and changed her life. At that moment, she'd decided she would develop a better method to treat end-stage organ failure. And being away from the OR had given her the time she needed to begin putting the pieces together.

She frowned. *No more thinking about Rylan.* It had annoying and unwelcome physiological effects like quickening her heart rate and inexplicably making her want to smile for no reason at all.

Nadia sat back against the leather seat and looked out the window, forcing herself to watch the dark silhouettes of trees and buildings flash by, thinking of nothing else for the rest of the drive.

Once they arrived at the community hospital, she and Li dragged the equipment inside. She went through the motions as they were pointed in the direction of the locker room to change into scrubs. The hallways in the main hospital were almost completely empty at this hour, and their footsteps filled the silence. But as they approached the operating rooms, a deafening rhythmic banging of something hard hitting the floor began offending Nadia's ears.

It was a familiar noise, a harbinger of doom that accompanied every donor recovery. It was the sound of solid ice being crushed into slush for cooling down the organs.

Nadia's attention sharpened as the organ coordinator went over the donor's medical chart with the teams. Three other surgeons were there to harvest the kidneys and liver.

"The donor is ready to be transported to the OR, but"—Liz, the coordinator, looked at the doctors—"the family has some questions first. They would like to speak to one of the surgeons."

No one offered. They all looked in every possible direction but at Liz. Nadia understood their reluctance. None of these doctors was the boy's treating physician. They were there to fight for life, but it wasn't the boy's life they were going to fight for. He was past saving. Their job was to try to do something good despite his untimely departure.

The silence droned on embarrassingly long. Something inside Nadia made her say, "I'll do it."

Her senior colleagues looked at her and shook their heads. Nadia would usually disapprove of her actions too. It was better not to know the donor, not to see the suffering family. Focusing on their own patients' interests should be their priority.

But the thought of ignoring the donor family's request made her sick to her stomach. She set her jaw and stood by her words.

"Thank you, Dr. Keating. They're in the ICU. Follow me."

As Nadia stepped toward the double doors, Li jumped after her. "What are you doing?"

"What does it look like I'm doing?" Nadia forced her voice into unshakable confidence.

"Dr. Singh said never to do that. It's in poor taste."

He was right, of course. But Singh wasn't there, and Nadia had made up her mind. And like most surgeons, she stubbornly stuck with her decision. Without breaking stride, she said, "Then don't tell her I did it."

Nadia and Liz arrived at the ICU a moment later. A middle-aged man and woman stood next to the donor's bed. The woman's face was puffy and her eyes were red. The man's face was stoic, reminiscent of a soldier. Nadia tried to mirror his expression, despite her heart sinking at the sight.

In an attempt to steal a moment to compose herself, she glanced at the donor. It was a mistake. Except for a bloody bandage wrapped around his head and the breathing tube sticking out of his mouth, the handsome young man looked healthy. His chest rose and fell rhythmically as if he were breathing. He wasn't. A ventilator was forcing air into his lungs, giving his cells the oxygen he needed to survive. But his brain had been too damaged by the fall for him to ever gain consciousness or breathe on his own again.

Nadia quietly cleared her throat, trying to chase away the overwhelming sadness that had built in there. "Hello. My name is Dr. Keating. I'm one of the transplant surgeons."

The woman began sobbing, piercing Nadia's heart. She instantly regretted being there. How could she offer any support to them when her own legs were giving way?

The father stepped forward and shook Nadia's hand. She tried to draw strength from him.

"I'm very sorry for your loss." Nadia's voice was soft. "I understand you have some questions about the donation process."

"We want to know about the patients who will receive our son's organs."

"I told them the recipient information is confidential," Liz whispered in Nadia's ear.

Nadia reached for the donor's chart. She had no interest in reciting the rules of nondisclosure to this family. She wanted to ease the couple's suffering, not add to it.

She pulled up a chair next to the mother. The chart included codes for the organs' destinations without identifying the recipients.

On the sheet for one of the kidneys' recipients it was written *PCKD 62*.

"One of your son's kidneys is going to Utah for a patient with polycystic kidney disease, a genetic condition that destroys a patient's kidneys, making them look like soap bubbles. The patient experiences a lot of pain and needs dialysis to survive. The prognosis is poor, and a new kidney is the last best hope for a normal life."

She flipped to the next page, where it read *Post-Strep GN 25*. "The other kidney," Nadia continued calmly, "is going to Minnesota. This recipient is about the same age as your son. He was healthy until he developed acute kidney disease after a streptococcal infection, likely a sore throat. As a result his own immune system turned against his kidneys, leading to acute glomerulonephritis. Most of the time the condition resolves on its own. But sometimes it leads to end-stage kidney failure. He is dependent on dialysis, something no one in their twenties should ever have to cope with. Your son's kidney means this boy can go back to the life he knew."

Nadia flipped to the third page and reviewed the information for the liver recipient: *HCC 54*.

"Your son's liver is going to a patient in this state with hepatocellular carcinoma, a type of liver cancer. It's usually fatal within two years. With your son's liver, the patient could live another twenty years."

The man went to stand by his wife, gripping her hand. His own façade was breaking. Nadia looked away to give them some semblance of privacy and to hide her own sadness. She shifted in her chair, asking herself whether the information was helping or hurting the couple.

Finally, the father spoke. "What about his heart?"

"He has such a good heart. *Had*," the mother choked out between sobs.

Since Nadia's expertise was cardiothoracic—heart, lungs, and other organs in the chest—she knew the answer without looking at the chart. "The heart wasn't placed. It will stay with your son."

"Why? What's wrong with it?"

Nadia blinked, taken aback by the question. She was here for the lungs, not the heart. She flipped through the pages to buy time.

"There's nothing wrong with it. In fact, it's perfect." Nadia stared at the heart's page a moment longer before looking up. "But your son's blood type is unique, AB positive. There wasn't a recipient close enough to make the heart transplant safe and successful. A heart can't be without oxygen for more than six hours or it won't start beating again when it's transplanted."

"I don't understand. How can it run out of oxygen? It's still beating," the father asked.

"The only way to continually supply oxygen to the organs is to keep them in your son and transport him to every transplant center. But that's neither logistically nor ethically possible, so the surgical teams come to him. Once we take the organs, we keep them on ice to decrease their oxygen demand. Some organs can last longer on ice than others. The heart is the most sensitive."

Nadia stole another look at the heart's page, her fingers dancing on the lab values, then continued. "But his unique blood type is just what our twenty-year-old lung recipient needs." She closed the chart. "She has cystic fibrosis, which she's struggled with all her life. She's had pneumonia more often than someone in their nineties. She doesn't know what it's like to breathe easily. Your son's lungs will give her a chance to experience life the way it's meant to be experienced."

At the mention of life, the mother's sobs increased, drowning Nadia in helpless frustration. How was she supposed to offer the couple any level of comfort when she was trained to fight death, not accept it?

Nadia reached out and placed her hand over the mother's. "I know nothing I say will lessen your pain. It wasn't his time to go. But we're all here tonight because of him. His organs will make a difference in the lives of the recipients. His memory will live on in them."

The parents nodded, the man wrapping his hands around his wife whose sobs had quieted down. Nadia stood up and turned to leave, but the father touched her hand. "One more thing, doctor," he said. "Grayson hated suits, but we were told a T-shirt might not cover the surgical incisions."

Nadia nodded. However small, this was something she could do for them. "He can wear anything you like. I promise no incision will be visible."

The couple thanked her, although she didn't feel she deserved it. With one final look at the donor, Nadia headed back to the OR. Focusing on her breathing, she tried to get over the feeling of helplessness.

Why couldn't she be more like Rylan?

The simple truth was that Rylan would have done better in that situation. Her bedside manner was exceptional. She would have soothed the pain of that couple, not by what she said, but in the way she said it.

Nadia gritted her teeth. Her emotions were raw, and her unguarded thoughts swung back and forth between Rylan and the donor's family. Even without comparing herself to Rylan, focusing on the case after seeing the grieving couple was going to be challenging. *That's why you don't talk with the donor's family.*

Back in the OR, she found her colleague. "Li, have you ever done a clamshell incision for a lung recovery?"

He looked startled at the question. "I've never even heard of it being done."

"It normally isn't. It's time-consuming and not as straightforward as a median sternotomy," Nadia said matter-of-factly. "But since it's done below the nipple line, it allows for an open casket funeral even with the deceased in a T-shirt."

"I suppose we won't tell Dr. Singh we did that either?"

Nadia smirked. "Good man."

"The patient's hematocrit is twenty-three. Should we get a unit of blood?" Li asked.

They had opened the donor's chest and were working on stopping the minor bleeds.

"No point. We'll cross-clamp soon. And it's the *donor's* hematocrit," Nadia corrected sharply. Referring to the donor as a patient would only make it harder when she had to stop his heart. "Patients are alive. Donors are dead."

Once Nadia had put on her sterile gown and gloves, she returned to her detached objectivity. Her heart still bled for the family's tragedy, but her hands were steady.

They silently dissected the thymus, an organ that began shrinking and was replaced by fat after puberty. The fact that this donor still had a decent amount of thymic tissue left was yet another grim reminder of how young he was. Nadia glanced at her hands, where the cotton ends of her gown overlapped with her gloves. The protective gear was like armor, numbing any feelings the donor's age might evoke. With that reminder, Nadia returned to her work.

They opened the pericardial sac surrounding the heart, revealing a strong muscle with minimal fat and great function.

Nadia immediately thought of Singh's very sick patient who was still waiting for a heart. It was another detached observation that she only allowed in her mind but not her heart. *Still, it's a shame to throw away such a good organ when people are dying.*

Michael Sanders was likely to pass away very soon. It was a cold, hard truth that Nadia understood and acknowledged. But this donor's heart was not the right match.

Nadia snapped out of her thoughts. "Let's take a look at the lungs before we dissect the great vessels. Dr. Singh is waiting for an update." The heart was at this point just a useless organ that would be discarded. There was no reason to get sentimental over it.

Nadia and Li cut through the pleural sacs, revealing partially collapsed lungs. As they worked on recruiting maneuvers to fully expand the lungs, she quizzed Li on what the next steps were. When he executed some of the tests himself, she nodded approvingly. It was easy to be a good teacher when he knew the procedure so well.

"Would you take these lungs?" she asked after they had assessed everything to her satisfaction.

The laugh lines around Li's eyes gave away the smile behind his surgical mask. "With these lungs, our patient will be breathing on her own in no time."

"Yes," Nadia agreed. She scanned the room. "Liz, please let Dr. Singh know the lungs are good. We'll cross-clamp in about twenty minutes."

Nadia looked again at the beating heart. Despite her trained detachment, something stubbornly stirred inside her when she looked at it. The other organs were going to good use, but this heart would soon die and benefit no one. And there were so many patients that needed a healthy heart. It was a colossal waste that pierced right through her armor every time she glanced at it.

Gripping the forceps and the cautery more tightly, she returned her focus to the remaining steps of the lung recovery.

Twenty minutes later, she was ready to remove the lungs. The donor's blood was anticoagulated, and the teams readied the ice slush and cold solution to pour on the claimed organs as soon as Nadia arrested the heart. *The strong, beautiful heart that nobody can use.*

Nadia injected prostaglandin, a medication used for lung preservation, and watched as the heart struggled to beat. The drug disrupted its function. Regardless, the muscle kept trying to contract. For a moment, all the frantic noise of the people around her faded, and her eyes zeroed on the heart. She could almost hear the blood sloshing and pumping inside of it. Fighting. Wanting. Needing to live.

The heart is dead. She blinked the daze away. *There is no one close enough who can benefit from it. Arresting it would change nothing.*

She made decisive cuts in the correct targets, and blood began pouring out in the chest.

"Cross-clamp," she called out evenly as she closed the clamp around the aorta.

Li began suctioning the accumulating blood, struggling to simultaneously add ice to the lungs.

"Begin pneumoplegia." Nadia added a third task.

At the sight of his clumsy technique, she itched to intervene. Instead, she simply waited. He needed to learn to stay on top of things if he was going to do it on his own.

There was a pause while the lungs were being flushed with a cold solution. In the absence of active tasks, Nadia looked at the heart again. Against all odds, it still pumped, although every beat got weaker and weaker. Nadia looked around the room. Everyone else grossly ignored the heart's heroic efforts. They were focused on the lungs, the liver, and the kidneys. Why couldn't Nadia stay focused on the lungs?

An uncomfortable feeling of pity wrapped around her chest and began tightening, making it difficult to breathe. It was so unlike her to let her emotions overrule her in the OR. And yet, *it was such a handsome heart.*

Then a daring thought replaced Nadia's helpless feelings. She looked around for Liz. "Does this donor have a research consent?"

"Yes, the parents consented to everything."

"Is anybody taking the heart for research?" Nadia asked, although she already knew the answer.

"No, just leave it at the back table. We'll put it back in for the funeral." Liz sounded as if they were discussing grocery shopping. Nadia supposed her work had desensitized her to death.

"Can I take it?"

Liz starred at her wordlessly. Every organ, tissue, and cell had to be accounted for or its absence justified. People didn't just take things. But Nadia's illogical instinct to hold onto the heart made her ask anyway.

"Er...I can call and ask my supervisor."

This was a safe answer. If her supervisor denied Nadia, Liz couldn't be held responsible. Except Nadia wasn't in the mood for games. Instead of talking to some middleman, her best shot was to ask the director of the transplant network. She had worked with him on several recoveries, and they shared a mutual respect.

"Call Dr. Rodriguez and let me talk to him." She sounded calm and collected, but inside she was neither. "While I'm waiting, I'll proceed with recovering this heart as if I can take it. If he says no, I'll return it." Nadia scooped some ice slush from the nearby basin and dumped it onto the heart. She looked at Li. "We're going to follow heart recovery protocol to remove the heart. Set up the cardioplegia."

"Uh...okay."

Nadia appreciated that Li didn't ask her why. She wasn't sure what exactly her plan was, but she was going with her gut. Anything was better than burying this healthy heart six feet under.

The surgeons continued with the organ procurement, first removing the heart, then the lungs, and finally the abdominal organs. Nadia attentively packaged the lungs for transportation, fully aware she was overcompensating for the fact she had been enamored by the heart all night. The heart was a side project. Her priority was the lungs and their recipient.

But once the lungs were safely packaged, her attention returned to the heart that remained immersed in ice water on the sterile table. Nadia, still scrubbed in, stood beside it like a guard, her arms crossed in front of her. She rocked up and down on her toes, glancing impatiently at Liz, who was on the phone with somebody who wasn't Rodriguez. They needed to transport the lungs, the sooner, the better. Staying here for the heart was wrong, but still Nadia made no attempt to remove her gown. *Two more minutes.*

Finally, Liz approached her with the phone and held the receiver against her ear. It was Rodriguez.

He sounded half-asleep.

She glanced at the wall clock. It was past three in the morning. His utter lack of pleasantries supported her theory that he was acutely aware of the time.

She listened briefly to his monologue about how she wasn't following procedure, then interrupted him. "Dr. Rodriguez," she said sharply, "you have my word. You'll see my research protocol first thing in the morning."

He went on with his lecture as if she hadn't spoken. Nadia bit her lip. The longer she stayed, the worse she felt about not getting the lungs back to the hospital. But her mind was set on leaving with both the heart and lungs. She stood her ground, saying, "Yes, I understand," so often that it lost its meaning. She let him vent. He would say yes eventually.

Finally, he finished his lecture, adding, "But since you've proven yourself to be an excellent researcher, I'm willing to make an exception. In the name of science, of course."

"Thank you, Doctor." Her voice rang with triumph.

"And any publications that come out of this will have an acknowledgment to the OPO."

Nadia rolled her eyes. *In the name of science, my ass.* "Of course. I would never dismiss the help of the Organ Procurement Organization."

"And, Keating?"

"Yes, Dr. Rodriguez?"

"If I don't like one syllable in your protocol, I'll personally collect this heart from your lab. Now, let me sleep already."

Nadia smiled. "Good night, Doctor." She hung up and looked at Liz, schooling her features into a well-rehearsed neutrality that hid her cocky joy of getting her way. "I'm taking the heart. Let's not waste any more time and head back home."

Adrenaline pumped through Nadia as she strode to the ICU around six that evening. After the recovery early that morning, she had spent the entire day in her lab. She understood now why she had been so spellbound by that donor heart. Now she knew its purpose, and she raced ahead to share it.

She found Singh at bed eleven, next to Michael Sanders. On the other side of the bed, his wife held his hand. Their three small children sat quietly nearby. He had been in and out of consciousness for several days.

Nadia registered the scene with a learned detachment. Her chin no longer quivered, nor did her voice struggle to pass a lump in her throat. She had numbed herself to the sight of dying patients years ago. And yet, her lack of sleep, mingled with the thought that this time she could offer a sliver of hope, made her heart beat with foolish haste.

Nadia touched Singh's shoulder. "Can we talk?" It was a question, but the delivery left no doubt of the urgency.

Singh frowned but nodded and followed Nadia into the hallway.

By now, Nadia's heart pounded wildly in her ears. She took a deep breath.

"What is it?" Singh asked.

Nadia met her eyes with determination. She took another breath. "Forget about trying to get Sanders another heart. We're going to build him one."

Chapter 13

The Right Way to do End-To-End Anastomosis

ASHLEY DRUMMED HER FINGERS LIGHTLY on the keyboard. She'd lost her train of thought again. Finishing up an op note had never been this difficult. She added a few more lines and signed out. It was after six thirty, and she couldn't remember the last time she had been so eager to leave her office.

Nadia had been on her mind all day, but Ashley hadn't seen her at all. There was no harm in walking by the lab on her way out. Her heart fluttered in agreement.

She got as far as the elevator when the doors opened and Nadia appeared before her. "Good. You're still here. Follow me." Nadia was her usual self. No explanations. No pleasantries.

Her usual self was incorrigible and yet Ashley followed her willingly into the elevator. They stood in awkward silence while Ashley's cheeks burned under Nadia's gaze.

"Why do you always dress so…" Nadia gestured at what Ashley was wearing. "This is a hospital, not a fashion show."

Instinctively, Ashley ran her fingers across the long-sleeved ivory shirt that draped against her skin. It was tucked into a pair of wool slacks that hugged her figure. The dark suede pumps she had worn all day were beginning to hurt her feet, but she forgot about the discomfort when Nadia commented on her appearance.

"It would be far less distracting if you just wore scrubs like everyone else."

Amused, Ashley raised an eyebrow. "Just so we're clear, you wanted me to follow you so you could tell me I should change the way I dress so you won't be distracted at work?"

Nadia glared at her, but the blush in her cheeks was unmistakable.

"Or did you want to tell me why the director of the OPO called me at three in the morning?"

"Rodriguez called you?" Nadia asked in gentler, more worried voice. "What did he say?"

"Nothing much. He asked what research projects you were working on and if you had the appropriate BUA and IRB permissions for them."

"And what did you tell him?"

They stepped off the elevator. Ashley followed Nadia as she turned right, then left, then right again. The lab wing hallways all looked the same to her.

"I told him as far as I knew, your projects are all approved by the necessary committees and you have an excellent track record when it comes to compliance." Ashley smiled. "And that he should go with whatever crazy request you've made."

"That was nice of you." Nadia turned to look at her with a small smile.

Ashley licked her lips. It was so addictive to see Nadia's pleased expression.

"I don't want to talk about my research tonight." Nadia resumed walking briskly, stopping in front of the skills lab. Her expression was back to stiff again. "There's something else I've wanted to do ever since our talk yesterday, and I can't seem to focus on anything else until I've taken care of it."

"Oh?" Ashley's pulse quickened.

"Yes." Nadia cleared her throat. "You said you'd welcome respectful feedback."

Ashely nodded guardedly. This was not exactly heading in the direction she thought it would.

"Since we've become…friendly, I wanted to show you some ways you could improve your surgical techniques."

With her eyebrows shooting through the roof, Ashley wondered if Nadia had lost her mind completely. "Excuse me?"

"Look, you have the medical knowledge. Of course you do. There's a reason you got ahead so fast in your career." The words came out in a rush, Nadia clearly desperately listing reasons to justify her absurd suggestion. She paused and took a breath. "But surgery isn't just science facts. It takes a lot of practice. You cannot skip the line and expect to be as good as those who have put in the time. You completed an accelerated training program, so, naturally, some of your techniques are clumsy. We should work on them."

Ashley stared at her wide-eyed. She was joking. *Right?*

Nadia exhaled impatiently. "Let's make a deal—you come in with an open mind, and I'll answer your question from yesterday. And all your follow-up questions. Trust me, there will be many."

Ashley remained frozen in her place, torn between wanting to please Nadia and wanting to protest. Getting some adolescent story about Nadia's first time with a woman in exchange for professional critique from a subordinate was not a fair exchange.

They faced each other in silence, Nadia's expression hardening with every moment that passed and she didn't get her way. If Ashley wasn't feeling the pressure to give an answer, she would have laughed at her impatience.

"Fine, I'll go first," Nadia said angrily when Ashley didn't respond. She took another deep breath. "When you asked me what my first time with a woman was like—well, you should know—you were there."

Ashley blinked. That was not what she expected to hear. She swallowed, focusing her eyes on Nadia, who hadn't moved.

She needed to say something. Nadia had confided something deeply personal to her. The least Ashley could do was not freak out. She nodded to acknowledge that she'd heard, then willed her body to move toward the double doors. "Let's see what you think I'm doing wrong."

As they entered the lab, they were met with the sound of steel instruments clashing together.

Crap.

Immediately forgetting about Nadia's revelation, or how she should best react to it, Ashley froze. She didn't feel like explaining to anyone what she was doing there with Nadia at seven p.m. She reached for Nadia's arm.

Nadia momentarily stiffened but quickly regained her cool composure. "Relax," she said with a nonchalant smile. "It's just your favorite medical student."

Ashley rolled her eyes. Not yelling at someone didn't mean they were her favorite. It just showed she was a decent human being.

"Don't worry. I'll take care of it." She turned to Jack. "It's Jack, right?"

He jumped to attention. "Uh…yes, ma'am."

"Well, *Jack*, if you truly want to become a doctor someday, you will never call me 'ma'am' again."

Nadia's threatening tone didn't help Ashley "not to worry". She chuckled and immediately cleared her throat to mask it. For good measure, she frowned as well. She didn't really approve of Nadia's treatment of Jack, but her intimidation act was funny.

"Yes, Dr. Keating." The blood had drained out of his face.

Nadia approached the counter where Jack was working. "So, *Jack*, what are you doing here so late?"

Ashley watched, ready to begin CPR in the likely event Jack went into cardiac arrest from this conversation.

"I…I'm working on my subcuticular suture," Jack stammered. "Dr. Williams said I could close for him tomorrow during his CABG case."

Ashley rolled her eyes. Peter Williams was as lazy as they came. He let students close, not to teach, but to leave the OR quicker, careless for the cosmetic outcome of the incision.

"I see." Nadia's jaw tightened.

So the idea of Jack closing for Peter bothered her too. *Interesting*. She assumed Nadia admired his operating skills despite his character. She was glad to know she was wrong.

"And you have full knowledge of how to do a CABG procedure?"

Jack nodded.

"You've just divided the sternum. What's the next step?"

"Uh…I would open the pericardial sac—"

"No. Guess again."

"Uh…uh…I would stop the sternal bleeds with wax—"

"Jack, I don't have all night. Skip the minor details. What comes next?"

"I…I don't know, Dr. Keating." Jack looked as if he might start crying any minute.

Ashley was torn between letting Nadia handle the situation and the urge to intervene. But Nadia's plan seemed to be effective. Judging by the look of horror on Jack's face, he would bolt out of the lab any minute, and she would be alone with Nadia. *Sorry, Jack.*

"Then I suggest you go find out." Nadia's voice was barely above a whisper. "Surgery is more than a manual craft. Knowledge should always come first. If you want to merely cut things up, you should have looked for a job in the local butcher shop instead."

Nadia leaned in to inspect Jack's sutures while he stood next to her, scarcely breathing.

Even from a distance, Ashley could see the sutures were sloppy and not watertight. She braced herself, convinced Nadia would berate Jack, even though most medical students were at the same unrefined skill level.

Nadia straightened up. "What time is the case?"

"It's at eight in the morning…Doctor."

"Meet me here at seven. Be ready to walk me through the entire CABG procedure, and I'll show you how to do this suture properly."

Ashley blinked. Wrong in her assumption again. A smile replaced her surprise.

Jack didn't seem to appreciate the help, appearing too immobilized by fear.

"Go," Nadia said in a hair-raising voice.

He grabbed his backpack and hurried toward the door, nodding at Ashley as he passed.

Ashley motioned him closer. "The answer Nadezhda was looking for is harvest the LITA." She winked at him.

Ashley caught Nadia staring daggers at her as Jack fled.

"How is he ever going to learn anything if you keep giving him the answers?"

Ashley refused to take the bait. She didn't regret trying to help Jack, but given Nadia's stubbornness, there was a better chance of getting through a brick wall than convincing her Jack didn't need this knowledge. Instead, she said, "It was nice of you to offer to help him before the case."

"I did it to protect the patient. We both know the moment the bone wires are twisted together, Williams will leave the OR."

Ashley shook her head. "God, Nadezhda, will the world end if you appear to do something nice? You don't have to be mean all the time."

"You don't have to be nice all the time," Nadia fired back. "I'm teaching him how the real world works. You're doing him a bear favor by constantly coddling him."

Ashley smiled knowingly. She'd wanted to drop the argument, but that didn't mean she couldn't win it. "Do you know what specialty Jack wants to go into?"

"It doesn't matter."

"Psychiatry."

Nadia rolled her eyes.

"He won't need to know how to properly hold surgical instruments or suture to do his job. Not everyone is as passionate about surgery as you are. In time, you'll learn that a good teacher knows what her students need."

"But he needs to know the steps for the procedure he's doing tomorrow."

"He probably does but was too frightened to tell you."

Nadia stepped closer, forcing Ashley to take a step back against the wall. Her legs wobbled as she breathed in Nadia's addictive scent.

"So he would have told me what the next step is after the LITA is harvested?" Nadia's breath was hot on her cheek. "Tell me."

"Create a pericardial—"

Nadia *tsked*. She brushed a strand of hair away from Ashley's face, her fingers lingering. "Come on, Dr. Rylan. That was the med student's answer. You can do much better than that." She caressed her cheek.

"I'd expose the mid-LAD—"

"Mm." Nadia pressed against her, short-circuiting Ashley's brain.

Ashley gasped softly. A moan rather than words built up in her throat. She gulped, giving her mind a moment to collect itself. "—do an end-to-side anastomosis with the LITA and anchor the distal LITA pedicle with stay sutures to avoid tension or kinking of the conduit."

Nadia stepped back. "See? If the knowledge is there, you don't need excuses."

Ashley blinked. Being dumped into an ocean of frigid water would have caused a milder hypothermic shock than the one she was in right now. Somehow, she managed to stammer out, "It's not the same."

"Are you saying his fear was greater than your"—Nadia raked her gaze up and down Ashley's body, licking her lips seductively—"distraction?"

Ashley opened her mouth, but Nadia interrupted.

"Careful now. My ego is quite fragile."

Ashley burst out laughing. Nadia's ego could withstand an atomic bomb.

Twenty minutes later, Ashley wondered if she had ever done anything right in surgery.

Nadia scrutinized her every move, starting with the way she held the needle driver.

"You've picked up terrible habits from the general surgeons," Nadia said. "Palming isn't meant to be a standard grip. It's to be used in limited circumstances. There's a reason they put holes in the instrument. Use your fingers."

"There's more than one way to skin a cat, Nadezhda. Palming gives a better range of motion."

"The standard grip gives you finer movements. You want precision when you're working in a limited space like the chest." Nadia raised a challenging eyebrow. "Now, quit skinning cats, and show me the proper grip."

Once Ashley changed the way she held her instruments, suturing became more awkward. Ashley was tempted to throw the instruments on the floor and shout at Nadia, but the mere thought of doing so made her grip loosen. She had never lost her temper like that with anyone and wasn't about to start.

Besides, even though Nadia was testing her tolerance, they had a deal, and Ashley intended to honor it.

They settled into suturing a Dacron polyester vessel. Regardless of Nadia's opinion, Ashley had confidence in her surgical skills and knew that with minimal practice she could suture with any grip she liked. Still, she couldn't help but feel a twinge of pride when she finally met Nadia's high and *very* specific standards.

And once her hands picked up the task, it was time for Nadia to fulfill her end of the bargain. "So when we…it was your first time with a woman?"

"I believe we covered this," Nadia said dryly.

For someone who always kept her distance, she was standing quite close to Ashley, looking over her shoulder. Her words blew hot air into Ashley's ear, sending her nervous system into frantic overdrive. "Right." She struggled to keep her hands from shaking. After all, surgeons were supposed to have steady hands.

So many questions were racing through her mind right now, so many things she wanted to ask. She sifted through her thoughts to find the right one.

And then she recalled with horror how she had acted. "If I had known it was your first time, I wouldn't have been so"—*Dominant? Forceful? Selfish?*—"forward."

Nadia leaned even closer, her lips almost touching Ashley's ear. "Because you usually reserve ordering one to strip naked and crawl between your legs for the second time?"

The forceps gracelessly slipped from Ashley's hand and clattered to the table. *Must she always be so direct?* "I could have made it special for you." The words rushed out. "We could have taken our time. You didn't even get a chance to…"

"Turn your body when you do this part." Nadia stepped back, putting some distance between them. "It will give you a better angle to see what you're suturing."

Trying to make sense of Nadia's words, Ashley looked at the forceps on the table and then to the abandoned synthetic vessel. So they were back to suturing now?

She picked up the forceps and shifted her weight. As usual, Nadia was correct. The new position made it easier to work on the vessel. Ashley hated that her instructions were so…helpful.

"If your idea of special includes rose petals and candlelight, I'm glad I didn't tell you."

Ashley rolled her eyes. Nadia had a talent for making good things sound horrible. "I never would have guessed it was your first time," she blurted out. "You were so"—Ashley turned to face her—"skilled."

"Dr. Rylan, you should know by now I always come prepared," Nadia said, the words delivered with her typical austere control, but her pinched lips twitched, the hint of a smile unmistakably there.

Ashley faced the table to hide her grin. "I'm dying to find out what 'literature review' you did on the topic."

Nadia chuckled. "I bet you are."

"So, uh…" Ashley swallowed against the tightness in her throat. "Does that mean you're bisexual? Or was it a one-time thing and you're straight? If you're attracted to women, have you always known, or are you just beginning to figure it out?" Now that Nadia had opened up a little, the questions spilled out.

"It took you longer than I expected," Nadia said mockingly. "I'm impressed you restrained yourself as long as you did."

"You promised to answer my questions."

Nadia leaned over and tugged on the synthetic vessel. "Don't take even bites on both sides. You don't have equal diameter vessels. Correct the mismatch by taking smaller bites on the smaller cuff."

Ashley nodded and adjusted her needle bites. She suspected Nadia was using the instructions to buy herself time before answering. Or else she was truly obsessed with Ashley's suturing.

"I've thought about it for a very long time," Nadia said. "I used to think I knew the answer. But as it turns out, around you, I'm often wrong."

Ashley kept working on the half-sutured vessel in front of her. Years of experience in the operating room had taught her how to shift her focus seamlessly between her hands and her thoughts.

"I suppose I've always been attracted to women. But I never allowed myself to think about it too much. I was brought up to believe that heterosexuality was the norm, and I simply stayed on the path of least resistance.

"I've never found people that interesting anyway. So I attributed my lack of…feelings of fulfillment to the mediocrity of humanity rather than solely to men." Nadia paused and clicked her tongue. "Don't misunderstand me. Sex wasn't bad. It was just sex. Mechanical. Given the right stimuli, one can achieve sexual gratification regardless of the partner."

Ashley pressed her lips together to keep from commenting. A debate about sex at this point might inhibit Nadia from continuing her story, and Ashley wanted to hear the whole thing.

"So I stayed in the heterosexual box and had relationships with men only. And sex was…nice, but I wasn't that enamored by the act itself. I thought perhaps it simply wasn't as exhilarating as people made it out to be. Eventually, I decided that I needed to experience being with a woman. Surely, sex couldn't be that different. Maybe it would put an end to my naïve fantasies."

"That's a lot of pressure to put on a sexual partner, especially someone you don't know." Ashley tried to keep the judgment out of her voice. Her stomach clenched. If she had known any of this, she would never have agreed to be part of Nadia's experiment.

"And that's why I didn't tell you." Nadia's voice became lighter. "I didn't want it to affect your performance."

"Why are you telling me now?"

"I said I would answer your questions."

"You cannot seriously be deciding whether you're gay or not based on one rushed sexual experience. And I can't speak for all lesbians, but what happened was definitely not what sex with me is like. You never even—"

"Why do you keep bringing up that minor detail?"

Ashley put down her instruments and turned to face Nadia. "It's not minor to me. I didn't get to make you feel as good as you made me feel." Fixating on one particular aspect of that night was a lot easier than thinking about all the unfairness in their relationship.

"I made you feel good?"

Nadia's smug expression suggested she already knew the answer. Ashley rolled her eyes.

"Well, as it turned out, I was wrong," Nadia said. "Sex with you was different. And I mean it in every positive way."

The knot in Ashley's stomach loosened, letting hope sneak in. She held her breath, as if saying the wrong thing would make Nadia take the words back. And they were such *lovely words*.

"You made me realize sex could never be great when the psychological pleasure is detached from the physical one. And that's what I've been doing all these years."

Ashley's heart pounded with all its might. Despite the analytical detachment that made the words sound like a psychiatric dissertation, Nadia had just admitted that she *liked* Ashley.

Well, she had only said she liked having sex with her.

Or perhaps she meant she liked having sex with women in general?

God! Why does Nadezhda have to intellectualize everything? Ashley stared at Nadia, searching for answers to questions she was afraid to ask.

"Of course, I can't be sure the results would be replicable with other women. Perhaps my theory that gender is irrelevant for me would have been confirmed had it been any other woman." Nadia locked eyes with Ashley. "But it was you, and it was nothing like I expected."

The words made Ashley's entire body vibrate with giddy excitement. Emboldened, she stepped closer. "You know, a good scientist would never base a conclusion on a single test run. Give me a chance to show you how much better it could be."

Nadia recoiled as if the words were toxic. "We shouldn't."

Ashley's heart sank into her stomach, aching just as if it had been dipped in acid. "Why not?"

"You're still my boss."

"Oh." Ashley was at a loss of what to say or how to feel.

Nadia was the queen of mixed signals. One moment she was sharing her innermost thoughts and feelings with Ashley and the next she was quoting HR policy.

Hadn't Nadia told Ashley that their professional relationship wasn't an issue, that she could separate the two? Perhaps she didn't trust that Ashley could do so.

Ashley turned back toward the abandoned anastomosis and picked up the instruments. After the roller coaster ride Nadia had just taken her on, she was done talking. There was no point in trying to understand why Nadia kept looking for reasons to spend time with her when she wasn't interested in a relationship.

To her surprise, Nadia moved to stand next to her. They worked in silence as Ashley completed the suture line from both sides and inspected it. Giving a short huff, she shook her head in frustration. It was a damn good anastomosis.

"Are we done here?" Ashley asked, failing at keeping her voice even.

"I want to show you how to tie it first." Nadia had the audacity to look and sound her usual reserved self. "You make an unnecessary extra move when you do the first part of the square knot, and it slows down the entire process."

Ashley scoffed. If one were to believe Nadia's assessment, she had apparently failed to grasp what medical students learned in their first year. But despite the criticism, Nadia had held up her end of the deal, and Ashley would too.

Nadia guided Ashley's hands to tie the knot. The close contact sent shivers through Ashley's body. How could they be so close physically but so far apart emotionally?

The knot finished, Nadia stepped away and cleared her throat. "So how was your day?"

Frowning, Ashley turned to face her. "That was quite the one-eighty degree turn. Why do you ask?" She sincerely hoped they weren't going to dissect her administrative schedule next.

Nadia shrugged, looking away. "Don't friends ask each other about their day or whatever?"

"We're friends now?"

Nadia met her eyes. "We don't have to be if you don't want to." Her lips were set in a grim line.

Ashley had the irrational need to pull Nadia close and reassure her of how much she wanted her. But that wasn't what Nadia was offering. Instead, Ashley forced a smile. While she couldn't make Nadia feel the same way she felt, she would never deny Nadia her friendship after she had been so vulnerable with her. "I had a meeting with the chair to discuss Peter's refusal to adhere to the call schedule. Guess how that went."

Nadia's face relaxed. "The man's too spineless to ever do anything about it."

"He wasn't too spineless to direct me to be the guest lecturer instead of him this Friday."

Nadia laughed. "So you went in asking Bratton to take something off your plate and you left with more?"

"I'm glad you find it funny."

Nadia stopped laughing but a smile remained on her face. "What is the lecture about?"

"Anything. It's for the first-year med students. It only has to be surgery related. Unfortunately, all my other presentations were on LVADs and ECMO support, but they're too advanced for this audience. I have to come up with one from scratch in the next two days."

Nadia cleared her throat. "If I had known you were busy, I wouldn't have wasted your time tonight."

"You didn't waste—"

"I have a presentation you can use," Nadia said decisively.

By now, Ashley should have known better than to object when she was like this. But still, she hadn't told her so Nadia would do the job. "Thank you, but you don't have to—"

"It's what friends do," Nadia added quickly. "I'll email it to you tonight and we can go over it tomorrow morning."

"All right." Ashley smiled, gladly giving up.

It would be good to have another friend at work.

Except Nadezhda is more than a friend.

Ignoring the nagging thought, Ashley tried to pick up the conversation again, but she knew her voice was strained.

This will never work.

Chapter 14

The Four Surgeons

ASHLEY SHUT THE DOOR TO her apartment and kicked off her pumps. She was exhausted, and it felt like a hammer was smashing against her skull. Dragging herself to her bedroom, she slipped into pajama bottoms and a loose T-shirt depicting a tent against a mountain background with OUTSIDER printed underneath. She had bought it as a joke, but it was no longer funny.

Back in her living room, she dropped onto her sofa, sinking into the soft cushions. She was as tired as if she had just worked a triple shift. She closed her eyes and sat in the darkness.

It was quiet.

Too quiet.

Ashley became more aware of the ever-present hollow feeling that slowly grew inside her. The emptiness suffocated her as if she were at the bottom of an ocean.

She opened her eyes and flipped on the nearby lamp. It didn't take a medical degree to recognize the symptoms of loneliness. She had sacrificed everything for her career, accepting solitude as the tradeoff.

She looked around her living room. It was clean and ordered.

Too clean. Too ordered.

The apartment looked like something from a magazine rather than a place where someone actually lived. The living room contained luxurious furniture she hardly used, a large television she never turned on, and beautiful abstract paintings no one but her ever saw. It was the same in every room: home office, guest room, bedroom, and kitchen.

She turned back to look at the pristinely unused kitchen. She couldn't remember the last time she had prepared her own food or baked anything. Even if she had the time to do so, cooking for one wasn't exactly motivating her to jump out of her seat. In college, she had frequently had guests over for meals, but over the past sixteen years, her world had gradually shrunk. Now the only people she met were those suffering from heart disease or those treating it.

When was the last time she'd had dinner guests over? Was it when Pari had come over with her family? Or was it when she and Maya had still been together? Or maybe it was the last time her parents had visited.

The thought of her parents made Ashley's stomach drop. How could she have forgotten what day today was? She grabbed her phone and typed in,

Are you up?

Squeezing her eyes shut didn't stop the guilt from mounting onto her shoulders.

Her phone rang.

"It's official—I'm the worst daughter in the history of daughters. I'm so sorry."

She was answered with soft melodic laughter that eased her anxiety a little. "You're not the worst anything, Ashley. It's fine. We know how busy you are."

"No, it's not fine," Ashley protested. Her shoulders slumped lower. It wasn't work that had been consuming her thoughts lately. "And I promise to make it up to you both. Is Dad up?" It was past midnight on the East Coast and the chances were slim, but hope still trembled in her voice.

"He's making himself a sandwich in the kitchen. He just got back from fixing an emergent STEMI."

"Is the patient okay?" Ashley asked, although she could have guessed the answer. Her father was an excellent interventional cardiologist.

"Your dad is really good at his job. Besides, what better way to celebrate a birthday than by saving a life? I'm sure you know the feeling."

"I'm glad you see it that way, Mom. Most women would have been disappointed that he spent his birthday working."

"Are you speaking from personal experience?" her mother asked knowingly.

"It's, uh, it's been known to happen once or twice." *Or every birthday for the last twelve years.*

"The right person would understand. That's how you know they're right for you."

The words were like a sword through Ashley's heart. Her parents were a perfect example of what love could be, yet it seemed like an impossible standard for her to meet.

Ashley involuntarily wondered how Nadia would react in this situation if Ashley had to work on her birthday. She would likely be pissed off. Not that it was somebody's birthday, of course, but that she wasn't invited to the surgery. Ashley pinched her lips to avoid laughing at the image.

Her thoughts were interrupted when her mother spoke again. "Here he is. I'll put you on speaker."

"Hi, honey. I'm so glad you called. I've been trying to explain the PCI technique I did to your mom for the last half hour, but she doesn't get it the way you would."

"Hey, Dad. Happy birthday." Ashley squeezed her eyes shut in embarrassment. "Sorry it's belated."

"I promise I'll get another one in a year. But I may never see what I saw today. Get this: an eighty-five-year-old gentleman who had a TAVR a year ago now has a long LM lesion that extends distal to the bifurcation."

Ashley smiled. After decades of practice, her father still loved talking about his job.

"I injected some contrast only to find the left sinus between the valve's struts."

"Did you go through them?"

"You bet I did! The device reps told me it had never been done before. You should have seen their faces. The kissing stents I put in at the bifurcation did the trick, and the man's heart responded immediately. It was something else, Ash. I wish you could have been here to see it."

Ashley's smile faded. They all had their careers but being so far from her family only increased her emptiness.

Her mother cleared her throat. "Speaking of kissing, is there anyone new in your life?"

The question immediately distracted Ashley from her sad thoughts. And her cheeks intensely heated. Her mother was worse than Pari. Nosy didn't even begin to cover it.

"You do know that isn't what kissing stents means, Mom, right?"

"Close enough." Her father laughed. "You'd tell us if there's someone new in your life, wouldn't you? No matter how many babies your mother delivers, she still wants grandchildren of her own."

"Ethan!"

Ashley heard a light slap against clothes, and her father chuckled.

"Dad, I'm going to pretend you didn't just say that."

"So no new lady in your life?" her father asked. "What about the new fellow? Does she play for your team?"

Ashley's mouth dropped, her mind robbed of thoughts, much less words. This call was getting too personal for her liking.

"What new surgeon?" her mother asked.

"You know, the famous Nadia Keating. Ashley's new heart fellow."

Ashley gasped at the way her father phrased it. Nadia wasn't *her* anything.

"I met her when she interviewed with our group." Her father seemed oblivious to the impact he'd made. "Her CV is impressive, and her mind is razor-sharp. A typical surgeon though. She wasn't too impressed to be talking with a mere cardiologist. Thinks she's a godsend. I'd have loved to prove her wrong, but Ashley snatched her from us."

"I had no say in it. It was Bratton's decision." Anxiety flickered in Ashley's chest at the thought her parents might think she'd taken advantage of Nadia or somehow charmed her into being with her.

"Still haven't answered my question, hon," her father said.

Her mother chimed in. "Does she want children?"

Ashley's entire body burned with mortification. "That isn't something we ask in an interview, Mom."

"Maybe it should be."

"You do realize I'm her boss. I can't just ask her personal things."

"Oh, please," her mother said, unimpressed. "Your generation is so sensitive. I'm not suggesting you put your hand in her pants and see what happens."

As involuntary images of Nadia pressed against the wall in her office and Ashley doing exactly that flashed through her mind, Ashley was sure she was about to have a heart attack of her own.

"All I'm saying is, if you find someone who makes your heart skip a beat, take a risk."

Ashley bit her lip to stop a frustrated sigh from escaping. As uncomfortable as this conversation was, her mother had a point. Her heart did more than skip a beat whenever she was around Nadia. In fact, it was completely at Nadia's mercy. With every action or reaction from Nadia, it sped up or slowed down, grew heavy or became light, burned or froze. Nadia was arrogant and bold, distant and warm, and so different from anyone Ashley had ever known. She owed it to herself to explore if there was something worth pursuing.

"Can we talk about something other than my nonexistent love life?" Ashley set her mother's advice aside in favor of switching to less volatile topics. "Mom, how's work? Did you hire another MA for your clinic?"

As the three of them caught up on their professional lives, Ashley relaxed on the sofa.

After Ashley finally hung up, she felt better. Lighter.

Her parents had agreed to visit more often. They had even set a date in a couple of months. Granted, the time overlapped with a medical conference they were considering attending, but Ashley was just glad they were coming, whatever the reason. She looked around her apartment again. It was just as empty, but the emptiness didn't resonate so strongly in her heart anymore. Glancing at her wall clock, Ashley's eyelids grew heavy. It was already eleven p.m. But before she could make herself move, she thought what her mother had said about taking risks when it mattered. She fought the urge to pick up the phone and call Nadia right then and there to tell her that friendship wasn't enough, that she wanted more.

Why is Nadezhda so stubborn? Her refusal to let her guard down couldn't just be about their professional status. What was the real reason Nadia didn't want a relationship?

Ashley pushed herself to her feet and went to the kitchen. There was no point in thinking about this tonight. She needed to do something with her hands to forget it. She pulled out a container of flour, filtered water, and a scale to weigh out equal amounts of the two ingredients.

The sound of the spoon against the glass bowl echoed in the empty apartment as she stirred the flour and water together into a smooth texture. There was something beyond loneliness that carved into her heart tonight. She didn't want just anyone here with her. She wanted Nadia.

She covered the bowl loosely with a towel and pushed it aside. Maybe everything would make more sense in the morning. With a heavy sigh, Ashley headed to her bedroom.

"Did you go over them?"

Ashley looked up and stared at the crisp white coat collar that framed Nadia's lean neck. *Things are in no way making sense in the morning.* She shook her head. "Sorry, no. I only just saw that you emailed me the slides. Sorry." Knowing how much Nadia loved apologies, Ashley put an extra emphasis on the second one.

Nadia chuckled as she walked further into the office. "Actually, I wanted to see your reaction when you opened them. Do you have time to go over the slides now?" Nadia dragged a chair next to Ashley without waiting for the reply.

Ashley smiled. The confidence was definitely sexy. "Of course. Thank you. You're saving me a ton of time; the least I can do is go over the slides with you. Which, by the way, is really nice of you too. Thank you."

Regretting her babble, Ashley glanced at Nadia, who was looking at her, amused, her chin on her hand. "Are you quite done with the *sorrys* and *thank-yous*?"

"I make no promises." She looked back at the far-less-enticing computer screen and opened the file. The title was "The Nobel Surgeons." Ashley laughed. "It's the talk you gave as a med student."

Nadia tilted her head. "I thought you didn't remember."

"I, uh, might have gone back to the online archives and searched for your name." She felt warmth rise to her cheeks.

"Hm." Nadia's expression lingered on Ashley a moment longer before she reached across the keyboard, a familiar scent of floral shampoo wafting to Ashley, who sat back in the chair in the interest of propriety. Nadia clicked the mouse. "The first slide is pretty self-explanatory. You might say something like, 'Alfred Nobel, the chemist who invented dynamite, left the bulk of his estate to fund the Nobel Prizes. His will specified that the awards should be distributed annually to *those who shall have conferred the greatest benefit of mankind.*'"

"Sure." The med students would probably enjoy a historical view of the Nobel Prizes. "But I think I'll start with something a little bit more exciting to grab the students' attention, something like, 'During his life, Nobel was labeled the merchant of death due to dynamite's destructive nature. It wasn't the legacy he wanted to leave, so he sought to replace it with something good.'"

Nadia stared at her with a perfectly neutral look.

"What?" Ashley asked.

"This is supposed to be a lecture, not entertainment. Don't dramatize the facts."

Ashley chuckled, but Nadia's stone-cold expression remained unyielding. "Fine." Ashley raised her hands in a willing surrender. "Perhaps I should outsource the talk to you. You seem to be very…passionate about it."

Nadia shook her head slightly. "They asked Bratton because having a surgery chair as a guest lecturer is prestigious and gives the students a networking opportunity. They're getting a departmental chief instead, which is acceptable, but if downgraded to a fellow, I doubt anyone would attend."

Ashley laughed. She had a point, as usual. "I'm glad you find me acceptable." Seeing Nadia shift in her seat, Ashley stopped laughing and cleared her throat. She hadn't meant to flirt. "So, how many surgeons have you included in this talk?"

"Four. Technically there are nine surgeons who won a Nobel, if you count the ones with surgical training, but only four made an actual surgical discovery. Neither Banting's discovery of insulin nor Frossmann's invention of cardiac catheterization count. They're great stories, but they didn't advance the field of surgery."

"I didn't realize you knew so much about the history of medicine."

Nadia shrugged. "If you understand the mistakes of the past, you can avoid them in the future."

Ashley frowned as an unwanted thought charged into her consciousness. Was that how she saw their time together?

Nadia leaned across the keyboard again and clicked to the next slide. "The first Nobel Prize in surgery went to Emil Kocher. He developed a technique to remove the entire thyroid gland, but that's not why he received the prize. Because his technique eliminated high surgical mortality, doctors were able to study thyroid deficiency, showing that each organ had a specific function. That was his discovery. After that connection was established, scientists thought that maybe damaged organs could be replaced with healthy ones. Kocher himself tried to solve this, but Alexis Carrel took the next step in transplantation by figuring out how to suture vessels together."

Ashley nodded. Any cardiac surgeon knew that name. "Carrel laid the groundwork for heart surgery and transplantation. We use a lot of his techniques today."

"He didn't do it alone," Nadia pointed out. "He had collaborators, like Tuffier and Lindbergh, who helped advance heart surgery."

"Nobody succeeds on their own. Science is a team sport." *And so is life.* Ashley held Nadia's gaze. Their time together was not a mistake.

"He was also pro-eugenics," Nadia stated evenly.

Ashley chuckled. "Fine, you win. He was a terrible human being." Perhaps she was reading a message into Nadia's words that wasn't there.

"Unfortunately, eugenics was popular among elite circles at the time. It's a good reminder that someone intelligent, spiritual, and deeply humanitarian can also be so wrong."

Silence followed as Nadia's eyes became distant and Ashley's smile died out, as the same eerie feeling crept up again. Why did Nadia keep talking about mistakes?

Before Ashley could ask, Nadia clicked to the next slide. "Be sure to tell the students about Carrel's transplant experiments. He once implanted a dog's kidney into a dog's neck. The surgery was flawless, but it only worked if it was the dog's own kidney. If it was from a different dog, the kidney died."

"Because of immune rejection."

"Carrel suspected that some peculiarity of our bodies was halting the progress of transplantation. The study of replacing organs was abandoned for nearly thirty years until this peculiarity could be identified."

"Murray solved this," Ashley said. There was no trace of whatever worry was on Nadia's mind anymore, and her eyes sparkled with hints of excitement.

"But before that happened, another Nobel Prize was awarded to Antonio Moniz for his discovery of the therapeutic value of leucotomy."

Ashley frowned. "The inventor of the lobotomy got a Nobel Prize?"

"Yes. Although Moniz wasn't technically a surgeon but a neurologist, he was awarded the prize for a surgical discovery, so I thought it was important to mention him. His deciding experiment included operating on twenty patients. A third of them improved, a third worsened, and another third remained unchanged. He received the prize at a time when antipsychotic drugs were not available. Psychosurgery offered a solution where none had existed. The ice pick version was developed and popularized by other doctors."

"Another controversial laureate," Ashley noted.

"I guess he is." Nadia frowned. "Our field really needs better representation."

"A woman, perhaps?"

"Perhaps." A faint smile replaced the frown on Nadia's face. She continued. "And, of course, there is John Murray, who did the first successful kidney transplant in 1954. What is most remarkable is that immunosuppressive drugs wouldn't be discovered until the 1960s."

"Meaning he cheated."

Nadia laughed. "Right. It's a proof-of-concept award. Doctors suspected the immune system might be the culprit for organ rejection, but they weren't sure."

"Murray met identical twin brothers, one sick, one healthy." Ashley rested her back in her chair and fixed her eyes on Nadia. "Twins are natural clones. He gave the sick brother a kidney from the healthy one. The sick brother's immune system didn't recognize the other brother's kidney as foreign, so it didn't attack the cells. And today we're able to—"

"Now do you remember our conversation before the talk?" Nadia looked at Ashley intently.

The presentation was vaguely familiar, but Ashley still didn't remember talking with Nadia. Her stomach tightened with frustration at her own poor memory. She shook her head.

"It's okay." Nadia stood up. "You'll remember soon enough." She gave a confident smile and turned to leave.

"How about a little hint?" Ashley asked, although Nadia was already halfway out the door.

She waved her hand but didn't turn around. "I already gave you a hint. You have to figure out the rest by yourself."

The door clicked shut, leaving Ashley alone in her office. She huffed. Why did she always have to figure things out by herself?

She shut her eyes and rubbed her temples. She was nowhere near a personal breakthrough, and Nadia's hints at mistakes added to her confusion.

Ashley groaned. Why couldn't discoveries be easy?

Chapter 15

The Osteopathic Difference

NADIA RUBBED HER EYES, TRYING to push past her exhaustion. Promising to build a heart for Singh's patient meant she was spending twice the usual time in the lab. She was sleeping even less than usual, and the deprivation made it harder to focus on ignoring her silly and inconvenient crush on Rylan.

"Dr. Keating?"

Jack stood tentatively at the doorway. She gestured for him to come in. Since they had last met to go over Williams's CABG case, Jack's knowledge had improved, but his suturing skills were still lacking. It didn't matter if he wanted to be a psychiatrist, a pathologist, or an astronaut. If he was in the OR, he should know how to suture.

"Have you been practicing?" Nadia asked.

"I have." He pulled out a small silicone skin pad that was falling apart around the incision sites.

Nadia watched Jack shakily guide the curved needle through the fake skin. She frowned as Rylan's words echoed in her mind. It wasn't *nice* of her to help Jack; it was necessary. Nice didn't earn respect in the world of surgery. It didn't save patients. And it was not a quality she often saw in her colleagues.

Except in the chief. A warm feeling rose in her chest. Despite Nadia's efforts to concentrate, Rylan stubbornly refused to leave her thoughts.

Attempting to distract herself, Nadia stepped closer to the table, silently judging Jack's suturing technique. His shaking worsened, making her question her methodology. Maybe Rylan had a point. Maybe Jack would respond better to encouragement. She could give it a shot. "Good job getting here on time this morning." Even to her ears, the words were stilted and forced.

And as soon as she said them, the instruments flew out of Jack's hands and clattered on the ground. He looked at her as if she might set him on fire.

Nadia pinched the bridge of her nose, her hand hiding her amusement. Silently, he picked up the needle driver and forceps and resumed his work.

No, she was nothing like Rylan, and there was no point in admiring her for the qualities Nadia so clearly lacked. The thought brought unease that spread through her chest, formed knots in her stomach, and added tension to her muscles. Since when did she even entertain the idea to be anything like Rylan?

She cleared her throat and focused on Jack again. "Stabilize your upper arms against your body and keep the lateral part of your hypothenar eminences on the table whenever possible. It will help steady your hands. Right now, you look more like a Parkinson's patient than a doctor."

What bothered Nadia most was that she had never shared so much about herself with anyone else but Rylan. She didn't quite understand how she could have allowed it. There was nothing unique about Rylan that justified such a lapse. Sure, she was attractive, but so were a lot of other people. Appearances hardly accounted for Nadia's interest in Rylan, and Nadia refused to entertain the possibility that it was Rylan's compassion that encouraged her to open up.

So what was it then?

Reminding herself again she should quit asking questions she had no desire answering, Nadia reached forward to hold the suture line away from Jack's field of work. Her mind rebelled against her, recalling that it was the same thing she had done for Rylan a few days earlier. Her heart jolted at the memory of Rylan's mere proximity back then. Unlike the spike in her blood pressure because of Jack's clumsy execution, back then her heart had raced because of the fine movements Rylan's delicate fingers made and the inherently melodic sound her voice carried. Even when she had been stammering about sex in a delightful fluster.

Nadia shook off the memory. It was wrong. All of it. It didn't matter how her body reacted to Rylan. She was in control of her emotions, not the other way around. Gritting her teeth, she told herself to ignore all thoughts of Rylan's delicate scent, soft skin, or piercing blue eyes.

Abandoning her assisting duties, Nadia dropped the suture and crossed her arms tightly as if she could hold onto her fleeting resolve. Her emotions toward Rylan felt like an unresectable cancer—when it was impossible to recognize where the tumor ended and the normal anatomy began, there was little hope for recovery.

Ignoring the grim realization, she looked at Jack. He still held the instruments, but he had stopped working. His clueless eyes were wide enough to warrant a workup for brain damage.

She pinched her lips to hide a mixture of displeasure and amusement. "You have no idea what a hypothenar eminence is, do you?"

As Ashley drew closer to the coffee counter, her breathing rate sped up as if she were on the verge of a panic attack. *This is embarrassing.*

She had just finished giving the talk on surgeons who had won Nobel Prizes, and it had been so well received that she wanted to get Nadia a coffee as a thank-you. Except she had no idea what coffee to get.

"Hi, Ashley. The usual?" asked the girl behind the counter.

"Hi, Janet. Uh, yes." Ashley smiled warmly. "And…one more drink."

Janet waited as Ashley scanned the menu. *What does Nadezhda like?*

"Are you familiar with what other doctors drink?" Ashley asked. "The one I'm thinking of is about my height with brown hair. And she looks angry most of the time."

Janet shrugged. "Sorry, not a regular."

What were the chances this would work, anyway? Nadia probably made one of her minions in the lab fetch her coffee.

Ashley sighed. "I'll take your four most popular coffee drinks."

She made her way to Nadia's lab juggling a four-cup carrier tray in one hand and an extra cup in the other. The liquid in the cups sloshed back and forth, reflecting Ashley's mind. Torn between thinking coffee was a terrible idea in one instant and a great one in the next, she trudged to Nadia's lab.

"The sutures go from out to in and not the other way around. This won't do." Nadia was criticizing Sarah, her lab assistant and a first-year medical student, in a sterile area at the far end of the lab.

"I'll redo the anastomosis, Dr. Keating."

As Sarah picked up the required instruments, she knocked down a vascular stapler.

"My grant isn't intended to cover expensive mistakes," Nadia said with ice in her voice. "Scrub out and get me another stapler."

Ashley wanted to shake her head and laugh at the same time. Nadia's reaction was excessive, but it was also funny how she always had something intimidating to say. Still, the chances of Sarah finding any humor in the sharp remark were slim. The girl scrambled out of the sterile gown and headed toward the exit. On her way out, she met Ashley's eyes.

"I'm glad she's not my boss," Ashley teased, trying to calm the tensed girl.

Sarah's eyes got even wider before she scurried away.

"Do you have to be so hard on the poor girl?" Ashley frowned, despite amusement still dancing on her lips. "She's still learning."

"If you were the patient, you wouldn't want some clueless medical student practicing on you. Some mistakes are harder to tolerate than others."

Ashley chuckled. "You just love being the bad guy, don't you?"

"It's a welcome bonus," Nadia said with just a hint of a smirk. She stepped toward Ashley, tearing off her sterile gown in one motion. "I'm busy. What do you want?"

"I got you coffee," she said, though the sudden closeness made her breathe a little harder.

Nadia looked at the tray. "Which one is for me?"

"I'm not sure." Ashley's cheeks heated. "I had no idea what to get you."

Nadia took her time washing her hands, then gestured for Ashley to set the drinks on the bench closest to the exit.

Ashley complied, relieved to put the tray down. But now she had nothing to shield her from Nadia's assessing stare, and she shifted her weight from side to side.

Nadia didn't even bother examining the drinks. "I don't drink coffee."

"Ever?" Ashley's mouth dropped. Surgeons loved caffeine, but maybe Nadia preferred tea instead of coffee.

"No tea, cola, guarana, or whatever caffeine nonsense people have come up with these days." Nadia quickly disabused her of that thought.

Ashley frowned. "But you're here all the time. I've seen you pull double shifts without batting an eye. You mean to tell me you keep going out of pure stubbornness?"

Nadia shrugged. "I don't like stimulants. They create physical dependence. And I don't like to be dependent on anything."

The "or anyone" was left out, but Ashley heard it just as loudly. Disappointment wiggled through her and she reached out to retrieve the coffees. *Well, this was a stupid idea.*

"Leave them." Nadia touched her hand. "I'll give them to my staff."

Ashley's heart jumped at the contact, and she looked up with her eyes wide. Nadia quickly withdrew her hand, leaving a longing sensation from Ashley's skin all the way to her core. Ashley cleared her throat, ignoring the feeling. "I thought nice went against your nature," she teased.

Nadia visibly cringed. "I'm not…that." She picked up one of the coffees and examined it. "You guessed Sarah's drink."

Ashley smirked. "For someone who doesn't drink coffee, you know a lot about other people's coffee preferences."

Nadia's nonchalant shrug made Ashley wonder if she was allergic to compliments. "I'd say it's nice of you to know something about her, but I'm afraid you might go into anaphylactic shock."

Nadia scoffed and turned the cup to show Ashley where the barista had scribbled "soymilk" on it. "There was a study that looked into how what kind of coffee someone drinks can tell you about their personality. I decided to figure out if the data applied to my staff."

Ashley grinned. Of course, there was research involved. "And does it?"

"People who drink their coffee with soymilk tend to be detail-orientated. It's spot-on for Sarah." Nadia glanced in the direction of where Sarah had been working. "That is if she remembers to suture the graft the right way."

Ashley chuckled at Nadia's dry tone. "And the rest?"

Nadia picked up the remaining drinks one by one. The PhD graduate student working with her was creative and motivated, which was reflected by his preference for cappuccino's rich and sophisticated flavor. The straightforward general surgery resident drank black coffee. The

Frappuccino drinker was more likely to take risks in life, as evidenced by the fact that he was the only staff member who ever argued with her.

"It also means he doesn't make healthy choices, but I don't need a study to tell me that, given the amount of sugar he consumes."

Ashley laughed, thoroughly enjoying Nadia's masterful ability to balance humor and discipline. For someone who rarely engaged in chitchat, her ample knowledge of her staff filled Ashley with addictive curiosity. "And what about this one?" Ashley placed the fifth cup on the table. It was Ashley's drink, a latte.

Nadia's face stiffened as she stared at the cup.

"What?" Ashley asked.

"Nothing. I have to get back to work."

Ashley grabbed her hand. "What just happened?"

"It's nothing. It was a dumb study conducted by an armchair psychologist. It hardly qualifies as science. Forget it."

Ashley realized what the problem was. "Now I have to know about latte drinkers."

Nadia crossed her arms. "I'm not going to tell you."

It was childish and yet adorable how Nadia tried to protect her feelings. Ashley pulled out her phone. "Fine. I'll find out for myself." How many studies linking personality traits and coffee could there be?

With a few taps, she found a blog post that referenced the study in question. She couldn't imagine Nadia ever reading a layman article about a scientific paper, but if any time was appropriate to cut corners, it was now. A summary table contained personality characteristics of the various coffee drinkers. She found the list for lattes: people pleaser, neurotic, indecisive. She snorted. "Yeah, that's pretty much how you see me."

"No." Nadia reached out but then retracted her hand to her side and made a fist. "You also add an extra shot. I think that description is more accurate."

Ashley looked back at her phone again. The traits for espresso were leadership and hard-working. She smiled. The whole study was silly, as Nadia had said, but it was nice of her to try to make Ashley feel better. And it was totally working.

"I'm changing my coffee drink," Ashley announced with all the seriousness she could muster.

Nadia chuckled. "I don't think you should change anything."

The words made Ashley's breath hitch. She stared at Nadia. Those intense brown eyes made her entire body flare with want, need, and something that words could never describe. No "friend" had ever looked at her the way Nadia did.

Nadia looked away, breaking the connection. "Except, of course, the way you tie your surgical knots," she added dryly. "I hope you change that to save some OR time."

Ashley forced a laugh. Nadia had made it clear they couldn't be together. She had to guard against emotional lapses like the one that had just happened. "If I do all my knots the way you want, it might save me fifteen seconds," she said, recovering. "And that is an optimistic estimate."

The door swung open. It was Sarah, returning with the stapler. Nadia snapped back into rigid aloofness.

"It's about time. Did you go all the way to India to get that stapler?"

Ashley stepped away. The moment had passed, and it was time for her to get back to work. She turned to Sarah. "Let me know if she's too hard on you, and I'll have a stern talk with her."

"Dr. Keating is a great mentor," Sarah protested promptly. "It's a privilege to work with her. She's inspiring, and her pioneering research is going to change the world."

Ashley looked at Nadia, who was smiling arrogantly.

"Did you hear that? It's a privilege to work with me."

Ashley snorted as she walked out. "I'll try to keep that in mind."

Nadia shifted in her bed. The mattress felt as if it were filled with stones, not made of memory foam. She had made significant progress on her project today, so why was she restless?

Her osteopathic background gave her the framework to build a heart, but the knowledge wasn't limited to one field. How did Ashley put it? *Healers explain the same world from different perspectives. Ideas are bound to overlap.*

Ah, boundaries.

Boundaries were good. They helped people operate within preset parameters. Emotions were complicated, unpredictable, and undesirable in a neat universe of rules.

But it is human nature to feel.

Nadia fluffed up her pillow, frustrated at how logic kept slipping through her fingers.

Ashley. When did she start thinking of Rylan by her first name?

She pushed the thought away and forced herself to think about her experiment. A heart, like any other organ, grew within a body. Osteopathy taught that the body functioned as a whole and should only be understood as a unit. The irony was that when it came to her relationships, Nadia had dispassionately compartmentalized her life. But they were artificial walls. What if she broke them down?

Nadia rolled over again. Why couldn't she have the same clarity in her personal life that she had in her job?

Squeezing her eyes shut, she tried to chase away the moonlight that peeked into through the window shades. She was ready to admit that her insomnia had nothing to do with her experiment. Not her *laboratory* experiment, anyway.

She couldn't say the same for her social experiment. Boundaries had been crossed, lines had blurred, and feelings had developed. She could no longer ignore the way her heartbeat quickened every time she saw Ash—no—Rylan.

She turned over again. It was hopeless. Fighting her feelings was a battle she had lost before it began. She was naïve to think she could separate her emotions from her actions. The truth was obvious: Nadia had deep, sappy, gut-wrenching, chest-tightening, butterflies-in-the-stomach feelings. For Ashley. *Yes, Ashley.* Because no matter how much she denied it, Nadia couldn't think of her in any other way anymore.

It was never just sex. And if Nadia kept burying her emotions, her heart might break.

Literally.

The only sensible course of action was to allow herself to feel her feelings instead of pushing them away.

The mattress shifted on the other side of the bed, and she fought the urge to slither away as an arm wrapped around her. She gently pushed the arm off and slipped out of bed. She stared at the handsome face in the dim light, guilt rotting inside her. Why couldn't she feel for him what she felt for Ashley?

Her mind flooded with frustration over her emotional ineptness, and her eyes dampened.

She couldn't keep going like this. She had to come clean. To everyone. And maybe Ashley would appreciate her honesty. Maybe she would understand—and forgive her.

Even if she didn't, Nadia could no longer keep secrets from the people she cared about. Telling the truth was the right thing to do. *For everyone involved.*

Chapter 16

The Imperfect Male

ASHLEY SWUNG BY THE PHYSICIANS' lounge on the way to her upcoming surgery. Dan was assisting her today, and she was in no hurry to see the usual hurt mixed with a glimmer of hope whenever he looked at her.

The lounge was almost empty at this hour—seven a.m. At this time, doctors were usually getting ready to or were already rounding on their patients. A rich aroma of coffee flooded her senses. Her mouth watered, and she swallowed enviously. Indulging in a second cup just before a four-hour surgery with nowhere to go wasn't a sound idea. She reluctantly looked away from the coffee machine and saw Pari at a computer station talking to Jason. They must be discussing their first case for the day. Ashley approached them.

"Come on, Dr. Singh," Jason pleaded. "Let me start the case. You let Nadia do so much more than me. It's embarrassing. She's a year behind me."

Pari didn't look away from the computer screen. "Keating knows what she's doing. You don't."

Jason huffed. "She certainly thinks she does. That's why she acts like a royal bitch all the time."

The words scorched Ashley's ears. "If I ever hear you say anything like that again, you'll be out of this hospital for good," she told Jason, unaccustomed rage pounding in her heart.

Jason turned to face her, startled. His expression told Ashley she had used the appropriate tone for the occasion.

"Dr. Rylan, I didn't realize you were—"

"Never talk about a colleague like that again. Is that understood?"

Jason nodded, mortified.

Pari turned in her chair. "Jason, go prep the patient. I'll assist and you can open. Go."

Jason scrambled out of his chair and out the door.

Ashley narrowed her eyes at Pari. "You reward his behavior?"

Pari stared at her blankly. "What's gotten into you?"

"Nothing," Ashley snapped. She flopped down in the chair that Jason had vacated, crossing her arms across her chest. "I just hate it when people are mean."

Pari snorted. "Then why are you defending the meanest of them all?"

"You think Nadezhda deserves it?" Ashley frowned. "I thought you liked her."

"I like Keating just fine. But even on a good day, she comes off as bitchy at best."

"She isn't," Ashley protested. "Just because she hides her feelings better than the rest of us doesn't mean they aren't there."

Pari tilted her head to an inquisitive angle. "Why are you Team Keating all of a sudden?"

"I'm not." Ashley scrambled to recover. "You told me to give her a chance, remember? I agree with you—she's extraordinary." Her cheeks got warm. "Extraordinary to work with."

Pari stood up. "I have to go make sure we still have a case. Jason's bedside manner leaves much to be desired." But instead of leaving, she turned back to Ashley. "By the way, what was the name of the woman you met online?"

"Why?" Alarms went off in Ashley's head.

Pari grinned ear to ear. "No reason. I'll catch you later."

Nadia's heart pounded, but no matter how much anxiety she felt this morning, she was determined to tell Ashley everything. With every step she took, her legs shook and her chest burned. It didn't matter.

As she approached the elevator, her phone rang. Her jaw tightened, but her heart began to slow down to a more comfortable rhythm. It was a welcome interruption—anything to postpone facing Ashley, even if only for a couple of moments.

"Keating speaking."

"Pari needs you in OR ten. Now!" It was Melissa, one of the operating room nurses. Her voice was urgent.

A familiar sense of calm replaced the tightness in Nadia's chest. There were clear steps to follow in medical emergencies. It was controlled chaos. Unlike her personal emotions that ran rampant, she could handle this.

Nadia hurried into the elevator and pushed the button for the OR floor. Patients always came first. Ashley would have to wait.

Tapping her foot repeatedly in a futile attempt to make the elevator go faster, Nadia sincerely doubted Singh had had time to ask Ashley to release Nadia to help with whatever emergency was going on there. No matter. She would deal with the consequences later.

The operating room looked like a bloodbath. Singh's face and gown, the floor, the lamps, and even parts of the walls were spattered. Singh was frantically working on the patient. Jason stood paralyzed on the opposite side of the table, a suction device in his hand.

"What happened?" Nadia quickly rubbed on the waterless surgical scrub to sanitize her hands, then self-gowned and gloved. The surgical barrier was like protective armor that numbed her mind to the likely outcome of this case. Fear had no place in the OR.

"Take off my loupes, Melissa. I can't see a thing," Singh shouted. Then to Nadia she said, "It was supposed to be a simple valve repair. You need to cannulate the femoral vessels so we can get him on bypass stat. He's losing blood faster than we can replace it."

Nadia pushed Jason aside and quickly made an incision in the patient's groin area. Her hands were steady despite her heart pounding as if she were the one fighting for her life.

She began exposing the femoral artery, and her surgical field disappeared in a pool of blood. It was surprising the patient had any blood left in his body at this point.

"Assist me," she hissed at Jason who remained uselessly frozen next to her.

"I just did a median sternotomy as I always do," Jason said. "I don't know what went wrong."

He still wasn't moving. Nadia glanced at Singh, who was too preoccupied to pay attention to his words.

"Iatrogenic tears are rare, but they do happen," Nadia said. "That wasn't your fault. Losing this patient because you're not doing your job will be your fault." She dragged Jason's hand with the sucker to the pooled blood and repeated, "Assist me."

"I need a Weitlaner retractor." Jason finally snapped out of his shocked state.

With the added help, Nadia quickly cannulated the artery and vein. It probably took her less than a few minutes, but every second dragged out with painful awareness that the patient was still losing blood. Once circulatory support was established, she breathed a sigh of relief. Singh clamped the aorta, containing the blood within tubes and vessels rather than it spilling out of the patient's chest.

Ignoring Jason, Nadia stepped opposite Singh to assist her with repairing the damage.

"You can go wash up, Jason," Singh said. "Keating's got this."

Jason stood, frozen, his hands pressed against his upper abdomen. When he stepped closer to the table as if to say something, Nadia shook her head. It was best he didn't speak. Singh had kept her cool for the patient's benefit. He shouldn't test her limits. As if reading her mind, he nodded and left.

"I can't stand to look at him right now. He condemned this poor man," Singh said through gritted teeth.

Nadia could have jumped to her colleague's defense but didn't. He probably hadn't done the blunt dissection under the bone with his fingers, so he had failed to detect the sternal adhesions and simply had run the saw carelessly, pushing through the resistance of the fused tissue.

"Thank you for coming in," Singh muttered.

Nadia nodded without saying anything back. The ghastly scene was captured in her mind, so this was no time for inconsequential niceties. She focused on the next step of the operation and the one that followed. She quietly assisted as the aorta was patched up and the valve replaced.

Once they began closing the layers, a task any cardiac surgeon could do in their sleep, Singh looked up. "Can we have some music?" Melissa jumped to her feet and tuned in Singh's favorite soft rock station. The nurses and anesthesiologists followed Singh's example and relaxed as light chatter replaced the eerie silence.

While Nadia was relieved the patient was stable now, her mind drifted back to her impending meeting with Ashley. Dread gripped her heart.

Singh scanned the room, and Nadia mirrored her in a desperate attempt to keep in the present. There was a tremendous amount of blood on the floor and walls. Singh sighed. "The only weapon with which the unconscious patient can immediately retaliate upon the incompetent surgeon is hemorrhage."

Nadia eyed her mentor. "William Halsted." She identified the author of the quote. "The man who introduced subcuticular suturing, among other things."

"Right." Singh chuckled. "Only you would know this about—"

"—one of the Big Four founding physicians of Hopkins. I know that, of course, but why lead with the obvious?" Nadia smiled cockily under her mask.

Singh chuckled as she looked back down at her work.

Emboldened by Singh's improved mood, Nadia decided to address a more pressing matter. "I hope you'll explain to Dr. Rylan why I've disobeyed her orders."

Singh looked up to meet Nadia's eyes. "Oh, I'm sure you two can reach an agreement all by yourselves. I'd hate to be the third wheel."

The "third wheel" comment made Nadia's ears burn. Refusing to acknowledge it, she busied herself with the next layer of tissue to close. Surely, Ashley would never tell Singh about them.

"So you're a fan of history," Singh added cheerily.

Nadia swallowed against a dry mouth. It would be best to remain silent until she knew where this was going. She continued to intently work on the subcutaneous layer closure. *One more to go* and she would be out of this OR.

"Let me ask you a question, then," Singh continued. "Given that the history of surgery is riddled with discrimination and preconceived ideas of what a surgeon should look like, it's not surprising that, in the past, being a woman and being a doctor were mutually exclusive. So who do you think was the first modern female surgeon?"

Nadia dropped her forceps. *Damn it.* "Jose, I need new pickups." She spewed the words at him harsher than intended. After all, he wasn't the one at fault.

Nadia searched Singh's face. The mocking expression in her mentor's eyes made it clear she knew something. "Mary Walker." Pleased that at least her voice came out cool and steady, Nadia maintained eye contact.

"Nope," Singh said. "Walker is considered to be the first female surgeon in the United States, but she's not the one I had in mind. Think further back."

"Elizabeth Blackwell?" suggested Jeffrey Floyd from behind the anesthesiology curtain.

"Nope. Blackwell was the first female physician in the States, but she lost sight in one eye, so her desire to do surgery remained but a dream," Singh explained. "During the time that Blackwell and Walker were fighting for the right to attend medical school, the surgeon I'm thinking of was at the peak of her very impressive career."

Nadia tried to focus on her work, but her blood was boiling.

"Come on, Keating. I'm sure you know the answer."

Nadia could answer Singh's question or she could leave the OR. But the last time she had walked out, she had regretted it. "James Barry," Nadia said. It wasn't the name Singh wanted, but it wasn't incorrect either.

Floyd laughed. "That's a guy's name."

"Ah, but Jeff, she's right." Singh was leisurely securing a chest tube, offering little technical help to Nadia. "James Barry was a woman ahead of her time. She lived in the early nineteenth century when the good people of England still honored the words of King Henry VIII on the matter of who could be part of the Company of Barber-Surgeons."

Nadia rolled her eyes. Had Singh prepared an entire lecture?

"Henry decreed that no carpenter, smith, weaver, or woman should practice surgery. That meant if Barry wanted to be a surgeon, she had to become a man. So she did. And she practiced surgery for fifty years."

Floyd whistled.

It was impressive to commit to a lie for such a long time. Nadia's anger simmered down as she wondered if Barry regretted what she did. How great were the sacrifices? Was she lonely all her life?

"She did some pretty badass stuff," Singh continued. "She implemented sanitation in the OR before lack of sterility and infections were linked. She also did one of the first C-sections where the mother and baby survived. But despite all that she accomplished, her life is remembered as *a supreme deception.*"

The words brought Nadia's anger back with a vengeance. She clenched her jaw. "You know, Barry gave clear instructions before his death on how *he* wished *his* body to be handled and buried. His wishes were ignored." Nadia's voice had a warning tone intended to make Singh finally shut her mouth. She glared at her for good measure.

Singh returned the look evenly. Her eyes slowly crinkled with the smile hidden under her mask. "Oh, but if the good doctor's wishes had been honored, that would make for a very dull story, don't you think?"

For a moment, Nadia and Singh simply stared at each other. Anger, embarrassment, and more anger piled up inside Nadia as she held her steely glare. Her life wasn't some story to entertain Singh. She should leave.

"So nobody knew he was a she until the body was being prepared for the funeral?" Floyd's question broke the silence.

Nadia returned to her work without a word. *Damn it*, it was a simple sternotomy closure. She should have been done by now. She tried to ignore Singh, but her voice carried in the almost silent room.

"After the funeral in a letter, Barry's doctor pretended he didn't know his patient's sex, implying that Barry might have been an imperfectly developed man, a hermaphrodite, or an intersex. As if there was no way a woman, lacking a Y chromosome, could ever achieve what Barry did. Because an imperfect male made more sense than a perfect female. Back then, men believed exposure to gore posed a risk to the health of delicate females. Apparently, they weren't aware that women deal with blood on a monthly basis."

Everyone in the room burst out laughing.

Nadia had no interest in joining. She was done with closing the incision, done with this surgery, and, most importantly, done with Singh. She stepped away from the table, ripped off her bloodied gown, gloves, and mask, and shoved them into the trash.

"My favorite part of the story is when Barry was charged with having a homosexual relationship with a governor. The governor's wife was appalled by the accusation. Not that the truth would have been any more reassuring." That comment elicited another round of laughter.

Nadia resisted the urge to strangle her superior. She kept her voice even as she said, "Thank you, Dr. Singh, for the history lesson. It has been very entertaining."

"Keating, before you leave, I have one more question for you." Singh stopped Nadia in her tracks. "What was the real name of James Barry?"

Nadia wished she had left her mask on. Betrayal. Indignation. Anger. Humiliation. Her emotions were running rampant, and, courtesy of Singh's unrelenting insistence, she could barely keep her face impassive.

Two things were becoming clear. One, using an obscure historical figure as a profile name for an online dating site wasn't as amusing as Nadia had once thought it would be. And two, trusting that women wouldn't discuss their sex lives with their best friends had been a colossal mistake.

She was going to kill Ashley.

Nadia turned to meet Singh's gaze, her nostrils flaring. "Her real name was Margaret Bulkley." The words were quiet but firm. And final.

She stormed out of the OR. Her anger had a new target now.

Someone burst into Ashley's office, slamming the door behind them. Startled, Ashley jumped in her seat and looked up from her computer to find Nadia with a murderous expression glaring at her.

"Why did you tell Singh about us?" Her voice was low but chilling.

"What? Pari knows?" Ashley's stomach dropped.

Nadia closed her eyes, took a deep breath, and opened them again. "James Barry?"

Ashley waited for Nadia to elaborate. When she didn't, Ashley asked, "Who?"

Nadia scoffed. "Margaret Bulkley?"

The name took Ashley's breath. "I didn't…this isn't your name," she said unintelligibly. There was no connection between that particular name and Nadia. Right?

"What exactly did you tell her?"

"I…uh, nothing that would identify you."

"What. Did. You. Tell. Her?"

Ashley glanced around as if the right thing to say was lurking in her office. She thought about what she had shared with Pari, and that her and Nadia's relationship had been turning into a positive one. Had Pari ruined it?

No, not Pari. It was Ashley's fault.

"I told her everything." Ashley looked down.

"What does 'everything' mean?" Nadia asked through gritted teeth. "Did you tell her we had sex in your office?"

The question hammered in her head, crushing any excuse. "I didn't say it was in my office, and I didn't say it was you. But yes, I told her we slept together."

"We didn't sleep together; we had sex," Nadia hissed.

Ashley rolled her eyes. Semantics.

"Did you give her any details?"

With the blood draining from her face, Ashley mumbled, "Yes."

For a brief moment the anger in Nadia's eyes was replaced by pain. "Did you tell her it was my first—?"

"No." She wasn't a complete monster.

Nadia said nothing else for several minutes while guilt gnawed at every nerve of Ashley's body. Could she ever make things right between them?

"I'm so sorry—"

"Stop." Nadia's expression hardened, the molten lava of her anger setting in. "I thought I could trust you." The cold words tore through Ashley like bullets.

She wanted to scream that Nadia could trust her, but she had no right to say that.

"You should have kept your mouth shut. You embarrassed me in front of someone I respect. You told me you could be discreet. You have no idea the humiliation I had to endure in the OR. She—"

"Wait. You were in the OR?" Ashley found her voice.

"There was an aortic tear. Jason was freaking out and—" Nadia paused. "You know what? Take it up with Singh. She was the one who asked me for help." She glared at Ashley, challenging her to disagree.

"I certainly will." Ashley held Nadia's gaze for a moment and then sighed. "At least now I know why you have blood all over your face. I thought you might have murdered Pari." Ashley handed Nadia an antibacterial hand wipe. "Tell me what happened."

Nadia sat down on the chair opposite to Ashley and began cleaning off the blood, blindly wiping her face and neck. Ashley gripped the armrests of her chair to resist the urge to help.

"We managed to get the bleeding under control. She kicked Jason out. He was in no way capable of operating. You should check on him. Singh was mad."

Ashley nodded absentmindedly, her fingers still itching as Nadia wiped the last bit of blood from her face.

"When we were closing, out of nowhere, she started talking about Margaret Bulkeley and implying things in front of the entire OR. Why the hell would you not keep your private life private?"

Ashley squirmed under Nadia's icy glare. "Who is Margaret Bulkley, and how is she relevant?"

Nadia went on as if she hadn't heard. "You shouldn't have shared anything about me with her."

"She won't tell anyone. I know Pari. I'm sorry you had to go through her immature behavior. I'll talk to her."

Ashley braced herself as Nadia's scowl only deepened. For a long moment, neither one of them spoke. By now, she had a pretty good idea what Nadia might say next. Something along the lines of how she could fight her own battles, or how Ashley had done enough, or how she didn't depend on anyone for anything.

Finally, Nadia broke the silence. "This was a mistake," she said quietly. "Nothing should have happened between us. We're not friends. We should stop acting as if we are."

The words hit Ashley like a dagger to her heart. She would much rather Nadia yell and fight with her than walk away.

Then Ashley stood up from behind her desk. She was the supervisor, and she had more to lose than the subordinate if their relationship became public. Indignation stiffened her spine. Nadia had dictated the rules from the beginning, and she had followed along. It was time to re-establish herself. "Have it your way," she snapped. She balled her hands into fists. "Oh, and in light of your most recent insubordination, your OR privileges are revoked until the end of the month."

Nadia set her jaw. "If that's how you want to handle it, *Dr. Rylan*." The fire in her eyes made her look more like a sociopath now than when she'd had blood on her face.

She sprang to her feet, flung open the door, and stalked off.

Ashley stood frozen in place. There was nothing else she could say at this point, and she wasn't even sure she wanted to.

She turned back to her desk, not bothering to shut the door. When she looked up again, Pari was standing in the doorway, grinning. She invited herself in, closing the door behind her. "Anything you'd like to tell me?"

"Nadezhda's OR privileges are still suspended. You used my fellow without asking me."

"You fucked your fellow."

The bluntness stung Ashley's ears. She winced. "It's not what it looks like." She sat back in her chair. "I had no idea who I was meeting until I got to the bar. And after that I…may have developed feelings for her…a little."

"Feelings? Is that how we justify sleeping with the help?"

It was a clumsy attempt at humor. The fellows were all adult professionals at the end of a long and highly specialized training, and they were all very independent. But there was no need for Ashley to point that out.

"I wasn't supposed to tell you about that." Regret renewed its attack on Ashley's heart. There was nothing comical from where she was standing.

"Tell me what?"

"Tell you that we had sex. Nadezhda's mad at me for not being discreet." She dropped her face into her hands. All the rules about what she could or couldn't say were—complicated. "I probably shouldn't have told you she's mad either."

"You do know I'd never jeopardize your careers, right?" Pari's voice became serious.

"I know that. I'm sure she knows it too." Ashley looked up to meet Pari's eyes. "But you're her superior after all. How would you feel if your boss knew details about your…personal stuff?"

"He wouldn't. I'd know better than to act impulsively."

"So you wouldn't have dated Phillip if he was working with you? You wouldn't have married him or had children with him?"

"No, I wouldn't have," Pari responded without hesitation.

"Even though he was the one?"

"Is that what Keating is? *The one?*"

The question made her heart cramp in her chest. *Is she the one?* "Of course not. She can't stand me, let alone like me." Ashley voiced the painful truth for herself to hear it as much as for Pari.

Neither one spoke. Pari stared at Ashley expectantly, as if she were about to reveal some big secret. But Pari already knew Ashley's secrets. There was nothing left to reveal.

Pari broke the silence. "Ashley, you do know that what you did was wrong, right?"

Hearing Pari say what Ashley had been struggling with from the start fueled her with a determination to prove them both wrong. "It's not like I'm picking favorites. Nadezhda and I are completely professional at work. What I do in my personal life is nobody's business."

Pari raised her eyebrows and waited.

"Fine. I know it was wrong," Ashley admitted. "But it didn't feel wrong. It felt right. And it hasn't felt right for a long time." She shook her head. "It doesn't matter. I told you; she doesn't even like me. Especially now."

Pari regarded her quietly for a few moments. "I didn't mean to stir things up between you two. I was just joking around in the OR. I'd never—"

"It's okay, Pari. I don't think it was you. You were just the excuse she was looking for to end this. It's been that way from the start. One step forward, ten steps back."

And with those words, her heart caught up with what her mind had known all along. Her relationship with Nadia had been doomed before it began.

She frowned at Pari. "But for God's sake, quit teasing her about it."

Pari grinned. "I make no promises. Even for your girlfriend."

Just picturing how Nadia might react to hearing that word made Ashley wince again. "She's not my girlfriend," she protested although she was sure it fell on deaf ears. The word caught in her throat and she cleared it. "One more thing."

"Yes?"

"Who, pray tell, are James Barry and Margaret Bulkley, and what do they have to do with Nadezhda?"

Chapter 17

Mocking the Creator

Nadia sat in the lab with the lights off, embracing the silence. The staff had left half an hour ago after a twelve-hour day. She would have kept them longer if she could have.

She lost her sadistic smirk, spun in her chair, and looked at the doorway, gripping the armrests. Nobody was coming. Looking at that damned door wasn't going to change anything.

It had been two days since the incident in OR ten. While that patient was doing well, the same couldn't be said about Nadia's ego. After her confrontation with Rylan, she had retreated to the lab like a wounded animal.

Yes, *Rylan*. It had always been Rylan, and it should have stayed that way. And she shouldn't expect her to come here and apologize. Even if she did, it wouldn't change anything. Nadia's lust had blindsided her to Rylan's untrustworthiness. With a low growl, Nadia spun back to face her computer.

Whatever false feelings her treacherous heart harbored, she should ignore them and focus instead on the heart she was building for Singh's patient. Her groundbreaking work was going to change the world. That wasn't a dream but an inevitable reality.

Nadia smirked. Okay, so humility wasn't her thing. But false modesty had never helped anyone.

"How is our patient doing?"

She nearly jumped out of her seat when she heard Dan's voice. He wasn't the person she wanted to see, and she had no intention of hiding her displeasure at this. She scowled at him. "The heart isn't a patient, and it certainly isn't yours."

Dan hoisted himself up on a nearby counter. "So you say, but I think we should discuss my coauthorship." He smiled charmingly.

His boyish looks and muscular physique, evident even under the baggy scrubs, surely got him a lot of attention. Why he chose to obsess over the one woman who wasn't remotely interested in him was beyond Nadia's comprehension.

Well, not entirely beyond. She could certainly see the appeal.

"Come on. I've been here every night. Surely, I've done enough to be listed as the second author."

It was true that Nadia had cultivated Dan's curiosity, especially at night when her staff personnel weren't at the lab. He, like most surgeons, was hopeless at translational science, but his skilled hands were good for the technical setup.

Nadia raised an eyebrow. "I might add your name in the acknowledgments section."

Dan huffed in exaggerated indignation and Nadia smiled. They both knew that section was useless in a scientific paper.

"That is, if there is any space left," Nadia deadpanned.

Dan grinned widely and pressed his hand against his heart. "It's what every doctor ever dreams of."

Nadia rolled her eyes at his theatrics.

"Have you eaten today?" He reached into his bag and tossed a sandwich in her direction.

"You really want that coauthorship, don't you?" Nadia teased. But she was, in fact, starving, and she devoured the sandwich in a matter of minutes.

With her hunger satisfied, her thoughts drifted back to Rylan. "Are we friends?" she asked Dan.

Dan looked at her, puzzled. "We're, uh, friendly"—he grinned—"*ish.*"

Nadia scowled. "And yet you consider our acquaintance sufficient to share personal information with me?"

Dan frowned. "Hey, I don't make a habit of sharing my sad personal life with people at work. But I have feelings; I need to vent sometimes."

He looked away. "Besides, my feelings for Ashley were hardly a secret. You already knew I liked her."

"Ashley?" The name, coming from his mouth, jarred her ears. "On a first-name basis with the chief, are we?" He had no right to call her that. "You're still a fellow. You should refer to your attendings with their titles. Or am I missing something?" She knew very well she wasn't missing anything. "Has there been a new development you haven't told me about?" She studied his face. "Did you turn Rylan straight?"

Her conscience tugged at her for a moment, but a deeper sense of irritation prevailed. If he showed Rylan the necessary respect, Nadia wouldn't have to remind him of it.

Dan blushed. "Please stop. You've made your point. It's Dr. Rylan. And nothing happened. I've been trying to avoid her ever since I asked her out." He hung his head, then looked up at her. "Anyway, it's in the past. Why are you bringing this up?"

Why was she?

Every time Nadia thought of Rylan and Singh talking about Nadia's bedroom—or rather office—performance, she felt humiliated all over again. It was something she didn't want to imagine, yet her cruel mind kept circling back to it.

Nadia crossed her arms. "I'm trying to understand why people feel the need to share private information with third parties when it's none of their business." She was trying but failing to sound dispassionate.

"Uh…because that's how friendships work? You share things, try to support one another, show mutual trust. That kind of thing."

"I know what friendship is," Nadia said curtly. "I meant, if you were seeing someone, would you talk about her? Not with me, because, apparently we're on friendly-ish terms at best, but would you share things with your actual friends?"

"Why wouldn't I tell my friends about somebody I'm seeing? I'd be excited for them to meet her."

"No, I don't mean that. Like—" Nadia pinched her lips together. Dan was missing the point. "Like intimate details. Would you share those?"

Dan gave her a lopsided smile. "What kind of details are we talking about here? I may need a few examples."

Men are so immature. Nadia's mind unhelpfully flashed back to her time with Rylan. She shook off the memory. "Never mind. I already regret talking with you at all." She was happy her voice was fixed with indifference. She might not be able to deny to herself how much Rylan's actions affected her, but she sure as hell wouldn't let it show.

"Fine, don't tell me. It's not like you ever shared anything about yourself before. And judging by how much time you spend in this hospital, there probably isn't much to tell." Dan eyed her carefully as if blinking would make him miss some tell-tale sign she would make.

Schooling her features into an emotionless mask, Nadia met his gaze as if she had nothing to hide. "Is that comment supposed to provoke me into telling you something about myself?"

"Is it working?"

Nadia scoffed. "Forget I said anything."

"A gentleman would never share intimate deeds," Dan said, apparently deciding to quit teasing her. "But not every man is a gentleman." He shrugged. "When guys get together and have a couple of beers, they talk. Sometimes they talk about their conquests. And sometimes they can be real assholes."

Recalling Rylan's recent betrayal, Nadia swallowed against the rise of unhealed memories. Evidently, being an asshole wasn't exclusive to men.

Dan tilted his head. "What prompted this line of questioning?"

Nadia had never talked about her personal life with anyone before. Even though Dan was the closest thing she had to a friend at work, that wasn't going to change.

She swung her chair away from him and faced her computer. "Go away. I need to focus on my work."

Dan got up. "For a minute there I thought we might be having a non-work-related conversation. Good thing you put an end to it."

His footsteps grew distant as Nadia pretended to read what was on her computer screen. Her muscles tensed when she heard Singh talking with Dan just outside the door.

Her instincts sent her into a frenzy of fight-or-flight indecision. Desperate to avoid dealing with her superior, she called out, "Dan, where are you going? I need you to assist me." He probably thought she was a lunatic, telling him to leave one minute and calling him to stay the next.

But if Singh had no issue throwing innuendos in public, Nadia didn't dare imagine how their conversation would go in private.

"Uh…you told me to go." Dan turned to look at her.

Good. He was still there.

"Keating, I'm happy to assist you." Singh invited herself into the lab. "Dan needs to get some sleep. He has a long case tomorrow morning."

Nadia set her jaw. Singh was too accommodating to mean it.

Dan turned to leave.

"Dan, you know what I need to do next. Stay and help me." Nadia breathed the words out with an air of desperation.

"Dan, go." Singh's tone left no room for discussion.

He looked back and forth between Nadia and Singh.

"Last time I checked, I was your superior, not Keating," Singh said. "When I say go, you go."

Her words helped him make the wrong choice. Nadia's stomach twisted as she helplessly watched him walk off. She turned back to her computer, hoping for Singh to leave.

She didn't.

After an awkward silence, Singh asked, "Do you need help with something?"

Nadia gave her the most menial task she could think of, hoping it would deter her from staying. Instead, Singh sat at the counter, methodically pipetting cells from one tube into another, in no apparent hurry to leave.

"Does your project have any chance of succeeding?"

Nadia relaxed a little. Singh was here to talk about work. "I'm cautiously optimistic."

"Michael doesn't have much time left. I'm planning to sedate him and keep him paralyzed to minimize the load on his heart."

"I know why we sedate patients." Nadia bit her lip.

"If we put him under," Singh continued, "it would be only to buy time for you to make this heart. If there's no chance of it working, I won't deny his family the few days they have left together."

"Let's see what he wants to do." Nadia willed her heart not to react at the prospect. What if the patient said no? Or worse—what if he said yes and she failed? She didn't want to offer the family false hope. Chasing away the doubt that threatened to overwhelm her, she focused on the facts. "If it were up to me, I'd have sedated him yesterday. If he expires, it doesn't matter if the heart works or not. I can't give it to anyone else." She looked toward the bioreactor chamber. "It's custom-made."

When Nadia had decided to do this, Sanders was already signed up for multiple experimental trials, and the group Nadia was collaborating with was in the process of growing his stem cells. So she had stripped the donor's heart from its native cells and added Sanders's to the scaffold. The new heart was built for him alone, and it was already showing evidence of contractile activity.

"So get sedated and either wake up with a new heart or die without ever seeing your family again." Singh summarized the patient's options. "Good thing I don't have to tell him that. You will. Tomorrow morning. It's your idea, so you pitch it to them. If it works, you'll be a hero, and if it doesn't, you'll be the one who denied his four-year-old child one more day with her father."

The words were harsh, but Singh was simply preparing her for the reality of being an attending.

"First thing in the morning," Nadia repeated.

Singh nodded and continued working. Nadia stared at her computer screen, thinking about what Singh had said. Her first responsibility was to the patient and his family, yet instead, she had spent her energy hating Rylan for her indiscretion. How trivial that now seemed compared to human life.

When Singh pushed aside the rack with tubes, Nadia returned to the present.

Dread knotted her stomach when Singh made no attempt to get up. She knew what the next topic of conversation would be. Trivial or not, she still had no interest in talking about it.

"I met Phillip in undergrad."

And there it was. Nadia stiffened. Mentioning her husband all of a sudden was an ominous sign.

"We had English literature together, and I tell people this is where we met. I actually met him at a party during my freshman year. I wish I could say it was love at first sight, but I was too drunk after losing a beer-pong tournament to see anything but a handsome guy."

Nadia shifted uncomfortably. Why did people have the need to overshare?

"What happened after that is fuzzy. But I do remember finding myself half-dressed in someone else's bedroom that night, vomiting all that alcohol onto Phillip's lap." She shook her head. "Imagine my horror when I found out that he had told his sister about it. I was mortified and very angry with him. I couldn't understand why he would do such a thing. But to him it was all a funny story. I suppose it was easy to see it that way when you weren't the one throwing up. But I let it go. If I hadn't, I wouldn't have married the love of my life and had three wonderful children with him."

Nadia frowned. It was an obvious ploy to get her to forgive Rylan. But Singh didn't know the first thing about Nadia. It was none of her business to find out either.

"So," Singh continued, "I think this makes us even."

Nadia blinked. "Even?"

"Now that you know something embarrassing about me, you can use it if you think I've overstepped." Singh stuck her chin out, challenging Nadia to disagree.

"I would never do that," Nadia replied categorically. She frowned at how little Singh thought of her. An eye for an eye was not her style.

"Good. I'd never overstep either, so you and I have nothing to worry about. You don't need to freak out every time we're alone together, and you can focus on your job instead."

Despite her desire to stay professional, Nadia snorted. "That was the point of your story? To improve my work productivity?"

Singh shrugged. "I said what I came to say. I can't help it if you take some other meaning out of it." She left as quickly as she had appeared.

———— •••• ————

Nadia stood at the foot of the patient's hospital bed. Singh and the Sanders family were all staring at her.

"The heart is incubated in an automated bioreactor system that maintains artificial environmental conditions and keeps it supplied with nutrients. For the cells to fully develop, we need at least thirteen more days." Nadia paused, gritting her teeth. She wasn't using the best layperson language, but under the scrutiny of the family, her brain went on autopilot. Medical terminology was just another layer that protected her from her emotions.

"Dr. Keating, I'm not sure I follow." Sanders spoke with difficulty.

Recognizing conversational dyspnea as a dire sign, a sense of helplessness stirred up in Nadia. Taking a deep breath to combat the feeling, she reminded herself that she was here to offer a solution—or at least the hope for one.

Before she could answer, Sanders turned to Singh for clarification. "Are you saying you've built a heart for me?"

His wife stood on the other side of the bed. She had been by her husband's side at all times, and with each passing day, the weariness on her face took more permanent root. Nadia's heart fluttered as she watched the faces of Sanders and his wife look at Singh with complete trust. Singh gently touched his shoulder.

"Kea—uh, Dr. Keating is working on it. It's not ready yet, and there are no guarantees it will work, Michael. She needs more time to make it. Thirteen days. The problem is that you may not have that much time." The grim words were softened by the warmth in Singh's voice.

Nadia wished she were more like Singh. The flutter in her heart morphed into a wanting ache. She was never comfortable talking to patients, but usually she was better at explaining things. There was just too much at stake here. And her insecurities bled through.

"We can buy you some time if we keep you sedated while we build it." Nadia tried again. *Simple, straightforward words.*

Sanders turned back to face her, his eyes drooping, and her resolve evaporated.

"We'll paralyze your muscles so you don't exert more energy than you have to." Nadia pressed her lips together. Okay, maybe he didn't need to know that. *Keep it simple.* "You won't remember anything. You'll just go to sleep until the heart is ready."

Sanders nodded.

Excitement bubbled inside Nadia at the prospect of succeeding, but she kept her expression neutral. If she smiled, it might give him false hope, and it wasn't a sure thing.

"Mr. Sanders, if we sedate you, today will be the last time you're conscious with your current heart. There are three possible outcomes: One, the new heart works, we transplant it, and you wake up feeling like a new man. Two, we do the transplantation, but it doesn't work. Three, we cannot develop the heart enough to even attempt the surgery. In the last two scenarios, you never wake up. Understand that this procedure has never been attempted before. There are no guarantees it will work."

A tear escaped from his wife's eye and landed on Sanders's hand. Nadia tried not to flinch at the sight. They had been through so much, and it pained her she couldn't promise more.

"What do you think I should do?" Sanders looked at Singh again.

"Michael, you know I can't make this decision for you," Singh said gently. "If you decide to go ahead, you should say goodbye to your family now."

"But do you think it will work?" he pleaded.

"I don't know that," Singh said. "What I do know is that I'm only considering this option for you because Dr. Keating is the one making the heart. She has worked tirelessly, and she won't give up even if there's only a one percent chance that it will work. If I had to bet my life on anyone, I'd bet it on her."

Nadia glanced at Singh as warmth overwhelmed her. It was the first time she had expressed so much trust in anyone except herself.

At this praise, everyone's attention was drawn back to Nadia. She blinked to clear her eyes. She should keep it together.

"Your first name is Nadia?" Sanders breathed out.

Nadia nodded, not trusting her voice just yet.

"Short for Nadyezhda?" He pronounced the name the way a Russian would.

Nadia flinched. Only one other person in her life ever said it that way. Her chest tightened to a suffocating pinch, but she fought to breathe through it. She met Sanders's eyes. "It is."

"Dr. Singh, did you know Nadyezhda means *hope* in Russian?"

"No, I didn't."

Sanders struggled to catch his breath. "You have brought me *hope*, Dr. Singh." His lips twitched upward. "I'd be a fool to say no to her."

No one spoke as the words sank in. Then Nadia's soft gasp was fortunately drowned in the light chuckle coming from Singh and Sanders's wife. The play on words sparked a battle inside Nadia. On one hand, she was arrogant enough to believe she could bring much more than hope for

Sanders. On the other, the pressure to succeed threatened to crush every ounce of confidence she had.

"I want to see my children first. They're coming in this afternoon. After that, we can do your plan."

Nadia's heart jumped. The trust, the hope, the responsibility—it all gripped her chest. It wasn't about her anymore. It wasn't about her staff, or the research money, or the hospital. It was about Sanders. His life was in her inexperienced hands. Her mouth went dry. She nodded, keeping her face neutral.

"And Dr. Keating?" Sanders held her gaze. "Thank you."

Yawning, Nadia walked into the dark and empty lab a little before midnight. She had spent the past two weeks practically living there. Building a heart was a slow, tedious, and mostly passive process. Still, just being close to it helped her peace of mind.

And gave her a lot of time to think about what she wanted.

A silhouette of a woman's back made her pause as she drew closer to the bioreactor. The free-falling blond hair, the high heels, and the wrinkle-free white coat told her it was Rylan.

Ashley. Nadia smiled tenderly and her heart began to race. Maybe she wasn't as done with the name as she thought she was.

Ashley was facing the machine, appearing too immersed in admiring the heart to notice Nadia. It was the first time they had been in the same room since their office disagreement. Nadia had stayed in the lab, focused on her work—and foolishly hoped Ashley would appear.

And here she was.

Nadia stepped closer. There were no grudges left in her, only an inexplicable sense of fulfillment that had nothing to do with her experimental heart passing all tests with flying colors today.

She tried to mask her smile with a neutral expression as she crept next to Ashley. "Frightful must it be, for supremely frightful would be the effect of any human endeavor to mock the stupendous mechanism of the Creator of the world."

"What?" Ashley asked, startled.

"It's the preface to Mary Shelley's *Frankenstein*. Dr. Singh enjoys drawing a parallel between me and the protagonist."

The melodic sound of Ashley's laughter filled the void of the last two weeks.

"You're a lot cuter than Frankenstein."

Nadia kept her eyes on the bioreactor. "Victor Frankenstein is the name of the doctor. The creature he builds never gets a name. It's just referred to as the monster." She clamped her jaw shut. This wasn't a book club meeting.

"I did know that. I stand by my assessment." Ashley's voice changed to low and husky, and she cleared her throat. "So your work is challenging God, huh?"

Nadia turned to meet her eyes and smirked. "Life reanimation is a godly business."

Ashley turned her attention back to the machine. "I hope your creation does more good than the one in the book."

Nadia stepped closer until their shoulders brushed. The feeling was electric, but she had no interest in pulling away. Together they stared at the heart—the heart that held enormous potential for Sanders, for other transplant candidates, for otherwise terminal patients who had lost all hope. She blinked the vision away. "I hope so too," she whispered.

"I had to come and see it for myself. It's remarkable what you—"

"I missed you." The words slipped out before Nadia had the good sense to stop them.

Even when Ashley turned to her, wide-eyed, she didn't regret saying them. They were honest. They were the truth.

After a moment, a warm smile replaced Ashley's shock. "I missed you too." She kept her soft eyes on Nadia. "But I wanted you to focus on your work without any distractions. You were pretty upset the last time we talked. I wanted to give you space and time. It is far too important for whatever is happening between us to screw it up."

Nadia couldn't decide if the statement was selfless or patronizing. Part of her wished Ashley had not made this decision for both of them. In a way, she wished that Ashley had walked through the door much sooner. But instead of saying anything, Nadia opted for her usual neutral expression, revealing nothing.

"What you did here goes beyond research," Ashley continued. "You're revolutionizing transplantation. All transplantation. If this works, thousands of lives could be saved." She turned back to the heart.

Nadia looked at it too. It beat rhythmically, maintaining a stable flow rate. Ashley's words were filled with tenderness and pride, and mixed with Nadia's own sense of accomplishment, they made her heart soar. "I know."

Blindly, she reached for Ashley's hand. She wanted her to know things were good between them.

Ashley returned the squeeze, the warmth enveloping more than just Nadia's hand.

"You know"—Nadia kept her eyes on the heart— "the reason *Frankenstein* had such a tragic ending had little to do with the way the creature looked. The monster murdered Victor's fiancée because Victor refused to take responsibility for his actions. If he had owned the consequences of his discovery, things might have turned out differently."

Nadia paused, her heart pounding.

Finally, she continued. "I was wrong. The last time we talked… I overreacted. I was the one who initiated things between us. I did it in your office, no less. That is the opposite of discreet. It was unfair of me to expect you to say nothing to anyone. I knew your best friend was my direct supervisor when I kissed you. I had no right to censor whatever you said to her or to anyone else, for that matter."

"I would never have told her anything if I thought she might figure it out," Ashley said softly. "I'm really sorry."

Neither Nadia nor Ashley looked at each other, but Ashley's quiet voice, filled with so much regret and pain, eradicated any trace of anger that still lingered in Nadia. "I know."

They stared back at the heart, their fingers intertwined. Nadia knew she shouldn't allow such intimate contact to exist between them. Regardless, there they were, observing a miracle together and holding hands.

"Hey, wasn't Victor's fiancée his foster sister?"

"Hush," Nadia scolded. She firmly pressed her lips together to keep from smiling. "You're ruining the moment."

Chapter 18

There Are No Happy Endings in Surgery

"Use extra UW solution to flush any remaining clots," Nadia reminded Singh as she wheeled the perfusion device that carried the bioengineered heart.

The thought of missing Sanders's surgery made her stomach turn over. So even though she knew that Singh was an excellent surgeon, she couldn't stop herself from regurgitating the basic guidelines.

Singh's fed-up expression finally broke through Nadia's jittery feelings, and she shut her mouth.

"Are you done yet? Is it out of your system?" Singh asked.

"Yes, I believe so." Nadia's eyes darted around. "It's just that…I made this heart. I can't help but feel protective."

They reached OR five, and Nadia stopped. "Please, take good care of it."

Singh waved her hand. "Quit acting like you're sending your baby off to college! Get your priorities in order before you go in. There's a real human in there."

"I'm not going in." Nadia wasn't overstepping the chief's orders again. It was more than sheer stubbornness that kept her rooted in her place. She couldn't bear the thought of doing more things that would disappoint Ashley.

"Even the great Nadia Keating cannot operate from outside the OR. The primary surgeon must be present for the entire case. I thought you knew the hospital's policies, given how much you love to break them."

Nadia blinked. "I'm the primary surgeon?"

Singh grinned.

A rush of adrenaline flooded her system. Every cell in her body came to life as she tried to process what she had heard. A first-year fellow leading an actual cardiac case was unheard of. Then something else occurred to her. "You shouldn't have talked with the chief."

Ashley hadn't mentioned anything last night about restoring her OR privileges. As much as Nadia wanted to be in that surgery, she couldn't bring herself to ask. It wasn't right to take advantage of Ashley like that. And the last thing Nadia wanted was for Singh to interfere.

"Oh, relax," Singh said. "I didn't ask your girlfriend."

Nadia glared. The word stripped down all the intricate and complex feelings she had for Ashley to something mundane and ordinary. Besides, it was none of Singh's goddamn business.

"You two are so obsessed about not displaying any bias that it is ruining your career. We both know Ashley is overcompensating by coming up with the stupidest reprimands in the history of surgery."

Nadia clamped her mouth shut. She couldn't take full credit, but Ashley would never have reprimanded her at all if not for Nadia's urging.

"What kind of surgeon-in-training is forbidden to do surgery for over a month?" Singh challenged. "You have only three years to master bypass surgeries, aortic replacements, valve repairs, tumor debulking, transplantations, lobectomies, pneumonectomies, and all other sorts of 'ectomies. But instead, you're hiding in a research lab. You might as well throw in the towel and transition to bench science. Building a freaking heart in less than three weeks is genius for science, but it's wasted time for a surgeon."

Nadia bit her lip. Admittedly, if it were anyone else, she would have handled the situation differently, but it was Ashley. There were a lot of things Nadia wished she'd done differently, but giving up a few cases for her felt like a small price to pay.

"If you weren't so busy trying to avoid looking like she owes you favors just because you had sex with her, you'd have filed an HR complaint demanding Ashley be fired. Instead, both of you are pretending to play the roles you think you're supposed to play."

Okay, Nadia wouldn't have demanded people to be fired. A reprimand, perhaps, for wrongful management would have sufficed.

Nadia looked away. She would never admit it out loud, but Singh was right. Her judgment had been clouded from the moment she had seen Ashley in the bar. But instead of dealing with the wreckage of her emotions, she had erected a wall, trying to keep the two worlds apart. She had only made things worse.

"So I did your job for you," Singh continued. "I went to the chair of surgery and demanded he overrule Ashley's decision. He was more than willing, given you're making history in his hospital today."

Nadia frowned at the thought of more people knowing her business. "What exactly did you tell him?"

"Don't get all strung up." Singh waved her hand. "I didn't tell him anything that would get either of you in trouble. I just said that, in my humble opinion, our young chief is too hard on you. Also, you did follow my orders, so the second incident was on me. You shouldn't have to pay for it for an entire month, especially given that you're a stand-up physician with an exceptional work ethic."

She raised her eyebrows, and Nadia rolled her eyes, before choosing to ignore the implication. "The chair told you I would be the primary surgeon?"

"No, he simply restored your OR privileges. Sanders is my patient, and it was my decision to make you primary on the case."

"Thank you." The simple words were all she could think to say.

"No need to thank me. You've earned it. As you said, this heart is your baby. It's only fair for you to see it through. I'll be assisting, but you'll be calling the shots. You deserve the credit."

Nadia nodded. The surgery was everything she had ever dreamed of. The years of study, the sacrifices she'd made, the people she'd met that had paved the way for her—it all amounted to this defining moment. Here. Now.

But then she thought of Ashley, and all her excitement ground to a halt. "I should check with Dr. Rylan before we go in."

"What for? She has no say in this. You don't have to worry about your precious professionalism."

"It's not that."

"Then what is it? Do you think you'll get in trouble?"

"No." Nadia looked away. She knew Ashley well enough to know that she hated being overruled. And Singh had done exactly that. Despite feeling the pull toward the OR to take her rightful place in there, Nadia remained frozen in the hallway. The surgery of a lifetime wasn't worth the cost of betraying Ashley. *Not again and not anymore.*

"I see." Singh had that annoying smirk again. "You're worried about hurting your girlfriend's feelings."

Why did she keep using that word? "Just give me a minute to go talk with Dr. Rylan, please."

"No. You're to go to your patient right now. Focus on your case."

Nadia hesitated. Should she listen to her mentor who had arranged her return to the OR with a splash, or should she make sure Ashley was okay first?

"Why are you in the middle of the hallway? What's the holdup?"

Nadia's heart sped up at the familiar voice. *Such a disloyal organ.* She turned to face Ashley.

"The holdup is that your girlfriend refuses to do her job without seeing you first," Singh said matter-of-factly.

"She's not my girlfriend."

"I'm not her girlfriend," Nadia said at the same time.

She turned back to Ashley, her scowl softening. "Dr. Singh told me I'm the primary for the case. I had nothing to do with it. I just found out."

"I know."

Nadia swallowed against a lump of nervous tension. "Are we okay?"

"We're more than okay. You'll do great. I'm sure of it. I'm glad I caught you," she added. "I wanted to tell you something that finally came to me last night."

"What?"

"Our first meeting, seven years ago. I remembered."

"It's about time." Nadia smiled.

"Pari had just left the conference, and I had some time to kill. That's when I saw you sitting alone in the café with your nose in your laptop. You looked so anxious that I had to help."

Nadia interjected dryly, "The savior of all med students."

"Not that you needed one," Ashley said. "After delivering the entire presentation by heart without stumbling even once, you told me you weren't going to go into transplantation because immunosuppression was a barbaric solution to the problem of organ rejection."

"And you asked me if I had a better idea."

"You thought you did. You were so arrogant."

"She still is," Singh interrupted. The two women turned to glare at her. "Don't stop on my account, Ashley. The story is just getting good."

Ashley turned back to Nadia. "Anyway, I challenged you to develop your idea, to come up with a better solution for transplanting organs."

"You called it *science fiction*. You didn't think I could do it." Nadia smirked. "I had to prove you wrong."

"And here we are."

Time stood still as Nadia gazed into Ashley's beautiful eyes that seemed to hold every dream she had ever dreamed.

"Aw, that story is so sweet it's giving me diabetes." Singh's voice broke through their bubble.

"Pari!" Ashley gave a high-pitched protest.

Nadia cleared her throat, trying not to laugh. This was a hospital, not Luna Park. Despite her reserved behavior, she was beyond happy at that moment, and it had little to do with the fact she was about to become a legend. All she could think of was how much she cared for Ashley. Why had she wasted time by not telling her exactly that—and the truth?

Guilt gripped her chest, and Nadia knew she had to rectify her mistake immediately. It couldn't wait a second longer.

"Dr. Singh, would you mind if I had a moment alone with Dr. Rylan?"

"Really? Now?" Singh frowned.

"Pari, give us a minute," Ashley said.

Nadia didn't wait for Singh's permission. Her pulse racing, she grabbed Ashley's hand and led her to a nearby empty substerile room between two vacant ORs.

When the door closed behind her, Nadia turned to face Ashley.

"I've had plenty of great sex before I met you."

Ashley's brows drew together in a quizzical frown. "O-kay."

Nadia huffed, annoyed at herself. "What I mean is, it's not just about the sex. It's everything. You're talented and smart and so beautiful. You're the complete package. I'm a fool for not realizing it sooner." She stopped to catch her breath. "I was naïve to believe I could have sex with you and pretend like it never happened. It did happen. It was amazing. And I want it to happen again. But more than that, I want you. I want you so much that I'm neglecting a once-in-a-lifetime opportunity to tell you this."

Ashley stared at her. "I want to be with—"

"No." Nadia cut her off. "There's something else I need to tell you. Something I should have told you a long time ago." Her voice trembled. She paused, swallowed hard, and forced herself to keep talking, even though her heart was racing. "You won't like it, but I have to say it. You should know that I—"

"What are the main steps in a heart transplantation?" Ashley interrupted. She spoke as if she were quizzing a trainee.

"Why?" Nadia demanded. Her voice no longer trembled.

Ashley gave her an unflinching look. "Indulge me."

Nadia scoffed. She hated being treated like an incompetent intern. But then again, she loved indulging Ashley. "I'll do a median sternotomy." As she began explaining the steps, the surgery clearly outlined in her mind, her heart slowed down.

"You won't cannulate the IVC?" Ashley asked halfway.

Nadia shook her head. "It's a redo. I'll cannulate the femoral vein instead so I can have more room for the IVC anastomosis later." She completed outlining the procedure, then added, "I'll do the anastomoses in the following order: left atrium, PA, aorta, IVC, and SVC." She locked eyes with Ashley. "Would you like me to keep going, or are you satisfied?"

"Good." Ashley smiled. "It's a big responsibility to be the primary surgeon. And I know you'll do great no matter what because you're you. But I want you to focus on what you're about to do. Everything else can wait."

Nadia smiled back effortlessly. This incredible woman understood her in a way that no one else did. Ashley had known exactly what she needed to hear. "Thank you," Nadia said, stepping forward. She leaned at the same time Ashley did. Their mouths met.

She didn't intend it, she certainly hadn't planned it, but the kiss happened all the same. Ashley's lips were soft, her scent sweet and inviting. Her body pressed against Nadia's, setting every nerve ablaze. At that moment, nothing else mattered. Nadia pressed her tongue, exploring Ashley's mouth with fervor, injecting the passion she had been denying herself all this time. Ashley moaned deep in her throat.

"Really, Keating? You're delaying the surgery of the century for a tonsillar exam?" Singh stood in the open doorway, grinning.

Nadia jumped back, heat burning her cheeks. She thought she might make the textbooks one day, but being caught in a textbook example of unprofessional conduct wasn't what she had in mind.

"I don't know if you deserve to be the primary on this case, since you clearly don't have your priorities straight. Or anything else, for that matter."

"Pari!" Ashley's voice went up an octave. "Stop teasing her."

"What? I'm pretty sure there's a policy against kissing in a substerile room. Wouldn't you agree, *Chief*?"

Ashley sighed dramatically. "Was there a reason you couldn't wait outside?"

"There's a horde of scientists, doctors, and PR reps gathered in the waiting area. They all want to see the surgery you two have been deferring for a make-out session."

"I want essential personnel only," Nadia said firmly, ignoring Singh's silly grin. Contrary to what had just happened, she didn't want to be the center of a public spectacle. "The less foot traffic, the better. Door openings disturb OR airflow, increasing the risk of wound contamination." Singh probably didn't need to hear infection control guidelines, but Nadia had to give some justification.

"Right," Ashley said. "You two go start your case. I'll deal with Nadezhda's fan base." She caressed Nadia's arm. "You can give autographs later."

Left atrium, PA, aorta, IVC, and SVC. Nadia repeated the order of the anastomoses in her head, willing herself to concentrate on anything but the electric touch that immediately brought the fire back in her body.

When she stepped out of the substerile room and toward her lifetime dream, a different type of fire rose in her chest.

"*Thanks*, Ashley," Singh said and followed Nadia.

Nadia glanced around the operating room until she spotted the perfusion device with the engineered heart. Her gaze lingered, but she resisted the urge to run over and check on it. As Singh had reminded her earlier, there was a patient, and Nadia was the primary surgeon.

The captain of the ship.

She saw the patient, *her* patient, lying sedated on the operating table, blue drapes covering everything except his chest area.

The familiar beep of the pulse oximeter monitor was drowned in chatter. Nadia frowned. There were more people in the OR than usual, all claiming to have essential roles to play. Somehow, a second anesthesia resident and two extra circulating nurses made sense in this OR.

"Why are they all staring?" Nadia asked Singh. The attention pricked at her nerves.

"They're waiting for you to say a few words. You know, being a pioneer and all."

Her mouth went dry. "Please tell me you're joking."

The last thing she expected when she woke up this morning was to be standing in a room with a dozen pairs of eyes waiting for her to deliver a speech. She cleared her throat. Surely, she could think of something meaningful to say.

Her mind drowned in thoughts, but nothing intelligible distilled from them.

"I can't do this. You should say something." Nadia pleaded with Singh.

Singh scoffed, then turned to the room. "Okay, everyone, let's get going. This isn't the Emmy Awards. Quit looking for a show and get to work. Now."

Singh's words were harsh and abrupt. And devoid of any inspiration. Nadia's nerves loosened a fraction. She couldn't do worse than that.

"In 1944, Alfred Blalock performed the first successful heart surgery on a baby with tetralogy of Fallot." Nadia's voice filled the room, silencing the chatter. "Nine years later, John Gibbon performed the first open-heart surgery with a heart-lung machine maintaining the circulation of blood and oxygen. In 1967, Christiaan Barnard performed the world's first human-to-human heart transplantation." Nadia looked around. All eyes were fixed on her, and her stomach flipped.

"These are just a few of the pioneers whose extraordinary achievements have advanced medicine. Without their efforts, we wouldn't be here today. But their stories are about surgical success. What they fail to tell is how

Eileen Saxon, the blue baby Blalock operated on, died a few days before her second birthday. Or how Louis Washkansky survived only eighteen days after his new heart began beating in his chest. And while Cecelia Bavolek survived for over thirty years after her heart-lung machine surgery, the patient before her, a fifteen-month-old child, died on the table in a failed attempt of the same procedure." Nadia nodded toward her unconscious patient. "The history of medicine is riddled with human sacrifice and failures. Even when success is reported, it doesn't guarantee a happy ending."

She swallowed, her mouth still dry. "You may think today is about pioneering the next step in human transplantation." The agreement, admiration, and undivided attention from every set of eyes in the room gave her unparalleled strength. "You're wrong. Our only goal today is to save Michael Sanders's life. Let us focus on that and that alone."

Nadia looked around, her own words resonating in her heart, but the feeling was short-lived. Her impromptu speech was, unfortunately, too good. She sensed the inevitable round of applause that was about to erupt.

"The first person who claps will find themselves on the other side of these doors." The startled expressions, even with her colleagues' masks on, were evident. Nadia bit her lip. That might have been a bit harsher than intended. "Clapping disturbs the airflow, increasing the risk of surgical site infection."

The staff returned to work and she sighed. They would just have to get used to her people skills.

"Not bad," Singh said.

"People are easily swayed by inspirational words. And they needed to be reminded that they're not here for a sensation but to do their jobs."

"You don't believe what you said?"

Nadia smiled. "Every word I said is undeniably true." Her emotions had been on a roller coaster all day, and right now, she felt at the highest peak, fear and excitement blending together in a thrilling sensation that skyrocketed her confidence level. She felt invincible. And in the mood for a joke. "But let's not fool ourselves, Dr. Singh. Today"—Nadia looked into the distance—"I become God."

Ashley sat at her desk, fidgeting, her nerves too frayed to concentrate on work. After dealing with Nadia's fan base, she had called OR five every fifteen minutes for an update. She had probably driven the circulating nurses insane. But this was the biggest, most groundbreaking surgical case since Murray had performed the first successful kidney transplant in 1954, only this case was led by a first-year fellow rather than a seasoned surgeon. So she had told the nurses this was the reason she needed an update. Every fifteen minutes.

The truth was, Ashley had complete confidence in Nadia's abilities. And with Pari by her side, it was a dream team for the patient. But her heart ached at not being able to witness Nadia's life-altering moment. Ashley wanted to be the one helping her succeed, not stopping her every step of the way. But because she was supposed to be the hard-ass boss who disciplined discordant fellows, she was kept away from the person who moments earlier had set her world on fire with three simple words: *I want you.* Ashley closed her eyes and ran her tongue over her lips, savoring the memory of Nadia's burning kiss.

"Dr. Rylan." The voice of Claire, her administrative assistant, brought her back to the present. "There's another gentleman at the front desk asking for Dr. Keating."

"Is it a reporter?"

"I don't know. I'll ask—"

"No, it's fine. I'll take care of it." Ashley needed a distraction from the inappropriate celebration scenarios she was running in her head. Might as well be useful.

At the front desk in the waiting area outside the ICU, a crowd of mostly female staff members had gathered. They seemed enthralled with a raven-haired man wearing jeans and a tight-fitting black T-shirt that showcased his muscles.

Ashley stepped closer and pinched her lips, trying not to chuckle at her colleagues' lustful faces. He could probably use some saving.

"May I help you?" she asked.

He turned to face her with a charming smile that revealed perfect white teeth and a strong jawline. "I don't believe you can. I'm waiting for a surgery to end."

"Are you here for a patient?" His relaxed expression didn't fit someone waiting for a loved one to get out of surgery.

"Oh no. Nadyezhda isn't getting surgery. She's doing it." His Russian accent gave the name an exotic and beautiful sound.

Ashley cringed, realizing she had been butchering Nadia's name all this time. "So you're looking for Na—" *Nope.* There was no way she was going to embarrass herself. "You're looking for Dr. Keating. She'll be in surgery for at least several more hours. It will be a long wait."

The man's carefree expression didn't change. "Not a problem. I'll wait for as long as it takes. I have a gift for her, and I want to give it to her in person," he said, indicating the festively wrapped box on the counter.

Do people give gifts for such occasions? "Well, she is making history today." Ashley cleared her throat, trying to filter out her confusion. "It's nice to know she has friends outside the hospital who appreciate that."

The man tilted his head. "What history?"

"The transplant she's doing right now. Wait, why are you bringing her a gift?"

"It's her birthday!" He grinned. "I didn't know about the big surgery. That calls for a double celebration."

Ashley smiled. His enthusiasm was infectious.

"Come to think of it, she did mention that she'd be unavailable this past month, but she used big words that went over my head. Is she doing a brain transplant?"

Ashley continued to smile pleasantly, fighting the urge to burst into laughter. Did Nadia really have a friend who thought a brain transplant might be possible?

"Uh, no, it's a heart transplant. She made the heart using the patient's own cells so the body won't be as likely to reject it."

"Oh." He stared at her blankly. "That's cool too, right?"

"Yes, it's very...cool."

"Then I'll definitely wait for as long as it takes. Is that all right, Dr... uh?"

"Rylan, but please call me Ashley."

His eyes widened. "Oh, you're the chief."

Her smile faltered. How did he know about her when she knew nothing about him? Had Nadia told him about their relationship, or had she complained about her boss? Knowing Nadia, it was probably the latter.

"You seem so ni—"—he stopped himself—"so young!" He smiled sheepishly.

Definitely the latter.

"Right." Ashley cleared her throat again. If they were going to start seeing each other, she would have to repair her image with Nadia's friends. "I have to go back to work, but it was nice to meet you, Mr...?"

"Evgeni Petrov. Please call me Evgeni." He extended his hand. They both gave a firm handshake. "It's nice to finally meet the person who's been keeping Nadyezhda up for the last month."

"What?" Ashley felt a blush rise to her cheeks. Maybe he did know what was going on between her and Nadia.

"She's been working almost every night lately."

"Right. *Working.*" Her face grew hotter. "So how do you know Na—"—*damn it*—"Dr. Keating?"

"We've been together for almost ten years."

The words wrapped around Ashley's chest like a boa constrictor. She couldn't breathe. Her mind shut down. She vaguely registered one of the nearby women ask what "together" meant. Ashley's chest tightened further still. She knew what it meant.

"Excuse me, I have to go back to the OR." She forced the words out.

Ashley wasn't sure if any reply followed. She felt submerged in water. Her vision blurred, her hearing diminished, and her body began starving for oxygen. She turned and walked away. Her legs carried her on autopilot to an unknown destination, her mind too muddled to fully comprehend anything.

Chapter 19

The Birth of a Discovery

"Happy birthday."

Ashley's voice sounded hollow and distant, which made Nadia pause in her work to steal a glance at her. Her eyes seemed unfocused. Nadia resisted her first instinct to go to her but instead returned her attention to the open chest. This should be her focus. "I suppose it is today." She settled for keeping the conversation going.

The new heart was already placed and contracting rhythmically, but Nadia's nerves were stretched. Weaning the patient off the bypass machine was a relatively passive step for the surgeon, but it was an important moment for the heart. Only if it was strong enough to pump blood on its own they could safely take the supporting machine off.

Nadia shook her head and frowned. Ashley herself had told her to focus on the case. Why was she distracting her with such trivial nonsense now?

"Aren't you curious about how I found out?"

Nadia kept watching the open chest. "Go to one liter," she told the perfusionist. "It's probably in my employee file." She answered Ashley's question evenly without looking up.

"Evgeni Petrov told me."

Nadia froze. Her mouth went dry. Her heart began to race violently. She looked up to meet Ashley's cool gaze. Then she returned to the midline incision. The bioengineered heart was her priority. "Dr. Rylan, I need to focus on my surgery. Anything else can wait," she said, reciting Ashley's words from earlier.

Straining her ears, Nadia waited with paralyzed dread, refusing to look back up. A moment later, she heard Ashley leave the room noisily.

At that moment, Nadia's poorly held defenses crumbled. Her hands began to shake. *Damn it.* They never shook during surgery.

She tried her usual breathing technique, reminding herself that she was in control of her body, but her hands kept shaking.

A momentary pause in the act of death. It was how John Collins, a nineteenth-century surgical giant, had defined shock. Nadia's hands stilled as she turned the words over in her mind.

She glanced at Sanders's vital signs. *Stable.*

Another prominent surgeon, Samuel Gross, had said shock was a *manifestation of the rude unhinging of the machinery of life.* And Furneaux Jordan would describe a patient in shock *as pale, as motionless, as indifferent to the outward world as if the injury had already terminated in death*—a perfect description of what Nadia was experiencing right now.

So that was what her brain was trying to tell her. It wasn't the patient who was in shock; it was Nadia. She was the one who felt *indifferent to the outward world*, rudely *unhinged* from it, who had paused *in the act of*—

"Keating, what was that about? Who's Evgeni?" Singh's voice broke through her thoughts.

Nadia forced herself to make eye contact. "My boyfriend." Unlike her crumbling existence, her words were detached, cold, and factual.

Singh's eyes widened.

A loud cheer from the OR staff drew their attention. The heart was officially pumping the patient's blood on its own. That meant the bypass machine could be safely removed, but Nadia felt no excitement. She was utterly *indifferent to the outward world.*

As Singh resumed her work, it was all Nadia could do to hold back her tears. She was incapable of continuing the operation she had so desperately wanted to do. She was too emotionally compromised and physically shaken. Operating in that condition would only put the patient at risk. The responsible thing to do was to let Singh finish the case without her. Perhaps they could call Dan in to assist.

"I don't like working with *medical* doctors in the OR." Once again, Singh's voice broke into her thoughts. "Do you know why?"

Nadia said nothing, afraid her voice would break.

"I'll take that as a no," Singh continued. "Years ago, I went to procure a donor heart. A cardiology fellow scrubbed in to assist me. It was a big mistake. In the middle of the case, she hit the heart with the Yankauer and induced V-fib. We never got the heart back into sinus rhythm and had to discard it. The fellow dropped the sucker and began crying. When I told Ashley the story, I couldn't help but laugh."

Nadia shuddered at the mention of the name.

"The nice person that she is, she didn't find it nearly as entertaining as I did. She said the cardiology fellow must have felt awful. Perhaps she knew the patient who was supposed to receive the heart. Maybe she felt terrible being the reason the patient wouldn't get it. But we both know Ashley doesn't understand surgery the way we do. Accidents happen, and sometimes people mess up during operations.

"The point is that such behavior isn't acceptable during surgery. Doubt and regret have no place in the OR. It takes a certain kind of person to handle difficult situations the right way. No surgeon wants to be remembered as the doctor who cried over a mistake while operating"—she looked pointedly at Nadia—"if for no other reason than to avoid contaminating the field."

Singh finished securing a chest tube. "That's what makes a great surgeon: the ability to remain calm when there's chaos." She looked at Nadia again. "Do your job and finish the case. Deal with your mess later."

The impromptu lecture was like an electric spark that jump-started Nadia's body and mind. Gross was wrong. Shock wasn't a process of dying but rather—as Crile, another giant, had put it—*a marshaling of the body's defenses in the fight for life*. Nadia took a deep breath and slowly let it out. She looked at the new heart in her patient's chest that was beating because of her. Nadia wasn't about to give up. She was a great surgeon, and she was ready to prove it.

She picked up the Yankauer suction instrument and examined the bypass tubing. Time to take the heart's crutches off.

An hour later, the surgery was over. The patient was wheeled to the recovery unit in stable condition. Nadia understood the importance of this surgery for the patient, for the medical community, for the world. But her heart wasn't in it. How could she feel any joy at all when she was haunted by Ashley's pain?

While she sat with the patient in the ICU, Nadia took time to think. Once his immediate postoperative chest X-ray and lab results confirmed everything was stable, she headed to Ashley's office. Her unexpected appearance in the operating room meant only one thing—she wasn't interested in talking about it. Why else would she choose a public place to tell Nadia what she had learned?

It was clear that Ashley wanted nothing more to do with her. And who could blame her? Nadia blinked back her tears, ignoring the sense of hopelessness. She had no right to be hurt. It wouldn't be enough to say how sorry she was. The best thing she could do now was give Ashley a clean break. She owed her that and so much more.

As Nadia passed the waiting area, she spotted Evgeni amidst a small crowd. He waved at her. "Nadyenka!"

Nadia forced a smile and moved toward him, nausea rising in her throat. How could she do this to him?

At the exact same moment, Ashley walked out of the telemetry unit. Nadia stared straight ahead, refusing to acknowledge her.

"Evgeni." Nadia stopped just out of reach from him.

"Happy birthday, Nadyenka," he repeated the affectionate Russian nickname. "I got you a present."

<hr />

Ashley stepped out of the telemetry unit just in time to see Nadia walking over to greet Evgeni. Bile rose in her throat. She hated Nadia for putting her in this situation, and she hated herself for acting rashly and unprofessionally by storming into the operating room earlier. Knowing that the transplant had gone without a hitch was bittersweet. She was relieved that her behavior hadn't caused a disturbance, but it was clear that Nadia had been completely unaffected when Ashley told her what she had learned.

Ashley tightened her fists and found herself impulsively heading over to confront Nadia once again.

Evgeni was still surrounded by admiring women, but Nadia was smiling at him, seemingly unconcerned by their attention. And why should she be concerned? Judging by the way he looked at her, it was clear he had eyes only for one woman.

Ashley fought back tears threatening to fall. Nadia had told her earlier she wanted them to be together. She had sounded so sincere, and it had made Ashley's foolish heart swell as if she were in a fairytale. Why had the knight in shining armor shown up?

"She's going to cure cancer," Evgeni declared proudly.

Ashley barely stifled a snort. She was sure she was about to witness the infamous Keating shredding the man to pieces for making such unintelligible comments.

Except Nadia didn't even bother to correct Evgeni's blatantly wrong statement. She just kept looking at him and smiling, stamping out any hope that the situation was different than it appeared.

"Last week I was curing AIDS. I see I've shifted my focus to oncology," Nadia joked.

The words were like a gut punch, and Ashley's stomach revolted at how seamless Nadia's affection was. She cleared her throat loudly. "Dr. Keating, can we talk?"

Nadia's warm expression instantly morphed into the ice statue-esque one Ashley was accustomed to seeing. "I'll be right back, Zhenya. I have to take care of some work."

The cold words stung Ashley's raw emotions. *Work?* So that was how Nadia categorized their relationship. Ashley stuffed her bitter anger and disappointment down for now and led the way to her office. She had already acted impulsively today. Nadia's footsteps followed closely behind her as she wondered what was with the Russian diminutive name parade.

"Do we really need to talk?" Nadia asked as soon as Ashley shut the door behind them.

Ashley's blood reached a new boiling point. She glared. "Are you serious?" It had probably been naïve to think that Nadia could portray, let alone feel, guilt. Or that she would beg for forgiveness. A sting of anger at her own naïve self jarred through Ashley. She should have known better.

"What would be the point?"

"The point is that I'm giving you a chance to explain yourself!"

"Is there any explanation I can give you that wouldn't end with us being over?" Nadia asked robotically.

Ashley blinked back the tears that welled up. "No," she whispered.

There was no part of her that wasn't completely broken. How could she ever find it within herself to forgive such an awful betrayal?

"Then what is the point in having this conversation?"

Nadia's cold indifference only made Ashley's insides burn hotter.

"Why would you—?" Ashley's voice was brittle. She paused and tried again. "I need to understand how you could do something like that. Not just to me, but to the man who's been waiting for you for the last four hours. What you did was wrong, Na—" She stopped, frustration suffocating her heartache. Evgeni had ruined the name Ashley had been using for Nadia. She left the syllable hanging.

"Leave him out of it. He has nothing to do with any of this."

"How can you even say such a thing?" Ashley clenched her fists as if that might help to keep her voice down. "He has everything to do with this. You cheated on him, and you made me an accomplice. How could you?"

"What's the point in me trying to explain myself? As you agreed, we're done. There's no point in torturing ourselves with this conversation any further."

The words were cold and uncaring as if the woman saying them were made out of stone. "Nade—damn it!" Ashley's tears rolled freely now. She sat on her couch, turning her face away. "I'm sorry," she said reflexively. "I didn't mean to do this in front of you."

"Please don't apologize to me," Nadia whispered. She waited in silence awhile until Ashley collected herself. "You don't want to say my name. Why not?" Her tone had softened.

Ashley wiped her tears and turned to face her again. "I don't want to mispronounce it. You should have corrected me when we first met."

"What makes you think you're mispronouncing it all of a sudden?" Nadia asked.

Ashley gave her a frustrated what-do-you-think look.

"Ah." Nadia nodded tightly. "He says it the Russian way. I'm not Russian, so he's the one who mispronounces it. I've never corrected you because you pronounce it the way it was meant to be said." She spoke as if they were in the midst of a casual cultural discussion.

"You're not of Russian descent?"

"Russia isn't the only Slavic country that has *Nadezhda* as a name." She pronounced it the way Ashley usually did.

"I don't know you," Ashley said, her anger rising again. "I don't know your ethnicity, I didn't know you were straight, and I had no idea you have a boyfriend!"

"I'm not straight."

"It doesn't matter. You lied and cheated on your partner. I don't want any part of it. I don't know why I expected so much better from you."

Someone knocked on the door. Neither one of them had raised their voice, so whoever it was, they wouldn't have overheard anything.

Ashley wiped her face and cleared her throat. "Come in."

Dan entered, followed by Evgeni, still carrying his gift for Nadia.

Both men looked at Nadia, but Ashley still half turned her face away to hide her eyes.

"I'm sorry to interrupt. Nadia, I thought you might want a moment with your boyfriend before you speak with the reporters." Dan spoke cheerfully, oblivious to the drama that had taken place in Ashley's office. "A lot of people want to hear about the first custom heart transplantation. Dr. Singh has been holding down the fort, but they want to hear from you. Why are you hiding in here?"

Nadia walked past Dan and stood before Evgeni. "A month ago, I had sex with somebody else. Now you know."

Chapter 20

The Reward Pathway

No one moved or made a sound.

What was Nadia thinking? Why had she told Evgeni about the affair now? Here? Like that? Had she no mercy?

Ashley glanced at Evgeni. He looked as if he might start yelling or crying any minute now. Guilt stabbed at her, and she looked away before she had to meet his eyes.

"I'll go now," Evgeni said, his voice barely audible. He set Nadia's present on a nearby chair and left.

Nadia turned to Ashley. "Satisfied?" she hissed.

Ashley was too stunned by what had just happened to think or articulate any type of response.

Without waiting for one, Nadia looked at Dan. "Where's the press?"

"Uh, in the conference room."

She marched out, leaving Ashley alone with Dan.

"You had an affair with Nadia," he said quietly.

Ashley looked away. "I didn't know she was in a relationship."

"So you just had sex with your junior fellow?"

"You wouldn't have complained if it had been you!" Ashley snapped, her eyes boring into him.

Dan stepped back and his shoulders slumped. Ashley immediately regretted raising her voice at him. He wasn't the one she was mad at. "Look, I'm sorry," she said the words on reflex.

"Sorry you did it or sorry you got caught?"

Both? Neither? Helplessness dampened her eyes, and she blinked. The only thing she was really sorry about was how this had ended. She was naïve to think Nadia might tell her it was all a mistake. That Evgeni meant nothing to her. That she hadn't lied to Ashley all this time. That she hadn't tricked her into falling for her.

She turned away from Dan and closed her eyes. She heard him walk away, and the door to her office closed.

Once again, Ashley was alone with her thoughts. Exhaling, she gave herself permission to feel the anger, disappointment, and hopelessness that filled her as if a dam had broken. The tears began streaming freely down her face.

———————————

Nadia marched to the elevator and punched the button. She was shaking violently. She dug her fingers into her hands, summoning every bit of strength to keep herself from collapsing. The startled look on Evgeni's face and Ashley's pain-filled eyes flashed before her in alternating images.

That wasn't how this was supposed to go. She had never meant to hurt anyone.

Her vision became blurry as the elevator doors opened and she stepped in, holding back her tears. She could do this. She could keep herself from falling apart until the doors closed.

At the last second, a hand stopped the doors, and Dan stepped in through the opening. Her short nails dug even deeper into her skin, the biting pain holding her together.

"Are you able to speak with the reporters?"

Nadia looked straight ahead, blinking away the moisture in her eyes. She willed herself to appear indifferent to the recent scene in Ashley's office. "Today, I made custom organ transplantation possible." She focused on that fact, although it brought her no joy. "I'm more than capable of speaking with the press."

Dan scoffed. "All that groundbreaking surgery and you still had the time to break two mortal hearts today."

Nadia took a deep breath, still refusing to look at him. "Evgeni will forgive me." She didn't believe that, but she wouldn't give Dan the satisfaction of seeing her cry.

"He might, but Ashley won't."

Nadia tensed further. Did Dan know about her relationship with Ashley? "Why would I care what Rylan thinks?"

"You slept with her."

Nadia clenched her jaw. On top of everything, she had threatened Ashley's reputation.

"You knew how I felt about her, and you said nothing." Dan's voice seeped with bitter anger. "All this time, you were laughing behind my back."

"Jealousy doesn't suit you, Dan." Nadia tightened her fists, giving her a sense of control. She turned to meet his eyes. "It wasn't my place to tell you about her sexual orientation, and I sure as hell don't owe you an explanation about mine."

"She must be a great lay for you to put up with being out of the OR for a month!" Dan spat out.

"You're out of line!" No amount of self-control was worth letting him speak of Ashley that way.

"I'm not the one who fucked our boss!"

Nadia's entire body lit with fire. She stepped through the opening elevator doors reminding herself that yelling at him in public could only hurt Ashley further. "This conversation is over."

She needed to clear her head of everything she had said and done tonight. Evgeni and Ashley deserved better. She had intended to do better. Her head throbbed, and her heart ached with regret at the mess she had left behind.

She took a deep breath and let it out slowly. In…and out. It was too late to fix things with Ashley now, and thinking about it wouldn't change anything. She needed to push down her emotions and focus on the bioengineered heart she had developed. It was an accomplishment she had worked toward her entire career. It should bring her happiness. Instead, all she felt was heart-wrenching despair.

— • • • —

Nadia walked around the block, a lump in her throat. It was past midnight, but the lights in her apartment were still on. *Their apartment.* She would have to face Evgeni soon, but she kept walking, trying to gather enough courage to face the man who had faithfully followed her wherever her surgical training took her.

Faithfully. She had been anything but faithful to Evgeni. The invisible weight on her chest grew stronger, and she had to fight the suffocating pain to breathe.

Nadia Keating didn't make mistakes. She certainly didn't make rash emotional decisions in the spur of the moment. She hadn't planned on telling Evgeni about her affair in such a heartless way. He deserved better.

Everything had seemed clear earlier today. Once she had shared her feelings with Ashley, she planned to tell her about Evgeni. It would have been the hardest conversation she had ever had, but delayed honesty was the best she could offer Ashley at that point. And as soon as she had told Ashley, she would have talked to Evgeni. It didn't matter what their reactions would be, what mattered to Nadia was that she finally be honest with both of them. It was a simple plan.

She had spent a lot of time convincing herself that sex was just sex, a physical interaction. And that monogamy was an artificial concept. She wanted to believe that. But she hadn't factored in Ashley's reaction. With one look, the lies Nadia had told herself disintegrated.

Her eyes filled with tears again. She should never have cheated on Evgeni. She shouldn't have lied to Ashley. Had she known better what she wanted, she wouldn't have hurt the people she cared about. They would both be better off without her.

She blinked the dampness away, but her agony persisted. Evgeni had texted her hours ago, shortly after he left. He said they needed to talk. That was all. She had stayed at work longer than necessary to postpone the inevitable, but she couldn't delay it any longer.

Stopping at the entrance, Nadia stared at the door. She had told Dan that Evgeni would forgive her, but the truth was she didn't know that. The thought of him resenting her made her pivot on her heel and begin to circle the block yet again.

He valued a monogamous relationship too much to simply overlook her infidelity. Or at least she knew he valued a monogamous relationship with her.

When she and Evgeni first met, he was handsome, charismatic, and popular. His blue eyes and shampoo-commercial-worthy hair made women swoon after him.

But not Nadia. She had always had little interest in the opposite sex. She had dated boys because…well, that was what girls did, right?

Nadia smiled at the thought of the first date she'd had with Evgeni. He had openly flirted with the waitress right before thoroughly examining Nadia from head to toe. Nadia had decided chivalry was an extinct quality in that boy.

But he had persisted, and his persistence had made her feel wanted.

She thought about their first kiss. At that moment, she had considered how pressing one's lips against another's should trigger the reward pathway of the brain—a track of neurons that led to feelings of pleasure. Kissing was supposed to raise adrenaline levels and release serotonin and oxytocin, the neurotransmitters that promoted bonding and happiness.

Nadia huffed. Physiology should have been the last thing on her mind. And even though Evgeni was attractive and she had been flattered by his attention, her knees didn't wobble and her heart didn't fall out of rhythm when they kissed. No, her feet had remained firmly planted on the ground and her heart beat steady.

Then there was her first kiss with Ashley. It had been rushed and unexpected, and it had taken her breath away. It had been beyond any first kiss magic she had ever experienced or heard about before. Nadia had been completely at the mercy of her desires. Her brain had shut down, and her body had pulsed with need.

Even though she had never experienced that with Evgeni, he had slowly crept into her life and her heart. Behind his pretty boy façade, he was kind, generous, and caring, always there when she needed him, knowing when to leave her alone. She felt safe with him. Maybe that was enough?

Every time she had wondered, Nadia found in his eyes the conviction she lacked in her heart. His unwavering affection had carried their relationship for so long.

Nadia's heart tightened. He loved her so much.

A familiar ringtone jolted Nadia out of her ruminations.

"Keating speaking."

It was Singh with an update about their patient. Unlike Nadia's state of turmoil, Sanders was doing exceptionally well for a man in his condition. Perhaps Nadia should consider building a heart for herself next. Nadia thanked her and ended the call before it wandered into territory that was none of Singh's business.

She reached the entrance to the apartment building again. Their light was the only one still on. She took a calming breath and opened the door. It was time to face Evgeni.

Chapter 21

The Tenth Circle

THE APARTMENT WAS QUIET EXCEPT for the sound of fists rhythmically hitting a punching bag in a distant room. Nadia's stomach knotted. She and Evgeni loved their home gym and often exercised together when her schedule permitted it. The thought of ruining their shared life made her sick all over again. She followed the sound, nonetheless.

Evgeni was circling the bag between punches, sweat running down his naked chest. Despite wanting to run away, she walked to the other side of the bag and stabilized it, giving extra support for the punches to land on.

"Who is he?" Evgeni asked between jabs.

"Does it matter?"

"Is he one of your colleagues? Someone as smart as you?"

"Nobody is as smart as me," Nadia joked, but the words fell flat. "And *he*"—filled with unwanted apprehension, she met Evgeni's eyes—"is a she."

Evgeni stopped punching and stared at her. Nadia held his gaze, and a moment later he resumed punching the bag.

"She's a doctor, but that's irrelevant." Nadia spoke to fill the silence.

Evgeni stopped punching again. "So that's it? You're a lesbian now, and that makes it okay to cheat on me?"

"That would be a lousy excuse," Nadia said.

"Agreed." He landed a few hard punches.

Nadia bit back the apology that instinctively came to her. Saying sorry wasn't going to make up for what she had done. It was a selfish response intended to ease her guilty conscience. Her vision blurred, and she did her best to blink the tears away. Evgeni had every reason to hate her, and that was that. "Nothing I can say will make it okay, Zhenya." Her voice cracked. "I cheated. That's it."

"Was it something I did?" He reached out to steady the bag Nadia had abandoned, pleading with his eyes. "Tell me the truth, Nadyezhda. What did I do wrong?"

It could never be that simple. He had no character flaws to justify her actions. There was no way for him to repair their relationship because she was the broken one.

Nadia sank to the floor, resting her back against the wall. She closed her eyes as if she could erase the image of his hopeful face from her mind. The darkness only made things worse, her aching guilt shining even more clearly. She opened them again and saw Evgeni sink down across from her, his piercing eyes still waiting for her to respond.

"I love you for assuming it's your fault."

"If it is, I can fix it."

"What if there's nothing to fix?" Nadia's eyes watered at the thought that she could always be herself with Evgeni. He loved her for who she was.

"Do you love me?"

"Yes, I do." She said it without hesitation. Evgeni had always been the one constant thing in her life, someone she could rely on, trust, respect, know. What else was love but the unwavering sense of security?

He touched her hand. "Then there is something worth fixing."

She burst into tears. "Why are you so good to me? I don't deserve you."

He moved swiftly to sit next to her and wrapped his arms around her. Her sobs grew louder as guilt tore through her all over again.

"Hush, Nadyenka," he whispered soothingly. "So smart and yet so silly. Don't you know you deserve all the love in the world?"

"Come in." Ashley wiped away her tears in response to Pari's knock on her open door. She was still in her office, despite it being past midnight. "How's Sanders?" she asked.

"Remarkably well. If I didn't know better, I'd say it was a miracle." Pari took off her shoes and sat back on the sofa. She rubbed her temples.

"Why can't it be both? Science and miracles don't have to be mutually exclusive."

"Because, Ashley, God makes miracles. The only thing Keating makes is a mess."

"Ah." Ashley stood up from her desk and moved to sit next to Pari. Raw wounds flared with fresh pain inside her, but she didn't try to change the subject. "I was wondering how long it would take you to bring her up."

"That was quite the stunt in my OR. You shouldn't have done that. Your drama could have waited until after the surgery."

"It wasn't your OR. You let your junior fellow be the primary surgeon, remember?"

"She deserved it, and you know it. Don't try to take it away from her just because she acted like a jerk."

Ashley sighed. Pari was right. "I shouldn't have done that, but it wasn't like it mattered either way. I doubt that Nadezhda cared enough to lose her focus."

"You're wrong."

"Oh?" Ashley's curiosity piqued despite the deafening voices of anger in her head screaming she was done with Nadia and didn't want to know anything about her ever again.

"After you left, she froze. I wasn't sure she'd snap out of it. In fact, I thought she might drop everything and run after you. Imagine if she'd done that."

A kindling of want sparked through Ashley at the thought of Nadia going after her, of Nadia fighting for her. She shook the thought away. "But she didn't. She ran to her boyfriend." Ashley was well aware that she was exaggerating, but accuracy wasn't her primary concern right now.

"What happened?"

"I saw them together. She acted like a whole different person with him." Tears streamed down her face as she recounted the event. "As soon as we were alone, she said it was over between us. Just like that. She didn't offer an explanation. She said there was no point because I'd never forgive her."

"Was she right?"

Ashley frowned between sobs. Pari's ability to find plot holes in one's story might be a great diagnostic skill, but it sure as hell wouldn't win her any friendship awards.

"She should have at least tried. I would have," Ashley muttered. "Instead, she gave up. I told her what she did was horrible, and then *he* showed up with his birthday gift. Which she left here." She gestured toward the untouched box on the chair that she wished to burn.

Pari jumped to her feet and grabbed it.

"You can't open it," Ashley blurted out even as the sound of wrapping paper being torn filled the room. "It's not yours."

"Really, Ashley? After everything she did to you, it's my actions that are bad?"

Maybe Nadia wouldn't care. Not caring seemed to be Nadia's specialty.

Pari whistled.

"What is it?" Ashley asked.

"It's the best pair of loupes I've ever seen. Mine look like crap compared to them."

Ashley snuck a quick peek at the magnifying surgical loupes and huffed. "Great." For somebody who didn't know the first thing about surgery, Evgeni sure had done his research on loupes. "In addition to being absurdly handsome, he's thoughtful and generous." But who was keeping score? Ashley was certainly not competing with him. "You can give them to her when she comes to work tomorrow."

"Oh no." Pari dropped the opened box on Ashley's desk. "This is between you and her. Besides, if I take these loupes, I'm keeping them for myself."

"And how do I explain the fact that her present is unwrapped?"

"You'll figure something out." Pari returned to the sofa. "So she just left with him, huh? That's bitchy, even for Keating."

"Not exactly..." Ashley conceded. "I told her what she had done was wrong and, worse, that she had made me an accomplice. It must have rattled her because when he came in, she went straight over to him and said she'd had an affair." Recounting the events didn't help her make sense of them, nor did it numb the pain in her chest.

"She said what now?" Pari's jaw dropped.

"She didn't say who it was with, but she was cold and deliberate, and he was completely crushed. Then he left, and she went to talk to the reporters." Ashley sniffed. "To make matters worse, Dan was here too. He put two and two together."

"I am sorry," Pari said softly.

"I'm sorry too." Ashley had no more energy left to cry. "I'm sorry I fell for her."

"You love her?" Pari asked evenly, but her face was heavy with worry.

"I can't love her after today…" Ashley shook her head, fighting the contradictory feeling inside of her with every ounce of her being. "I can't."

"Good luck telling your heart that." Pari took her hand and patted it. "It's late. Come with me. You shouldn't be alone."

"No." Despite the void in her chest, Ashley had had enough company for one night. "I need to be alone. Go home to your family, Pari."

———————

"Do you love her?" Evgeni asked when Nadia finally stopped crying. His words were those of a broken man.

Nadia swallowed against a rising tide of fresh guilt. "I seem to have developed feelings for her." She didn't want to hurt him anymore, but she couldn't lie to him either. "It was never my intention to become emotionally attached."

"Then why did you do it?"

The question was inevitable, but regret muddled her well-rehearsed thoughts and burned through her throat. Nadia took a deep breath. "I convinced myself it was something I had to try before I"—she hesitated—"before we moved on with our lives together."

"You mean before you married me?"

Nadia flinched at the words. Right now, the thought of marrying Evgeni felt as if it were from another life. "Yes, that."

"How many times have you told me no already?"

"Four times. And it was never no, rather 'not right now.'" Rotting guilt renewed its attack on her heart. She knew "not right now" was all Evgeni needed to stay.

"Are you sure? I can only think of three."

"On the day I got my bachelor's degree, after earning a DO degree, after my general surgery residency, and most recently this past New Year's Eve." Nadia delivered the words with newsroom-worthy precision. How could she ever forget them? Every time was etched in her mind with unfathomable sorrow. She had been selfish, knowing she could never love him the way he loved her and yet not being able to let him go.

"Did I really propose to you at New Year's?"

"We went to New York, even though I didn't want to," Nadia said. "We were at the Empire State Building when you shouted at the top of your lungs, pledging your eternal love for me." She smiled. "You were drunk."

"Good thing I don't remember, then."

"It was sweet."

"But not sweet enough. You didn't say yes, and you went on to sleep with someone else." He paused, inhaled a deep breath, and blew it out slowly. It was the same centering technique that Nadia used.

"You know, I always knew," Evgeni said.

"Knew what?"

"That you liked women. I figured it out on our first date."

"How?"

"The way you looked at Stephanie when—"

"Who?"

Evgeni chuckled. "The waitress on our first date. I suppose you never got her name."

"I'm surprised you did." The fact that Evgeni had left their first date with the waitress when Nadia had shown no interest in going home with him hadn't bothered her as much as the fact that, when they met again, he stopped chasing women. He had changed for her and knowing this burdened her immensely. She couldn't change for him.

"Why? You thought I'd sleep with a girl without knowing her name?"

"Haven't you?" Nadia raised an eyebrow.

"Not that time." He smiled. "That was a memorable evening. It was the night I met you. I remember every detail, including the name of the girl I took home that night."

"How romantic." The sarcasm did little to erase the smugness off his face.

"When she spilled wine on you and tried to clean it up, you watched her the whole time."

"You know I don't like people invading my personal space," Nadia argued. How had he seen what she couldn't even admit to herself back then?

"Oh, you were definitely uncomfortable, but not for the reason you like people to believe. You enjoyed it. You were a little green with envy when I left with her, but you hardly even looked at me that night."

"That's quite the wild speculation." Nadia didn't want to admit how right he was. It stung that she had been unable to figure out her own feelings when they had been apparent to others.

"You had to see it from my perspective."

"So you thought I was gay, but you still pursued me. You liked the challenge?"

"No, it wasn't like that at all. I know better than to think a person's sexual preference can be changed."

Nadia raked her fingers through her hair in helpless frustration. Of course, he'd say that. He was the perfect man who always said the right thing. *Christ*, he wasn't making things easier for her.

"I wanted to get to know you because you were different from anyone I had met before. I hoped we could be friends." His voice grew quieter and broke at the end. He cleared his throat. "Anyway, when you kissed me, I thought you were into men too. Or, rather, I didn't think. All that mattered was that you were with me." He sighed. "I should have known better. You never paid attention to other men. But you noticed women. You may not want to admit it, but you did."

Nadia looked away. Evgeni had never been that perceptive, but he had seen a side of her that she had hidden from herself. Losing him would be like losing part of herself.

She turned back to look at him. "I chose you, Evgeni," she said softly. "Not some waitress or another guy or woman. You. I love you."

"If that's true, why are we here now?" He asked the question without accusation.

Nadia closed her eyes, embracing the darkness. "Because I betrayed us."

"Why did you tell me, Nadyezhda? Are you leaving me for her?"

"We're not together." Fresh tears welled up in her eyes again. "She didn't know about you until you showed up at the hospital. It's over between us."

"She didn't know?"

"Of course not." Nadia drew her knees up close to her chest and gripped her legs. At the thought of Ashley, her tears fell freely.

Evgeni wrapped his arms around her again. The familiar scent comforted her.

"It's your boss, isn't it?" His voice was still soft.

"It doesn't matter. She hates me."

"Nobody can hate you, Nadyezhda. I don't hate you. I love you. You know I do." He continued to hold her, his grip and words unwavering.

Along with Nadia's tears, the confession spilled past her lips. "It wasn't supposed to be her. It wasn't supposed to be anyone I knew. I was playing out a fantasy. I thought I could get over it if I acted on it. And when it turned out to be her, I knew we could never have a future together because we worked together. It felt like a sound decision at the time. But maybe it wasn't. Maybe I was looking for an excuse because I wanted her. I don't know anymore."

"What were you planning to do if she hadn't found out about me?" Evgeni gently lifted her chin.

"I was going to tell her. And then"—she met his eyes—"I was going to break up with you, Zhenya."

His face fell and he sat back against the wall.

"She's beautiful," he said quietly. "I can see why you'd fall for her."

"I haven't fallen for her," Nadia said it to herself as much as to him. "And you're the most attractive person I've ever met. Looks have nothing to do with it."

"And what about sex? Who's better—?"

"Evgeni, you're better than this."

He dropped his head into his hands. "I don't know if I am. She's smarter than me and richer than me. And you're throwing away everything we have together for her. I just… I don't know." Tears ran down his face.

His words landed on her like physical blows. She had no right to comfort him because she was the one hurting him. And she had hurt Ashley. Her indecision had hurt both of them. All she wanted was to curl up in a ball and cry until the ache in her chest subsided. The thought made her feel even worse. It was selfish to leave and it was selfish to stay. Torn with indecisiveness, Nadia remained passively seated.

The seconds turned into minutes that felt like hours. At last Nadia broke the silence. "Are you angry I cheated?" The question had been twisting inside her long before she had met Ashley. She had been indecisively postponing taking a self-destructive path because she doubted Evgeni would understand her. When it came to their relationship, it was all or none for him. It was yet another excruciating fact that grated her conscience.

"I'm hurt," he said, his voice quivering. "Wouldn't you be?"

She had no good answer. "I never meant to hurt you. I'm sorry."

"You rarely apologize."

"I mean it though. And I should have said it sooner."

"I forgive you. Of course I do," he said. "But that's not the point. Tell me honestly: if it's over between you and her, can we move past this? Can you marry me and live with me for the rest of our lives? Would you be happy?"

Nadia didn't have to think about the question. She had known the answer long before she had met Ashley. But only now had she found the strength she needed to admit it.

She looked into Evgeni's eyes, her heart sinking under the weight of the truth. Evgeni was a saint, and she didn't deserve him. Surely, there was a special circle in hell for people who hurt saints. But she knew what she wanted, and her eyes watered for the millionth time tonight. "No, I wouldn't be happy."

Tears rolled down Evgeni's face. "Then this must be the end for us."

"The end," Nadia repeated, the words piercing her heart. It was over. "I still love you," she whispered.

Evgeni met her eyes, a look of agony painted across his handsome face. "But you were never in love with me."

Chapter 22

The Odds of Ever Working Out

NADIA DROVE AIMLESSLY. EVEN AFTER everything she had done to Evgeni, he had insisted that she stay. He had even offered to be the one to leave. Nadia shuddered at even the thought of letting him leave the apartment he had picked out and decorated so artfully. The apartment she only lived in occasionally. Work had always come first, and Evgeni was an afterthought. *Unfairly so.* A lump of bitterness rose in her throat.

No, staying would only have made her feel worse. But leaving left her with no plan, and she was drained after an emotionally, physically, and mentally exhausting day.

To top it all off, her heart was pulling her in a forbidden direction. But Ashley was off-limits. *For good.*

Nadia blinked to clear her vision. In a single day, she had destroyed the two relationships that meant everything to her. *How supremely fucked up is that?* Never mind that she had also changed the face of transplantation for good. The irony that the best and the worst day of her life were one and the same brought fresh tears to her eyes.

She pulled off to the side of the road. The dark empty streets amplified her anguish. She tried to steer her brain in a positive direction and thought of Sanders, whose life she had saved. And then she thought of the person who shared this medical triumph with her. Surely, Singh didn't hate her.

Nadia pulled back onto the road and headed to an address she had been to only once seven months ago. Making an impulsive decision at three in the morning wasn't smart, but her mind was too wrapped up in misery to fight her tired limbs.

———————————

"It's three in the morning."

Pari's husband, Phillip, opened the door wearing only a pair of boxer shorts. He rubbed the sleep out of his eyes.

"I'm aware of the time. Is Dr. Singh awake?"

"She's barely had an hour of sleep. Can't whatever this is wait until morning?"

Nadia backed away from the door. She shouldn't have come here. Singh didn't hold the magic answer to her guilt-ridden insomnia.

"It's okay, Phillip. I'm up."

The voice came from inside the house. Nadia stopped in her tracks, shifting her weight from one side to the other. As much as she wanted the perspective of someone who had always been levelheaded and honest with her, she became uneasy when she saw Singh out of her scrubs and in a night robe.

"Well, I'm going back to sleep," Phillip muttered, turning away from Nadia. "Don't let her keep you up too long," he said to his wife. "Peyton has a recital tomorrow, and you better not fall asleep like you did last time." His amused tone suggested he hoped she would do that. He disappeared into the house.

"It's three in the morning," Singh reminded Nadia. She headed to the kitchen, flipping on a light.

Nadia followed rigidly, still torn between relief and unrest. "I didn't know where else to go."

"Right." A not-so-subtle smugness colored her voice. "I imagine your boyfriend kicked you out after the scene you pulled in Ashley's office."

"So she told you," Nadia said. If having a relationship with Ashley meant every single detail of her life would be reexamined under the scrutiny of her mentor, perhaps she had dodged a bullet.

The thought only made her heart ache more.

Nadia sighed. Who was she fooling? Even if Ashley told the whole world, nothing would stop her from wanting her. She bit back the urge to ask how Ashley was doing. She didn't deserve to know how she was doing.

"He didn't kick me out. He forgave me and wanted to marry me." Nadia sat down on a stool at the kitchen island. "But he wasn't the one I wanted to be with. I left so I wouldn't end up in Dante's eighth circle of hell."

Singh chuckled as she put the kettle on. "That's the one with the Bolgias? One of those Bolgias is reserved for hypocrites, right?"

Of course, she knew that. At this rate, they were dangerously close to starting a book club. Nadia rolled her eyes, letting her sarcastic thoughts distract her from her real feelings.

"You're aware you already qualify for the second circle?" Singh added not unkindly.

The adultery circle. Nadia should have seen that coming.

"Also the fourth, fifth, and sixth." Singh kept going.

Nadia dropped her head on the counter. She was too tired to trade witty remarks.

"You hurt my friend." Singh pulled two cups and some tea from a cupboard. "What makes you think it's appropriate to come to me?"

Nadia swallowed past the lump in her throat. How could she admit that the day's events had left her feeling vulnerable and exposed, that she just didn't want to be alone? "I saved your patient. I thought that might count for something."

"The fact that you're a brilliant surgeon doesn't give you license to do what you please. Actions have consequences."

"I'm aware of that," Nadia snapped. She took a few deep breaths to regain control. "Look, I never meant to hurt anyone. I heal people, I'm not supposed to break them."

Singh pushed a steaming mug in front of her. "Why are you here?" she asked softly. "Haven't you heard of a hotel?" As soft as Singh was capable of, anyway.

Nadia looked at her through half-opened eyelids, wishing the woman would understand her silent plea. There was no strength left in her to voice out that she needed the company. That for once in her life, she couldn't be alone. That the events from today had left her vulnerable and exposed.

"Fine," Singh said. "You can stay in the guest room tonight. But that doesn't mean I'm on your side. You aren't the victim here."

"Thank you." Nadia picked up her mug. The scent of chamomile filled her senses. A calm feeling spread through her that had little to do with the effect of the tea.

"Before I forget,"—Singh removed a drawing from the refrigerator door—"Sanders's kids drew this for you."

The simple drawing showed a bedridden stick figure and another stick figure with long hair standing next to the bed. Nadia's eyes lingered on the standing figure that wore blue scrubs and a white coat that appeared more like a cape. In one hand was a hammer, and it appeared that the hammer had broken the machines attached to the bedridden figure. In the other hand was a golden heart.

It's perfect. Warmth, excitement, sentiment, and positive feelings Nadia thought no longer existed within her threatened to flood her eyes with tears. She blinked them back and cleared her throat. Her emotions were too unguarded to be seeing this right now.

"The detail is remarkable." Nadia traced the drawing with her fingers. "The pressor pumps, the monitors, the iNO gas tank—everything is recognizable. They even drew the correct cannulation sites for the ECMO."

"They spent a lot of time by his side."

They marveled together at the primitive sketch. Despite her personal failings, Nadia had accomplished something good. It warmed her aching heart.

At last Singh moved. "I'm going back to bed. The guest room is down the hall, second door on the left. There are clean sheets and towels in the closet. Take the day off tomorrow and rest."

"Thank you," Nadia whispered.

"What for?"

"For not asking me why I did it."

Singh shrugged. "What would be the point? What's done is done. The only question now is what you'll do to fix it. You need to figure that out."

Singh disappeared up the stairs, leaving Nadia gripping the warm tea in her hands. *There is nothing left to figure out.*

⁕

Ashley toyed with the Dacron graft she had used to practice suturing under Nadia's tutelage. She folded and unfolded the polyester tube mindlessly. It was self-sabotage. She had promised herself to stop thinking about Nadia, about her betrayal. And yet every day—no, every minute—she failed miserably at keeping her promise.

She dropped the graft on the desk and pushed back against her chair noisily. Why was it so difficult?

Nadia hadn't come to work for the past two weeks, and yet Ashley couldn't stop thinking about her, grieving the loss of something she had never had. She should be happy Nadia had requested time off.

Ashley glanced at the door, her treacherous heart irrationally hoping Nadia would burst in any second. When she didn't, Ashley forced herself to look away. Despite Nadia's indiscretions, she missed her.

A knock on the door broke her out of her musings.

"Come in."

Claire, Ashley's administrative assistant, poked her head in. "Dr. Rylan, there's a gentleman at the front desk asking to speak with you."

"This early?"

"He doesn't have an appointment, but he'd like to know if it's a good time to meet with you."

"What is it about?"

"He didn't say."

"It's a good time. What's his name?" It was probably another reporter.

"I, uh, didn't catch his name." Claire blushed. "He was very handsome though."

Ashley's mouth went dry. She knew of only one man who was capable of freezing a woman's brain like that, and her wounds were too fresh to risk talking with *him*. "On second thought, I'm busy." As she scrambled to come up with a reasonable explanation, her pager went off. At the same time, a code blue at the ICU announcement came over the speakers.

Ashley stood up, sighed, and immediately felt a kick of guilt in her stomach. She shouldn't be almost relieved that someone had gone into cardiac arrest even if it helped her avoid a meeting with her uninvited guest.

As she hurried down the hall, a man called after her. She charged ahead, stubbornly ignoring him.

In the ICU, she followed the line of people running toward the emergency. Her heart sank as she realized it was the patient in bed eleven.

"What happened?" Ashley shoved her hands into a pair of gloves.

Dan was doing chest compressions. "The patient started having acute shortness of breath and chest pain. And then his sats dropped. Next thing I knew, he was in V-fib."

"Paddles are charged to 200," a nurse said.

Dan grabbed the paddles from the defibrillator machine behind him and pressed them to Sanders's chest. "Clear."

Everyone around the patient stepped back. For a moment, the room stilled, and Ashley could only hear her own pulse ringing in her ears. Sanders's body jerked when Dan administered the electric shock.

The team rushed back to the bed to continue working on the patient. Ashley ignored her racing heart and joined them in the resuscitation efforts. The patient needed her focus not her fright.

"Tube is in!" a resident shouted. Ashley watched him squeeze the Ambu bag, ensuring he didn't squeeze too hard or too fast but delivered just the right amount of air into Sanders's lungs.

Dan paused chest compressions, and Ashley pressed her fingers against Sanders's wrist. His pulse was faint but steady. That much was good. But then she glanced at his neck. A cold rush of adrenaline surged through her at the sight of the profoundly distended vessels. "Get me an echo. Now!"

Dan jumped back. "What are you thinking?" he asked.

"Look at his neck."

"Pulmonary embolism!" Dan shouted out the life-threatening diagnosis.

The echocardiogram machine was wheeled to the bedside. Ashley was sure that a massive clot had traveled to his heart and was blocking the flow of blood to his lungs. No blood to the lungs meant no oxygen to the body. He could die within minutes. The fact made Ashley's heart double its efforts, as if it were her own life she was fighting for.

With unnerving impatience, she waited for Dan to conduct the test and thought of the last embolectomy case she had done. It was the night Nadia had kissed her…touched her…and told her they could never be together again.

Ashley's jaw tightened as her thoughts fast-forwarded to Nadia's words a week after that: *Embolectomy is declared a failure before an incision is even made.*

Failure. The word echoed in her mind. Nadia had called her insane for thinking she could have done the surgery at bedside. *Performing open-heart surgery outside the OR is a fool's errand.*

Any credible surgeon would agree with Nadia, and yet Ashley's gut instinct rebelled.

"My God!" Dan said.

Ashley's attention was drawn back to the present. The monitor confirmed what she had predicted. "We have to operate now or he'll go into another cardiac collapse." Her voice was steady. To hell with her doubts and with what Nadia had said. This situation demanded an aggressive approach, and if that made her a fool, so be it.

She stepped back long enough to put on a sterile gown and gloves and charged right back in.

"You can't open him up here," Dan protested.

"I won't let Nadezhda's miracle patient die on his way to the OR." Ashley splashed some betadine on the skin, trying to get the field as sterile as possible. Then she drew her scalpel across Sanders's chest, tracing the healing incision from his transplant surgery.

"We don't have a bypass machine," Dan said. "Ashley, this is insane!"

"I can and I will do this right here. And I don't need a bypass machine." Ashley worked urgently, and despite his objections Dan kept up with her. They cut and pulled the chest wires that had been neatly placed two weeks earlier. Sanders's chest gave in as each side of the sternal bone was pulled away from the midline. "We're going to do a modified Trendelenburg procedure."

"Ashley, that's a terrible idea. TP for pulmonary embolism has dismal outcomes."

He had a point. The odds of it working weren't far different from winning the lottery. Still, those chances would exponentially diminish if she didn't operate right now.

The miracle heart made a few pathetic attempts to beat before giving out completely. Despite her own heart pounding, Ashley's hands remained steady. She had expected that.

"Patient coded. Prepare to—"

"No, Dan." She clamped the aorta. "We do a modified Trendelenburg, and the patient survives. Follow my lead. We have to move quickly."

Ashley had once read an article about a gunshot wound case. *The aorta was clamped, the pulmonary artery incised at its bifurcation, the shrapnel removed, and the pulmonary artery closed—all in 5 minutes. The patient survived.*

She intended to follow the same exact steps to evacuate the stuck clot.

Only the sound of breathing disturbed the still air as everyone waited as Ashley and Dan worked frantically.

"Time elapsed since the heart had stopped: one minute," a nurse said.

Ashley widened the incision, ignoring the pressure in her chest. *The patient survived*, she reminded herself the last part of that article.

"Time elapsed: two minutes."

Ashley's hand jerked, but the clot was out. *The patient will survive.*

"Three minutes."

Her vision became less crisp the longer she stared intensely without blinking, but her hands didn't need the input. They were guided by muscle memory. She closed the pulmonary artery. *My patient will survive.*

"Four minutes."

Ashley glanced up at Dan. "Now you can restart the heart." She pulled the suture strings, ready to tie the knot as soon as circulation was restored.

Dan removed the clamp, and blood spurted out, completing the de-airing maneuver. He cleared the field with the suction tube, and Ashley secured the knot.

The heart began filling up with blood. As it resumed beating, Ashley allowed herself a deep sigh, blinking to get the blurriness out of her eyes. The heart kept beating strong and maintaining a steady rhythm, as if it wanted not only to live but to thrive. It truly was a miracle heart.

"Sir, you absolutely cannot be in here."

Someone drew the curtain open. Ashley looked up and froze as she found herself face to face with none other than Evgeni Petrov.

His determined expression was quickly replaced by a wide-eyed look of pure horror. She understood why. Her appearance at the moment was less than stellar. Her surgical gown and face were covered in blood, and she was elbows-deep in a man's chest.

Fortunately, it became clear she wouldn't have to engage with the intruder. As his eyes rolled back in his head, the pale man wobbled and lost his footing and ultimately the battle against gravity.

As he fell, he reached out instinctively for the nearest object and tipped over the nearby tray of surgical instruments. The sound of metal hitting the floor rang out with deafening roars. In the process, a scalpel lacerated Evgeni's hand. He hit the ground hard.

Amid the shocking scene, Ashley's mind kicked back into gear. "Someone take this man to the emergency." Her voice was calm and decisive. "And someone please replace my contaminated instruments. I have a chest to close."

"You're thinking about her again."

Singh's smug comment brought Nadia back to reality.

"I'm not thinking about anyone," she snapped.

Nadia had stayed at Singh's house for the past two weeks, unable to make any plans. The world might think she had defeated death by bioengineering a human heart, but all she remembered from that day was how her own heart had been shredded. And the longer she stayed away from everything she cared about, the more difficult it was to maintain her façade of confidence.

"You have been not thinking about anyone for far too long," Singh mocked.

"Now, honey, let Nadia take her time to sort out her feelings." Philip looked up from his newspaper.

"Dear," Singh said, her voice dripping with false sentimentality, "do not pretend that you are indulging her behavior for anything other than your own self-interest."

Philip gave a mischievous smile but said nothing.

In the two weeks she had been there, Nadia had noticed that Phillip was the one who held the fort, taking on the lion's share of responsibility for child-rearing despite working a full-time job himself. He and their three young children knew better than to interfere with Singh's career.

Helping around the house was the least Nadia could do. It didn't soothe her frayed nerves, nor did it give her a sense of purpose, but going through the motions was better than doing nothing.

"It suits me too," Singh replied, "but Keating didn't train for ten years to wipe noses and bake cookies."

Regrettably, Nadia had done both of those activities.

Singh's phone began ringing in the other room and she rose. "Which reminds me,"—she glanced at Nadia—"Parker has a doctor's checkup today. I'll text you the details to take him." She hurried to answer the incoming call.

Phillip snorted at Singh's directive. He clearly wasn't the only one happy to have Nadia pitch in.

"I don't mind helping out. It gives me something to do," Nadia told Phillip.

"I'm not complaining, but Pari is right. You can't hide here forever. Eventually you'll have to face your demons."

His voice broke through her numb mind, and Nadia hated how right he was. Fortunately, Phillip returned to his newspaper without pressuring her to reply.

Shortly after, Singh rushed back and picked up her bag and keys. "I just spoke with Dan. Sanders had a saddle embolism, and they opened him up at bedside."

"Did they have time for ECMO?" Nadia asked, her mind suddenly cleared.

"No."

Her stomach dropped. Without the benefit of mechanical circulatory support there was only one operation Dan could have attempted.

"Is he alive?" Nadia asked, bracing herself for bad news. Patients didn't survive a Trendelenburg pulmonary embolectomy, period. And no matter how good a surgeon Dan was, his chance of success was negligible.

"He is." Singh grinned. "Your girlfriend saved him."

Nadia's heart skipped a beat and a foolish smile threatened to overwhelm her. Ashley had pulled off the impossible.

"She's not my girlfriend," Nadia snapped. Even if she felt warm and fuzzy inside, she wished to portray neither of these emotions.

"And whose fault is that?" Singh headed toward the door. "I'm going to check on our patient before rounds. When I get back, I want to see your first draft of that long-overdue, prize-winning manuscript on how you changed the game of transplantation. Your self-pity party is over." She shut the door without waiting for a reply.

"Yes, ma'am. Right after I get your kid to his doctor's appointment," Nadia muttered.

"She's not being mean on purpose. Nice just isn't her thing."

Phillip stood up, still wearing his robe. He always woke up two hours earlier than he had to so he could have breakfast with Singh, even though she never seemed to notice. Most mornings she rushed out the door without even saying goodbye. Nadia wondered if she had treated Evgeni the same way. Had she taken him for granted all those years? Her heart began to ache once again.

"I prefer honesty anyway," she said before her brain registered the irony in her statement. *Great.* "I mean I don't like wasting time with superfluous niceties either. I just haven't been myself lately."

"Good to know apathy isn't your usual state," Phillip said, then left to wake up his kids.

Nadia took the two empty coffee mugs and her glass to the sink and began rinsing them, thinking about the conversation that had just transpired.

Her hands froze as the cold water hit them. She wasn't apathetic. Nadia's insides twisted as if to prove how deeply her feelings ran and how little control she had over them.

She had spent the last two weeks cowering, accomplishing nothing. She should have been the one who saved Sanders's life.

But I didn't. Ashley saved him.

A warm, yet unwelcome, feeling crept into her heart. By pulling off the impossible, Ashley kept proving Nadia wrong again and again. Nadia didn't mind it. She was happy Ashley was so good at her job. *And she was gifted with unmatched compassion and kindness.*

Unfortunately, those qualities no longer extended toward her.

Blinking away the burning sting in her eyes, Nadia reminded herself that she had no right to ask Ashley for anything. She should have told her the truth the night they met in that bar. But she hadn't and now it was more likely that Ashley would save another patient with her last-ditch Trendelenburg surgery than that she would forgive Nadia. At least those odds weren't astronomically unfavorable.

It was too late to salvage their relationship.

Nadia shook her head, her heart breaking. It was naïve to think they might have a relationship at all. *And indulging in fantasies never achieved anything.*

Nadia squeezed the glass she was rinsing. She heard it crack and watched her blood swirl down the drain before her brain registered the deep cut and she felt the sting of the wound.

Fan-fucking-tastic.

———— •••• ————

As Ashley stood at the doorway of the emergency department gathering the courage to enter, the doors swung open from the other side.

"What a surprise to see you here, Dr. Rylan. Are you here for a consult?"

Ashley forced a smile. "No, Dr. Hayes. I'm, uh—" What was she doing there? "I'm visiting a friend."

"I hope it's nothing serious. Let me know if I can be of any help." He smiled sympathetically.

"Thank you, Robert."

Ashley crossed the threshold, her nerves getting worse with each passing step. She studied the whiteboard of patient names. Petrov was in bed five. She fought the urge to bolt out of the room when she glanced to the bed and then back to the door.

Evgeni was alone, facing away from the door. He held a piece of bloody gauze against his hand. Good. This conversation would be easier without an audience.

She took a deep breath and headed toward him. With every step, she became keenly aware of the plain blue scrubs she was wearing. After her impromptu surgery on Sanders, she had to change out of her bloodied business outfit that brought her the confidence she so desperately lacked now. Instead, a cocktail of dread, guilt, regret, and jealousy swirled in her heart. But she kept walking. Running away wouldn't solve anything.

Evgeni turned to face her and his face lit up. "You're here."

She picked up his chart. "No concussion," she murmured. "That's good."

"I didn't hit my head."

"And no one has been here to look at your hand yet?"

"No, but that's okay. There was some big emergency earlier. I figured they're still busy with it."

Ashley pinched her lips. How could somebody so ridiculously good-looking be so nice and understanding? "This is an emergency department. It's their job to deal with emergencies. They should have fixed a simple laceration by now." She looked around. "I can take care of it, if you'll let me."

"That's very nice of you," Evgeni said, "but I'm sure the chief of cardiothoracic surgery has better things to do than to sew up simple cuts."

"Suture." She corrected him reflexively. "You wanted to talk?"

He nodded.

"You might as well let me fix your hand while we do."

His smile returned. "Yes, of course. Thank you, Dr. Rylan."

She nodded and grabbed a laceration repair kit before she could change her mind.

When she came back, she busied herself with setting up the equipment. The cut was deep, but no longer bleeding and no tendons or nerves were affected. Keeping her eyes on his hand only, Ashley cleaned the wound thoroughly, numbed the area, and began suturing.

After a brief awkward silence, Evgeni spoke. "I didn't know you could do surgery outside the operating room."

"We don't usually operate in the ICU." She glanced up to meet his eyes.

"But how come no one stopped me from going in? I just followed a group of doctors when the doors opened, and there were only curtains separating the patients. It should be harder to get in."

Ashley huffed. "This isn't a prison. We can't have security everywhere. The patients in the ICU need more attention than the floor patients, so the curtains make it easier for the nurses to monitor them. And they can have family visitors. It's not exactly a civilian-free zone."

"I'm sorry. I shouldn't have burst in there like that." Evgeni looked down. "I don't usually faint at these sorts of things either."

Ashley shrugged, focusing on her work again. "Vasovagal syncope is quite common actually. Some people faint even at the sight of a few drops of their own blood."

She glanced up when he didn't respond. He looked at her as if she had spoken an alien language.

Ashley smiled. "It's the medical term for what happened. You saw something disturbing, went into 'fight-or-flight' mode, and your blood pressure spiked. Your system overcompensated and your blood pressure dropped just as abruptly. Losing consciousness is a defense mechanism of sorts. When you're in a horizontal position, it's easier for your heart to pump blood to your brain."

Evgeni's blank expression told Ashley she was rambling. Her cheeks flushed, and she shut her mouth. Time to wrap up the lecture. "What happened was you saw a man's chest open, and you had a normal physiologic response. It wasn't because of any lack of masculinity." Ashley realized too late how that statement might sound to him. She hadn't meant to imply that was why Nadia cheated on him—although there had seemed to be a lack of sexual satisfaction. *God*, she looked away as her eyes bulged in mortification at her inappropriate thoughts.

"That isn't why I wanted to talk to you." Unfortunately, Evgeni seemed to catch on that topic much better than he had to the neuroscience lesson.

"What, then?" she asked, her mouth dry. Was she naïve to hope he didn't know who Nadia had cheated with?

"I want to talk to you about Nadyezhda. I know you were the one she slept with."

Ashley's heart jumped in her throat. She was naïve. "I didn't know she had a boyfriend until I met you. It was over as soon as I found out." She forced herself to meet his eyes. He had to know she was sincere. That no matter how she felt toward Nadia, she would never knowingly hurt him or anyone like that.

"Yes, she told me that." He waved his good hand.

Ashley stared in surprised confusion. He seemed far less angry than she might have been.

"I didn't come here to blame you," Evgeni continued. "Nothing like that."

Ashley's heart relaxed slightly. The conversation was going significantly better than she had imagined. But then again, her sole frame of reference was *The Maury Show*.

She met his eyes. "Then why are you here?" She held her breath. Did she want to know?

He looked her straight in the eye. "You should give Nadyezhda another chance."

Chapter 23

The History of Embolectomy

ASHLEY BLINKED. ONCE... TWICE... THREE times. Evgeni's eyes remained steady.

She could see why Nadia would choose him. It went beyond his physical appearance. It was his personality that truly shone. And it made Ashley want to punch him in the face. Nobody was that selfless.

"I love Nadyezhda. I've loved her since the first moment I saw her." Evgeni carried on with his absurd explanation as to why he would ask Ashley to forgive Nadia when Ashley didn't say anything. "But deep down, I knew she could never love me back the same way. I didn't want to lose her, so I never questioned her about it. It was selfish, I know, but having part of her was better than not having her at all. Only now do I realize how miserable staying together made both of us."

"But she cheated! How can you not be mad at her?"

Evgeni shook his head. "I'm sad but not mad. I know Nadyezhda, and she's not someone who would normally do such a thing. She must have felt so trapped and alone all these years." His voice cracked. "It helped me see that only in the last few weeks before we broke up, she was happy for the first time."

Broke up? The words reverberated in Ashley's mind but she shook her head, stomping down any forbidden thoughts.

"You're mistaken, Evgeni," she said, her voice trembling. "Nadezhda can't even stand me." She swallowed several times to steady it. "Ever since you showed up at the hospital, she has stayed as far away from me as possible. She hasn't even come to work. And work is her true *love*."

"Exactly!" Evgeni stared at her as if this explained everything.

Ashley tilted her head. He wasn't making any sense. She wished they could go back to talking about the physiology of vasovagal responses.

"Don't you see? She's so upset about what happened with you that she's staying away from what she loves the most."

Ashley shook her head. His explanation was far-fetched and didn't make sense. *Nadezhda doesn't care for me.* Ashley's heart squeezed with ache. *If she did, she wouldn't have lied.*

He sighed. "Remember when she had that, uh, stomach surgery thingy?"

"Appendectomy." Ashley smiled. Evgeni's lack of medical terminology distracted her momentarily from her inner turmoil.

"Yes, that. She insisted on working the next day."

Ashley nodded. "No one could convince her to take the day off."

"And what about the time she had to work with that medical student just because he was somebody's son?"

"The chair of surgery's son. He was here for eight weeks, and Bratton insisted Nadezhda train him since she was the best. She hated every second of it."

"And yet she came to work every single day. Even the days she was supposed to be off. And what about the time she was suspended from the OR?"

Ashley looked down, her cheeks warming. "She told you about that, huh?"

"She tells me everything. I'm her best friend." The unspoken *just her friend* lingered in the air. He paused and took a deep breath. "Nothing keeps her away from her career. But for you, she's ready to throw years of hard work in the gutter."

Ashley still held the needle driver in her hand. She clicked it open and shut rhythmically as she considered, then rejected his words. Her heart had been through so much already. Any flicker of hope frightened her. She held her breath to suffocate any trace of it.

No, Nadia had been so cold and indifferent the last time they spoke, it was more likely she had stayed away because she hated Ashley.

"Tell me this," he added when Ashley didn't respond. "Do you love her?"

Ashley froze momentarily, the sound of the needle driver abruptly dying. Her heart jumped in her throat, and she busied herself with discarding the used instruments. After she returned to dress the wound, she finally found her voice. "That isn't an appropriate question to ask me. We're supposed to be rivals."

"So you do want to fight for her."

"I didn't say that. I mean we shouldn't even be talking." Ashley jumped to her feet, her task complete. "I should go."

"Wait." Evgeni touched her arm. "I'm sorry if I crossed a line, but I'm not your enemy. I only want to fight for Nadyezhda's happiness."

Christ. Ashley pursed her lips. *Could he be any sappier?*

He looked at her with those deep blue eyes that made her jaw tighten. Why was he so charismatic and saying all the right things? It made hating him that much harder.

"I thought I was beginning to love her, but how can I after what she did?" The words slipped out unbidden.

"I think we can agree Nadyezhda is one in a million," Evgeni said softly, his eyes filled with pain. "If I thought I had a chance with her, I wouldn't worry about whether it's right or not. I would just be with the woman I love."

Ashley swallowed the lump in her throat. Her mind struggled to reject Evgeni's words. To believe that Nadia wasn't one in a million. That she wasn't worth challenging her integrity. That the mere thought of her wasn't making Ashley's heart violently ache with contradiction.

Ashley stepped back, completely lost at what she was going to do. She looked at Evgeni. "Come back in two weeks to have your sutures removed."

———— •••• ————

Evgeni's words echoed in Ashley's mind as she headed to the OR for her next case.

Nadia is no longer with him. The thought kept coming back again and again, and Ashley fought as hard as she could to push it away. That shouldn't matter.

What did matter was that Nadia had lied and she hadn't tried to explain. She hadn't even apologized.

For all Ashley knew, Nadia hated Ashley for making her tell Evgeni the truth. Although she couldn't exactly make Nadia do anything she didn't want to do.

Ashley considered other possible reasons Nadia had kept her distance. Maybe she was too stubborn to ask for forgiveness. That would be so Nadia. Besides, Ashley had told her that nothing she said would be enough. So if Ashley wouldn't listen, what would be the point in explaining?

She arrived at the OR to find Pari rummaging through packs of freshly autoclaved surgical instruments. "Are you stealing surgical supplies?"

Pari looked up at her. "Borrowing materials is hardly a crime." She returned to bagging the packs along with some sutures and disinfecting materials and shoved the bag into Ashley's hands. "And I'm not taking anything. You are."

"I have a case scheduled. I don't have time for riddles."

"Haven't you heard? Your case got canceled because I'm doing an emergency aortic dissection repair in this room now."

Ashley looked at her phone. "I haven't heard anything about that." She looked at the bag in her hand and asked, "Why do I need all these surgical supplies?"

"Because my day just got busier and yours got freer. You'll take them to my house instead of me."

"I don't follow." Ashley frowned.

Pari was tapping on her phone and didn't look up. "Keating cut her hand. She said she needs stitches but refuses to come to the hospital. It doesn't sound too serious, but you know she likes to underplay things."

Ashley gawked at her, trying to process the statement Pari had just so casually delivered. "She's at your house?"

"Yes."

"And she's been there how long?"

"For the last two weeks."

"And you didn't think to mention this to me until now?"

"That's right."

"Because…?"

Finally, Pari looked up. "Because I thought you two would have figured things out by now. Instead, you're doing risky surgeries on my patient, and my star fellow is babysitting my children instead of watching said patient. She's also depressingly pining over you in my guest room."

From the array of emotions that swirled in Ashley's mind, curiosity won over. "She's been pining over me?"

Pari huffed. "Go talk to her. It's clear how you two feel about each other, but you're both too stubborn to admit it. Figure out your drama, please, so she can get back to work." Pari nodded at the bag Ashley was holding. "I need her to be able to use her head and hands. She's useless to me as the bloody, sniveling mess she is right now."

It was Ashley's turn to huff. Pari had a flair for the dramatic. It was biologically impossible for Nadia Keating to snivel. But then another thought took over. "You told me having a relationship with a fellow is wrong. Why have you changed your mind?"

"I'm still very much against attendings and fellows screwing around. But, Ashley, this isn't about office policies anymore. This is about your heart. You've never shown so much interest in anyone before. And I'll personally kill you if you ever mention this to Keating, but she's a fellow by title only. I trust her judgment more than I trust half of the attendings here. Besides, you two have already created so much goddamn drama around not dating, I can't imagine it getting any worse if you do actually date." Pari pushed her gently toward the door. "Stop looking for reasons not to talk to her and get it over with already."

Ashley gave a weak sigh of surrender as they reached the door. Pari was right. She owed it to herself to hear Nadia out. A conversation was long overdue.

"Good luck with your case," Ashley said as she stepped out of the room.

Pari grinned. "Don't need it. I'm the surgeon, so the patient will do great."

With an exaggerated eye roll, Ashley thought, *Does everyone around here have a God complex but me?*

As she hurried away, Pari added, "And it will go a lot smoother without having fellows challenge my decisions."

Ashley shook her head. Having her decision challenged in her OR were simpler times. There was so much more at stake now than her ego.

Her feet hammered the floor, and she ignored whatever other witty remark Pari hurled after her. Every cell in her body brimmed with energy and hope flickered inside her. This time she didn't fight her feelings. She let them grow and evolve into a burning desire that maybe, just maybe, things would work out at the end.

————— ••• —————

Nadia tapped her fingers on the table beside her keyboard. She reread the first sentence of the introduction: *Heart transplantation remains the only curative treatment option for end-stage heart failure (HF)*. She growled, her fingers accelerating their drumbeat. She had started the whole heart-out-of-scratch idea because Ashley had dared her to do it seven years ago.

And she'd had time to finally do it because she was banned from the OR.

Her fingers stilled and she thought of how her first time with Ashley had happened because she apologized. Could it really be as simple as apologizing and being forgiven? She shivered. She had never felt so attracted to anyone else before. And it wasn't only because of Ashley's gender. Nadia's heart didn't go wild for just any woman. Only for Ashley.

Nadia sat back in the chair. There was no point in working on the manuscript draft when she lacked focus. And it was obvious why she was unable to do anything productive or even leave the house. She was ready to admit that Ashley was different from her past lovers because she was the only one Nadia had ever loved.

Her heart ached with the hopeless realization. Who in their right mind would want a relationship with a liar?

Nadia tried so hard to feel differently, but her heart refused to listen. Maybe she should build herself a new one.

The sound of keys turning in the front door lock jolted her back to the present. Singh had texted that she had an emergency and wouldn't be able to deliver the medical supplies she needed to suture her cut, but maybe something had changed. It would have been easier to go to the hospital like a normal person, but Nadia refused to take the chance that she might run into the woman who was presently plaguing her heart and mind.

"I didn't expect you so early." Nadia kept her eyes on the screen, pretending to work, as footsteps approached. "Parker went to sleep half an hour ago, so please stay out of his room."

"You're switching careers to a full-time nanny, Nadezhda?"

Nadia's heart began pounding in her chest. She turned to face Ashley. "I thought you were Dr. Singh," she said unintelligently.

Seeing Ashley standing in Singh's living room made Nadia want to apologize profusely for all the things she had done wrong. Instead, she focused on her breathing. Apologizing wouldn't change anything.

"She's busy. She wanted me to give you this." Ashley tossed the biohazard bag on the table.

Neither one of them took their eyes off each other. How could Nadia look anywhere else? Against all reason, her foolish heart had been hoping Ashley would show up and forgive her. And blinking now could only take the moment away.

Ashley's presence doesn't mean she's forgiven you, a small voice at the back of her mind insisted. The thought grew loud and unrelenting, and Nadia's face stiffened to contain the raw emotions bubbling under the surface. "Thank you," she hesitated, "Dr. Rylan."

"Really, Nadezhda? I think we're well past formal titles."

Nadia clamped her mouth shut. What was the point of irritating Ashley further?

Breaking eye contact, she picked up the bag and laid out the contents methodically in preparation for repairing the laceration. Her breathing returned to normal as she carried out the familiar task.

Under the weight of Ashley's intense stare that set her skin prickling, Nadia cleaned and numbed the wound. She picked up the needle driver with her left hand and began awkwardly placing sutures.

"Want me to help you with that?" Ashley asked knowingly.

"I'm perfectly capable of suturing a simple cut. I don't need your help." It was easier to pick a fight than to talk.

Not that she had the right to be angry. Her mind was frazzled, and it instinctively took her down the familiar path of self-destruction. Nadia gritted her teeth, reminding herself that keeping quiet was for the best.

Ashley watched Nadia stubbornly suture herself using a single-hand technique with her nondominant hand. Despite the awkward grip, Nadia was succeeding with astonishing grace. Her dogged competence was typical—and so infuriatingly sexy. Ashley sighed. "Why are you fighting with me?"

Nadia said nothing.

Why was she pretending to be indifferent? If Pari and Evgeni hadn't convinced her of Nadia's remorse, she would have thought Nadia had none. Why she insisted on portraying this cold-hearted being was beyond Ashley.

Then it dawned on her. Nadia had told her there was no point in torturing themselves by talking since their relationship was over. She did that a lot—shut down every time things got emotional. Ashley relaxed her shoulders, letting go of her frustration. This time Nadia's defense mechanism wouldn't work.

She pulled out a chair and sat next to Nadia, extending a gloved hand.

After a moment of hesitation, Nadia surrendered the needle driver, then looked away.

It was a tiny gesture of relinquishing control, but it gave Ashley a cautious hope. She focused on the deep wound rather than the delicate hand surrounding it.

"The last time we talked," Ashley said, "you were right."

Nadia turned and looked at her.

"I was determined to hate you. There was nothing you could have said to make me change my mind. Because I wasn't ready to listen." Ashley lightly touched Nadia's hand, carefully avoiding the cut. "I am now."

Nadia closed her eyes. When she opened them again, they were filled with tears. "I never meant to hurt you."

Ashley gripped the needle driver. "It's a little late for that now," she said softly.

"I know." Nadia looked down, her tears wetting the table.

"That day in the substerile room…before Sanders's surgery, you wanted to tell me, didn't you?"

"I wanted to tell you long before that," Nadia said. "But it's easy to put off admitting something that will only cause pain. Especially something you don't believe can be justified."

Ashley blinked, clearing her eyes. She began suturing Nadia's hand. "No, I don't believe there is any justification for cheating."

"As soon as I realized how I felt about you, I thought...I hoped that if I told you personally, you might at least trust me."

The tears in Ashley's eyes intensified and she paused. Nadia was right. She didn't trust her.

"By the way, I heard about Sanders's bedside surgery."

At the sudden change in topic, Ashley looked up. Perhaps Nadia was simply avoiding her feelings again. But it was a welcome distraction.

"He's stable," Ashley said.

"You pulled off a miracle; you know that, right?"

Ashley gave a tight smile. It was extremely rare for patients to survive such a near-death experience. If Sanders did, perhaps she and Nadia could also beat the odds.

"Do you know the story of this surgery?"

Ashley shook her head. She knew the highlights, but Nadia had a way of bringing a story to life.

"When Trendelenburg came up with the procedure in 1908, it was thought to be a great discovery. And it was—in theory. In practice, it was so unsuccessful that a patient had to be actively dying before a surgeon could even attempt it. Trendelenburg himself never saved a single life with his procedure.

"During one case, a young surgeon helplessly watching his patient die realized the procedure would never work unless there was a way to keep the blood flowing during surgery."

"John Gibbon's cardiopulmonary bypass machine," Ashley noted quietly.

"Yes, his invention changed everything. But Gibbon first developed the miraculous heart-lung machine in 1953. What were surgeons supposed to do before that? The Trendelenburg procedure was the only solution they had at the time. A surgeon's efforts were almost always futile, but what other choice did they have but to try to make it work?"

Ashley dressed the closed wound and looked up to meet Nadia's eyes. "Why are you telling me this?"

"I want you to understand how something that appears adequate at one time may prove to be severely deficient in retrospect." Nadia paused as if searching for the right words. "I chose Evgeni because he checked all the boxes. He understood me, he supported me, and he is the kindest man I've ever met. And he loves me so much. But like Trendelenburg's embolectomy without Gibbon's machine, my relationship with him was doomed to fail. It was like the anecdotal successes of Trendelenburg's surgery. It was just enough to fool me into believing it could work. But in the end, it never did."

"Because you were missing a pump machine?"

"Because I was with the wrong person," Nadia said in a rush, her red eyes pleading for understanding. "But I didn't know of any alternative. So I made do with what I had."

Ashley frowned. "You were with Evgeni because you thought he was your best option?"

"It sounds bad when you put it that way. I wasn't using him, but I couldn't reciprocate his feelings either...at least not in the way he deserved. But I stayed with him because..." Nadia pressed her lips together. "This is a lot harder than I thought it would be."

Ashley touched her hand. "You're not the first homosexual to try to make a heterosexual relationship work." She gave a shaky smile. "Although you're probably the first one to use the invention of the bypass machine as a metaphor for it."

Nadia groaned. "You'd think the person who discovered the right way to do organ transplantation would have figured out her sexual preference by now."

"The *right* way, huh?" Ashley teased. "I'm glad your lack of humility is still intact."

"I don't know about that." Nadia turned her opened laptop toward Ashley without meeting her eyes. "It would appear you've reduced me to a mess incapable of writing a simple paper."

Not that there was such thing as a simple paper in medicine. Curious, Ashley scanned the title: *The First Successful Transplantation with a Bioengineered Human Heart on Donated Extracellular Matrix*. It was a catchy heading. For a dry scientific article, anyway.

She examined the authorship block next: *Nadezhda R. Keating, DO; Riku Sato, PhD; Dan S. Myers, MD; Sarah M. Ross, BS; Li Wei, MD; Robert J. Stevens MD; Ashley Rylan, MD; Pari J. Singh, MD.*

She reread her name. Based on her previous articles, Nadia typically gave authorship solely based on merit. Naturally, Ashley gasped when she saw her name right before Pari's, the senior author.

"My middle initial is 'C,'" she said and smiled. "It's for Christina."

"I'll be sure to add it," Nadia said matter-of-factly. She cleared her throat. "Just so you know, I didn't have an ulterior motive when I added your name. I'd have done the same for anybody who rescued the subject from a saddle embolism."

"Noted," Ashley said, mimicking Nadia's businesslike tone.

The rest of the draft wasn't as reasonably thought out. The introduction began with a coherent sentence, but then shifted to drawing a bizarre parallel between a physiologically broken heart and an emotionally broken one that had no medical treatment available. Ashley was glued to the screen, biting back laughter at the absurdity of what she was reading. It seemed like nothing that Nadia might have written. "If I had known the discovery of the century would allow you to change the format of these papers, I'd have tried to come up with one myself."

The faintest smile brushed on Nadia's lips before sadness drowned her face. The smile never reached her eyes.

Soon Ashley's amusement died out. The text was full of self-hatred and harsh appraisal. It was how Nadia approached her work—criticizing, discouraging, and condemning mistakes—and apparently it was also how she approached her personal life.

Ashley closed the laptop and looked at Nadia, who stared at her bandaged hand, refusing to meet her eyes. Nadia's brain might not be hardwired to forgive, but Ashley found herself wanting to do exactly that.

If only it could be that simple.

"If you had told me about him, how did you think I would have reacted?" Ashley tried to keep the accusation out of her voice. "Or were you planning to stay with him if I had turned you down?"

"No…" Nadia looked up to meet her eyes, her face streaked with dried tears. "Of course not. He deserves better than to be the consolation prize. My impulsive announcement in your office…just sped up the inevitable. We broke up." Nadia looked down again and began picking at the edges of her dressing. "I don't expect it to make any difference, but for what it's worth, after you and I… Well, I haven't had sex with him since. I couldn't. It just felt…wrong."

Ashley sat in stunned silence. Nadia had been in her lab practically 24/7 when she was building the heart but it was still hard to imagine her avoiding Evgeni completely. Ashley knew that if she were sleeping next to Nadia, she wouldn't be able to keep her hands to herself for a single night, let alone weeks. And yet Nadia seemed sincere in volunteering the information. Despite everything, she had never actually lied.

She just neglected to mention some essential details.

The omission was enough to keep Ashley's distrust alive, even if she liked the idea of Nadia not sleeping with Evgeni. The feeling that she might always feel such distrust chilled her.

"What is it?" Nadia asked.

"You cared for him, and yet you betrayed him. How can I trust you wouldn't do the same to me?"

Nadia grabbed Ashley's hand and pressed her fingertips against the side of her neck, sending an instant shiver down Ashley's spine.

"Can't you feel it?"

The feeling of Nadia's rapid pulse at the carotid artery made Ashley's heart pound in response.

"It's what you do to me. Without a miss, my heart wants to break out of my chest at the mere sight of you. Every. Single. Goddamn. Time. This has never happened to me before. *Ever.*"

Ashley resisted the urge to extend her hand and curl up her fingers behind Nadia's neck. With all her might, she fought her desire to kiss her. Because when had that ever solved anything?

"I don't want to ever lie to you again," Nadia said, her eyes fixed on Ashley. "I can't promise I won't screw up. I'll never do anything like that again, but I'm sure I'll do something equally stupid to sabotage this relationship. I'd be a fool to promise I won't fail. What I can promise is that if you give me a chance, I won't stop trying to be better. Because even though you're giving me constant heart palpitations I want to be with you more than anything I've ever wanted. Including surgery."

Ashley gasped. Nadia's words were all the encouragement she needed. Pulling her close, Ashley savored her scent before capturing her mouth with hers. Nadia responded breathlessly, pulling her even closer.

The kiss felt like the rightest thing in the world, igniting a passion Ashley had forgotten existed. Her skin burned with desire, seeking more of the contact, and her insides melted into liquid lava that extinguished any trace of doubt.

At last Ashley pulled away and looked into Nadia's dark eyes. "You can always build yourself a new heart."

Nadia's lips curved into a cocky smile. "Now that is something I can definitely do." She leaned in and kissed Ashley again.

When Nadia's hand made its way under her shirt, stroking her skin and leaving a trail of goosebumps, Ashley was sure her heart pounded faster than Nadia's ever could. Her body pushed forward to meet Nadia's touch, humming her encouragement when Nadia found her breast.

When her phone rang, Ashley snapped back to reality. Resisting her first instinct, to fling the damn thing at the wall, she reminded herself that they were in Pari's dining room. Something that Nadia seemed oblivious to, her hand still wandering against Ashley's skin.

"Wait." With great effort, she pulled away from Nadia, who gave a choked gasp of protest.

Ashley mouthed *sorry* and answered the phone. It was Claire with a list of meetings Ashley needed to attend.

"You have to go," Nadia said matter-of-factly once Ashley hung up.

Ashley nodded, fighting the burning need to stay. She had responsibilities. "I had a case that got canceled, so now I have to attend the meeting I was going to skip. And apparently, when the chief leaves work in the middle of the day, everybody freaks out. So maybe I shouldn't have done that…"

"I'm glad you came." Nadia touched her arm, terminating her ramblings.

Ashley smiled. "Me too."

Nadia's smooth face, free of any lines, of any negative emotions, made Ashley want to call in sick. She even began mentally composing a list of plausible acute illnesses.

But with a sigh, Ashley let go of that plan. Even if she somehow managed to ignore her own sense of duty, she doubted a workaholic like Nadia would respect her if she pulled that stunt.

"Let's pick up from where we left off tonight. Text me your address." Nadia's smoldering brown eyes held Ashley's.

Ashley pushed down the urge to agree. "No."

Nadia frowned. "We can meet back here, but I can't promise my performance won't be hindered if Singh is in the other room grinning like an idiot."

Ashley laughed. "A definite no to that."

"Hotel?"

Ashley shook her head. "We tried it your way. Now we'll do it my way."

Nadia crossed her arms and quirked an eyebrow. "And what way is that exactly?"

"The food-at-a-public-place way."

"Aren't we past that?"

Ashley smiled broadly. "We're *exactly* at that." She mimicked Nadia's instructions for their first meeting. "We meet this Friday at seven at a restaurant. There will be food. There will be drinks. We will talk and get to know each other. And in case that isn't clear enough, we will go on an honest-to-God, old-fashioned date."

Nadia sighed theatrically. "Do we have to?"

Still a bit heady from Nadia's passionate display a moment ago, Ashley challenged. "Do you want me?"

"Yes," Nadia replied without hesitation.

"You have your answer."

Nadia huffed. "Fine. We'll do it your way." She smiled with mischief. "Let's see how long you can keep your hands to yourself."

Ashley chuckled as she turned to leave. "Oh, I don't think it's my hands we need to worry about."

Chapter 24

The Attending-Fellow Relationship

IT WAS PAST TEN WHEN Nadia heard Singh's footsteps approach. The children were in bed, and given the first draft of her manuscript had been embarrassingly unusable, she had been working on rewriting it from scratch ever since Ashley left.

She looked up from her laptop. "Did your case go well?"

"You would have loved it. I did your favorite—a valve-sparing aortic root replacement," Singh teased, reminding her yet again of the incident that had got her thrown out of the OR. "And I see Ashley has fixed your hand," she continued, pointing to Nadia's bandage. "Good. I was certain you cut yourself on purpose to avoid her for two more weeks."

"I'm capable of suturing a simple cut on my own," Nadia said flatly.

"Does that mean you two didn't figure things out?"

Nadia said nothing. She had no desire to share anything about her private life with Singh.

"Fine, don't tell me. I'll see it on the nanny cam anyway."

Heat rose to her cheeks. "You don't have a nanny cam." Nadia ended the sentence more like a question rather than a statement, earning herself a teasing smile from Singh.

"I'm beginning to think I should get one."

"Nothing happened," Nadia insisted.

"*Something* happened, or you wouldn't be blushing so hard."

Nadia looked away as Singh laughed at her lack of composure.

"Well, regardless of what transpired in my home earlier, I'm happy for you two! You're both intelligent, stubborn, and perfect for each other. It would have been a shame if you screwed it up."

"I told you, nothing happened here, Dr. Singh." The statement was mostly true although plausible deniability wasn't worth the sacrifice.

"So I don't have to arrange a sitter for the kids tomorrow?"

Nadia frowned. When had she turned into Singh's nanny? "I'm going back to work tomorrow, so you'll need to find someone else to raise your children. Try one of the medical students. That will keep them out of my way."

Singh chuckled. "I'm glad to see you're back to your usual self."

"That reminds me, I'll email you the draft of the article on the bioengineered heart later this week. We should submit ASAP. Let's aim high, like *The Lancet* or *JAMA* or—"

"Stop changing the subject, Keating," Singh interrupted. "After I put up with you moping in my home for two weeks, I expected you to be a little more communicative. I suppose I could always ask Ashley. She *will* tell me everything."

"Fine." Nadia gave a long-suffering sigh. Singh was right. There was no point in being discreet. "Yes, we figured things out. But my personal life will not interfere with my work performance, if that's what you're worried about."

"Like it hasn't until now?"

Nadia gritted her teeth. Singh was on point, and she hated it.

"Oh, quit looking so miserable. I'm just giving you a hard time. I trust you won't let your girlfriend distract you too much during business hours."

Nadia snapped her laptop shut and stood up, ready for this conversation to be over. She headed toward the guest room.

"What? You're staying here tonight?" Singh called out after her.

Pausing, Nadia turned. "She wants to take things slow."

"Ugh."

Nadia stifled a laugh. "Tell me about it."

"I never had this problem with men."

"Mm." Nadia nodded before she could stop herself. Then she met Singh's eyes. "But she's worth it."

"Good. Because if you hurt her again, you and I will have a problem."

Singh had every right to want to protect her friend. But Nadia wasn't the enemy. They both wanted the same thing—for Ashley to be happy.

Instead of giving an overly emotional response that would probably embarrass them both, Nadia said, "Parker received his vaccination today. The shot was in his left shoulder. He can expect some site tenderness and generalized fever over the next couple of days."

Nadia's return to the hospital was greeted with praise and congratulations, as if she were about to usher in the Second Coming. The attention had a bittersweet ache to it. Although she basked in the glory, she longed for Ashley instead of the spotlight.

They both had hectic schedules complicated by maintaining a professional distance. There were no official policies against attending-fellow relationships, but no one thought it was a good idea, especially within the same department. Normally Nadia would have agreed wholeheartedly, but she had never before been one of the parties involved. *Well*, her case was the exception that proved the rule.

Since everyone knew relationships were bound to happen, the next general advice was to keep it under wraps. Until Nadia became an attending, they had agreed to keep their private life private. If people knew they were involved and brought it to the attention of the chair of surgery, the repercussions would fall on Ashley as the chief. That and the fact that Nadia had little interest in sharing information about her private life with hospital staff made discretion an easy choice.

Getting ready for their Friday night date was a little more difficult. Simply choosing what to wear was driving her insane.

Nadia sat on the edge of the bed in her rented studio, looking at every pair of pants in her closet and rejecting every single one of them. She had done the same with her skirts, dresses, blouses, and shirts. Nothing seemed to be good enough.

She rubbed her temples. Getting ready to go out had never been this difficult before. But when it came to Ashley, every fleeting thought or action was magnified and reexamined with scrutiny.

Nadia stood up and went to her closet to confirm her lack of choices.

Ashley always looked amazing in her stylish professional attire, and there was no doubt she would look beautiful tonight. Nadia raked her hair. Why couldn't Ashley wear scrubs at work like everyone else?

Her eyes darted to a neatly folded pair of scrubs and then she looked away. No, she couldn't wear those.

Why had Ashley insisted on this getting-to-know-each-other charade? Nadia had spent enough time with her by now to know who she was. Her nerves twisted with a rising sense of dread. It felt like a test she was doomed to fail.

Nadia closed her eyes and reached randomly into her closet, pulling out a navy-blue pantsuit. She rolled her eyes. Great, she was ready to have a do-over of her interview with Ashley. She sighed and tried again.

———

Nadia watched a server wearing a tux carry a tray of food to a nearby table. Each table was adorned with immaculate white tablecloths, and there were too many flatware options to know which one to start with. Classical music played softly through the overhead speakers.

She picked up her phone and texted,

I am here.

The reply was instant:

Running late. Sorry! Be there in 10.

She slammed her phone down on the table. *Late and apologizing.* A combination she still deeply detested in a person. Why did she keep tolerating it in Ashley?

"You know, I always wondered how angry you were when I was late for our first date," Ashley said, appearing out of nowhere. "That bad, huh?"

Nadia's irritation instantly dissolved at her appearance. "It wasn't a date," she pointed.

"But this is."

Instead of replying, Nadia examined Ashley thoroughly, her eyes moving slowly from Ashley's face down to her legs and back up again. She was stunning. Perfectly tousled layers of long blonde hair fell freely on her almost-naked shoulders, and her dark green dress clung to every curve, testing Nadia's control to reach out and run her fingers against it. The grace Ashley carried herself with made her sexy high heels appear almost comfortable. It all worked in harmony to enhance what she undoubtedly hid under the layers.

Nadia smiled, happily conceding. "Yes, this is a date."

Ashley sat across from her. "You look beautiful."

Nadia blushed under Ashley's lingering gaze, partly because of the embarrassing amount of time she had spent choosing the shirt and slacks she was wearing. Uncomfortable with her uncharacteristic shyness, Nadia did what she did best—she rolled her eyes and scoffed. "And you, of course, look gorgeous as always. Are we done with the compliments portion of this event? What's next? Do we exchange tips on how to best apply eye shadow?"

Ashley chuckled. "You're really bad at this."

"There's a reason I don't want to go on dates."

"You never went on dates? Not even with Evgeni?"

"No." Nadia looked down. Hearing Ashley say his name was like a punch to the gut.

"It's okay," Ashley added kindly. "I said I wanted to get to know you better, and I meant it. You don't have to pretend that your life with him never happened."

Nadia's chest tightened. She hated talking about her failures and showing her imperfect side. But she knew that was not why Ashley had asked and forced herself to open up. She met her eyes and nodded. "We had one dinner date when we first met. He ended up sleeping with the waitress. Whenever he attempted to bring up going on a date after that, I'd remind him. After a while, he stopped asking."

Ashley chuckled, shaking her head. "Weirdly, that story is so you."

Nadia relaxed a little and leaned back in her chair.

"Let's try something else. What do you think of the restaurant?"

Nadia opened her mouth to tell her exactly what she thought about a place that didn't list prices on the menu, because they were likely to give the customers a heart attack but Ashley held up her hand. "Before you answer that, I want you to consider a few things."

"Like what?"

"Like the thought I put into choosing this place and the fact that it's our first official date. Also consider that, despite a hectic day at work, I still found the time to go home to get ready."

Today had been Ashley's clinic day, and in addition to seeing outpatients, two urgent CABG cases had popped up on her schedule. She was still running between the OR and the clinic when Nadia left the hospital.

"So you want me to be nice rather than honest?" Nadia asked.

Ashley covered Nadia's hand with hers. "The two don't have to be mutually exclusive."

Easier said than done. Being nice didn't fix things. Telling people what they did wrong did. Nadia bit back the retort and took a deep breath. "It's a very clean place." She could think of nothing else to say that would meet both requirements.

Ashley burst out laughing.

"But," Nadia continued, "I need to point out that I hate seafood."

Ashley stopped laughing and the stunned expression on her face was worth losing the we-already-know-each-other argument. "Why didn't you say something?"

Nadia shrugged. "You were so excited when you suggested the place. And I knew you put a lot of thought into where we should go. I didn't want to ruin it for you." She sipped from her water glass. "Anyway, they always have a chicken option for people who get dragged here against their will."

Ashley glanced around, then added, "I'm actually not a big fan of seafood either."

"Then why did you choose this place?" Nadia glared in shocked confusion.

"I don't know. This is one of the best places in town. I guess I wanted to impress you."

Nadia took Ashley's fidgeting hand and squeezed it gently. "That's adorable but unnecessary. I'm beyond impressed already. All you really have to do is be yourself."

The shy smile Ashley gave charged Nadia's entire body with need to reassure her with more than just words. She continued to hold Ashley's hand.

"Besides," Nadia added, "I'm a low-maintenance woman."

Ashley burst out laughing again. Nadia slapped her hand lightly, feigning disapproval.

The server appeared at the table and asked if they were ready to order.

Without looking at the untouched menus, Nadia declared, "We'll both have the chicken option."

———

Ashley and Nadia spent a good part of their date going over the seventeen rules Nadia had prepared. Apparently, gifts were absolutely forbidden, and even though Ashley had asked her out, she somehow lost the argument about who would pay for dinner.

Ashley wasn't sure why she was surprised. Categorizing and quantifying everything was part of Nadia's DNA. So she simply relaxed into her chair and chuckled at Nadia's opinion about the appropriate length of time before contacting someone after a first date. The fact that they would see each other at work tomorrow was moot.

But when it came to personal interests, the conversation quickly derailed. Ashley tried listing typical activities that people did together. "Hiking?"

"It's a waste of time rather than calories."

"Yoga?"

"Stretching is the warm-up, not the actual exercise. People should stop pretending otherwise."

"Cooking?"

"More wasted time."

"Reading?"

"I thought the point was to find something we can do together. Should we take turns reading out loud?"

Ashley was stumped.

"Look," Nadia said, touching Ashley's hand again, "stop worrying about what we will or won't do together. I already know you, and this won't be a problem."

Ashley bit her lip. "But that isn't true. Outside the hospital, we don't know each other at all."

"I disagree." After a pause, she sighed as if she were forced to reveal a dark secret. "You use Biogel PI gloves because you have a mild latex allergy, and you prefer blue undergloves instead of green ones for no other reason but that blue is your favorite color. You always enter the OR before the patient is sedated to reassure them, and you make scalpel incisions before using the Bovie to minimize the scarring. You hold—"

"My favorite color was a lucky guess. The rest is all work-related stuff." Ashley looked down. She understood why these things mattered to Nadia because they mattered to her too. Still, she couldn't help but wish Nadia cared at least a little bit about the personal details of her life. "You're an observant assistant. That's hardly a romantic declaration."

Nadia frowned. "First of all, there's no need to insult me. Medical students are assistants. I'm an assistant surgeon."

Despite her disappointment, Ashley couldn't help but laugh at Nadia's distinction.

"And second of all, I *do* know you."

"But you don't." Ashley shifted in her seat. "What's my favorite movie?"

"How is that relevant to anything?"

Ashley opened her mouth to explain how this showed how little they knew about each other when Nadia held up her hand.

"Fine. You like people to believe it's *Little Women* because you think it makes you sound sophisticated, but I'd say it's *Professor Marston and the Wonder Women* because of the way you talk about it." Nadia smiled knowingly. "It's a lot steamier, too."

Ashley smiled back. "I'll never admit to it."

"And I bet your favorite book is *Cutting for Stone* because you like to ask every new medical student, intern, or resident what a Schrock shunt is."

"Fine, I get it. I talk a lot in the operating room."

"No"—Nadia squeezed Ashley's hand again—"I've just paid attention to you longer than I care to admit."

Having Nadia openly hold her hand and express her affection made Ashley's spirit rise immediately. But then the words set in. Ashley looked at her empty plate. "I don't know any of these things about you."

Nadia waved for the server to come over. "We're ready for dessert. We'll share the chocolate soufflé."

"It takes forty minutes to make."

Nadia smiled, looking at Ashley. "That should be enough time for me to explain why *The Magic Mountain* by Thomas Mann is the greatest book ever written."

The server left to fill their order.

"You know, Mann got a Nobel Prize in Literature," Nadia said, not taking her eyes off Ashley.

"Of course, you'd know that about him. And your favorite movie?" Ashley held her hand up. "Don't tell me. It's *Something the Lord Made* where Alan Rickman plays the cardiac surgeon. Or *Malice* because Alec Baldwin, as the trauma surgeon, says that when patients pray to God, they're really praying to him."

Nadia laughed. "Both good guesses. It's *Quills*."

Ashley shook her head slightly. The movie didn't sound familiar, but somehow she doubted that it was about feather pens.

"It's about the Marquis de Sade."

"The guy who popularized sadism?" Ashley chuckled. Yes, that made sense.

Nadia smiled. "It stars Kate Winslet."

Ashley rested her chin on her hand. "I'm listening."

By the time Ashley realized she had a throw pillow crisis on her hands, it was almost noon. Nadia would be here any minute.

Ashley paced back and forth. A proper sofa arrangement paired a base pillow with a smaller accent pillow with an extra interest pillow in the center to keep everything from looking too balanced. She was a pillow short, and there wasn't time to run to the store. She dropped onto the sofa with a sigh.

Their first date had ended unremarkably with a quick kiss outside the restaurant. Nadia had kept her distance throughout the week too.

Ashley appreciated Nadia giving her space and time to learn to trust her again, but it would have been nice if Nadia showed less…restraint. Patience was a virtue no surgeon typically possessed. For many, instant gratification was what attracted them to the field in the first place. Regardless of the outcome, surgery provided immediate answers.

But Nadia was displaying a patience unusual for any surgeon. Despite her active pillow crisis, Ashley smiled. Nadia was giving her the space she needed. The issue was that every time Ashley saw her, she wanted to satisfy her own inner surgeon's need for instant gratification.

The doorbell rang, effectively terminating Ashley's musings. She jumped up and quickly reshuffled the pillows, then hurried to answer the door.

Nadia stood behind a bouquet of red and white roses, looking stunning in a pair of black jeans and a loose-fit V-neck shirt.

"I thought no gifts was on your extensive list of dating rules," Ashley teased.

"I said I don't want any gifts. I never said I wouldn't give you any." A perfectly serious expression was firmly fixed on Nadia's face. "Besides, they'll die in seven to ten days. Or sooner if you don't cut the stems, use the flower food packet, and change the water every few days." She paused. "Come to think of it, I've created more work for you. Sorry." Stepping closer she held the bouquet to Ashley and smiled. "I just couldn't help myself. I've never gotten flowers for anyone before."

Ashley accepted the roses, breathing in the sweet scent. "Thank you…I think." She held the door open and stepped aside. "Come in."

Ashley found a vase and placed the flowers on the counter, her gaze lingering. She counted five white and six red roses. Nadia must have asked Pari about her taste in flowers, or it was a lucky guess. With a relaxed smile, she returned to the living room to find Nadia pacing.

"So,"—Nadia quirked an eyebrow—"do I get a tour of the place?"

Ashley showed her around, critically appraising her apartment with new eyes. She hadn't obsessed nearly enough about the pillows in the other rooms.

But Nadia didn't show a reaction about the pillows or anything else. It was what Ashley had come to expect from her, and the predictability eased her nerves a little. At least until they reached Ashley's home office. Ashley gulped as Nadia stroked the surface of the desk and looked at Ashley with a barely suppressed smirk. "Sturdy."

The simple word made Ashley's knees wobble. "We don't have to do this." Heat rose in her cheeks.

Nadia leaned against the desk, not taking her eyes off Ashley. "You said your plans for the day were to make bread. And I want to spend my day off with you"—she sighed theatrically—"no matter how impractical the activity might be."

"Can you ever say anything that is just nice?"

"I'm working on it." Nadia pushed herself off the desk and reached for Ashley's hand as they went back to the kitchen. "Have you already made the leaven for the dough?"

Ashley blinked. She wasn't surprised that Nadia considered baking to be a waste of time, but she hadn't expected her to actually know the steps to make sourdough bread.

"What? You thought just because I hate baking I can't do it? Please. I researched the topic *extensively*."

"Of course you did." Ashley laughed. "And yes, I made a starter three weeks ago and activated it yesterday. Today is the bulk fermentation, and tomorrow I'll bake it."

"Mm. You do realize it will take longer to make this bread than it took me to build a human heart, don't you?"

"It's not the same!"

"I agree," Nadia replied. "Mine wasn't wasted time."

Ashley shook her head, laughing. "You're impossible." She leaned in and kissed Nadia.

After a moment, Nadia pulled back and looked at her. "Did you use commercial yeast for the starter?"

"No." The moment passed, Ashley turned and pulled out flour, a scale, and a large bowl.

"Good. Commercial yeast overpowers the lactic acid bacterial fermentation, and the bread will lack in flavor, bioavailability, and bioactivity. That's because the creation of short-chain fatty acids are lost—"

"I said I didn't use commercial yeast." Ashley measured the water and flour, cutting short the biology lecture.

Nadia raised an eyebrow. "Tap water?"

Ashley groaned. "This isn't the first time I've made sourdough bread. I know better than to kill the bacteria with chlorinated water."

The comment didn't stop Nadia's inquisition. In fact, it didn't even slow it down. "It feels cold. You know, some bakers say the temperature should be treated as an ingredient—"

It appeared that baking with Nadia was much the same as operating with her, except Nadia had even less restraint in Ashley's kitchen than she did in the OR.

"This is supposed to be a relaxing activity," Ashley said tensely.

"And?"

"I'm very much the opposite of relaxed."

Nadia's attempt to look innocent broke as she smirked. "So you don't like it when people assume you don't know what you're doing?"

Then it clicked that Nadia was micromanaging on purpose to show how Ashley treated her in the OR. "I do ask a lot of questions, huh?"

"As the attending, it's your right to ask questions." Nadia brushed a strand of hair from Ashley's face and her fingers lingered. "Still, it would be nice if you gave me the benefit of the doubt from time to time. I sometimes know what I'm doing. And outside of work, I'm your equal."

"Well, then"—Ashley set down the flour sifter and held up her hands—"since you've done all this research, you should take over and impress me with your skills."

Several hours later—time spent talking about their childhoods, their journeys through medical school, and their residency experiences—two loaves of doughs were neatly wrapped and left to proof in the refrigerator overnight. They then ordered Thai food and sat down with a bottle of white wine to wait.

"You never told me what you think of my apartment."

Nadia took a sip from her white wine and made a show of examining the large sofa they were sitting on. She ran her hand suggestively across the sofa fabric. "Soft and big. Plenty of room for activities other than sitting."

She spoke in a low, breathy voice, and desire surged through Ashley. She leaned in and kissed Nadia, breathing in the scent of her hair. Savoring her lips against hers, Ashley's lungs began burning for oxygen, but her body starved for more. More contact, more friction, more Nadia. Ashley grabbed Nadia's hand and guided it to her breast.

Nadia broke away. "I have to go actually. I have to be at work early tomorrow."

Breathless, Ashley stared at her. *What just happened?*

Her chest and throat tensed, and she didn't voice the question. Instead, she muttered dubiously, "Sure."

Nadia kept her distance during their utterly awkward goodbye, and Ashley forced herself to emulate the same dispassionate appearance.

Only once she was alone in her apartment, she dropped back on the sofa, a single question trapping her mind. *What if it's a phase?* Nadia had told her that she had never been with a woman before Ashley. What if she decided this wasn't what she wanted?

Her thoughts raced until the doorbell made her jump. It took her a minute to remember she had ordered Thai food. Ashley answered the door, her stomach lurching. The food had arrived, but her appetite had left along with Nadia.

Chapter 25

The Marshmallow Experiment

Nadia glanced at Ashley again as Jason's presentation on the last consult for the morning droned on.

Normally she would be amused listening to Jason try to convince them that a patient who wouldn't tolerate any interventions was a surgical candidate, but right now, she was worried about why Ashley was so distant lately.

She shifted her weight. She had tried not to screw up things between them, but it seemed she had done just that. Again.

It likely had to do with her abrupt departure from Ashley's apartment a few days ago. But Nadia had promised to take things slow because she knew it was important to Ashley, and she knew by now that she would do anything for her.

But that promise didn't keep Nadia's body from pulsing with need every time they were close to each other. Nadia looked away from the group, heat at the memory of their last kiss rising in her cheeks.

To distract herself, she thought of the Stanford psychologist, Walter Mischel. In the late sixties, he conducted an experiment with preschool children. Each child was given one marshmallow and the option to eat it right away or wait fifteen minutes and be rewarded with an additional marshmallow. Then they were left alone with the tempting candy on a plate and nothing else to distract them. Some children waited; others didn't. When he followed up with the children's parents years later, he found that the children who had waited scored higher on SAT tests and were considered to be more self-reliant. The message was clear: self-control and the ability to delay gratification predicted greater success in life.

Objectively speaking, Nadia was the most successful person she knew. So self-control should be a walk in the park.

Then she glanced at Ashley and sighed. Theory and practice were two very different things.

"He wants a pericardiectomy as soon as possible," Jason concluded.

"Did the patient tell you that?" Ashley frowned. "Didn't you say he was delirious during the exam?"

Nadia pressed her lips together hard to keep from smiling. Ashley looked cute when she was confused.

"Well, yes," Jason said. "But he did express a strong desire to—"

"He also expressed a desire to marry a Martian. Shall we comply with that request as well?" Nadia's voice broke through. This meeting was taking too long. "He's internal medicine's problem. We drain the fluid. If it reaccumulates, we drain it again. Surgery isn't an option because of his advanced liver failure. He'll die on the table if we try to operate." Nadia paused, seeing stunned expressions all around her. Unfazed, she gave back a look that dared them to disagree. "We're done rounding."

Everyone looked at Ashley, who muttered her agreement and dismissed the fellows from the rounds. Then she pivoted on her heels, hurrying away from Nadia.

Nadia chased after her. "Dr. Rylan, can we talk?"

"What is it?" Ashley asked as they ducked into a nearby empty patient room.

"You've been avoiding me. Why?"

"I thought...at my place...I thought you wanted to...but then you left."

Nadia chuckled at Ashley's lack of vocabulary. When she didn't join in and her frown deepened, Nadia sighed. "Let me be clear." She met Ashley's eyes. "I want you. If we did this my way, we wouldn't be having idle talks and food preps. I already know you. But that's why I know the complete experience is important to you. You want the overpriced food, the dying flowers, the personality trivia." Nadia stroked Ashley's cheek, adding softly, "And I want to give you that experience and much more."

Ashley swallowed. "You're not having second thoughts? This isn't…a phase for you?"

"You think my attraction to you is temporary?" Surely, a blind person could see how much Ashley meant to her. "It's not."

Ashley appeared unconvinced as she chewed on her lip, avoiding Nadia's eyes.

Nadia exhaled heavily. It would seem women were a lot of work. "This isn't some teenage fling for me. Stop projecting your past experience onto us. I chose you." She dropped her hand and gaze to Ashley's shirt, lightly tugging at the edge. "Besides, if it was temporary, I wouldn't be summoning all my willpower just to stop myself from tearing your clothes off right now." She stepped closer, eliciting a soft gasp from Ashley. Yes, doing this here and now was inappropriate and rash. And the boldness of it was worthy of a gasp. Nadia's body quivered with the familiar need uniquely reserved for Ashley. "How about a kiss for now?" *Self-control be damned.*

Nadia leaned in, capturing Ashley's mouth with hers and interrupting her enthusiastic nod. Ashley grabbed handfuls of Nadia's scrubs, pulling her hard against her. Immediately, Nadia moaned, the sweet taste of Ashley numbing her inhibitions. It was insane to think, even for a second, that Nadia wouldn't want to spend the rest of eternity exactly where she was.

After a moment longer indulging in her indiscretion, Nadia tapped into her depleting power reserves to pull away. Ignoring the tormenting rush of arousal that surged through her, she glanced around to confirm they were still alone. "You're not working this weekend, right?"

Ashley nodded.

"I believe it's my turn to take you out. Besides, I'm afraid you'd want to go horseback riding or walking on the beach, if I left it up to you." She frowned. "Or worse—horseback riding on the beach."

Ashley rolled her eyes. "You know, you have a talent for making good things sound horrible." She smirked. "But I look forward to finding out what qualifies as a reasonable date for you. What time shall we meet?"

"Seven in the morning."

"You want us to meet that early on our day off?"

"Yes." Nadia had been picturing another date with Ashley ever since they had left that overpriced restaurant Ashley had taken her to. "Also wear something sporty."

Ashley's brows drew together. "Are we going to the gym?"

"Maybe"—Nadia lowered her voice—"or maybe I just want to see you in leggings." Immediately, Ashley's pale cheeks flushed and Nadia chuckled. Making Ashley blush was turning into one of her favorite things to do.

"In the meantime," Nadia stroked her cheek lightly, "I'm happy to continue dissecting our feelings over lunch today."

"I have a conference call at one," Ashley said apologetically.

"Since I'm on your service today, why don't I speed things up a little in the OR so we have time for lunch?"

Ashley smiled. "That sounds nice." She glanced at Nadia's hand. "How's your cut?"

In the operating room, Nadia had been covering her hand injury with Tegaderm, and her dexterity hadn't suffered one bit. Still, the fact that Ashley remembered to ask her about it made her heart skip a happy beat. She slowly raised her hand and wiggled her fingers. "My hand is fully functional." She winked.

Once again, Ashley's cheeks flamed as she shook her head adamantly. "That's not...why I asked."

Nadia nodded with a mocking seriousness. "Of course not."

They both looked up at the sound of approaching footsteps, a reminder of where they were. Nadia held her breath until the footsteps faded, then cleared her throat. "Also, I know it's a redo CABG, but I'm confident it can be done off-pump. It will be so much faster."

This time, considerably less shyly, Ashley crossed her arms and bore her eyes into Nadia.

"Fine," Nadia conceded. "It's your case; we'll do it your way." She smiled, appreciating Ashley's ability to stand her ground. Besides, Ashley might have won this round, but Nadia wasn't going to let her have the last word. "While you're waiting for the patient to roll in, look up Mischel's study on delayed gratification. We're discussing it at lunch."

Ashley's eyes narrowed. "Was that the marshmallow experiment?"

Nadia sat on an old wooden bench at the trailhead, breathing in the chilly morning air. It carried the distinct scent of the fresh grass and green trees that surrounded her. She breathed in deeply, exhaled, and watched a faint vapor of condensed water escape her mouth and dissolve in front of her. She caught sight of Ashley approaching from the parking lot and immediately smiled.

Ashley's workout outfit consisted of black leggings and a light gray hoodie made of the same slimming material. Nadia made a point of staring as Ashley walked to her. Just as with the green dress she had worn in the restaurant, Nadia fought the urge to reach out and touch Ashley. The visual feast would have to be enough.

Her eyes dropped to the pristinely clean white running shoes that completed an outfit that could grace the pages of a sports fashion magazine. "Did you buy these today?" Nadia teased.

"No." Ashley sniffed. "It was yesterday."

Nadia laughed, then indicated the path. "Shall we?"

They started off walking, surrounded by tall trees and unseen chirping birds. The paved road turned into dirt, and Nadia began hearing ocean waves crashing in the distance. Even though the trail was mostly deserted, Nadia stayed close to Ashley, their shoulders occasionally brushing. It was an overwhelming brand of serenity that made her want to walk next to Ashley for eternity.

Nadia did a few stretches and jumps to warm up and try to get back on track. Her body and mind were too relaxed to exercise. "The trail is a three-mile loop, supposed to be the most scenic in the area. It should make for a nice run."

"You don't run here usually?"

"No, I prefer a treadmill. But you mentioned an interest in hiking, so I thought we might compromise. Today is all about doing mundane, everyday things together."

Ashley looked at the trail anxiously. "Uh, I don't usually run."

Nadia snorted, glancing at the brand-new Nikes. "You could have fooled me." She touched Ashley's shoulder. "Come on. We'll take it slow. You can set the pace."

Ashley blushed, looking away.

"And we'll only do one round this time."

Nadia started jogging. Ashley hesitated briefly, then quickly caught up.

Every time Nadia glanced at Ashley, it disrupted her breathing, but she couldn't help herself. The view to the right was considerably better than the surrounding scenery.

The smell of saltwater grew stronger, and soon the forest to their left disappeared, replaced by blue sky and ocean that merged over the horizon. When they got to the beach, Ashley dropped gracelessly onto the sand, sucking in air.

"You shouldn't sit immediately after a run," Nadia commented, then turned to survey the scene. "The online reviews weren't exaggerating. The view is stunning."

"I wouldn't know," Ashley gasped.

Nadia laughed. "You did great for your first time."

"What's next? Skydiving?"

The dread in her eyes made Nadia wish she'd planned that. "Not today. I promised you a mundane weekend. Besides, I have to stop at the lab. I need to check on a perfusion experiment my staff is running today. We can go to your place first to change and get breakfast."

Ashley nodded, still gasping, and seemingly too out of breath to voice any objections.

Ashley had left Nadia alone to focus on her work for a few hours, but she found it impossible to stay away any longer.

As she entered the lab Nadia greeted her with a smile. "Did you miss me?"

Wide-eyed, Ashley glanced at Sarah, who was working on a computer next to Nadia. She tilted her head toward the student.

"Time for lunch." Nadia pretty much barked the order.

Sarah jumped in her seat. "It's okay, Dr. Keating. I don't eat lunch."

"In that case, go to the library and prepare a presentation on the evolution of membrane oxygenators. Now."

Guilt stirred in Ashley as Sarah hurried out of the lab. "Please don't give the poor girl a heart attack on my account." She wasn't sure *she* could deliver the requested lecture at an hour's notice, let alone the timid student.

"Don't worry. I don't really intend to listen her stumble through a talk she isn't prepared for. I'll share this news with her in about fifty-five minutes."

Ashley laughed. "You're such a jerk."

"Hm." Nadia's lips quirked in amusement. "Anyway, she wouldn't say anything. But I'll try to be more discreet next time. I just seem to lose my good sense around you."

Her intense brown eyes stirred all kinds of butterflies in Ashley's stomach. It would be easy to ignore her sense of propriety, close the distance between them and do much more than kiss Nadia. She shook the thought away. They needed to exercise caution and restraint in the workplace.

Ashley cleared her throat. "So where do you want to go for lunch?"

"I just ordered some Italian food. It's in the break room."

Ashley gulped. Alone time with Nadia in a tight space was sure to test her resolve to stay appropriate in the hospital.

"I heard you found a new place," Ashley said when they settled next to each other on the small couch.

"Why do we even need to talk when Singh tells you everything that's going on in my life?"

Ashley continued, undeterred. "She also told me it is—and I quote—a really shitty place. There's no kitchen, and the bedroom is the size of a shoebox."

Nadia stabbed a piece of ravioli with her fork. "A big tragedy, I know. All my culinary expertise will go to waste."

"Nadezhda, I'm serious. You should have told me."

"So you'd feel bad even though none of this is your fault?" Nadia met Ashley's eyes, and the intensity in them was far from the sexy kind. "No. It's fine. It doesn't matter. I spend most of my time here anyway. Let's talk about something else."

Ashley knew that Nadia's living situation wasn't her problem, but it gnawed at her all the same. Despite her recent success, Nadia still lived on a fellow's salary, and Ashley remembered how limiting that had been. Pushing the feeling down, she told herself that Nadia was a grown woman who didn't need a knight in shining armor to take care of her.

"Tell me something I don't know about you."

Nadia rolled her eyes. "This nonsense again?"

"We can always go back to talking about your studio."

"I've been sharing a lot lately." A smile replaced her grimace. "Why don't you tell me something about you?"

"Hm, let's see…" Ashley tapped her chin. "You were the first person I talked to on that dating website"—she licked her lips—"and you are the only person I've ever agreed to have sex with without getting to know first."

Nadia stroked Ashley's hand lightly. The contact was like an electric current that set her nerves tingling. "That's sweet," she said softly, "but those are hardly secrets."

"Hey!" Ashley slapped her hand playfully as Nadia laughed openly at her reaction.

The door opened, making Ashley jump, and she realized too late that she and Nadia were sitting quite close.

"Sorry… I thought you'd be alone," Dan stammered.

"What is it?" Nadia asked, her lips held in a thin line.

"It's not urgent. I'm sorry to interrupt." He hurried out of the room, flinging the door behind him shut.

Ashley sighed. "Here's a secret for you: a month ago, he asked me out."

"I knew that too," Nadia said, getting up. "I'll be right back."

Motivated by a burning need to set something right for once, Nadia caught up with Dan as he waited for the elevator. She met his eyes. "I'm sorry."

"What for?"

"Fine," Nadia said. "I'm not sorry. I wouldn't do anything differently as far as you're concerned. But if you care for Rylan as much as you say you do, you wouldn't torture her like this."

Dan frowned. "How am I torturing her, exactly?"

"You know—with your puppy-dog eyes and the pouting."

"Your pep talk sucks."

Nadia smirked. "I've been told that before."

"You're right though." He closed his eyes and gave a deep sigh before opening them again. "She shouldn't feel miserable just because I do."

"It's true," Nadia agreed. "I'm always right."

Dan shook his head. "And always so full of it." The elevator arrived and Dan stepped in, holding the doors open. "I came to tell you that we're discharging Sanders, if you want to say goodbye."

Nadia quirked an eyebrow. "Do you know who loves this type of emotional display?"

Dan rolled his eyes. "If I had known Ashley was here today, I'd have told her."

"I'll tell her to meet us there." Nadia pulled out her phone, but then paused and eyed him. "And it's Dr. Rylan."

When Ashley joined them at the telemetry floor, Nadia said, "Dan has something he'd like to say to you."

He looked at Ashley with that lovesick look he usually got around her, and Nadia felt a familiar sense of jealousy course through her. She ignored it. This wasn't about her.

"I'm sorry for making things awkward between us," Dan muttered.

Nadia cleared her throat.

"Dr. Rylan," he added.

"Great," Nadia said. "One awkward emotional situation down. Let's go to the patient's room for another."

Nadia charged ahead, ignoring their stunned expressions.

She didn't understand why everyone made such a big fuss about Sanders leaving. He would be back in a week for a follow-up appointment. In fact, there were a series of appointments ahead of him to see how the heart would do long-term. Her steps faltered when she thought about the long road ahead for Sanders and his new heart, but she quickly picked up her pace again. She needed to maintain healthy detachment instead of connecting with patients. Levelheadedness was what saved lives.

"There she is!"

Singh, Sanders, his wife, his children, and a few other people Nadia didn't recognize applauded. She smiled uncertainly. Mrs. Sanders charged forward to hug her, but Nadia managed to step aside in time to avoid her. She swiftly pointed to the surgeons who had walked in behind her. "You remember Dr. Rylan and Dr. Meyers? They did the bedside operation that saved your husband's life."

"Yes, of course. Thank you so much, doctors!" The woman hugged them each in turn, then lunged toward Nadia. "Don't think I've forgotten you, Dr. Keating. You get a hug too!"

Well, at least Nadia had tried to avoid it. She stood still, waiting to regain her personal space and trying her best not to flinch.

"Ready to get out of here?" Ashley asked Sanders.

"Never felt readier. The view from my home window is considerably better than this one. No offense."

Ashley smiled. "None taken."

After everyone had shaken everyone else's hand, the staff accompanied the family to a side exit to avoid any media reporters and said their final goodbyes. Nadia let out a sigh of relief as the weight of balancing politeness and suitable distance lifted off her shoulders. At last she found herself alone with Ashley again.

"That was exciting." Ashley grinned. "What's next on your date itinerary?"

Nadia glanced around to make sure that the hallway was empty. She stepped forward and looked into Ashley's brilliant eyes, her heart rate speeding up. "Next, I ask you if I might come over to your place tonight. And just to be very clear—there will be no baking involved."

"Does that mean I've waited my fifteen minutes and I can eat the marshmallow now?"

With a different meaning in mind, Nadia raised her brows.

Ashley immediately turned crimson. She closed her eyes. "That's, uh, that's not what I meant."

Nadia fought the laughter rising in her chest. "I'm going to do you a favor and give you one more chance to answer my question."

Ashley groaned and covered her face with her hand. "Yes. Please come over."

Nadia touched Ashley's hand, already missing the sight of her pretty face. "I know I promised you a mundane day, but I can't promise you a mundane night."

Ashley continued to blush.

Nadia stepped back. As delicious as toying with Ashley was, they shouldn't act so familiar at work. "I'll come by at seven, Dr. Rylan."

"Uh, Nadezhda?"

Nadia paused in mid-pivot.

"You should really call me Ashley."

The thought of voicing out the name awakened an entire swarm of butterflies in Nadia's stomach. But after Ashley's repeated insistence for Nadia to say her name, saying it in the middle of the hallway felt anticlimactic. She would have to prolong this sweet torture just a little while longer. For Ashley's sake, of course. She smiled deviously and said, "I'll think about it."

Chapter 26

Beauty is in Symmetry

When Ashley left the hospital, a mixture of anticipation and anxiety began coursing through her. Why was she so apprehensive about Nadia coming over? They'd had sex before.

But that time was different. For one thing, it had been impulsive. She hadn't had the time to think about what could happen and what it might mean.

Which was all she could think about ever since she had arrived home. After scanning her living room, she went to her bedroom for the third time tonight and began nervously fluffing pillows and smoothing the covers on the bed.

The first time had been so life-altering for Nadia that she had eventually broken things off with her long-term boyfriend. But that encounter was out of character for Ashley. She wasn't usually so...dominant. She had been fueled by anger, but could she deliver such a performance if she wasn't angry?

Was Nadia expecting a similar performance?

The ringing of the doorbell pulled her out of her thoughts. On her way to answer the door, she glanced at the throw pillows on her sofa. She shook her head. Now was not the time to worry about interior design.

———— •••• ————

"You're here!" Ashley's voice came out as a nervous squeak.

Nadia stepped in with a smile that poorly masked her own nerves.

Ashley seemed determined to play the perfect hostess. "Would you like something to drink? I have wine, red and white, beer, whiskey, bourbon—"

"No."

"How about something nonalcoholic? Water? Soda? Tea? I'm sure I have—"

"Stop." Nadia placed her hands on Ashley's shoulders. "Why are you so nervous?" Knowing she had that effect on Ashley did bring her a certain degree of satisfaction.

"I don't want to say the wrong thing. I don't want to chase you off."

"I've made it clear that I'm here to stay. But if you need verbal reassurance, I promise not to leave unless you ask me to." Nadia moved mere inches from her. She softened her voice. "Would you relax now?"

The apprehensive expression on Ashley's face deepened. "I don't think I'll ever be able to relax around you."

Nadia leaned in, lightly brushing her lips against Ashley's. She pressed in, meeting her lips again and deepening the kiss. She sucked on Ashley's bottom lip, savoring the sweet sensation. It wasn't the novelty that excited her, for the thrill of the new was gone. It was that sense of the familiar that compelled her to crave the impractical urge to want to kiss Ashley forever.

Eventually, Nadia withdrew far enough to meet Ashley's eyes. "Better?"

Ashley shook her head.

Nadia chuckled. "Am I that intimidating? Shouldn't it be the other way around?"

Ashley said nothing for a moment, then abruptly straightened up as if she had come to a decision. "Clothes off," she commanded.

The words immediately made Nadia's core throb with need. It was the voice Ashley had used the first time, when Nadia had agreed to let her be in charge. No, not agreed—*challenged.* She hadn't thought Ashley had it in her. As so often occurred lately, she'd been wrong to assume Ashley lacked leadership skills.

But this time, Nadia had something else in mind, and it made her entire body quiver with excitement.

She pushed Ashley to the nearest wall and pinned her there. "I love your bossy side. I *really* do. But it will have to wait. I have an injustice to address first."

"Oh?"

Nadia leaned in closer, schooling her features into neutrality. "The last time we had sex, I distinctly recall being the only one without any clothes on."

Ashley stared at her for a moment then burst out laughing. "Right, as usual, Dr. Keating. A great injustice indeed."

"One I plan to remedy in the next thirty seconds."

With one swift move, Nadia lifted Ashley's top over her head and threw it on the floor. She swallowed hard, feasting her eyes on the black, lacy bra. It contrasted with Ashley's pale breasts that were rising and falling with each breath. Nadia's hands twitched with need. She had to see more.

She stepped closer and reached behind Ashley's back to find her bra clasp and undid it in another swift motion. With her other hand she unbuttoned her pants, then slipped her hand inside, pushing them down around her hips.

"Impressive," Ashley purred.

"It gets a lot more impressive than that."

Ashley pushed Nadia away long enough to step out of her pants and pull off her bra. Nadia's heart pounded as she realized she was only one clothing item away from keeping her promise.

She dropped to one knee and slid Ashley's black bikini down to her ankles. Ashley stepped out of them, then reached for Nadia to raise her back up.

Nadia paused and examined her thoroughly. Ashley looked uneasy. *Why should she?* Her body was exquisite.

As an osteopath, Nadia was trained to look for invisible asymmetries that signaled structural dysfunctions. The muscles in the back alone could alter the spine's curvature, set the shoulders askew, and change the way a person walked.

But Ashley's body took her breath away. She drank in the visual feast. The pale, smooth skin of her breasts contrasted with erect nipples, and Nadia's mouth watered. Her eyes traveled along with the flowing contours of Ashley's magnificent body. Her abdomen was flat and slightly toned. Nadia followed the delicious subtle line that ran in the middle of her abdomen to her navel. Then her gaze went further down to a triangle of neatly trimmed blonde hair between Ashley's legs, and Nadia licked her lips.

Ashley's body was pure femininity. It was a stark difference from any of the features of her former lovers, and yet it was a familiar anatomy. It was a paradox of known and unknown that left her burning with a fire she had never before experienced.

"Uh, Nadezhda, I know this is new to you and all, but do you plan on just staring at me all night long?"

Nadia raised her gaze, meeting Ashley's expressive blue eyes that seemed to promise her the world. She smiled. "I intend on doing a lot more than that."

She stepped closer to Ashley and brushed tentative fingers across her breast, the sensation of the soft flesh and the firm nipple at its peak sending a series of shivers to her core. Tracing her hand motions with her tongue drove her body wild. She licked and sucked Ashley's nipple, throaty moans encouraging her exploration. Addicted to the sounds, Nadia cupped Ashley's other breast, squeezing, kneading, loving it. Loving this…loving *her*.

She reached down, her fingers trailing across a silky smooth skin.

Without warning, Ashley intercepted her hand. "I don't think so. You corrected your injustice, but I have one of my own." Ashley smiled slyly. "I owe you an orgasm."

"Are you keeping score?" Nadia teased. She longed to continue exploring Ashley's anatomy.

"There is no score." Ashley laughed melodically.

Gorgeous. "You sure?"

"Positive. Still"—she pushed herself off the wall, gripped Nadia's shoulders, and swung her around—"nothing would please me more than to see you lose count."

Clearly, Ashley was past her initial uneasiness. "What do you have in mind?" Nadia asked, her body and voice humming with desire to please her.

Ashley smiled. "Strip."

Nadia obeyed without hesitation, dropping her clothes to the floor. The sudden cool air raised goosebumps on her arms, and she moved to press against Ashley, craving her warmth. Before she could do that, Ashley grabbed her hand, pushed her onto the sofa, and leaned in for her own exploration, licking, kissing, gently biting every square inch of her neck.

"You're perfect," Ashley murmured in Nadia's ear.

Nadia moaned as her body responded, her back arching against the sofa. She needed more.

"I've been dreaming about this," Ashley said as she kissed her way down Nadia's neck and across her breasts. She began mapping Nadia's areolas with her lips.

"Yes?"

"Yes."

Ashley's mouth settled on her nipple, and Nadia closed her eyes to gather her fleeting thoughts. "What exactly did you dream about?" she managed to ask between gasps.

"How about I show you rather than tell you?"

She began sucking on Nadia's sensitive nipple hard.

"Yes." Nadia moaned. "Show me." Her body throbbed as she writhed underneath Ashley.

Ever so slowly, Ashley moved her licks and kisses lower and lower, never breaking contact with her skin. It took all of Nadia's self-control to stop herself from groaning in frustration. She needed more.

When Ashley finally made her way between her legs, Nadia held her breath in aching anticipation of what was to come.

But instead of helping her, Ashley began kissing Nadia's inner thighs, alternating from one leg to the other. The unaddressed tension continued to build in Nadia, harsh and desperate, tightly winded and challenging her ability to control her breathing. As Ashley began moving even farther away from where Nadia desperately needed her to be, Nadia threw her head back and gave a guttural groan.

Ashley looked up. "Something wrong?"

Nadia pushed herself up on her elbows. "Do you need a refresher on female anatomy?"

Ashley grinned mischievously. "No, thanks. I aced that test." She continued teasing Nadia, now with feather strokes across her burning flesh.

Nadia bit back another groan. "Then I suggest you apply some of that knowledge in action."

The tips of Ashley's fingers grazed Nadia's sensitive clitoris for the briefest of moments. She pushed her hips forward in vain, desperate to ease the tension that smoldered like a volcano.

"You seem to be focusing an awful lot on a minor detail." The fake innocence in Ashley's voice didn't mask her amusement. Her fingertips repeated the teasing action.

As the tension inside her continued to coil, Nadia cursed the day she had spoken those words in the skills labs weeks earlier. "Now I understand. You've been dreaming of torturing me."

Ashley chuckled. "It's within your power to change it."

"You want me to ask you nicely for an orgasm?" Nadia challenged, ignoring the fingers that purposefully strayed from the correct destination. The throbbing in her sex assured her she was ready to be nice—just this time.

"Not exactly." Ashley leaned down closer to the very sensitive bundle of nerves between Nadia's legs. She blew on it lightly, sending shockwaves of pleasure up her spine. "I want to hear you ask *me*." Ashley breathed every word slowly and purposefully close to her clitoris, just to tease.

This is what this is about? With a dismissing scoff that more resembled a groan, Nadia pushed herself up on her elbows. "No more teasing, *Ashley*. Please. I need you."

Ashley wasted no time. Her mouth pressed into Nadia's center and Nadia cried out. She threw her head back and shut her eyes tight. She reached for Ashley's head, her fingers lost in her blonde locks and greedily drawing her closer.

When Ashley's fingers moved inside her, Nadia gave up on whatever dignified self-control she wished she possessed and let out a throaty moan. And another one. And another one. With every thrust, curl, and rub, Nadia's pleasure intensified exponentially and pulsed as her muscles tensed and relaxed harder and harder, desperately seeking the release that was so close.

"Come for me," Ashley growled between her legs.

A shuddering explosion immediately overcame Nadia. Her eyes rolled back, her body stiffened, and intense waves of pure bliss spread through every inch of her. The tension was gone, replaced by an indescribable sense of floating and melting at the same time.

Rooted in her spot, Ashley waited for Nadia to catch her breath. Then she resumed licking and kissing Nadia's thighs, softly and slowly at first, from one side of her body to the other. The pressure grew stronger as she returned to the source of Nadia's pleasure. Still recovering her strength, Nadia could do little else but moan her encouragement.

She sure knows how to make full use of a woman's capacity.

Of course, Nadia was familiar with the concept of multiple orgasms. What she hadn't anticipated, though, were the earth-shattering sensations that accompanied the phenomena.

Her body reacted readily, reaching greater heights of pleasure than she thought possible.

Desire, arousal, climax, and resolution. Kaplan's linear model of sexual activity appeared far too simplistic to account for what she was intuitively responding to at these glorious moments. The steps circled back and forth, blended and repeated in an endless loop of pleasure. If Ashley's goal was for Nadia to lose count of how many times she orgasmed, well then, *mission accomplished.*

Nadia arched her back and moaned more loudly than she cared to admit. Losing control wasn't her thing. Or it didn't use to be. Right now, she couldn't care less about it.

Eventually, the stimulation culminated in a final powerful orgasm that left Nadia gasping for air.

Ashley pushed up beside her, draping an arm around her. For a moment, they simply lay together in afterglow until the panting and trembling subsided.

"Best lover ever?"

It took Nadia a moment to register the question as her body and mind were completely liquefied by Ashley's heavenly actions. Then unchecked laughter erupted from her mouth.

"What?"

"You're joking, right? Isn't that the kind of question a man would ask to stroke his ego?"

Ashley furrowed her brow as if in deep thought. "Mm. Nope, I'm pretty sure it's not patented by one gender only." She smiled. "Besides, the female ego needs stroking too."

"Oh, is that so?" Nadia teased.

Ashley nodded.

Putting on her serious face, Nadia said, "Well, if this was a competition, you would be disqualified."

"How come?"

Still fighting valiantly to keep a straight face, Nadia said, "As a woman and a doctor, you are using your better knowledge of the subject to obtain more effective stimuli. It wouldn't be a fair comparison."

Ashley giggled. "What I'm hearing is that I win."

"Then you're not listening," Nadia scolded. "Because what I'm saying is that you should compete against someone equally versed in the matter." Regaining some of her strength, she shifted her weight and hovered over Ashley.

"Oh, and you're an expert now?" Ashley challenged with a goofy open-mouthed smile.

"Not yet." Renewed desire coursed through Nadia's body. "But practice makes perfect."

⸻

Ashley wrapped her arms around Nadia, loving the feel of her weight. Her tongue and lips explored Ashley's breasts, and her knee pressed gently but deliberately between her legs. Instantly, Ashley's senses became dull to everything around her but Nadia.

In that moment, all Ashley could smell, feel, see, and hear was Nadia. She wanted to breathe in her scent, feel her touch on her body, hear her moan whenever they connected.

When Nadia stopped abruptly, it took Ashley a few seconds to realize why. Her phone was ringing, interrupting the moment again. She clenched her jaw, muffling a groan of protest. Why did this keep happening?

"Are you on call?" Nadia asked, scowling.

"No, but when has that stopped anyone?" Bitter coldness replaced the warmth in her chest. It wasn't that she didn't love the job she had trained so hard for, but her colleagues demanding undivided attention 24/7 tested that love.

Ashley bit back the indignation that rose in her. Such was the responsibility of being the chief of cardiothoracic surgery. She reached for the phone, but Nadia grabbed it before she could pick it up.

She checked the screen, then looked at Ashley. "I can make this go away."

Ashley hesitated.

"Just let me handle it. Please...*Ashley*?"

When Nadia said her name, Ashley nodded, surrendering any illusion of control. She might regret it later, but right now, all she wanted to do was to please Nadia.

"Can this wait?" Nadia barked.

Ashley glanced at her, frowning. Did Nadia answer her own phone like that?

In the quiet room, Ashley could make out parts of the conversation. Her face burned hot as she realized Nadia was talking to Dan.

"That simply will not do. I'll call you back in a minute."

Nadia hung up, dialed a number, then winked at Ashley. *Uh-oh*.

"Yes, I'm aware of the time, Dr. Bratton."

On the other end of the line, Ashley heard a string of words and her eyes widened. She was frozen in shock as if ice-cold water had just been dumped over her head. Why had she allowed Nadia to answer her phone? And why was Nadia calling the chair of surgery?

Instead of focusing on the very imminent disaster, Ashley was distracted by Nadia suddenly kneeling between her legs. Her heart jumped in her throat as she looked at Nadia and silently mouthed, "What are you doing?" It was a stupid question. It was quite obvious what Nadia was doing.

Nadia pressed the phone against her bare skin to mute her reply. "Testing a theory," she said in a hushed voice.

Bratton was still talking. Likely lecturing her on her impertinence for calling so late.

"What theory might that be?" Ashley whispered back.

"That given the right stimuli, I can make you forget all about work."

When wandering fingers pressed between her legs, Ashley knew that proving Nadia wrong would be a lost battle. She moaned.

"Hush," Nadia murmured against her thigh. She traced soft kisses where her hand had been. "You have to be really quiet."

The prospect of letting Nadia be in charge sent adrenaline pumping through Ashley's body, tunneling her mind to a single purpose. Nadia's theory was confirmed: Ashley no longer wished to do anything else but sit right where she was.

Nadia withdrew her mouth, ruthlessly chuckling as Ashley suppressed a groan by biting her lip.

Once the phone was back to her ear, she added authoritatively, interrupting Bratton's monologue. "And actually, it's Dr. Keating speaking."

The barrage of words on the other end paused, and Nadia smiled arrogantly. Apparently, Bratton had more respect for Nadia than he did for the chief of the CT surgery department, a realization that would have typically bothered Ashley had she not been so thoroughly distracted right now.

"I understand Dr. Williams has decided not to be on call tonight." Nadia carried on evenly. She held the phone with her right hand so that her left one was free to pick up where her mouth had left off. "I'm sure he has valid reasons as I also understand he is with you right now."

Ah, so that was what Dan had told her. He had probably tried to deal with the situation himself and called Peter directly when he had likely told the staff to contact Ashley instead. Peter's typical behavior, abusing his friendship with the chair, made Ashley roll her eyes in frustration.

"You see, I'm having a meeting of my own with *Dr. Rylan*," Nadia said, stressing the name as her free hand pressed at just the right spot.

Ashley shut her eyes and placed her hand over her mouth in a desperate attempt to keep quiet.

"And she's been working *really* hard to convince me to take a permanent position at your hospital after my training is complete."

Ashley's eyes flung open. Did Nadia just offer herself a job?

Of course, they would be lucky to have Nadia working as an attending. She was now a star doctor, which meant other hospitals would be fighting for her. They might even offer her a better opportunity to finish her fellowship. Ashley shuddered at the thought of Nadia leaving, which temporarily took her mind off her building pleasure.

"But how can I ever consider such an offer here when all I can think about is that, in three years, it would be me covering for the attendings who refuse to take calls when they're supposed to? And if I'm covering all the time, I won't be able to work on the many research projects I have lined up."

The words were delivered with the necessary respect, but the message was clear: *I won't stay if you don't play by my rules.*

Witnessing Nadia's thrilling ability to maintain a calm voice while simultaneously giving professional ultimatums and conducting very personal business drew Ashley's full attention back to those talented fingers that plunged inside her.

Grabbing a nearby pillow, Ashley muffled her primal moans with it.

She vaguely registered an inaudible mutter over the phone, Nadia's triumphant smile, and some insincere pleasantries being exchanged.

When Nadia called Dan again, she sounded only too pleased to inform him that Peter Williams was suddenly available to do his job. A thumb joined Nadia's long fingers, drawing circles against Ashley's clitoris, seriously testing her ability to remain quiet. The steady pressure building inside her exponentially increased, and she panted heavily into the pillow.

"Call me if you run into any trouble with him." She listened for a beat, then grinned widely. "Make that two. At least." Tossing the phone to the side, she looked at Ashley. "Dan assured me no one from work would bother you for the next two hours." She looked at Ashley with those smoldering brown eyes that conquered worlds and rendered Ashley completely at her mercy. "Let's make them count."

"How is it possible you're so good at this?" Ashley asked.

She was stretched out luxuriously on her sofa, Nadia aligned next to her. They were covered in a plush blanket that was as soft as velvet.

"Mm. It seems you inspire me to do more than build hearts." Nadia's smile faded as she added, "I hope I didn't overstep."

"What?"

Nadia caressed strands of blond hair away from the face of Ashley— the woman who had spent the last three hours redefining the meaning of pleasure for her. "The call from Dan earlier?"

"Oh, that! Hm." She pushed herself up to face Nadia. "That was completely unprofessional, Dr. Keating," she scolded half-heartedly.

Nadia bowed her head in an attempt at remorse she wasn't feeling.

"But seriously," Ashley said without humor. "You do know I can fight my own battles, don't you?"

Nadia considered her response. There was a time she would have said no without hesitation. It wasn't that her opinion had changed, but now she felt a need to protect and support Ashley rather than discourage her. Ashley's success meant Nadia's success.

"I know you could have handled it…if handling it meant abandoning me before I had the chance to even the score," Nadia said bluntly. She could always try to be nice next time. "So I assure you, *Dr. Rylan*, my intentions were entirely selfish." She leaned in and softly brushed her lips against Ashley's cheek.

"Did you mean what you told Bratton? Are you considering staying as an attending?"

"I just played the game. He wanted something—me—and I used that as leverage to get what I wanted—you." She stroked lightly the cheek she had just kissed. *Softer than the blanket.* "I don't know where my career will take me, and I refuse to be bound to this hospital forever. And you shouldn't either. But I'm here for the next two years, and after that, we'll make our decisions together."

Ashley's eyes grew big. "You think we'll be together in two years?"

"I plan to be with you for as long as you'll have me," Nadia said. It was a promise she had never made to anyone else because it had never felt right before. But the promise came from her heart. "Does that scare you?"

Ashley looked away.

Nadia gently brought her head back. "I won't go away no matter what you tell me, *Ashley*. Please."

"The last time we… It was different." She blushed. "I was afraid you would be disappointed if it wasn't the same."

Nadia took a deep breath before speaking. "When you took charge—well, it was nice. *Very* nice. I've never let anyone be in control like that before, not with a man, and I don't think I would have with any other woman. But it was you, and I wanted you to. That doesn't mean you have to pretend to be someone else because you think that's what I want. I want the real you, because, Ashley, I love *you*."

She hadn't intended to say that out loud—not yet—and it made her heart pound. She looked to see Ashley's reaction: she was staring at her like a deer in the headlights.

"This shouldn't be news to you," Nadia said, trying to bring her focus back.

"But, Nadezhda, we barely know each other!"

"I don't need more time to know how I feel about you. I *know*. But if you need more time, it's fine. Or you never have to say it. That's fine too. It doesn't matter. It's just a word." Nadia sighed, aware that she was rambling. "Just…don't make this harder than it has to be. We can simply enjoy each other's company. It doesn't have to be more complicated than that. Let's not overanalyze it. It's not surgery; it's just dating."

Ashley smirked. "You've been talking to Pari."

"She gives great relationship advice," Nadia deadpanned. "You should listen to her."

Ashley chuckled, but the forced sound died out quickly. "I'm not ready to say it."

"And I said that's okay." Nadia squeezed Ashley's hand.

While her chest ached with the tiniest bit of hope Ashley would feel the same, she had never expected her to say it back. It was just how she felt right here and right now. Not hearing those three words back didn't change that.

Ashley bit her lip, undoubtedly doing exactly what Nadia had just told her not to do—overanalyze things. "How about if I offer you another relationship step instead?"

"I'm listening."

"My parents are coming to town for a conference next week."

Nadia nodded slowly. Judging by Ashley's upbeat attitude, she probably grew up surrounded by unconditional love and hot cocoa to go with it. "I'm not afraid of meeting your parents." Nadia was proud her voice didn't waver. "What conference?"

"Ob-gyn."

Ashley was closely watching for a reaction, so Nadia did her best not to roll her eyes. In her accurate opinion, ob-gyn doctors were the worst. They had limited training in surgery, yet they naively believed that theirs was a surgical subspecialty.

"It makes sense that your parents are doctors." Nadia opted for the benign, if boring, answer. "You were exposed to medicine early in life, and that's why you're so advanced in it."

"My mom is a gynecologist. My dad is an interventional cardiologist."

This time, Nadia sighed theatrically. "You're not going to make it easy to love you, are you?"

Ashley laughed. "If it helps, they're both big fans of your work."

"Well, then," Nadia said, "perhaps there's still hope for them. Which reminds me…" She stood up and retrieved her backpack, pulling out several typewritten pages stapled together. "I've been keeping this from Singh for a while now. I want you to be the first to read my manuscript. It's only fair, given that you inspired me to do it." She flopped back onto the sofa. "More importantly, I want to make sure you know I can write a proper journal article."

Ashley plucked the pages out of Nadia's hands, plumped up the pillows behind her, and settled in to read. "Do you have—?"

Reading her mind, Nadia handed her a pen. "You do realize this is nothing more than a nice gesture. The paper is perfect as it is. *I* wrote it."

"Oh, but I wouldn't be a good coauthor if I didn't make a few minor tweaks," Ashley teased. She studied the first page. "Are you in love with the title? Because I was thinking of something catchier like *The Dawning of Customized Medicine.*"

Nadia scoffed. "I already regret giving it to you."

She reached out and half-heartedly tugged on the pages, but Ashley just gripped them more tightly. Her brows knitted as she began reading and editing along the way.

Nadia relaxed and watched as Ashley worked next to her. This was the woman who had challenged her to go into transplantation and change the course of medicine. Random chance had led them to meet again, and this time Ashley had challenged her to change her personal life. It was Ashley who appeared in all the important moments of Nadia's life, and Nadia's love for her filled her heart.

Indeed, there is beauty in symmetry.

Chapter 27

The Dawning of Customized Medicine

Five years later

The ring of her cellphone at 2:26 in the morning sounded like a drumbeat in Ashley's head. Rubbing her eyes, she reached toward the nightstand.

Still half-asleep, she pieced together that she was being called in on an emergency case. *No surprise there.* Ashley twisted her mouth into a frown. "Williams is on call today, Casey."

"Peter's repairing an aortic aneurysm," Casey, the nurse manager, said curtly. "He said it would be at least four hours before he could do another case."

Ashley clenched her teeth to muffle an irritated sigh. "What about Singh? Isn't she the backup surgeon?"

"Pari is at a conference promoting bioengineered organs in Las Vegas, remember?"

Ashley might have remembered if the nurse had called at a decent hour.

"Dr. Keating said she'd cover for her," Casey continued, "but she's doing lung transplantation right now."

Like most registered nurses, Casey referred to every other surgeon by their first name. In fact, everyone treated Nadia as a deity, rising above the mere mortals she worked with. Few people knew the wonderful person she was outside the operating room.

"Have the patient in the room, but tell anesthesia not to sedate him. I'll be there in twenty minutes."

Ashley hung up and stretched out to wake up her body. Still in a sleepy daze, she got up, quickly changed, and was about to leave when the phone rang again. Hanging onto those last drops of drowsiness, Ashley wondered why the ringtone sounded muffled. And then she smirked, realizing that the meticulous Nadia Keating must have forgotten her phone when she left for the transplant case.

She found it lodged between the mattress and the bed frame. She glanced at the screen and squinted. It was an unknown foreign number. "Hello?"

"Hello, am I speaking with Dr. Na-dez-da Keating?" The cheery voice with a Swedish accent mangled Nadia's name.

Ashley's eyes widened as comprehension dawned. *Now* she was fully awake. "She's in the middle of surgery right now," she stammered.

"You might want to get her on the phone. This is a very important call. A. Very. Important. Call." He enunciated each word. "From Stockholm."

"I hate waking up alone."

Chills ran down Nadia's spine when Ashley's breath warmed her ear. The words were whispered so quietly that even the nurse next to them wouldn't hear. Despite the distraction, Nadia kept her focus as she continued working on the right pulmonary artery anastomosis with skillful confidence.

"Suction," she ordered the surgical fellow. She closed and de-aired the vessel. "Clamp off." The lung began to pink up, and she smiled under her mask. Keeping her eyes on the surgical field, she asked, "Dr. Rylan, I heard you had an emergency case. What are you doing in *my* operating room? Are you here to observe how I'm pioneering care for this patient?"

"I don't doubt that you are, Dr. Keating," Ashley responded with equal dramatics. "But as you so astutely pointed out, I have my own emergency to take care of. In fact, I'm not here to talk to you at all."

"Oh?"

"Contrary to popular belief, the world does not revolve around one Nadezhda Keating."

Everyone in the room laughed.

With the iciest glare she could muster, Nadia immediately put an end to it. She briefly turned to lock eyes with Ashley, quirking an eyebrow with amusement. If she could silence the room with a single look, perhaps the world should revolve around her.

Ashley chuckled melodically and turned to speak with the circulating nurse. Nadia couldn't make out the hushed words, but she didn't pay attention to them. She had an operation to finish while also teaching Christopher, the junior fellow, how to do the surgery—something he appeared to have no clue about. She also had to keep an eye on the medical student next to Christopher, whose lack of knowledge about basic sterile techniques was a contamination risk she could simply not tolerate in her OR. Nadia took effective teaching seriously, even if she secretly enjoyed intimidating her trainees.

Just as Ashley moved away from the circulating nurse, the student bumped the instrument table, knocking a perfectly good—and quite expensive—stapler onto the ground and making it useless for this procedure.

"Do me a favor, Jessica—"

"Janelle," the girl squeaked.

"Whatever. When the time comes to choose your specialty, don't choose surgery. The world has enough problems as it is."

The room chuckled and the girl looked as if she might start crying. Nadia clicked her tongue with annoyance. That would certainly contaminate the surgical field.

"Be nice, Nadezhda," Ashley said, stepping close behind her again. "She's just learning."

"How about she learns in your OR, then?"

"Come straight to my office after you're done here." Apparently, choosing to ignore Nadia's remark, Ashley whispered instead. "Do not talk to anyone or listen to anything anyone says. Understood?"

Nadia nodded, her heart fluttering. Ashley rarely asked—or rather ordered—her to do anything, but when she did, it usually ended with a lot of sexual gratification for Nadia.

"Excellent," Ashley purred behind her.

She left the room just as Janelle elbowed Christopher. He dropped the cautery on the floor.

Giving a long-suffering sigh, Nadia pondered why she was always assigned the incompetent ones. She would have to take it up with the chief.

As soon as Ashley left, the whispering started. Nadia heard the circulating nurse answer the phone and say, "Dr. Keating is busy at the moment, and she can't take any calls even if they come from the Pope himself."

When Nadia demanded what was going on, everyone pretended there was nothing to tell. Nadia returned to her surgery, deciding curiosity wouldn't take the better of her. If it was that important, she would find out eventually.

Once the case was over and the patient was stable, she hurried to Ashley's office. The sunlight gave the dull hallways she crossed a deceptively fresh appearance. It was already morning, and although Nadia had been awake for hours, she didn't feel tired. Time had no meaning in the OR, and at the end of every case, her sense of accomplishment won out over her exhaustion.

Unfortunately, with the sun came the people.

Nadia walked past colleagues just arriving to work, replaying Ashley's appearance in the OR. Now that the case was over, she had time to wonder why Ashley had whispered orders in her ear.

A general surgeon whose name she couldn't remember grinned widely as he walked toward her. "Congratulations!"

Nadia nodded, then frowned after she passed him. He was the third person who had said something like that this morning. Normally she would have stopped to ask what was going on, but Ashley's instructions were clear.

Nadia entered Ashley's office, locking the door behind her. "You know better than to come to my OR and order me around. You broke a rule, and I'll have to do something about it."

Ashley's chair spun around, but it was Dan who faced her. "Do tell what happens behind locked doors when Ashley misbehaves." He wore the biggest grin in the history of grins.

Nadia drew her brows down, hiding her wide-eyed shock at her slipup. "Wouldn't *you* like to know?" She quickly recovered after the involuntary blush. "What are you doing here, Dan?"

"Your girlfriend asked me to go with you to that school meeting since she's busy with a surgery," Dan clarified in such a badly rehearsed manner it guaranteed he was hiding something.

Nadia overlooked his behavior in favor of deciding what bothered her more: the fact that people referred to Ashley as her girlfriend or the fact that Ashley didn't trust Nadia to keep an appointment.

"I don't need a chaperone," she said. "I told her I would take care of it, so I will." Nadia decided the girlfriend reference was worse. Ashley was so much more than that.

"She told me to tell you this was nonnegotiable."

Nadia scoffed. Ashley was being unusually bossy today. "And you can't refuse anything the original Rylan asks, can you? What version of her are you dating this week, Dan? Shy Rylan? Hot Rylan? Naïve Rylan? I liked Hot Rylan. She was…well, hot."

A couple of years ago, Nadia had pointed out that Dan's girlfriends were all versions of Ashley: blonde, blue-eyed, and in medicine or another high-achieving profession. The difference was that they were actually interested in him—a very important distinction that had made Nadia eventually overcome her jealous feelings so she could keep her friendly-ish relationship with him. Besides, the fact that Dan had passionately denied her astute observation made it impossible for Nadia to resist teasing him every chance she got.

"Madeline isn't even blonde, so joke's on you."

"Ah, so it's Brunette Rylan."

Dan stared at her, a familiar unimpressed, fed-up look firmly glued on his face. "Are you quite done? We should go."

Nadia smirked. Clearly, he had failed to think of a good comeback.

"Did Ashley give you my phone?"

"No phones. Boss wants you to go straight to the meeting. Don't even think about changing your clothes."

"She is not my boss anymore, and neither is she yours." Nadia sighed as she considered the tedious meeting she was about to attend. "Since when do people care if a four-year-old is eligible for first grade? Don't kids at that level just finger paint all day anyway?"

Nadia pretended to examine a brochure about child-rearing as she waited to meet with the principal. Without a phone, she didn't know what to do with her hands. Dan spent the time texting and making goofy faces. His new girlfriend must be hilarious.

After twenty minutes, the assistant returned to say that the principal insisted on meeting with both parents.

"You can't be serious." Nadia's voice raised.

"Okay," Dan said. "I'll call Ashley and see if she can make it."

Nadia made herself control her breathing since she couldn't control anything else.

Dan made the call and put his phone away. "How come you had a transplantation so early this morning? I thought they were all done during business hours now, ever since you reinvented the field."

After the success of Nadia's bioengineered heart, transplant science had made some major leaps. A French team developed a protocol to remove HLA markers, the proteins that the immune system attacked as foreign intruders. Building on that development, a Japanese group created a method to reseed a kidney scaffold with HLA negative stem cells, making it a universal organ that worked for any recipient. Mass production of organs meant that getting an organ for transplantation was now as simple as ordering hospital bed sheets.

"Now and then we get an emergency," Nadia said, the change of topic softening her temper. Knowing she had started it all brought a satisfying smile to her face every time. "The patient this morning was a fire victim. He had inhaled so much soot that his airway was wrecked. He couldn't oxygenate even on maximal support. A new pair of lungs saved his other organs from becoming too hypoxic to function properly."

Dan nudged her shoulder playfully. "Look at you, being the hero and—"

"I'm here." Ashley rushed breathlessly into the waiting area.

"Where's my phone?" Nadia asked dryly despite her heart becoming its usual tachycardic self at the sight of her partner.

Ashley approached the front desk, evidently choosing to ignore the question. "I'm so sorry to be late. May we still keep the appointment?"

"Certainly, Mrs. Keating." The assistant smiled warmly.

The preposterous way the assistant addressed Ashley made Nadia cringe. Hearing a *missus* in front of her name alone hurt her ears. She glanced at Ashley, whose smile only grew bigger as she thanked the assistant.

"I guess my services are no longer needed." Dan stood up. "I'll see you both at the party tonight."

They were all planning to attend Evgeni's engagement party. Dan and Evgeni had become friends after they met in the waiting room five years ago. Nadia would never understand how men made friends at the drop of a hat.

And despite everything that had happened between Nadia and Evgeni, he had stayed in her life. He had dated casually for a couple of years, then met a former model who rivaled his good looks, which was an achievement on its own. Evgeni had pointed out she was a lot like Nadia, but Nadia couldn't see it. In her opinion, the woman was cold, aloof, and too direct. Despite that, she always softened around Evgeni, so Nadia was happy for them.

She would have never predicted she would be attending his engagement party as a guest, let alone be bringing Ashley along with her. But Evgeni had put the past behind them. Nadia couldn't do that. She blamed herself for the pain she'd caused both Ashley and him. She couldn't see herself marrying anyone either. It was something she had tried to promise Evgeni, and going through it with someone else felt like committing yet another betrayal.

Of course, Ashley—being Ashley—had accepted Nadia's position when she told her. Still, she couldn't shake the feeling that her partner was disappointed.

Ignoring the pang of pain her straying thoughts brought, she followed Ashley to the principal's office. The principal wasn't there. *Unbelievable.* Nadia shook her head and huffed, but her anger had simmered down the moment Ashley had appeared. Besides, she didn't mind the alone time because she could ask Ashley about her strange behavior earlier.

"Where's my phone? Are you holding it hostage?"

Ashley looked as if she had been caught with her hand in the cookie jar. "Don't be paranoid. It's in my car."

"And what if there's an emergency?"

Ashley laughed. "There's no such thing as emergency transplants anymore. Anyway, I told everyone at the hospital that you're taking the rest of the day off."

Nadia frowned. First, Ashley had barged into the OR when Nadia was working. Then she had stood her up in her office. Now she was changing Nadia's schedule. Plus, she was shifting in her chair as if she had ants in her pants. Something was going on.

• • •

"You're acting weird today."

"Hm?" Ashley pretended she had no idea what Nadia was talking about. She glanced at the door, hoping the principal would show up. She wasn't good at hiding things from Nadia.

"You heard me." Nadia narrowed her eyes at Ashley. "And don't think we won't have a serious talk about your inappropriate behavior this morning."

"Did it turn you on?" Ashley smiled suggestively. There was a time when she would have mistaken Nadia's attitude for hostility. She knew better now. For Nadia, icy was a form of foreplay. "Did it make you wish you could drop to your knees right then and there and—"

"I'm sorry about the wait." A woman entered the room.

Ashley jumped in her seat, her cheeks flaming. At the corner of her eye, she could see Nadia's lips twitching as she visibly struggled to contain herself from laughing. At least somebody was having fun.

"Dr. Keating, it's an honor to meet you in person." The principal shook Nadia's extended hand. Indeed, only people who'd spent the last five years in a cave didn't know the name of *that* surgeon. "And you must be Mrs.... uh..." She trailed off as she shuffled through her papers.

"It's *Doctor* Rylan."

"Ashley."

Nadia and Ashley spoke simultaneously. The difference was that Nadia appeared to be about to skin the woman alive. Ashley smiled, partly to soften the situation and partly to hide her amusement at how intimidated the principal already looked.

While Ashley appreciated Nadia fighting for her respect, she didn't like using her title outside work. It felt elitist. Which was why Nadia insisted on it.

"We're not married," Nadia added rigidly.

Ashley's smile faltered a little, but she quickly recovered. Thankfully, Nadia kept looking ahead at the principal and didn't notice.

Ashley had made peace with Nadia not wanting to marry, even though it was a dream she'd had since childhood. She shook the fleeting thought away. It was a small price to pay for what Nadia had given her.

"Oh." The woman cleared her throat. "I'm Ms. Grey. I understand you want your daughter to be in the same grade as her brother."

"That's correct," Nadia said simply.

Immune to Nadia's intimidation tactics, Ashley rolled her eyes in further amusement.

The principal shuffled papers frantically, searching for something.

"She's a year and a half younger, but Katya is a very bright girl," Ashley said. "I'm sure she's passed the necessary tests to—"

"What seems to be the issue here?" Nadia challenged.

"I'm so sorry. I can't seem to find the right file. The only Keating here is your son."

Nadia glared at her. "Her. Name. Is. Ekaterina. Rylan."

"Oh." Grey shuffled through the stack of papers again until she found the page she was looking for. "You're correct. Your daughter has passed all tests with flying colors. In fact, she's more than qualified for that level, as is her brother. You should be proud of having such smart children."

"We really are—"

"Are we done here?" Nadia interrupted impatiently.

"No, there's one more thing, Dr. Keating." Grey straightened up. "When a child enrolls at an upper level, there are other considerations. Children her age lack emotional maturity. Studies show that expecting too much from a young child can lead to increased stress and poor mental health."

"Are you suggesting we're bad parents?" Nadia's voice was chilling.

This time, Ashley's glare matched hers. Grey didn't know anything about their family, and she certainly shouldn't make insinuations about their parenting style.

"No, not at all, Dr. Keating."

"Then do not quote statistics to me, Ms. Grey." Nadia didn't back down. "I can assure you, as the top scientist in the country, I've made my due diligence—I am familiar with the current child-rearing guidelines."

Ashley stepped in with a kinder explanation. "When we first met Katya and Rai, they had already been through so much. They were forced to grow up fast, but at least they had each other. We believe that keeping them together whenever possible is the right thing to do."

"Of course. Rai's story is quite remarkable. He was the second patient to ever receive a bioengineered heart. Dr. Keating, you operated on him before adopting him, correct?"

"Ms. Grey, both my children are *quite* remarkable because of their personal traits, not their medical histories."

Despite the curious look on Grey's face, Nadia didn't elaborate further and Ashley held her tongue. Nadia was even more overprotective of the children's privacy than her own.

There was more to the story, of course. Rai began as Nadia's patient, but after building him a heart, Nadia had decided that returning him to the foster care system he came from would be as cruel as when his biological parents had abandoned him and his sister.

When Nadia had first brought Rai home and announced that she had begun the adoption process—a life-altering decision made on her own—Ashley had been speechless with anger. The most infuriating part had been Nadia's solution: to include Ashley by telling her to adopt his younger sister. When Ashley had tried to explain that children weren't puppies, Nadia said she would adopt the little girl herself.

Despite what had looked like an impulsive decision, Ashley eventually came to realize that Nadia had indeed thought this through. And by the time the adoption process was complete, Ashley couldn't imagine her life without their children. Their adoption wasn't about filling some kind of void—one that by now was a distant memory—that had existed in Ashley's life. It wasn't about having a purpose or even about indulging Nadia's insane level of insistence. It was an unfamiliar yet burning sense of belonging that lit her heart with conviction that their family was meant to be together.

As if proof that this was meant to be, the small Ecuadorian boy that was referred to Nadia as a patient was named Rylan. During the adoption, Ashley had altered their daughter's name from Catherine to its Slavic version, Ekaterina, so that the children shared something with both their parents.

"We have carefully weighed the impact that enrolling Katya in an upper level will have on her psychological development," Nadia carried on in her usual cool tone. "I'm happy to provide you with my research, if you are interested in reviewing more recent studies on the topic. Now, is that all, or is there something else you would like to discuss?"

Grey's shoulders slumped. She silently handed them the required consents and waiver documents to sign. Ashley bit back a snort.

Nadia gave a new meaning to the phrase *God complex*. She was powerful and merciless, and if she was to start quoting research papers, Ashley might melt from the sheer hotness of her commanding voice. After her graduation as an attending, Nadia was offered the position as the new chair of surgery, a title the hospital board had presented to her as a publicity stunt no doubt. Little did they know that Nadia would use her new position to make this hospital the best healthcare center in the country, possibly the world; knowing Nadia, it would likely be the latter.

The memory always made Ashley smile with pride. At first, it felt strange to have their roles reversed, but after some trial and error they had found a working balance without stepping on each other's toes too often.

After they signed the forms, they headed home to get ready for Evgeni's engagement party. Ashley was happy for him, but her happiness wasn't entirely altruistic. She felt responsible for his breakup five years earlier despite Nadia repeatedly reminding her everything was her fault. But now that he was moving on, she felt...lighter.

"Mommy, you're home!"

A small girl with dark hair and blue eyes ran to Ashley and threw her arms around her legs. A small spark of jealousy coursed through Nadia. Her daughter always ran to Ashley first. Granted, Nadia didn't possess Ashley's natural warmth, but she still wished Katya recognized her deep affection for her.

"What are you two doing up?" Nadia asked, her lips pressed in a thin line. "It's well past your bedtime." Hearing herself, she sighed in amused resignation. She could see how playing the bad guy wouldn't win her any parent of the year awards.

"We couldn't fall asleep without a story." A little boy with dark wooly hair and bright eyes emerged from behind the sofa.

On the living room table behind Rai, Nadia could see the half-built jigsaw puzzle of an anatomically accurate human thorax the children must have been working on until now and smiled with pride. Of course, when she had brought it home, Ashley insisted it was inappropriate for a six- and four-and-a-half-year-old. The disturbed look on their sitter's face suggested that he wasn't on her side either. But the children loved it. Besides, it was educational. People didn't get *scarred for life* by education, as Ashley had so dramatically put it.

"Am I to understand that James doesn't know any stories?" Nadia asked her son before giving the sitter a quick wink.

"He doesn't know the story we want." Katya finally let go of Ashley and clung to Nadia's legs tightly.

Nadia's heart instantly got a few degrees warmer. *Better late than never.* After ungluing her daughter from her legs, she bent on one knee to meet her at eye level. "And what story might that be, Katya?"

"We want the surgeons' story!"

Nadia smiled. The first night the four of them had been together as a family, she had told the story mainly for Ashley's entertainment. The children were too young to understand and fell asleep likely out of boredom rather than Nadia's storytelling skills. But they wanted the same story the next night and the night after that. It was probably more about Nadia's enthusiasm than the content, but she still loved to hear them ask for it.

"Okay, but you might have to help me."

Katya and Rai began jumping up and down, yelling enthusiastic yeses.

"Go brush your teeth and put on your pajamas first," Ashley said.

After they paid the sitter and waved him goodbye, Nadia went to their bedroom to change. She slipped off her black cocktail dress and put on a pair of bottom scrubs and a T-shirt that felt much more comfortable. Unlike Ashley, even when Nadia became an attending, she rarely dressed in anything but her blue scrubs. Ashley, though, seemed to be in no hurry to change out of her sexy dark red dress that complimented her complexion beautifully. Nadia's eyes had been glued on her all night, and she'd had to exercise great restraint during the party to keep her hands on PG-friendly places.

"I can put the kids to bed if you want to change." Nadia pressed Ashley against the countertop and ran her hands down her back. She leaned forward and kissed her.

"I love you," Ashley murmured into Nadia's mouth.

Even though Ashley had said those words plenty of times by now, Nadia felt an exhilarating thrill of pure happiness every time she heard them. And she always gave the same answer back. With her best self-assured smile, she breathed, "I know."

Without looking away, Nadia sneaked her hand into Ashley's purse that was on the countertop. "I think it's time for you to return my phone."

Ashley playfully slapped her hand. "Enough with the phone obsession. And I'm coming with you to make sure you spare the gory details you so love to fill up our children's heads with."

Nadia rolled her eyes. She kept her stories very kid-friendly. "Yes, ma'am."

Her hands lingered on Ashley's body a moment longer, then Nadia willed herself to let go and headed to her daughter's bedroom, where both children were nestled in Katya's bed. Rai always stayed with his sister until she fell asleep. He was fiercely protective of her. Nadia sat on the bed with them while Ashley leaned at the doorway.

"Once upon a time," she began, "there was a rich king who wished to reward his bravest and smartest knights. The king's name was—"

"Nobel!" Katya yelled out.

Nadia smiled as she pushed a strand of hair back from her golden-brown face. "And what did King Nobel do, Rai?"

Her son furrowed his brow, thinking. "He came up with the Nobel tournament where knights fought against evil monsters and the bravest ones got a big prize."

"Can you name the five tournament categories?" It was a tough question for anyone, let alone a six-year-old, but while Nadia adored seeing Rai emulate her self-assuredness, she wanted to teach him confidence should always be backed up by knowledge.

"There's one for physiology and medicine, uh..."—he scratched his head—"and one for chemistry, and three more for physics, literature, and peace." Rai beamed.

"It's physiology *or* medicine, not *and*."

"Nadezhda."

Nadia shrugged, then added, "But good job naming all five categories." She continued the story. "In the medicine tournament, the surgeon knights were the coolest and fiercest fighters in all the land." Without looking back,

Nadia knew Ashley's eyes were rolling. "And the first knight who fought and won against the Goiter monster was—"

"Kocher," the children yelled in unison.

Nadia smiled uncertainly. They were always excited to fill in details, but they had never volunteered names before. "And what did *Dr.* Kocher do, Katya?" Nadia could almost hear another warning for asking such hard questions.

"He sliced off the Goiter monster with his sword because it was making people sick."

"That's right. He performed a thyroidectomy in goiter patients."

Rai interjected. "But Rejection monster attacked them, and the people got sick again."

"But before they could fight Rejection, another knight defeated the Bleeding monster."

"Dr. Carrel," Katya yelled.

Nadia smiled approvingly. Her daughter had picked up on her correction from earlier to call the surgeons "doctor." It was never too early to learn professionalism as far as she was concerned.

"So both knights got the tournament prize for their awesome victories." Nadia moved the plot along. "But despite taking care of the Goiter and Bleeding monsters, an even scarier monster terrorized the kingdom and made people sick."

"Rejection monster!" Katya and Rai said together.

"And the brave knight who defeated it was—"

"Dr. Murray," Rai shouted. "He didn't defeat Rejection, but he blinded him so Rejection couldn't see what to attack."

"That's right." Nadia smiled at her own ingenuity to explain how Murray had done kidney transplantation between twins in a way her children could understand. "Where are your kidneys?" Nadia asked the seemingly random question to add some education to the story.

Rai and Katya both pointed to their flanks at the anatomically accurate kidney location.

"Right again. So Dr. Murray might not have defeated Rejection, but he did show it could be done. It's called proof-of-concept."

"There's another surgeon knight," Rai said.

Ashley had repeatedly cautioned Nadia against talking about the Lobotomy monster while the children were still so young. "You're right, but that knight was rewarded at the tournament because his fight seemed like a good idea at the time. Like when it seems like a good idea to eat all your Halloween candy in one sitting, but then it makes your tummies hurt."

The children giggled knowingly despite shaking their heads in denial.

Rai spoke up again. "We still need one more knight to defeat Rejection."

Nadia looked at him and then at Katya. They were snickering together, their eyes darting to each other and they weren't the only ones. Nadia turned to look at Ashley.

Ashley cleared her throat, visibly trying to keep a straight face. "I concur with Rai's assessment, Dr. Keating. You can't have a good story without a happy ending," she carried on with the plot's criticism. "Rejection must be defeated for good and the hero rewarded."

Everyone but Nadia was having a lot of fun with a private joke she wasn't in on. Yet. Despite her bubbling curiosity, she maintained a calm face for the sake of playing along. "Katya, do you agree with your mother and brother?" She looked at the youngest conspirator.

"Yes! We need one more knight *lawyuate* for a happy ending."

Nadia felt a thrill of pride that Katya knew the word *laureate*, even though she mangled the pronunciation. "Well, Rejection was defeated, but the jury is still out on the reward part." Nadia hinted a smile, more toward Ashley than the children.

"Kids, make a note of this moment," Ashley said dramatically. "As we all know, Dr. Nadezhda Keating is rarely wrong, but this might be one of those rare occasions."

At last Ashley returned Nadia's phone to her. It was opened to a news page that declared *Nadezhda Keating, DO, is this year's Nobel Laureate in Physiology or Medicine.* Nadia looked up at Ashley, then turned back to the phone and read the second line: *for her discoveries concerning bioengineered solid organs in the treatment of human disease.*

Nadia blinked. And blinked again. Her mind was frozen, her nerves shaking. Her children began jumping up and down on the bed, screaming with excitement—a perfect reflection of everything that was going on in her heart.

Ashley took the phone out of Nadia's rigid hand and pulled her into a tight embrace as if to prove to her that this was not a dream. "Congratulations, Dr. Keating," she whispered.

Suddenly, Ashley's bizarre behavior made sense. "You knew about this all day." Nadia spoke softly. She glanced at her hyperactive children and back to Ashley. With a smile, she raised an eyebrow. "Did you orchestrate this whole storytelling?"

"After I finished my case, I came home and we practiced." Ashley grinned. "I wanted this day to be more special for you than a stranger calling you from Stockholm. I wanted you to find out from your family."

"It's perfect." Nadia gave Ashley a light kiss.

As the children continued to make noise, Ashley leaned closer. "The night's not over yet," she whispered, her voice laced with promises of things to come. "As your superior, I have to make sure all this fame doesn't go to your head."

"But, Dr. Rylan, you have not been my superior for quite some time now."

"I'm still the chief of CT surgery, and last time I checked, you were still a CT surgeon."

One could argue that a chair of *all* surgery trumped chief of a department of surgery, but Nadia would save that territory battle for another day. Instead, she said, "Yes, ma'am."

"I like the sound of that." Ashley's voice became huskier. "You know, I've never had a Nobel laureate kneel before me."

Nadia's heartbeat instantly sped up. "We should address that oversight immediately."

But first, it was time to get the children into bed. She pulled back, effectively terminating their playful banter for the moment.

"Mommy told us you're the first female surgeon to ever get the prize," Katya said as she settled down in bed.

"I suppose that's true." Nadia tucked her in. "But you shouldn't judge people's accomplishments as more or less based on their anatomy."

"You're also the first DO to get the prize," Rai added as he rubbed his eyes.

"True, but DOs and MDs are the same where surgery is concerned."

"I got it," Ashley said as she stroked her son's hair. "Nadezhda Keating is"—she paused for effect—*"the fifth surgeon."*

Nadia considered the words. Hearing her name amongst the giants in medical history brought an unimaginable pride to the very essence of her soul. A smile spread slowly across her face. "That will do."

Other Books from
Ylva Publishing

www.ylva-publishing.com

L.A. Metro
RJ Nolan

ISBN: 978-3-95533-041-5
Length: 349 pages (97,000 words)

Dr. Kimberly Donovan's life is in shambles. After her medical ethics are questioned, first her family, then her closeted lover, the Chief of the ER, betray her. Determined to make a fresh start, she flees to California and L.A. Metropolitan Hospital. When she meets Jess McKenna, L.A. Metro's Chief of the ER, the attraction is immediate. Can either woman overcome her past to make a future together?

Falling Hard
Jae

ISBN: 978-3-95533-829-9
Length: 346 pages (122,000 words)

Dr. Jordan Williams devotes her life to saving patients in the OR and pleasuring women in the bedroom.

Jordan's new neighbor, single mom Emma, is the polar opposite. Family and fidelity mean everything to her.

When Emma helps Jordan recover after a bad fall, they quickly grow closer.

But neither counted on falling hard—for each other.

Irregular Heartbeat
Chris Zett

ISBN: 978-3-95533-996-8
Length: 261 pages (94,000 words)

When drummer Diana Petrell leaves her rock-star life to return to ER medicine, she won't let anything stop her—not even falling for aloof mentor, Dr. Emily Barnes.

Emily isn't happy having to babysit an intriguing resident with a ten-year gap in her résumé. But then the lines blur.

What happens to their careers when Diana's secret comes out?

A lesbian romance that asks how much we'd risk for love.

Major Surgery
Lola Keeley

ISBN: 978-3-96324-145-1
Length: 198 pages (69,000 words)

Surgeon and department head Veronica has life perfectly ordered...until the arrival of a new Head of Trauma. Cassie is a brash ex-army surgeon, all action and sharp edges, not interested in rules or playing nice with icy Veronica. However when they're forced to work together to uncover a scandal, things get a little heated in surprising ways.

A lesbian romance about cutting to the heart of matters.

About Faith Prize

Growing up, Faith Prize had two dreams: to become a doctor and to write a book. She spent the last decade traveling the United States in pursuit of the former while neglecting the latter. Her sole writing experience consisted of generating bone-dry research articles. Fortunately, she came to her senses and decided that the two fields were not mutually exclusive. In fact, medicine is and always will be her muse. However, unlike her nonfiction work that is restricted by tangible facts, her fictional stories are filled with possibilities limited only by her imagination.

CONNECT WITH FAITH
E-Mail: faithprize.author@gmail.com

The Fifth Surgeon
© 2021 by Faith Prize

ISBN: 978-3-96324-543-5

Available in e-book and paperback formats.

Published by Ylva Publishing, legal entity of Ylva Verlag, e.Kfr.

Ylva Verlag, e.Kfr.
Owner: Astrid Ohletz
Am Kirschgarten 2
65830 Kriftel
Germany

www.ylva-publishing.com

First edition: 2021

Credits
Edited by Hayley Price, Julie Klein, and Michelle Aguilar
Cover Design and Print Layout by Streetlight Graphics

9 783963 245435